Shadowy Reflections

Shadowy Reflections

William G. Anderson

First Published in Canada 2014 by Life Journey Publishing

Book Cover Design: Marla Thompson
Typeset: Greg Salisbury

Library and Archives Canada Cataloguing in Publication

Anderson, William G., 1956-, author
    Shadowy reflections / William G. Anderson.

ISBN 978-1-77141-065-6 (pbk.)

    I. Title.

PS8601.N4494S43 2014   C813'.6   C2014-904727-4

For Conrad,
who showed me that the way to defeat adversity
is to rise above it.

Testimonials

"This is a gripping, readable story of interesting characters easily visualized, in an expanding human drama, with a twist. It is a fine tale, full of surprises."
Conrad Black, Former Newspaper Publisher *(The Daily Telegraph, Chicago Sun Times, etc.)*

"A book as large, powerful, and mysterious as the mighty Mississippi River which wends its way through the background of this passionate and artfully constructed coming-of-age story. "Energy," said William Blake, "is eternal delight," and William G. Anderson has peopled 'Shadowy Reflections' with characters full of the raw over-abundance of burgeoning self-awareness and the dark turbulence of sexual longing. A capacious, humane, and insightful meditation on the exigent metabolism of adolescence."
Roger Kimball, Editor and Publisher, *The New Criterion*

"You have to make only one decision about William G. Anderson's book 'Shadowy Reflections': decide to pick it up. Once you do, you will never put it down until you are finished."
George Jonas, Author of *Vengeance* (basis of Steven Spielberg's film *Munich*)

"'Shadowy Reflections' embodies the enlightenment and catastrophe that occur in adolescence. William G. Anderson reveals in exhilarating detail a bold, raw, coming-of-age drama intertwined by three characters' perspectives. My heart has never raced so much by turning pages. Truly a pleasure to read."
Uno Adams, Producer of the Award-winning Short Film, *Stuck*

"*Relationships define our existence as human beings. It is the relationships with those who survive us that define who we are remembered as when we are gone and it is relationships that define 'Shadowy Reflections.' William G. Anderson's novel not only allows you to peer into the lives of its well-defined characters but also different types of relationships. The writer experiments with relationships between best friends, lovers and families, but perhaps the most compelling is a relationship that he creates between characters and readers.*"

J. Cole Lansden, Independent Filmmaker

Acknowledgements

Firstly, thanks to my family for their love and support.

My deepest appreciation to Conrad Black, who continues to serve as my teacher and mentor and without whom this book would never have been written.

A special thanks to Alana Black, James Wing, Linda Vann, Jonathan Black, Joan Maida, Fiona Dudley, Cole Lansden, and James Black for taking their time to offer insight and encouragement to a fledgling author.

Many thanks also to Margaret Atwood, Roger Kimball, and George Jonas for taking the time to read this book.

Bennett Coles, my editor, was as amazing as he was patient.

Julie Salisbury, Alina Wilson, Gulnar Patel, Marla Johnson, Lyda McLallen, and all of the wonderful staff at Influence Publishing were and are phenomenal.

I want to also express my continuing gratitude to two very gifted and talented young men–Zac Adams and Ethan Lewis–for their extraordinary efforts in support of my work.

The changing of sunlight to moonlight
Reflections of my life,
Oh how they fill my eyes.
The greetings of people in trouble
Reflections of my life,
Oh how they fill my eyes

I'm changing, arranging, I'm changing,
I'm changing everything;
Everything around me.

THE MARMALADE

SUMMER

While the air is filling;
It carefully takes the step;
Reaching beyond all measures;
Extending past all depth.

Transcending the flowing waters;
Eclipsing the stars and space;
Evolves a spiritual vacuum;
In search of an unwary place.

This new and dark dimension;
Defying what's thought to be real;
Light fails in becoming fragmented;
Dissolving with time standing still.

Promoting an age of obscurity;
Maintaining a perilous stride;
Exposing a fragile formation;
Where deep-seeded fears reside.

BLAKE

Chapter One

BLAKE

People underestimated the power of the spell cast when sitting astride a John Deere ride-on mower in a seemingly never-ending series of left turns. It engaged the average sixteen-year-old boy of the early twenty-first century in the kind of deep mental exercise I was currently undertaking: was it a yard, or a lawn?

I thought "yards" was more of a southern term, which gradually turned into "lawns" as you traveled west of the Ozarks, east of the Appalachians, or north of the Mason-Dixon Line.

Of course, I was tucked away in southeast Missouri, which left me in the middle of a cross section of cultures. Maybe that's why they called Missouri the "show me" state. Not being really sure where we fit in the great American socio-political, geographic landscape, we developed that "show me" attitude, rather than accept things as socially, politically, or geographically correct.

I was usually engrossed in my music thanks to the marvels of modern technology, which had given us high-powered headphones that plugged into my iPod. The iPod was a gift from my family for my sixteenth birthday, just two days ago. I was a rap music enthusiast, which separated me from most people around me except for my best friend, Marsh. My father had made it clear that he identified rap music as the work of the devil. If that was the case, the devil was accumulating royalties in record amounts. Seriously, my father, one of the stalwart deacons of the First Baptist Church of Gardner, was just expressing the views of almost all the members of his generation. My mom just worried. She did that a lot.

My love of rap music also created some problems with my peers. Being a product of the black music scene made rap a foreign entity in Gardner. Of the fifty-eight members of my class

1

moving up to Gardner High School, only nine were minorities. Five of them were black. Prejudice knew no boundaries and certainly had its place in our small, rural community. I guess our love of rap made me, Marsh, and a handful of other white kids our own minority. Nonetheless, I reveled in the sounds of Snoop Dogg, Jay-Z, DMX, and more.

The sounds of Cash Money currently served as a background for my thoughts as the left turns started occurring a little more often. As I rolled along, I often glanced across at my best friend, Marsh. He was manning the gas powered weed eater and was plodding along the border of the driveway. He had already completed this task along the front walk and the flower beds. I'd manned the weed eater earlier, policing up around the back patio and the pool fence.

The yard (lawn or whatever) we were mowing and manicuring belongs to Marsh's grandparents. His grandfather, Mr. TM, had hired Marsh and me to work for Gardner Grain Elevators for the summer. He owned the elevators, and most the rest of Gardner as far as I could tell. He owned thousands of acres of farm land across southeast Missouri, an investment company in Sikeston, and other properties. He was a great guy who was wonderful to Marsh and treated me like one of the family. I had no memory as vivid as the day Marsh's father was killed in a car wreck. We were ten years old. Ms. Becky, Marsh's mother and our elementary principal, pulled Marsh out of class that morning. When I got home that afternoon, my mom told me what happened. I remember going to my room and staring out the window trying to figure out what to do. Later that evening, Ms. Becky called and said Marsh wanted to come over and stay the night. When he arrived, we sat in my room and played video games for a while. I remembered looking at him as tears started rolling down his face. We both cried and hugged each other. Nothing had come between us since.

Anyway, Marsh and I did a variety of jobs all over the place.

We had a weekly stop here, of course. It was our favorite stop because we always got a good lunch courtesy of Ms. Doty, Marsh's grandmother. Then, to top it off, we got to go for a swim in their pool when the job was done. As far as the job went, I managed to pocket two hundred a week plus a monthly bonus of one hundred dollars, which came out of Mr. TM's pocket. He called it a slush fund and swore us to secrecy. My lips were sealed.

This helped me manage my new bevy of expenses, which sprung to life on my recent birthday. Mom and Dad came through on a Chevy Colorado, which they purchased at the dealership in Sikeston. Mr. TM was the majority owner of the dealership, although I wasn't sure how that affected the price. Once again, my lips were sealed. I was given the responsibility of taking care of it and supplying my own gas. Dad took care of the insurance which, since he owned an insurance agency, probably got us a pretty good deal, even for a sixteen-year-old driver. Marsh and his mom gave me a bed liner and a bed tarp. Mr. TM and Ms. Doty gave me two hundred dollars of gas credit at the T-Mart in Gardner, which Mr. TM also owned. It was the biggest birthday I had ever had.

I had narrowed my mowing trek down to a ten-by-ten foot square and was forced to come out of my trance. The finishing touches required shifting into reverse a few times. I noticed Marsh was on his final run up the far side of the driveway. Finishing the last strip of grass, I rode over to the storage shed to store the mower. After completing that task, I grabbed the push broom and started clearing the stray grass clippings from the front sidewalk and the driveway.

To say that Mr. TM's home was impressive was an understatement. An expensive red brick home with a front entry highlighted by four large white columns gave the home a somewhat majestic look compared to the other homes in the area. It was two stories and, according to Marsh, measured about seven thousand square feet. A large covered patio sat in the back, adjoining a very large, fenced-in pool and pool house. It was in a plush neighborhood just south of Sikeston, close to Sikeston Country Club, about a fifteen to twenty minute drive from Gardner.

"You want me to grab the other broom?" Marsh asked, as he walked the weed eater back to the storage shed. It was hard to miss Marsh because of his blond hair. I mean it was really blond.

"No, I got it. It won't take me long."

"Okay, you want me to get your CD and headphones?"

"Yeah, just put 'em in the floorboard. And check my cell phone for messages, will ya'?"

"Got it."

I swept away the last of the loose grass and returned the push broom to the shed.

"You want me to lock the shed?" I asked, as Marsh fumbled around in my truck.

"Yeah, go ahead. I've got the key. No messages. I'm grabbing our bags—anything else?"

"Nope bro, that oughta do it." I waited in front of the breezeway, which led to the pool. Marsh joined me, bags in hand, and we made our way to the pool. Ms. Doty had left the pool house open for us along with some fresh towels, so we could shower before we hit the pool.

"You boys want me to bring you something to drink?" Ms. Doty yelled from one of the kitchen windows.

"No, that's okay, Grandma, we have water," Marsh replied.

"Thanks, anyway," I chimed in.

"Alright," she called back, "You boys swim as long as you like and stay out of the beer."

"Man, does your grandma have ESP or somethin'?" I asked laughing.

"No, bro, I just don't think she trusts you," Marsh said with a solemn face as we entered the pool house.

"Me! Me! She doesn't trust me? We get almost every ounce of liquor we drink by you sneakin' it outta here. The rest we get from your cousin, Ray, along with the weed we smoke. And she doesn't trust me?"

"Well, it's a matter of family loyalty and honor. Because we're her grandsons, it's easier for her to suspect you than either one of us. Besides, you actually are a slippery, deceitful, and amoral dude. But, I love ya," Marsh stated in a very matter-of-fact tone.

"I'll prepare a suitable response to such outrageous allegations as soon as I find out the meaning of "amoral," I responded, trying to sound like my dad conducting a business deal.

"So as not to contribute to your less than desirable, delinquent qualities," Marsh countered, "While you jump in the shower, I'll get the beer."

"I appreciate your touching concern," I said, while coming out of my grungy tennis shoes and ragged socks. Stripping down, I jumped in the shower. One thing that was probably different about Marsh and me was our lack of modesty when it came to undressing in front of each other. Even guys in the basketball locker room were private about the others seeing them naked. In junior high, this was somewhat understandable because some of the guys were just really starting puberty. But when you got a little older, it sounded more like a phobia to me. I had beat Marsh to full-scale puberty growing a bush of pubic hair midway through my thirteenth year. He trailed me by four months or so. We were probably unique in our worlds in that we openly discussed such things with one another.

I had more of an athletic build than Marsh, standing about five-eight and weighing about one-fifty-eight. The weight work we did in off-seasons basketball had given me better body definition. Marsh came in a couple of inches or so taller, but eleven or twelve pounds lighter. One notable feature he had that I really envied was a long, dangling pecker. I worked hard—when I was hard—to push six inches. He beat that by a good inch. I liked to think I was bigger around, but that was a very biased opinion.

"What're you doin' in there, jackin' off?" Marsh asked loudly, as he came back into the pool house.

"Does it really matter?" I yelled back, spitting through the water.

"No, I'd rather you did it in there than in the pool."

Ms. Becky had pulled me aside at my party the other day. She thanked me for being such a good friend to Marsh over the years. She said he had such great respect for me and loved me like a brother—he would be lost without me. I thanked her and told her I felt the same way about Marsh, and I would certainly be lost without him.

"Well, that sure feels better," I said, emerging from the shower. "Be sure and watch where you step."

"Very funny," Marsh smirked, as he stepped around me and into the shower.

The swim was refreshing on such a hot afternoon. After straightening up and loading up, we checked our cell phones, hopped in my truck, and headed for Gardner.

"So, bro, what're you and Krista doin' for her birthday tomorrow?" Marsh asked.

"Well, here Mom's bakin' a cake. She asked Krista if she wanted to have some friends over, but she declined. She wants me to take her to dinner and a movie."

Krista and I had been doing the girlfriend-boyfriend thing since the end of school. She was the most beautiful girl in school in my very qualified opinion. Being a normal teenager with raging hormones, my goal was to bring an end to our virginity. Unfortunately, she had very definite ideas about that subject— many of which were founded in her Catholicism. I was facing a fight through the Vatican to make any headway. I was a life-long Baptist. We apparently didn't believe in premarital sex either. Hell, I didn't want to believe in it; I just wanted to do it.

"I think dinner and a movie's a very mature thing to do," Marsh said, using his solemn tone again. "It shows the two of you are building a relationship based on trust, devotion, responsibility, and sound judgment."

"Jesus, Marsh, that sounds like an oath to join the Boy Scouts," I mumbled in exasperation. "I'm tryin' to get laid here."

"Boy Scouts probably get laid; of course it's probably with some wild animal or maybe even with each other," Marsh stated calmly.

We cut the conversation to soak up some classic Tupac for a few minutes. I decided to turn the focus on his recent female exploits.

"How're you and Ciera doin'?" I asked. Ciera and Marsh had been going together for at least six months and I was jealous of the foreplay they had already engaged in.

"Oh, about the same," he said. "We're still doin' the touchy feely thing when she comes over. My mom gives us more privacy than her folks do. So I get to rub her tits and between her legs, which she really gets into. At the same time, she has a really strong hold on my boner and works it good—almost too good. Last week, in the midst of some heavy makin' out, I almost came all over myself. I pleaded with her to let us both have some relief, but she said we had to wait."

"Wait for what?" I asked.

"Hell, I don't know. I guess for my dick to bust out of my pants."

We were finally pulling into Gardner, a thriving metropolis of about twenty-five hundred people. Not much here that would catch anyone's attention. We had a couple of old doctors, a dentist, and some shops downtown. We had one restaurant, a Dairy Freeze, and a Subway. The Subway was another Gramps thing. My dad's insurance agency was the only one with an office in town. The most recent and impressive feature in our community was our recreation park. It was built four years ago and had something for everyone, including baseball/softball fields, a small skateboard park, which Marsh and I had frequented from time to time, tennis courts, a soccer field, and a nice walking track.

We were passing the park when Marsh spotted Ciera over in the parking area. "We got time to pull over and say hi, bro?" he asked.

"Of course."

"Be nice," he said, cutting his eyes at me.

"Without a doubt," I replied as I pulled in. Ciera spotted us and came running over with a couple of friends. She's a cute girl. She had a kind of round face, which I didn't care for, but a nice well-rounded ass, which I did care for. She was also stacked really good. She cut her sandy colored hair a little shorter than I liked, but it was still attractive. She made it to the passenger side door before Marsh could get the window down.

"Hey, Marsh," she said with a bright smile, leaning in the now open window. "You guys just comin' in from work?"

"Yeah; it's been a hard day," Marsh replied with a smile of his own, trying to keep her from smelling the beer on his breath. "What's goin' on here?"

"Oh, nothin'; just another boring summer day," she said with a drab look. "Oh Blake, I just love your new truck. Aren't you excited?"

"Yeah, it's nice," I said. "You know Ciera, we were just talkin' about you."

"Blaaake...," Marsh said, eyeing me carefully.

"Oh really," she said with a big smile. "I hope it was somethin' good."

"Well, actually..."

"Careful," Marsh warned.

"Ciera, do you realize how sexually frustrated Marsh is?" I asked, just before receiving a whack on the shoulder from Marsh.

"Well, uh...," Ciera stuttered, blushing brightly.

"He's just bein' an ass; makin' stuff up," Marsh quickly said. "There's nothin' to what he's sayin'."

"There's nothin' to his sex life, either," I said, quickly shifting to avoid another strike from Marsh.

"Well, our relationship is our business, Blake," she said, glaring angrily. "We happen to have a proper approach to our feelings for each other. You obviously have issues of your own, so don't take it out on us."

"He's been tryin' to get you to take it out...," I managed to get out before Marsh cupped his hand over my mouth.

Before anyone could say anything else, the sound of squealing tires caught our attention. To everyone's dismay, Matt Perdue wheeled in the parking lot in his red Silverado, pulling around to my side of the truck. Matt Perdue was, in my opinion, the biggest prick in school. He would be a senior this year and was universally regarded as an arrogant asshole. He was also a six-foot two, two-hundred pound-plus arrogant asshole, which made him dangerous. And as bad as I hated to say it, he was a pretty good basketball player. On top of all this, he'd had a crush on Krista and hated me.

"Well, well, well, Coleman," he started, showing off the depth of his vocabulary, "You've finally landed a ride. You have a baby truck."

"Chill out, Blake," Marsh said quietly, before I started to reply.

"Did that thang come with trainin' wheels?" Perdue asked loudly, drawing laughter from the two Neanderthals riding in the truck with him. One of them was his constant companion whom everyone called Mutt. Mutt was even bigger and stronger than Perdue.

I was seething inside, squeezing the steering wheel, while working hard to show an expression of indifference.

"No really, I guess it fits you pretty good," Perdue continued. "It's small, dark, and plain—just like you." He drew more laughter from his captive audience.

Before I could say anything, Marsh jumped in, "Yeah, Matt, we can't all drive a big red fire truck like you."

"I don't believe I was talkin' to you, Williams," Perdue said, eyeing Marsh.

"Damn, Matt," Marsh said, "Someone tries to pay you a compliment and you get all rude about it. You really make it hard for people to be nice to you. Even in Gardner, there is such a thing as proper etiquette, even though I'm sure you have no idea what that means. So why don't you, dumber, and dumbest go look it up."

You could see the fire building in Perdue's eyes. "You better mind your own business, you little faggot," he blasted out. "Just 'cause your granddaddy owns the town don't mean shit to me. I'll stomp your squirrely ass without blinkin' an eye. And the same goes for your 'wigger' friend with his 'wigger' lips."

He struck a nerve with that "wigger" remark. One of my unique physical qualities was my thick lips. The girls really seemed to like them, but the rednecks viewed them as a common characteristic of black people. I prided myself in the fact that I didn't have racial prejudices and was glad I was raised that way. The term "wigger" was a racial slur, and a very personal one.

"Y'know Perdue, I've tried to ignore everything you've said, which is good advice for anyone who runs into you. I'd call you stupid and obnoxious, but as Marsh points out, you don't take compliments well." Out of the corner of my eye, I saw Marsh gently move Ciera away from his door, as I continued to lash out. "And concerning your comments about my lips, I never criticize your lips when they're wrapped around my dick every day."

That did it. Perdue kicked his door open as his buddies grabbed him, trying to keep him in the truck. I used the opportunity to quickly throw my truck into gear and squealed my tires as we sped out of the parking lot.

"You know, bro, one of these days he's gonna kill you," Marsh said, "Leavin' me with one hell of a problem."

"What's the problem? I'm the one gettin' killed."

"Because if he kills you, then I'll have to kill him. The problem is figurin' out how to get away with it."

We both managed a laugh, but a wary one. We cruised out on what we all called the "main drag" which cut through the rapidly shrinking downtown area of Gardner. I kept checking my rearview mirror, but there was no sign of Perdue. As I slowed at an intersection, Marsh spoke up.

"Hey, bro, there's Krista waving from the Fresh Market."

The Fresh Market was the last surviving grocery store in town. Krista was standing beside her mom's car in the parking lot. I cut the corner pretty sharp—and way too quick—to whirl back into the lot. I eased up to her as I lowered my window.

"What's up, Krista?"

"Not much, baby," she replied. "Hey Marsh."

"Hey Krista," Marsh answered.

"Shopping with mom?" I asked her. God, she was so damned hot. She was wearing a skimpy white t-shirt and some really snug jean shorts. My shorts started getting a little snug too.

"Yeah," she said. "I wish she'd c'mon. She's in there gabbing with Mrs. Tacker"—her smile broke out again—"I'm makin' big plans for tomorrow night."

"Yeah, me too," I said, smiling back at her.

At that moment, Mr. Dailey pulled in to park across from us. He was an attorney who worked here and in Sikeston. He and his wife had a little girl and Krista did most their babysitting.

"Hey Krista; hey guys," he said, emerging from his car, still wearing a suit.

"Hello, Mr. Dailey," Krista answered and Marsh and I waved. Mr. Dailey kept himself in great shape and the girls, and women, around town just couldn't resist gawking at him. I had to admit to being a little jealous and a whole lot envious.

"Everything still good for Saturday?" he asked, smiling.

"Yes sir," Krista said. "I've got it on my calendar."

"Good deal," he said. "You guys take care."

With that, he hurried toward to the store, stopping for a quick word with Krista's mom who had just come out.

"Well, there's Mom, finally," Krista said and then leaned in to give me a quick peck on the cheek.

That was my cue to go and we cut out. As we turned north on 1st Street, making our way to Marsh's house, we could see the huge grain elevators rising against the skyline to the east. They towered over the town.

"You need anything from the stash for you and Krista tomorrow night?" Marsh asked, breaking into Jay-Z on the radio.

"No, I've still got some vodka in the flask behind the seat. That's all she'll want. You know she won't smoke weed."

"Well, maybe the vodka'll loosen her up."

"It always loosens her up," I said, showing a little exasperation. "We'll get into some having makin' out, but that's all we'll get into. So, after the heat of frustration, I'll dutifully take her home. Then, I'll go home, go to bed, and, once again, relieve myself."

"A truly romantic experience in which you enhance your ability as a point guard," Marsh stated, "by skillfully handling your own genitals."

"Kiss my ass, Marsh."

"It wouldn't help."

KRISTA

"Krista, is that you?"

"Yes, Mom!" I yelled back sternly. "Who else would it be?"

I was relieved I got no response to that last question. It was five minutes before midnight: my curfew, even on my sixteenth birthday—and Mom was still waiting up. I should have saved myself the trouble of even trying to be quiet coming into the house. Plus, Mom didn't exactly sound sober.

Working on my own sobriety, I completed a successful search in the fridge for some grapefruit juice and, with glass in hand, started to my bedroom. I made it about half way.

"You kinda pushed your curfew, didn't you," Mom said as she met at the entry of the hall.

"I made it before twelve, Mom." I had to keep steady here. Plus, it was obvious that she wasn't very steady. "Look, Mom, I'm tired and ready to go to bed. Everything's cool—okay?"

"Well, I think twelve is a little late for someone your age, but your father thinks it's okay. But I know what teenage boys are like. You just remember that I'll be watching."

"Watching! You sure what you're drinking won't cloud your vision?"

"You watch your mouth, young lady," she said firmly. "I'm an adult and I know how to drink responsibly."

"You know how to drink every way imaginable," I snapped back.

"You know better than to talk to me like that," she said with an exaggerated frown on her face.

"It's okay, Mom," I said calmly. "I doubt you'll remember it in the morning."

She started to say something, but I quickly walked past her

down the hall and into my bedroom, shutting the door behind me. I leaned back against my door and took a few deep breaths. One day, something would have to give with my mom. My dad— my loving, hard-working dad—seemed at a loss to deal with it or was afraid to. I just didn't know. My mind moved to more pleasant thoughts.

I had a great night out with my love, Blake. He was so hot! He wore his beautiful black hair over his ears, but not too long. His enchanting eyes had their own special sparkle. His ears and nose were perfect, along with the soft slender contour of his cheeks, which sprouted a few stray whiskers that were still really no more than "peach fuzz". His thick lips were beautifully shaped; they were so tender they made me melt. He had a sweet smile that was the most engaging I had ever seen. His body was perfectly proportioned. For someone with such a macho make-up, his hands were firm, but tender and soft. He was also fun to be around and just reckless enough to make life more exciting. He weighed heavy on my mind as I quietly undressed and slid into bed, with absolutely no intention of going to sleep.

I grabbed my cell phone and called my best friend, Cheryl. The first ring never finished.

"Hello," she said in a voice that clearly indicated she was not asleep.

"Hey girl, how're you doin'?"

"Not near as good as you are, I'm sure," she replied, "I'm all set to hear about the birthday girl's big night out with Blake the snake."

"Now, cut that out, Cheryl. He's a great guy who's dedicated to our relationship. He has normal desires and so do I, but he respects what we have together."

"Get real, girl!" Cheryl said, raising her voice. "Blake's a nice enough guy as guys go. But the only thing he's dedicated to is getting into your pants and out of his. You can see it in 'im. All guys are like that to a degree, but Blake's degree is extreme.

I know you don't like to talk about his ex, Tammy, but she's a pretty straight-up girl. She doesn't talk about her relationship with Blake much, but we had a good talk the other day, and you need to know some things."

"What if I don't want to hear what probably amounts to sour grapes from Blake's ex?" I asked, sounding defensive, I'm sure.

"Well," Cheryl fired back, "I guess you can hang up then."

I went mute for a few seconds, leaving the door open for her to continue, which she did.

"Okay, Tammy said in the weeks leading up to their breakup earlier this year, Blake was persistent about having sex. She said she gave in to the point of some foolin' around, but he wanted more. It seems clear now that Blake was already making discreet moves in your direction which, based on what you've told me, seems to add up."

"Maybe he was tired of her," I said, "and wanted a change. There's nothing wrong with that."

"Oh, he wants a change," she responded. "He wants to change outta his clothes and get you to change outta yours."

"Oh come on, Cheryl."

"No, I'm not through. Look, you're my best friend in the world. Now you're fallin' for a guy who is mindlessly driven by his hormones. I just think you're settin' yourself up to get hurt. If you wanna like Blake, then like 'im. But be prepared to go to bed with 'im. That's okay, too, if it's what you wanna do. Just come to terms with what you're dealin' with."

"What do you mean by comin' to terms?" I asked.

"Just this," she continued, "Blake is hot; he's gone from a cute kid to a good-lookin' guy. He's goin' into high school, which makes him more available and acceptable to even the older girls. He's determined to have sexual experiences, and he's gonna have 'em. I do think he really likes you a lot, but I seriously doubt it'll keep 'im loyal. Krista, you still there?"

"Yeah, I'm just running through my mind some of the things

you just said. I really like Blake; maybe love 'im. Help me out here, Cheryl. What should I do?"

"Do you really want an honest answer to that question?"

"Yes, I do," I replied, trying to sound bold. In reality, I was shaking. My mind was racing back to earlier this evening with Blake. My God, he was making me melt inside. His kisses were so deep. His lips set me on fire—I wanted him so bad.

"Well, girl," she declared, "You're gonna have to decide what you're willing to give up. If you can sacrifice your virginity, then your situation's settled. But I know that involves religious issues for you. Another option is to allow for some heavy foreplay. You're the new girl and he's crazy about you, so that would hold 'im for a time. How far you go with that and how intense it gets, you'll have to decide. These are dangerous waters. For what it's worth, that's how I see it."

"Yeah, I've got some big decisions to make."

"Well, how about we discuss another subject?" she said. "How's the babysitting comin' along over at the Dailey's?"

"The job's goin' fine. Cindy's a typical three-year-old, and she likes to get into things. But, after lunch, I play with her in the pool for an hour or so, then she naps down for two solid hours. That gives me some great sun time out by the pool, so it works out good."

"That's great. Now for the important question. How often does Mr. Dailey come around? He's really hot!"

"Yeah, he's a dream," I said. Ted Dailey, an attorney, was thirty-one but had the body of a twenty-year-old decathlon champion. Standing about six-one and weighing whatever perfect was, he was the definition of a hunk. He ran ten miles a day, shirtless and in running shorts during the summer. His wife, the luckiest woman I knew, worked for a consulting firm in Sikeston. "As a matter of fact, as much as I'm crazy about Blake, he's not in the same league with Mr. Dailey."

"I think Mr. Dailey's in a league by himself," Cheryl added. "I could have some great dreams about being a player in his league. Hey, are you ready for the big Williams' end of July bash next week?"

"Yeah, it's always crazy, but my new love'll be there, which makes it a little more bearable."

"Maybe, but Marsh'll be there too," she said. "Which means the two of them will be in the same place at the same time. They're more dangerous than a terminal illness. Are you sure you're ready for that?"

"Let me, once again, clarify somethin' for you, girlfriend. There is no way for anyone to have anything to do with Blake without accepting Marsh and vice versa. Their friendship is the only one I've seen that's stronger than ours. I have no doubt if I were to offer Blake my body if he would give up his friendship with Marsh, he'd tell me to get lost."

"Wrong!" Cheryl exclaimed. "He would take your body first, then tell you to get lost."

I couldn't help but laugh at that. "You may be right. Good night girl, love ya'."

"Back 'atcha." The call ended.

Well, I guess my relationship with Blake was already reaching a crossroads. Cheryl read people as well as anyone I knew, and she felt strongly that she had Blake pegged. Damn, why was liking a guy so hard? Why were the rules set the way they were? I had no answers. I thought I'd just decide when the time came—a "spur of the moment" type of thing. Spontaneity was a road to adventure. Of course, life with Blake Coleman could easily be spontaneously combustible.

Chapter Three

MARSH

If Blake ever showed up on time, it was because someone was chasing him. I tossed my bag on the floor and kicked back in the recliner. Actually, knowing Blake so well had managed to teach me some important lessons in dealing with other people. For one, never have expectations because you were setting yourself up to be disappointed, angry, disillusioned, or a combination of the three. Also, people were inherently selfish. They usually found it impossible to see past their own self-interest, even though they loved to claim they were doing so. Spending time with Blake provided examples of these lessons on a frequent basis. But he was my bro and I loved him.

"Marsh," my mom said, as she entered the den, breaking up my useless train of thought, "I thought you guys were leaving at eight-thirty."

"Blake lives in a world where time is irrelevant. As a matter of fact, I'm not really sure if much of anything is relevant in Blake's world."

"I'm sure," Mom agreed. "Now, Marsh " —Uh, oh—"I want you guys to lay off the booze out there. I know your gramps doesn't care much as long as you're at his place, but the fact is it's illegal, not to mention dangerous. Your gramps and I don't always see eye to eye when it comes to you, but I'm your mother, and I have the final say."

"Come on, Mom," I said, "We just drink a little beer. No one's payin' attention—they're all plastered."

"That may very well be, Marsh, but that doesn't change the fact that guys your age have no business boozing it up, even if you're surrounded by irresponsible adults exercising poor judgment."

"We're in a safe place, Mom. We're not out drinkin' on the road or someplace we could get in trouble with the law or anything."

"What about the lake?" she countered. "It's very dangerous drinking and boating on the lake. And the park officers patrol the lake."

"Alright, Mom, we won't drink any booze on the boat and," She started to say something, but I kept going, "We'll just slip a couple of beers or so at the cookout."

"I've stated clearly how I feel about all of it, Marsh. And if your Dad were here, he would feel the same way."

"Well, he's not here, is he?" I snapped back, regretting it immediately.

She turned and looked out the window. "No, he's not," she said, her voice breaking a little.

I was on my feet in a second and ran to her. Wrapping my arms around her, fighting the tears, I held her close.

"Mom, you know I didn't mean that. And I know you're right about how Dad would feel." I released her, but kept full eye contact. "I don't wanna start lyin' to you. You know Blake and me drink now and then. We occasionally smoke a little weed, but we're not stupid about it. I know there are risks, but I'll face more and more risks now. I'm still workin' on bein' a teenager, so my thinkin' gets a little out of whack. There are a lot of things I'm unsure about. But two things I am sure about are that I have the greatest mom in the world, and I love her with all my heart."

She managed a smile and gave me a big hug just as a horn sounded. It was hard to believe that someone as unreliable as Blake could manage such good timing. Grabbing my bag, I made a dash out the door. Mom said something, but I didn't quite catch it. I felt sure it was something like "behave yourself," but it sounded like "I love you". I liked that better.

We loaded up in Ms. Kathy's—Blake's mother—Oldsmobile. I sat in the front seat on the passenger side; Krista was behind the wheel, with Blake sitting between her and the driver's side door. Okay, maybe that was a bit of an exaggeration, but things were pretty snug over there. Boy, was I a third wheel or what? Ciera went with her family to her uncle's in West Memphis, Arkansas. I was invited, but had to beg off. I wasn't about to miss this summer bash at the Williams lake house. I kept my eyes straight ahead or looking out my window, to avoid staring at Krista. She was really hot and it was almost more than a guy like me could take. Besides, it got a little quirky trying to nonchalantly hide a boner in such close quarters.

As we stopped at the last intersection on our way out of town, Matt Perdue, in his big red pickup, crossed very slowly in front of us. I couldn't help but notice Blake's hand squeezing the steering wheel. I also noticed a quick change in Krista's facial expression, no doubt feeling the tenseness in Blake. It had been over a week since our rec park encounter with Perdue, and this was an obvious attempt to intimidate and he was fairly successful. We moved on quickly.

The drive to the lake house usually took less than an hour and a half. On the way, we argued about music—our rap verses Krista's soft rock—and anything else we could come up with to fuss about. Blake was actually a pretty good driver, he just hid it well. Krista stated at least three times in the first hour that Blake and I were insufferable. It was an appropriate description of the way we acted sometimes.

"Hey Marsh, you think your gramps is really upset with me about yesterday?" Blake asked.

"What happened yesterday?" Krista jumped in before I could respond.

"Fred felt I was guilty of reckless driving at the elevators," Blake answered.

"Who's Fred?" Krista asked.

"Fred," I said, "Is the office manager. Your dad knows 'im. He told Blake and me to move some grain trucks to the back lot."

"And," Blake said, "He said to be quick about it. He doesn't think we earn our money. He's probably right, but it's none of his business. Plus, I have hell shiftin' gears on those trucks and he knows it. Some of the guys around there think it's funny."

"Anyway, Blake and I get started," I said. "Blake's problem is gettin' through first and second gear without the engine dyin'. Those are old trucks and you have to be pretty good at negotiatin' the clutch and the accelerator. You'd think a skilled basketball player would be a little better coordinated with his feet."

"The floorboards are so damned deep in those trucks," he said, "I have to use my toes to get the clutch in. Marsh manages that well due to his secret love of ballet and his fetish for wearing tutus."

"Nothin' wrong with a healthy fetish," I said.

"Plus," Blake continued, "All the guys stopped what they were doin' to watch the show for shits and giggles."

"So, anyway, Blake decides enough is enough. He decides, once he gets in third gear, he won't shift back down for any reason. The problem with that is the turn around the front office building needs to be taken at no more than twenty miles an hour. Third gear hits at about thirty or so. Therefore, when hot-rod-Henry over there makes the turn, the grain trailers swing hard, throwin' gravel everywhere and creating a miniature dust storm. This, of course, scatters the audience and sends everyone runnin' for cover."

"Yeah, and then Fred comes out screamin' at me," Blake said. "He tells me to stop that shit and drive right."

"Well, did ya?" Krista asked with a smile.

"Of course," Blake replied. "I didn't do it again 'til I moved the next truck. I'd found my niche and conquered the curse of the grain trucks."

"Then red-faced Fred stomped out and said he was gonna call Gramps," I said. "To which Blake responded by askin' if he'd wait a couple of minutes because he had one more truck to move."

Krista laughed out loud and we joined in. Senseless laughs were always cool.

"What did Fred tell Mr. TM?" Krista asked, cutting her eyes at me.

"I'm not sure," I replied, "But he probably said somethin' like Blake and me were insufferable."

The family lake house sat on a small bluff on the east bank of Lake Wappapello. It was built many years ago in a clearing of a deeply wooded area. Behind the house, there was a path which led through the woods and down the bluff to a private boat dock, which housed a two-seat fishing boat, a ski boat, and pontoon, which could handle up to ten or twelve people, depending on the number of adults and children.

The house itself had four bedrooms, a bonus room which could sleep more, a game room, a party room, and enough bathrooms to go around. We arrived about ten-thirty, before most of the family and friends got there. But one vehicle caught our attention quickly. It was a light blue Lexus with elaborate chrome plates. That vehicle belonged to the craziest person Blake and I had ever known—my cousin Ray.

Ray Conroy, now eighteen, and a recent high school graduate, was the son of my Aunt Tricia and Uncle Hal. They were really good people, which made it one of life's great mysteries that they somehow spawned Ray. He was one weird son of a bitch. How he had managed to escape the clutches of law enforcement, I would never know. He speeds recklessly, drinks incessantly, and drugs out uncontrollably. Yet, he still lived a charmed life and almost everybody liked him. Well, I liked him a little and Blake really didn't like him at all. He called me Cuzzy-Wuzzy and called Blake, Blink. The only thing that made him somewhat tolerable was he got our weed for us; and booze, if we couldn't swipe it from Gramps.

Blake parked off the drive, under a nice shade tree.

"Look, guys, before we get out, I need ya to know I told my mom we wouldn't be drinkin' on the lake," I said. "She gave me the 'concerned parent' talk this morning remindin' me that I'm not old enough to partake of alcoholic beverages despite the festive occasion."

"That's good by me," Krista said. "My folks'll be here later and I don't wanna give 'em any reason to monitor me any closer than they do now. Mom'll get sauced, as usual, but Dad will be ever vigilant."

"Well, my folks will not be here," Blake said. "But in accordance with my devout Baptist principles, I'll be bound by abstinence. Therefore, I wouldn't consider any activity which would put my soul in danger of eternal damnation."

"I wish I could be as devout in our faith as you are, Blake." I said, trying not to roll my eyes. "But does all that bullshit mean we agree not to drink on the lake?"

"Of course," Blake said, turning off the ignition. "We can make up the difference on land."

We made our way into the house and went through the ridiculous greetings, which adults always seemed to treasure but we found stupid and unnecessary. Blake and I had worked out a strategy which would allow us to avert the worst of this. We'd planned our arrival to be before noon, thereby beating most of the hordes of family and friends to the party. Next, we got the keys to the pontoon from Gramps. The only issue here was we had to work through Ray and whoever he showed up with. He would want to ski first while he could still stand up, so he'd start in the ski boat and we'd take the pontoon. The trick was to stay out on the lake for about three hours. We'd then return to the cookout, which would be in full swing with most of the guests totally shit-faced or well on their way. That way, we could maintain some semblance of anonymity.

Having accomplished the first part of our plan, we set out for the back patio to find cousin Ray.

"Cuzzy-Wuzzy!"

We'd found him.

Ray came over and gave me a quick, unsolicited hug. "How've you been? What's it been—almost two weeks?" Ray was a couple of inches taller than me and had an almost miraculous athletic build considering his lifestyle. I could tell he was already high on something.

"I think so, Ray," I said. "That's a long time to remember exactly."

"You are so right, Cuzzy-Wuzzy—that's life in the fast lane. Jodie! Pam! Paulie! You guys come over and meet the kids."

Jodie was Ray's latest flame. She was a looker—brunette, pretty face, fair tits, and great legs. Pam, who I was seeing for the first time, had long brown hair, a good build, and a nice ass. Paulie was tall and lean; he was also totally zonked out on something.

"Guys," Ray blurted out, "This is my favorite Cuzzy-Wuzzy, Marsh, and his good friend, Blink." Blake flipped Ray off, which went unnoticed by everyone but me. "And this is, ahh—I apologize, sweetheart, but your name escapes me."

"Her name is Krista Baker," Blake said firmly.

"Oh yeah," Ray said, "I thought I recognized you. You're John Baker's daughter." He turned to his friends. "John Baker is the manager of the elevators and oversees Gramps' farm operations." He then turned back to Krista. "I'm not good with names, but I always remember a beautiful face like yours." He gave Krista a quick wink and smile.

"Ray," I jumped in before Blake could, "We wanna hit the lake before the crowd gets here. Are we close to a move?"

"Slow down, Cuz, we're gettin' there," Ray said. "Kids, these are my friends Jodie, Pam, and Paulie." They all managed a nod in our direction. "Now, let's get organized. We have to have a legal adult on each boat. I'll ski first, so we'll start with Paulie driving the ski boat. Jodie will be in the boat with us. Pam, you'll need to start out on the pontoon with the kids. Cuzzy-Wuzzy can drive the pontoon, but you'll have to be there, so we're legal."

"Fine by me," Pam said, "As long as the gin's on the pontoon, I'm cool."

"That's my girl," Ray continued. "We'll rotate from that point, so whoever wants to ski will get all they want. Does that sound good to everyone?"

"That's a great plan, baby," Jodie said, leaning her head on Ray's shoulder. "Only you could set it up so well."

"Yeah, Ray," Blake said, "I really admire your ability to organize."

"Thanks Blink," Ray said with a coy look.

"And," Blake continued, "The way my dick fits in your mouth."

"Well, I never!" Jodie exclaimed.

"You can if you want to," Blake said, earning a nudge from Krista.

"Blink, you shithead," Ray said, stepping towards Blake, his face turning red, "I don't care if you're just a punk kid; I'll drag you down to the lake and kick your ass."

"Didn't you mean 'kiss' my ass?" Blake asked, not giving an inch.

"Alright, alright," I said, stepping in. "You guys can insult each other some other time. We need to get movin' before everybody starts gettin' here." Ray was still glaring at Blake, who was staring right back. "Okay, Ray, we'll grab the ice chests and take 'em down to the pontoon. Ray, you get the keys and we'll meet you down by the dock."

After a few seconds, Ray turned to go and noticed his friend, Paulie, had a big smile on his face.

"What's so funny, Paulie?" Ray asked.

"That Blink's a punk kid, but you gotta admit he's got balls," Paulie said.

"He knows I got 'em," Blake said. "He holds 'em in his hand all the time."

Blake then grabbed Krista by the arm and bolted for the kitchen, with me close behind. Boy this was going to be a hell of a day.

Damn, it was so good to finally be on the lake. It was a hot day but felt good out here on the water. I was a little concerned about the tension between Ray and Blake. They kept trading discreet glares at one another while we were loading up at the boat dock. I knew the Perdue sighting as we left town had made Blake uneasy and probably put him on the defensive. For Ray's part, he was just being an arrogant ass. He was really good at that—one of the few things he was good at.

While Krista and Pam caught some sun at the back of the pontoon, Blake was chillin' up front with me as I navigated the pontoon listening to some Eminem. Pam was already doing the gin and tonic thing.

"Bro, that thing with you and Ray almost got out of hand," I said.

"Well, he brought it on and you know it," he said. "He's always tryin' to make us look bad by talkin' down to us, and he does it in front of his friends, our friends, or whoever. We're not little kids anymore and I'm tired of it."

"I know, Blake, but you took a pretty hard shot at Jodie and that was not cool."

"Maybe so; but he started it by makin' a pass at Krista, and I didn't like it. Besides, what was that shit about 'I think that is a great plan, baby'" —said with a high pitched voice, making a sour face—"Hell, it wasn't like he was plannin' the Macy's Thanksgiving Day Parade."

"We both know Ray's a jerk and basically full of shit," Marsh said. "But he does help us out from time to time."

"Are you talking about the booze and the weed?" I asked. "Hell, Marsh, we pay 'im top dollar for that shit. Besides, we can go to other sources and save money in the process—plus not have to deal with his sorry ass."

"Speaking of his sorry ass," Marsh said, pointing off to our right, "Here he comes."

One thing about Ray—he could water ski. Blake and I could too, but not like Ray. He loved to show off and was capable of doing it. The ski boat went by within about twenty yards of the pontoon. As Ray passed, he flipped us off and, then, patted his butt, relaying the "kiss my ass" message. Boy, cousin Ray was an amazing piece of shit. To make him a worthy member of society, the bar would have to be lowered so far it would be a hole in the ground. Well, here he came again. As he moved closer, he was waving at the girls. At that moment, a bottle rocket exploded a few feet over his head. Ray ducked, looked around in all directions and barely managed to stay up. As the ski boat made a big turn to circle back, I whirled around to see Blake with his homemade bottle rocket gun. We'd fought many wars with that thing, but this was insane.

"What the hell are you doin'?" I yelled.

The girls jumped up to look from the back as Blake fired his next round. Ray fought to keep his balance as the second rocket flew past him. This time he wasn't so lucky and took a beautiful spill.

"Dammit, Blake, are you nuts?" I asked, as I killed the motor.

Both Krista and Pam were laughing so hard they almost fell off the pontoon. As the ski boat whirled around to pick up Ray, I could see Paulie laughing, too.

"Hell, Marsh, that was so cool," Blake said, keeping a wary eye on Ray as he swam to the boat. "I wasn't firin' right at 'im; there was no way he was gonna get hit. He says he's an acrobat on skis, so I gave 'im a chance to prove it. I have to give 'im credit, he can wipe out with the best of 'em."

"Blake, you need to cut this shit out with Ray, or we won't get through the day," I said, raising my voice to reinforce my point.

The ski boat slowly made its way closer to us. Paulie killed the motor, so they could drift along with us. To my surprise and everyone else's, Ray was smiling.

"That was pretty good, Blink, if I do say so myself," Ray said. "I must be gettin' rusty or lazy, wiping out like that. Who knows? Anyway, I'm gonna pull Paulie a few rounds. You doin' okay, Pam, baby?"

"Yeah, enjoyin' the fun," she replied. "That was a great plunge."
"Cool!" Ray exclaimed, as he started the boat. "There's always excitement at a Williams' lake bash. Later." He then revved up the motor and they took off.

Tired, but refreshed, I climbed slowly up the boat ladder and into the boat. I had just taken my turn on the water skis, and it was exhilarating, as always. Ray knew how to drive a ski boat, making good turns and allowing for good cross action. Once again, this represented one of his ever-shrinking positive attributes. Blake was in the water putting on the skis for his turn. I had been a little apprehensive about Ray pulling Blake. But Ray had actually been decent since the bottle rocket fiasco an hour or so ago. Maybe Jodie hanging all over him had him distracted, so there was little interest in the events earlier in the day. Blake appeared ready and flashed me the thumbs-up signal. I told Ray to gun the motor and Blake was up.

I'm pretty good on the water skis, but my bro was better. Blake was a really good athlete. His body, though not real big, was well chiseled. His arms, chest, hips, and legs were toned well. Even his size ten feet were perfectly contoured compared to my long, slender elevens, which appeared to be still growing. The only place I could best him was on the golf course, and he was a pretty good golfer. I had a super golf instructor and also had the advantage of Blake having a low level of patience with a slow paced game.

It was amazing to watch the grace in which he glided across the water. It was almost hypnotic and—

Suddenly, the motor choked down hard, as Blake was gliding across to the right side. Just a moment later, Ray revved the motor back up full throttle, creating a whip action on the ski rope and jerking Blake forward with great force. Blake was airborne, losing a ski before he released the rope and hit the surface of the water face first and hard. It happened so fast, I was frozen for a moment.

"Oh shit," Ray said.

"What the hell happened, Ray!" I yelled, as I crossed to the driver's side of the boat. "Did you do that on purpose? You did, didn't you?"

"He did no such thing," Jodie said, jumping in between us.

"Look, Cuz, the motor choked down. It does that sometimes, and we've been runnin' for over two hours," Ray said.

"Yeah, I bet it did Ray!" I responded angrily. "You must think I'm a total idiot to swallow some horseshit explanation like that!"

"It's a good explanation!" Jodie chimed in.

"You would think so!" I fired back. "And you stay out of —"

Oh, my God, it hit me. We hadn't turned to go back for Blake.

"Turn the boat around Ray! Now!" I yelled. "And go back for Blake!" I was almost shaking, as I looked back. I couldn't see him.

Ray turned the boat immediately. "How could I turn the boat with you yellin' in my face?" Ray shouted back at me.

"Just hurry up, Ray—Now!"

I could finally see him. We got back close to him pretty quick. As we eased up to him, I could see his nose was bleeding and his face was red. I immediately dove in the water and swam to him. As I reached him, I grabbed his arm—he was trembling. He had a strange blank look on his face. And his eyes—I did a double take—man, there was a weird look about his eyes; or maybe I was seeing things.

"Blake, you okay?" I asked, facing him.

"I blacked out or somethin', I guess," he stammered, breathing unevenly.

"Are you hurt anywhere other than your nose?"

"My right shoulder hurts, but it seems to work alright," he said, rotating his arm and wincing.

"Okay, bro, assume the lifesaving position," I said. "I'm gonna swim you over to the ladder." Blake normally wouldn't let you help him much, but he offered no resistance now, which concerned me a little. Positioned behind him, sliding my left arm under his armpits and around his chest, I eased him over to the ladder.

"Ray, help me get 'im back in the boat!" I yelled.

"Okay, I'm here," Ray said, as he appeared at the top of the ladder.

We eased Blake in the boat. I slowly laid him down, placing a life preserver under his head and noticed he was still shaking a little. I started grabbing towels—everyone's towels—and covering him up.

"Hey, that's my towel," Jodie said.

"Shut up," I said, grabbing some tissue and packing his left nostril to stop the bleeding.

Ray eased the boat over to pick up the skis. He killed the engine and leaned over the side with a boat hook, bringing in one ski at a time.

"Is he okay?" Ray asked, as he secured the skis.

This was my chance. "He better be Ray, for your sake."

"Look, Marsh," Ray said defensively, "I can't be held accountable for a mechanical malfunction. These things happen."

"Mechanical malfunction!" I yelled, jumping in his face. "You're a total malfunction! You're a freak of nature, Ray. God fucked up when he came up with you, and He's probably regretting every bit of it."

"Now, hold on!—" Ray started, but I was too quick.

"You hold on, you idiot!" I blared out. "You could've hurt 'im real bad, Ray, maybe even killed 'im. With your stupid, cocky attitude, you're just enough of a man to make everyone sick. You serve no positive purpose in life." I knew my face was turning redder by the second, and my eyes must've been on fire, because Ray looked dumbfounded. "You could've killed 'im, you stupid motherfucker! Do you hear that? Killed 'im! He's worth more than a million of you! So, if you want trouble, then your trouble is with me!"

"Listen Marsh, cousin or not, I'm real close to knockin' your teeth out!" Ray said starting to get red-faced himself.

"Then do it, Ray! You may kick my ass, but you've got it to do!

So, let's go right now, you worthless piece of shit! Well, what're you waitin' on? Let's rumble, Cuzzy-Wuzzy!"

Ray glared at me, but I didn't back up an inch. Suddenly, he whirled around and got behind the wheel of the boat. He cranked the engine, put it in gear, and we made for the pontoon. I sat down quickly beside Blake. No one in the boat was saying a word when Blake nudged me. I turned toward him and caught his eyes again. I was kind of drawn to them, which was weird.

"Remind me never to piss you off too bad, bro," he said. He managed a little smile, which mirrored mine.

Chapter Four

BLAKE

I didn't want to talk about my big spill and told Marsh to let it go. Ray could have his bullshit explanation. What Ray said or thought didn't mean a damn thing to me. I could tell Marsh was really pissed. He'd sit with Krista and me for a little bit and then just get up and wander around the cookout—then come back.

Ray, his girl, Marsh and me were the only ones who knew what really happened. That had changed a few minutes ago when I told Krista the whole story and swore her to secrecy. I knew it worried her a little, but I honest to God was feeling better every minute. I'd eaten a rack of ribs and a huge burger. Plus, Marsh had already slipped me a couple of beers. Hell, my shoulder didn't hurt anymore.

On top of all that, it was like some kind of energy was stirring inside of me. I felt like I could sense things in other people. Like a few moments ago, I could sense Krista was troubled about all this—I could damn near feel it. Her eyes were so warm when I looked at them. Warm? How could that be? I felt the same thing when I caught Marsh's eyes while sitting with him on the boat after my spill. Damn, I should be drinking more beer.

"It's pretty hard to imagine Marsh doin' that," Krista said, returning from a brief visit with her parents.

"Yeah, Marsh was ready to go toe to toe with cousin Ray," I said, feeling a lot better now.

"I'm not sure how smart that was. Ray's bigger and stronger."

"Never doubt, baby, that if Ray had taken Marsh down, I would've grabbed the boat hook and beat the holy shit out of 'im," I said and meant it.

"Well, Ray's a big jerk anyway. But I know this is tough for Marsh because of the family situation."

"Marsh'll be okay. He's a lot tougher than people think he is and, all in all, Ray's no match for 'im."

"You must be right, baby," she said, putting her arm around me. "I'm just glad it's all over and you're okay. I was really scared at first. I just care about you so much."

I turned to her, gave her a quick kiss and said, "I'm crazy 'bout you, baby. You're my special girl."

I was almost frozen looking into her eyes. I suddenly felt a huge surge and I knew what was driving this one. My dick almost sprang out of my shorts. I wanted her so bad. But what was different was I could sense her desire for me. And I mean a strong desire. Where was this going? Damn…

"You guys about ready to load up?" Marsh asked, breaking up whatever this was.

"Yeah, it'll be dark in a few minutes," I said, turning away from Krista.

"It doesn't matter to me; whatever you and Krista want to do," Marsh said.

"That's up to you guys," Krista said, shaking her head a little. "I just need to escape this spiked punch because I'm not sure what's mixed in it."

"Yeah, that stuff gets stronger as the day goes on," Marsh said. "I think Gramps just grabs a bottle of somethin' and loads it every so often."

"Okay, let's ease outta here," I said, as I started clearing the table.

"Alright, I'll go tell Grandma we're outta here, and you guys start roundin' up our stuff," Marsh said, as he turned and walked back to the house.

Krista helped me finish with the table, and we went over to the garage to get our bags. She looked so good in just a white t-shirt and khaki shorts. She showed just enough to cause my hormones to go crazy. Nature could be a bitch.

"Blake, do ya think Marsh would mind drivin' while we ride in the back?" she asked, with a little apprehension.

Wow! This just kept getting better all the time.

"Sure, baby," I answered. "I'll ask 'im. I'm sure he'll be cool with it."

"Well, whatever you think. I need to check out the ladies room before we go."

"Go ahead, baby, I'll take the bags," I said, and grabbed the bags and made my way to the car. I saw Marsh crossing the lawn to meet me.

"Alright, we're ready...where's Krista?" he asked.

"She had to stop by the little girl's room. Uh, Marsh, would you mind drivin'?" I asked, trying not to sound over-anxious.

"Not at all, bro. You've had a few beers anyway," Marsh replied.

"Would you care if Krista and me rode in the back?"

"No problem, bro. I don't think I can stand all the heat and passion anyway. Only one stipulation—tell Krista I'm jammin' to our music."

"You got it," I said, unable to contain a little laugh.

"Good thing we got your mom's Olds; lots of room in the back—you do have a condom, don't you?" he asked with a sly look.

"What the hell for? You'd have more use for one up there by yourself."

"No way," he said, "When it comes to jerkin' off, I like a 'skin to skin' hold on things."

We both got a laugh out of that.

"What's so funny?" Krista asked, walking up.

"We were just discussin' the advantages of gettin' a grip on things," Marsh replied.

After Krista gave me a puzzled look, I just shook my head and we all hopped in the car and headed east. It caught my attention when Krista laid her big beach towel on the bench of the back seat for us to sit on.

It didn't take Marsh but a couple of minutes to crank up some

Eminem. Krista started cuddling up to me—real close, real fast. She started licking my lips, which led to a warm, inviting kiss. Damn, she was hot. Our kisses got deeper and deeper. The heat was searing. We eased apart to catch our breath. Our eyes had adjusted to the dark and they met—

—My God, where was I? It was so dark. It was like some kind of corridor and I was floating. It was warm—a soothing warmth. I wasn't sure what was above me or below me. I couldn't get over how good it felt —

I moved to her neck and worked her firmly, but gently. She was moaning softly, and I could feel her body pulsing in rhythm with mine. We'd never been like this. She took my left hand and laid it across her breasts. Holy shit! My hand began running all over and gently squeezing. Our passionate kissing rose to a new level. As we broke again, our eyes came together once more—

—I was back in the corridor again. This time I could see that I was hovering over some kind of stream. The waters were dark and flowing and I was drawn to them —

There was a drive moving in me I had never felt before. I slid my hand under her shirt and there was no resistance. I carefully removed her bra. My hand found her rock hard nipples and gently pinched them. I slowly began undressing her and, once again, there was no resistance. Some kind of natural instinct was driving both of us. With no warning, she started undressing me. She was in some kind of fervor, almost tearing my clothes off of me.

Finding ourselves totally nude, we began a journey of exploration of each other. Our eyes became locked again—

—I was back in the corridor but was now descending to the dark waters. My feet slipped into the waters. My God, the waters were warm and felt so soothing. I started squirming, trying to fall deeper into the flowing waters—

I eased my hand up her inner thigh and began exploring her with my fingers. At the same time, she found me. I was so hard, it hurt. Her touch set me off. She moaned as she began a gentle but firm caress, which sent tingling sensations firing through me.

Somewhere in the background I could hear Jay-Z's GIVE IT TO ME, though it was fading. Our groans were like faint echoes. As I moved on top of her, our eyes found each other—

—I now began a gradual descent into the waters... to my knee... to my stomach... to my neck. My God, this felt so good I didn't know how long I could stand it. Suddenly, flames broke out on my right. They were bizarre, but not threatening. Then they broke out on my left as I continued to be carried by these amazing waters—

With her hand guiding me, I eased inside of her. Our groans were still echoes and seemed even more distant. Our dual movements became a peaceful, erotic motion. This was mesmerizing, beyond anything I had ever imagined. The flow was steady as the tide inside me began to rise higher and higher. She had her hands on my hips urging me deeper and deeper. We were totally out of control. I met her eyes again.

—Fire was everywhere, the feeling was so powerful; beyond anything I had ever known—

Neither of us could hold back. We exploded in tandem, surrendering all we had. My release went on and on. I closed my eyes as things became hazy and I could feel us falling, with no place to land...

I opened my eyes and saw Krista sitting up in the seat, putting her clothes on. I slowly eased up and started getting dressed. I could now hear the music blasting. Where had it been? Krista was folding the towel.

"Hey, Marsh!" I said, trying to cut through the blasting sound.

"Yeah," he said, turning down the volume.

"Thanks, you had it cranked pretty good."

"I was tryin' to hear over the noise comin' from back there."

"Oh, right, sorry."

"Don't be sorry, bro."

I leaned back and put my arm around Krista. She leaned into me, but didn't say anything. I just held her as we sat quietly for a few minutes.

"Okay, guys, decision time," Marsh said, after turning down the music. "We're comin' up on Fifty-Five. You wanna run to Sikeston or head on home?"

"Just take me home," Krista said. "I'm really tired."

"But, Krista," I said, but she cut me off.

"No, really Blake. You guys take me on home."

I could tell she meant it.

"Okay," I said, but didn't like the way it felt...

We pulled up to Krista's house just before ten. Holding her close, I slowly walked her to the front door. We held each other a moment. She offered only a quick kiss and then looked at me. "I love you, Blake."

"I love you, too, Babe," I said, slowly releasing her. She eased inside the door and I made my way back to the car. Marsh was getting out from behind the wheel as I approached.

"Hey, Marsh, would you keep drivin'? I'm zonked."

"I bet you are," he said with a chuckle.

I plopped down on passenger side seat, feeling uncomfortably weak.

"Well, you wanna go celebrate?" Marsh asked.

"She said she loved me," I said, looking straight ahead.

"Surprise, surprise," Marsh said.

"I told her I loved her, too."

"No surprise there either."

"But I don't."

We sat quiet for a moment when I felt Marsh's hand on my shoulder.

"Blake, you alright, bro?"

I put my right hand on top of his and turned to look at him. I swear I could see through his eyes—

—*I was floating in the warm waters again. It felt so damned good. Once again, fires began to break out all around me. The warmth continued to grow as I floated on and on...*—

Chapter Five

MARSH

I made my way into the pro shop to pick up a scorecard and some snack crackers while Blake put ice in the ice chest. I had hoped to hit the practice range before our round, but we were running late—thanks in part to my bro's roller coaster sense of timing—and the course was busy as hell. We also had the misfortune to be paired up with Mr. and Mrs. Burns for our round as it was the only morning slot open. They were actually okay golfers, considering they were in their sixties and losing their eyesight. The problem was we felt obligated to be on our best behavior, which could be tedious for me and an absolute stretch for Blake.

I was really anxious to play for a couple of reasons. One, I had managed some driving range time a couple of days this week and had hit the ball better and with more consistency than ever. Todd Little, the club pro who worked with me extensively, said he was amazed at how I had elevated my game and I needed to hit the course.

The other reason was more problematic and complex. My world was in a mess. Ciera and I were on the rocks. She hung up on me last night, which she had every right to do. But there was only so much monotony a teenage boy like me should have to take. Ciera loved to complain about how boring things were all the time. She couldn't seem to grasp the fact that we lived in a small town surrounded by small towns, which meant there just wasn't very much to do. Half the people of Gardner viewed Sikeston as a city. What did that make St. Louis or Memphis, small countries? Anyway, the point was things were just boring sometimes, depending on your definition of excitement.

I asked her to take a look at what we did as a routine. We went to each other's house, or one of our parents dropped us at the movies or something. We used our private time to make out and rub each other in all the right places. She continued to insist that we had to wait to further explore those places and that made our relationship stronger. I tried to remember that when I woke up each morning looking at the rise in my sheets and, as of late, trying to set new records for jacking off.

Another reason was that Mom and I were at each other a lot. I'd made myself a promise after Dad died that I'd be open and honest with Mom. Dad would've wanted that. The problem was sometimes Mom freaked out when I honestly answered some of her questions. She knew I fooled around with alcohol and weed some, and it really seemed to be a moral dilemma for her. I was also irresponsible about some things around the house, like my room. It wasn't that my housekeeping skills left a little to be desired; it's that I didn't have any. I loved my mom so much, which left me at a loss about what to do.

But, I was skirting the real issue and I knew it. Underneath all this typical bullshit was something that was definitely not typical. I couldn't get past what happened that night last week when we got back from the lake. It was all about my best friend, and I was scared as shit to bring it up.

As I left the pro shop, I ran into Todd who, along with being my golf instructor, had become kind of a mentor. He was a first class guy who had been really good to me. I'd started playing on the school golf team this past year, but my golf coach was the girls' volleyball coach, whose knowledge of golf would fit in a thimble. Todd, on the other hand, was a great teacher who had also become an adult confidant I could trust. He took extra time on many afternoons to work with me on my game and had helped me a lot. I also felt I could go to him if trouble arose concerning things that Mom and my grandparents wouldn't serve as good options. I hadn't had to play that card yet, but it was nice to know it was there.

"What's up, Todd?"

"Busy, busy, my friend. I was beginning to wonder if you guys were gonna make it."

"Well, we're movin' on Blake time, which is difficult to gauge."

"I bet that's right," he said smiling. "How's he doin' since his spill you told me about?"

"Oh, he seems okay to me." I really wasn't one hundred percent sure about that. He had been acting a little weird this week.

"When do you wanna come in again and work on your swing?"

"I can probably make it late tomorrow afternoon. I think Mom can bring me."

"Sounds good. Tell her she can drop you off, and I'll run you home afterward. Burgers are on me."

"That's cool. I'll check with her later today and give you a call if that's okay."

"Works for me," he said, and then looked just past me. "Well, hello Blake. I heard about your spill on the lake; you okay?"

"Doin' okay, thanks," Blake said.

"I'm glad," Todd said. "You know Lake Wappapello has somewhat of a sordid history."

"No, I didn't know that," Blake said, with a curious look on his face.

"Yeah," Todd said, smiling a little. "I'll tell you guys about it sometime. But right now go burn up the course. I've got to try to manage this madhouse—it's crazy today."

Blake actually took the news about having to play a round with the Burns without a complaint. There was clearly something going on, and whatever it was must be really bothering him. He'd said he needed to talk to me about some things as we drove over here this morning. There was also something I needed to tell him. Well, maybe our golf game would help both of us into a better frame of mind.

We met the Burns at the first tee and exchanged pleasantries for a couple of minutes. The tone for the round was set when Mr. Burns hit his drive up the right side of the fairway. It wasn't real long, but it was perfectly placed.

"Nice drive, Mr. Burns," Blake said.

"Thank you, Son," he responded with a smile. "It looked good the last time I saw it."

Blake cut his eyes at me, and we exchanged discreet smiles.

The club course was predominantly flat, and the fairways were lush green with almost perfect consistency. Groups of trees lined every fairway, adding to the beauty and difficulty of the course. There were three ponds, which came into play on seven of the holes. The greens were large, perfectly contoured, and surrounded by some pesky sand traps. Overall, it was a beautiful and unforgiving course.

It was busy, but we kept a good pace until we got backed up at the seventh tee. What was truly remarkable was that Blake and I were both at the top of our games. Blake, a great ball striker, played long but usually struggled with his short game. That wasn't the case today. He was one over par at this point. I was also playing well, and currently stood at even par. Maybe it was our focus. I couldn't remember the last time I saw Blake this focused, and it was definitely affecting my focus. To this point, our conversation had centered on our golf game and that helped, too. Having to occasionally play the role of seeing-eye dogs for the Burns had kept us from tensing up.

Now, we found ourselves looking at a fifteen-minute or so wait at the seventh tee. Blake and I used the opportunity to break out the snack crackers.

"Your golf game is out of sight today," I said, watching the group playing in front of us leaving the tee.

"Thanks, but even at my best, I can't match your game," Blake said, kicked back behind the wheel of our golf cart.

"Yeah, well, you're leavin' me no room for error. Your short game may be the best I've seen it. Have you been doin' some practicin' on the side?"

"No way, bro. You know if I'm playin' golf, it's with you," he laughed a little and appeared to be more relaxed than earlier.

"You know, the Burns are actually kinda cool people," I said, looking at them on the other side of the tee, sitting in their cart.

"Yeah, but Mr. Burns seems a little sad to me," Blake said.

"Jesus, Blake, he's been all smiles, laughin' and jokin' the whole round."

"I know, but there's somethin' about him that seems sad."

"I can't see how you figure that, but whatever."

"Marsh, I'm really sorry about bein' late today," Blake said, turning to face me. "Things are, well, a little out of sorts. But that's no excuse."

"It's all in the past, bro, so let it go. We're havin' a great day, so let's keep at it. We can dig into things later and work 'em out. Right now, I'm tryin' to beat your ass and it's tough."

Blake smiled, and we both hopped out the cart. It was time to tee off.

It had been a great round of golf. This was the absolute best Blake and me had ever played. I was currently lying two, just to the left of the eighteenth green. This was a par four finishing hole, and I was sitting even par for the round. To heighten the suspense, Blake was on the green in two, just about twenty feet from the cup. He was just two over par, which still gave him a shot at me. Providing a welcome contrast, Mr. Burns had just blasted out of the sand trap—on his second attempt—making reference to either his shot or his ball as a "goose-headed gopher". This didn't sound very profound until you considered the possibility of the existence of such a creature. If it did exist, I suspected you could find it somewhere between the Sci-Fi and National Geographic channels.

I was finally set for a short pitch to the green and hopefully in the cup. I took a short, easy stroke and watched as my ball ran past the cup about twenty feet. Mr. and Mrs. Burns, both with longer putts, ran their balls to within a two-foot radius of the cup, which constituted a "gimme". There was no official reference in any golf rulebook I knew of that mentioned a "gimme". Yet, I suspected it was one of the most common shots scored in a round of golf, and you didn't even need a club.

The showdown was now set. We decided I would putt first. If I made the putt, I would par a course for the first time ever. After determining my line, I putted the ball, which rolled slowly up to the lip of the cup and—dropped in.

"Yes!" I said as I thrust my right hand up in the air.

Mr. and Mrs. Burns applauded and my best friend came over and gave me a big hug. Blake missed his putt, but still managed the best score he had ever shot. The Burns offered their congratulations, telling us how much fun they had. We told them it'd also been fun for us and thanked them for everything. As we returned to our cart, Mrs. Burns walked over.

"Boys, I'd like to offer you special thanks," she said. "Last week, Mr. Burns lost his older sister. He was always close to her and has been deeply upset. This is the best day he has had since her death. I'm going to leave your names with the restaurant manager for you guys to have a meal on me. Thank you so much."

We both thanked her and told her how sorry we were for his loss. After she walked away, I slowly turned to Blake and started to speak, but he spoke first.

"The answer is," he said, looking straight ahead, "I don't know."

The sounds of T.I. rolled out in Blake's truck as he turned left off Highway Eighty on to a farm road, which ran east of a huge soybean field. This land belonged to Gramps. The road wound into an obscured clearing with a group of trees which surrounded an old, dilapidated farm house. This was one of "our spots" we used for the privacy we needed for our shady recreational activities. Today the activity was smoking weed. It was a hot afternoon, but the trees provided a cool, shaded area. He parked his truck around behind the house, further out of sight.

Blake and I took a seat on the back porch of the house, our

feet dangling off the edge. We began playing one of our favorite games, pass the blunt. Ray gave us a good deal on this stuff and said it was top of the line. I guess it was his way of saying he was sorry for the lake thing. No doubt it was more for me than for Blake. There was a strange feeling about the setting here today, probably because of some of the things we had to say.

"How're things goin' with you and Ciera?" he asked.

"Not worth a shit," I answered.

"Oh," he said weakly, obviously a little stunned by my terse response.

"Hell, Blake, she hung up on me last night and probably should have sooner than she did. I've been a real asshole lately, and not just to her. Mom and I seem to be going at it every day about something. Damn, I saw Rick the other day and was almost rude to him for no reason."— Rick Thomas was a classmate of ours and a good friend—"But, back to Ciera; you know how things are between us. She whines about her friends all the time and how everything's boring. I got tired of that and decided to bring up the point that our relationship was spinning its wheels. She took offense to that, as she should've. Then I snapped at you this morning for running a little late."

"That was my fault all the way, bro."

"Well, it didn't deserve that kind of reaction from me. That was my version of whining just like I'm doin' about everything else."—I pulled a heavy drag off the blunt—"Boy, Ray came across with some pretty good shit this time."

"You're right about that," he responded, obviously beginning to feel the potency.

"Anyway, I don't know what's goin' on with Ciera. I guess part of it is I've been so horny lately. Or I'm startin' to feel different— hell, I don't know. Maybe I'm jealous of what you and Krista have found."

"Well, don't be," he said, sighing a little. "Krista and I are on the ropes. I've been keeping that to myself because it's a strange situation. As much as I loved the amazing sex we had that night, I don't know if it was worth it. I feel like she's gonna dump me any day. And the worst thing about that is, for some reason, sometimes I find myself not caring very much. But Jesus, I don't want to lose her. Can you believe all this?"

"It does sound a little weird," I said. "But, I could tell somethin's been goin' on with you."

"I mean it's like I want the sex really bad, even though lately we haven't been very intimate at all. She turns me on big time. But there's a part of me that just—oh hell, I don't know. Am I losin' it, bro?"

"It's hard to answer that question not bein' real sure what 'it' is," I said, really starting to feel this high.

"My sanity, I guess," he said slowly, no doubt feeling a little high, too.

"You know, Blake, bein' adolescents gives us a little leeway on sanity."

"Really, how much?"

"Hell, I don't know."

"Well, I might as well tell you the rest," he said with some obvious apprehension. "Sometimes weird feelings seem to stir inside me. I don't know what they mean. Hell, I don't even know what they are. That thing with Mr. Burns today; I knew he was sad—I could feel it just looking at him. Damn, Marsh, that night in the car with Krista, I swear I could see inside of her. I know that's crazy, but I could," —he paused to take a hit—"and there's somethin' else, too."

I took a hit and said, "Okay."

"Bro, ever since that night with Krista I've been havin' wet dreams and I mean big ones."

"What's wrong with that?"

"How many have you had?"

"None, but I'm jackin' off like crazy."

"Well, I'm jackin' off a lot too," he said with more conviction.

45

"Hell, Marsh, I've only had a couple of wet dreams before, as far as I can remember, and now I'm soakin' my boxers every night."

"Well, I'll admit that creates a sticky situation."

"You're funny as shit, asshole."

"Okay, my bad, bro," I said apologetically. "Just tryin' to chill out about this stuff."

"I know, I'm just screwed up about all this shit." He took a toke, sighed and said, "Whadda ya think Todd meant when he said the lake had a sordid history?"

"Oh hell, Blake, he was smilin'; probably just makin' a joke."

"But ya know, Marsh, this crap did seem to start after my spill at the lake. You think I hit my head too hard or somethin'?"

"Well, if you did, I musta' hit mine on somethin' too."

"Whadda ya' mean?"

"You remember when we dropped Krista off at her house after the lake?" I asked, staring straight ahead.

"Vaguely," he responded.

"You came back to the car after walking Krista to her door and asked me to drive."

"Yeah."

"In the car, you told me Krista said that she loved you, and you told her that you loved her."

"Yeah."

"Then, you told me you didn't love her."

He didn't respond, so I turned to look at him and he was looking down, slowly nodding his head.

I continued, "So then I put my hand on your shoulder and asked if you were alright. You looked back at me."

"Okay."

"Well, my friend," I said with a sigh. "When you first returned to the car, the clock showed 10:05. When I started to back the Olds out of the driveway, the clock showed 10:40."

"What?" he said with a shocked expression.

"What I'd like to know," I said, gazing straight ahead again, "Is what the hell happened to those thirty-five minutes?"

Chapter Six

KRISTA

Hurry, hurry; she's always in a hurry. Mom knew I was working at getting organized, but that didn't matter. I took a deep breath. It was time to answer the call to breakfast. I finally found my way to the kitchen.

"I thought you got lost," Mom said, trying to be funny. Her eyes were a little red, no doubt from partaking of that infamous last martini.

"No, Mom, I'm just trying to get ready without having to rush." I took my seat at the table. It only took until I'd buttered my toast for the questions to start.

"What did you and Blake do last night?" she asked.

"Well, Mom, let's see. Where should I start? We went to Sikeston to eat at Branch Gardens. There were no movies we wanted to see, so we drove back to town and cruised around for a while. Then we went to his house and watched television. That about covers it. How we got it done all in one night, I'll never know."

She gave me her smug look, which showed she had noted my sarcasm. "There's nothing wrong with parents wanting to know what their daughter is doing out on her dates, is there John?" she asked, as my dad came into the kitchen and made his way to the coffeemaker.

"Wrong with what?" Dad asked.

"With us knowing what Krista did on her date last night," she replied, as Dad stopped by my chair and gave me a kiss on the cheek.

"In general terms, I guess. My baby girl has a good head on her shoulders, so I don't care much about the details."

"I just think knowing what's going on with my daughter falls under my rights as a mother," Mom stated, a little defensively.

"I told you what we did. It's just pretty drab stuff, Mom."

"Other than the obvious red hot date last night, how're things goin' with you, Krista? You've seemed quieter than normal lately," Dad said in his unassuming manner.

"Oh, Dad, I don't know," I said. "I guess I'm just thinking about school starting in a couple of weeks and all the things that go with it."

"Sounds like boy trouble to me," Mom said, rejoining the conversation.

"Well, Blake and I are doin' fine. So, I have no idea what you're talking about."

"I've got an appointment for us Wednesday," Dad said, looking at me and purposely ignoring Mom.

"You and me, Dad; what for?"

"We have to check something out at the Chevrolet dealership in Sikeston," he said with a solemn look on his face, which then turned into a big smile.

I was stunned for a moment. Then, it hit me, and I was up in a second. I ran around the table to my dad and hugged him with all the strength I could muster.

"Oh, Daddy, I didn't know if you were gonna be able to swing it."

"For my baby girl? Are you kidding?" he said, holding that big smile.

"Thanks, Dad, you're the best. You always have been. Oh, I've got to go call Cheryl; good breakfast, Mom."

I headed for my bedroom, trying not to trip on the way.

"Hey girl," Cheryl said, answering on the first ring as always.

"Get ready, girl, for the news of the day," I said anxiously.

"Alright, I'm ready. Let's hear it."

"Dad and I are goin' to buy me a car, Wednesday."

"Now that is the news of the day, girl! That's so cool!"

"I know. I wasn't sure if it would happen before school. You know how Dad budgets everything. It's a dream come true."

"Yeah, and you deserve to have some dreams come true. Have you told the 'snake' yet?"

"No, I've gotta sit for the Dailey's at noon for a couple of hours; then I'm goin' with my folks to the five o'clock Saturday mass. He's comin' over when we get back so I'll surprise him with it then."

"Well, goin' to mass before seeing Blake is probably a good idea."

"Oh, Cheryl, I don't wanna talk about Blake right now," I said. "I just wanna think about having my own car."

"Okay, girlfriend, what kind of car are you up for?"

"I'm not sure, but I know it'll have to be affordable first, and everything else, second. I'll call you later and we'll discuss some options. I've gotta start gettin' ready to go to the Dailey's."

"Alright, girl. I'll do some surfing for some ideas."

"That'd be great. Love ya', girl."

"Back 'atcha," she said, as she hung up.

Boy, I had given up on this happening before school started. Wow, I hadn't felt this good since...well, since... Why did I always end up backing up in this mess? It had been two weeks since that night. To say it had been a roller coaster ride would be vastly understating things. It just wouldn't go away. Fighting this was slowly becoming unbearable.

I loved Blake, but was convinced I didn't know what love was. When I was around him, I wanted him. I wanted him the way I had him that night. Then I started hating myself for feeling that way. The answer was probably to break it off with him, but in a weird sort of way, I was afraid to. This was where it really got strange. Something inside me gave me the feeling that if I gave up loving him, then it would be alright to have sex with him. Somehow, it wouldn't matter. This was so insane.

At first, I'd been so emotionally caught up in the moral implications of what we did, nothing else mattered. Finger pointing came next. I blamed Blake, the booze, Marsh, Ray, the bash—you name it. Hell, I even blamed I-55. Naturally, blame eventually found its way back to me. Honesty always did that. Then came acceptance. And, in accordance with my Catholic upbringing, there had to be confessions. With all of this stress, I felt like I must be suffering from some sort of spiritual virus. Of course, the fear of pregnancy had hovered over everything. But, thankfully, I'd had my period the other day. Then, something changed.

I began having extreme sexual urges. These urges were the kind I never knew existed. They seemed to be powered from deep inside me. I found myself having various types of carnal desires. Afterward, I was left feeling weak as they faded away. Sometimes they were so bad, I started rubbing myself and I had never done that.

To make matters worse, I seemed to have these strong sexual impulses when working around Mr. Dailey. I mean I'd always been captivated by his good looks. But now he could walk into the room and it was like the rumblings of unrestricted lust began. The longer he stayed in my presence, the more these feelings seemed to build. These feelings were new and so powerful, they would rise without warning.

The situation with Blake was completely different and really weird. My desire for him was strong because of my feelings for him. But this unprecedented sexual aggression did not rise up with him. It was like something inside me said "You really like this guy, so you can't go there." How much sense did that make? How much sense did any of this make? How could you find answers when you were afraid of the questions?

Well, I guessed it would be back to confession, where I could share that I had lusted about one hundred times over the past few days. I thought I'd ask if there was a way to reserve forgiveness in advance. That would probably be frowned upon by the "powers that be"—whoever they really were.

Chapter Seven

BLAKE

Getting out of the shower, I almost managed to slip and bust my ass. That would probably be a fitting start to every day for me. So much was going on with me, I didn't know if I was coming or going. The good news was I hadn't zoned out or lost track of time in a while. The bad news was I kept having strange or weird sensations about the people around me. Were they real? My association with reality, if there was such a thing, was slowly becoming a loose one.

The situation with Krista was becoming a little frightening. I was crazy about her, but I wasn't sure it had anything to do with love. Hell, what did I know about love anyway? But dreaming about our amazing sexual encounter was pulling me apart at the seams. I had reached a point, at times, that control became an issue. I mean, I was getting boners all the time. And I was still waking up with my boxers plastered to me about half the time. When I busted a nut, my release was always tremendous.

The big problem was every time I got really close to Krista, I could feel this anguish, like she was suffering from a great internal conflict and it was about me. At the same time, she was emitting some really powerful sexual vibes. On one hand, I was pushed back by my concern for her well-being. On the other hand, I wanted her so bad; I almost couldn't deal with it. Maybe leaving her was the best option, but I did not want to leave her. This bouncing back and forth was gradually becoming a real pain in the ass for me; I wasn't sure of much of anything, or so it seemed most of the time.

Then there was this thing with Marsh. We hadn't discussed again our mutual time lapse experience after the lake bash. It wasn't like us to shut down like that, but what were we supposed to do? How did you address an occurrence that there was no explanation for? I was a little concerned because I could tell there was something Marsh wasn't telling me. No matter how many times I'd opened the door for him to talk about it, he just shrugged it off. Whatever it was, I could tell he was uncomfortable about it. That might be what was behind the shift in his attitude. He continued to have bouts of conflicts with Ciera and his mom. We were doing okay, and his rapport with Todd was good. In the midst of all this, his golf game kept getting better and better. I couldn't figure that one out.

And now my mom and dad were joining the party. I easily sensed Mom was concerned about me. It was the depth of that concern that caught my attention. There was something that she felt, but couldn't seem to figure it out. Join the club, Mom. Dad, with his stalwart persona, wasn't as sturdy as I once thought. I could sense his insecurities. Also, he and Mom seemed to be in conflict about something to do with me, but I had no idea what it was.

What better day to be in deep thought about all those issues than today? It was a Sunday morning and I was getting ready to go receive my weekly dose of spiritual fulfillment, Baptist style. My bro would be in attendance with me, so maybe we'd both undergo a spiritual transition, which would give us answers to all our questions, including some that hadn't come up yet. But they would come up, because we Baptists were thorough.

I told Krista all the time that we had the Catholics beat on this confession thing. They did the private kind. Our whole service was a confession. There was a reason we were noted for our "fire and brimstone" services. We were making sure that everyone was prepared for their fate by knowing the directions to the place that majority of us were headed. This tried and true method was battle tested. We would receive official verification just as soon as we found someone who had survived the trip and could share their experiences with us.

Well, I had managed to carefully don my neatly pressed slacks that we Missourians referred to as "dress slacks". We Baptists dressed up for church as did most other church-goers in the region, except the progressive ones. They obviously weren't aware that God had a dress code. I worked with as much precision as I could to make myself presentable. This included a nice white shirt with a nice tie. If I could pass Mom's inspection, I was good to go.

"Son, are you decent?" my dad asked, lightly tapping on my bedroom door. I found the "are you decent" question to be almost ridiculous. But I'd come to accept it as a substitute for asking if you had your clothes on.

"Yes, Dad, come on in," I said, feeling just a twinge of discomfort.

"Well, you really look nice, Son," Dad said, scanning me quickly. "I'd like to talk to you for a minute."

He cleared a couple of CDs from my desk chair and took a seat. I hoped he didn't look at the CDs because I wasn't up for a "rappin' to hell" lecture at the moment.

"Sure, Dad, shoot."

"Son, your mom and I have been hearing some disturbing things about you, and I need to get to the bottom of it."

"Okay," I said, slowly taking a seat on the edge of my bed. This had an ominous feeling about it. Plus, I sensed Dad was having trouble with this.

"A couple of people have brought it to your mom's attention that you and Marsh have been drinking." He then shifted around uncomfortably. "And we hear that you two are smoking marijuana." He paused, looking at me for a second. Our eyes met—

—*I was surrounded by shadows, and a stiff wind was swirling around me. Something was in the wind and it hurt. It felt like sand and it had a sharp sting to it. I turned, trying to find a direction away from the wind and the stinging. It was hard to breathe. Fear began to grow as I looked for a way out—*

A shuffling sound shook me and I was staring at Dad, who had sort of a blank look about him. It passed in a few seconds. What the hell was that about?

"Anyway, Son," he said, clearing his throat a little. "You know your mother and I do not approve, nor will we condone you being involved in any kind of drug use. That includes alcohol, marijuana, or anything else. Now, I know how the rumor mill works in communities like ours, which is why I came to you. However, you should know that your mom has talked to Marsh's mom. She told your mother that Marsh said he has dabbled with drinking a little beer and has experimented with marijuana. She said Marsh has never mentioned you doing anything."

Good ole' Ms. Becky; I was sure Marsh told her about my involvement, but she wouldn't give me up. I always told Marsh what a great mom he had. But I had to play this right, which meant protecting Marsh as well as myself.

"Okay, Dad," I said, letting my eyes fall to the floor. "What Marsh told his mom is true about both of us. We've experimented a couple of times with beer and pot. I know it's not right, but that's what happened."

"Well, Son," Dad said, "I appreciate your honesty, but we still have to find a way to resolve this. We trusted you enough to buy you a truck and now we find out about this."—Now, he was getting flustered—"So, here's what we're going to do. You can drive your truck to church and to work. Other than that, it stays parked and so do you until school starts."

I wanted to protest loudly, but I could sense Dad was on the edge of exploding and things could get out of hand. I decided to play it close to the vest for now. I'd take it up with Mom later.

"What about people comin' to see me?" I asked.

"I don't have a problem with that," Dad said, "As long as it's not every night; and let's put a ten o'clock cut-off on it. All company must be out by then."

I remained silent, continuing to look down.

"And one more thing," Dad said, as he got up from the chair, "I know you and Marsh are close, so I'm sure you wouldn't want to jeopardize your right to keep company with him by making the same mistakes in the future."

A sudden fury rose up inside me. Never in my life had I felt such anger. My eyes slowly rose and I glared at my dad.

—I was back in the swirling, stinging wind. I raised my right hand and swiped at the wind. Suddenly, the stinging stopped as the winds swirled away from me and they were screaming—

"No, Dad, I certainly don't want anything like that to happen," I said, in a tone of voice I didn't recognize myself.

My dad's face seemed to lose all expression. He took a step back and almost stumbled.

"O-okay, Son," he stammered and shook his head a little.

He then turned to leave the room, stopping for a moment to look back at me. My glare remained. He started to say something, but changed his mind and left the room, gently closing the door behind him. As the door shut, I laid back on my bed, staring at the ceiling. What I just felt inside of me seemed to be receding which, for some reason, I knew was a good thing. I had no idea where it came from and had no desire to go looking for it.

Chapter Eight

MARSH

"So, my mom snitched us out," I said, staring out the window of Blake's truck in exasperation.

"No, your mom snitched you out, bro," Blake responded, starting to brake as we approached First Baptist Church. "Look, moms are concerned about this stuff and ours know we hang together. Your mom, who is the coolest mom I know, lets you open up and tell her things without the threat of punishment hangin' over you. My parents still abide by the same principles they were raised to believe in, even if some of 'em are from the Stone Age. After all, that shit we do is against the law. Worse than that, the weed is almost considered an abomination by the church we belong to. So, in my situation, I just have to do better at hidin' it or keep a steady supply of alibis in reserve."

"Yeah, I guess you're right. Wonder who snitched us out?" I asked.

"Who the hell knows?" Blake replied. "We live in a small town. We're all playin' in the same sandbox. So, if you want to play outside the box, you take the risks."

We were slowly making our way into the parking lot of the church which, for various reasons, was never quite as full during the summer. Blake was facing the slings and arrows of the parental discipline for our ventures outside the sandbox. I was really impressed at how well he was taking this. There were some subtle changes about him I was just starting to pick up on. I had to wonder if they were related to the weird things that had been going on with him lately.

"I think you handled the thing with your dad really good, bro," I said, as Blake pulled into a parking space.

"Y'know, Marsh," he said, with a contemplative look on his

face, "I had one of those looks inside my father." He paused for a second. "I could sense the pain he was feelin' in havin' to deal with this. It backed me off a little."

"Yeah, well, those looks you have sometimes scare the shit out of me."

"Well, they don't scare you any more than they scare me, bro," he said, as we got out of the truck, "But you really should watch your language this close to the house of the Lord."

"You're right; I just lost my head there for a second."

"Yeah, you have to try not to fuck up around here."

We made our way inside and took our seats in the back pew on the right side of the sanctuary. This was the largest church in Gardner with a membership of, I would guess, close to three hundred. I would estimate half of these to be fifty years of age and older. About two hundred usually attended services on a regular basis, and we were a little shy of that today.

Sitting on the pew in front of us and over to our left were the McKay twins, Jana and Lana. They were a year older than us and nice-looking. Although identical twins, there were some differences in their looks. Lana was a little better looking. They were both average height with fairly impressive figures. They were a little light up top, but acceptable—acceptable enough that I could feel the swelling in my pants happening right now. The most prominent feature the twins had was their reputation. The word was they were always ready, willing, and able, which I was sure would come as a shock to their parents. Blake and I had always traveled under their radar. It would be interesting to see if that continued to be the case.

Our pastor was the venerable Brother Elias Conrad. We liked to refer to him as Brother Condrab, but only to each other. He was a big guy, standing about six-three and weighing in at about two-fifty—Jesus, I sounded like a ring announcer at a wrestling match. His hair was graying fast, even though he was in his mid-fifties. I imagined this job could do that to you. He had a strong voice that carried well—a great attribute for a Baptist minister. But, giving way to modern technology, he now wore a small microphone on his lapel for use with our new, state-of-the-art sound system. Seated behind him was the church choir. Your ability to sing was not a requirement for membership in the choir, which was often reflected in their performance.

I managed to make it through the first half of the service, though the hymns were a real challenge. It was now time to settle in and prepare for Brother Condrab's sermon in which he would relay his continuing message of salvation along with other, more subtle, spiritual tidbits.

"Good morning," he started, and the congregation dutifully responded in kind. "I wonder how many of us could make a list of the things we paid special attention to this morning?"

Now that was an interesting topic. How long did I have? Blake and I usually used this time to write ideas for rap songs on the church bulletins.

"...What we're eating for breakfast, a news program on television, what shirt or blouse to wear..."

I was getting a little flustered because none of those things would be on my list.

"...Of course, these are very normal things that we focus on because they have become part of our routine. We become conditioned to the normalcy of these areas which garner our attention—almost robotic..."

Now hold it right there. You had just introduced a term which had to be considered foreign to many in the congregation? Some of these people had heard thousands of sermons in their lifetime and I would wager, even though that was a sinful activity, that few of these devoted brethren had ever heard the word "robotic" used in a sermon.

"...Now, stop and think about all those things that have hold of our attention and how we've become so accustomed to them that they have become blinders to the other things around us.

Now, you may be asking yourself what other things I am talking about here..."

Actually, I was willing to forgo that question in fear of where it might lead.

"...Looked outside your window at the beautiful trees..."

Uh oh, his voice was rising.

"...Or stepped outside on your porch and breathed in the fresh air, felt the warmth of the sun, or watched the birds flying about in the..."

He was rolling now—this was building to an important point that would require him to drive it home with a lot of force.

"...The answer is NO! These are the things that represent the beauty of nature that our Father has provided. BUT! We are far too caught up in the other nuances..."

That word was also a reach for many in here.

"...That we allow to clutter our thoughts and distract us from the beautiful gifts that God has given us to revel in..."

We were on our way now and my interest was fading. I heard him say something about the Book of Matthew and my "Brother Conrad mute switch" was flipped on by all the evil forces that resided within me.

What had caught my attention was my good friend, Blake, sitting on my left. I had never seen him more attentive to a sermon in my life. Without any facial expression whatsoever, he actually appeared to be taking this in. Of all the strange things going on with my friend, this had to be the biggest. I also found it a little spooky to see Blake's attention drawn to a sermon about what you should be paying attention to. I was beginning to wonder, through all of this, if maybe the planets had fallen out of alignment or something. I decided it was time to chill out and start playing some Eminem in my mind...

"...So, in closing..."

Those words brought me back to earth. This was my favorite part of the sermon.

"...We will better ourselves and those around us by not allowing all our attention to be focused on the menial things we surround ourselves with. Instead (his voice rising), We should not forget to pay attention to gifts that God surrounds us with. It is those gifts that will sustain us! Amen."

Whew!

Following the closing hymn, Blake and I quickly scooted out the door so we could dodge most of the interaction with the brethren, who always wanted to stop and ask trivial questions and comment on how nice we looked. We exited the foyer and stepped into the bright sunshine.

"Hey guys!"

We both turned and saw the McKay twins walking quickly toward us.

"Well, Marsh," Lana spoke first, "Are you ready to step up to the world of high school?"

"I suppose, Lana," I said, "Though I'm not sure how someone really gets ready."

"Well, let me tell ya," Lana continued, "It's a big change. Sophomores are on the bottom rung of the ladder. They're last for everything. But, upper class students can make the transition smoother."

Wow, that came out of nowhere.

"What about you, Blake?" Jana asked, "Are you ready?"

"I haven't really thought about it," Blake replied, obviously trying to blow them off. "I don't see it as that big a deal. I didn't even know there was a ladder, much less any rungs."

"That's just typical sophomore ignorance," Jana said, with a smug smile. "You just don't know; but it helps to have someone older with experience to help get you through."

"I'll keep that in mind," Blake said abruptly. "You ready to go, bro?"

"Okay, thanks for the heads up," I said, looking at Lana.

"No problem, just give me a call," Lana said confidently. The twins then casually walked away.

Right after that interesting encounter, Blake and I hopped in his truck and made our way out of the parking lot. Blake started to turn on the CD player, but stopped and looked over at me.

"You're gettin' ready to swim in shark infested waters, bro," Blake said.

"Well, you know, it might be time for a swim," I said.

"You do know one indiscreet encounter, or even a discreet one for that matter, and you can forget Ciera—probably forever."

"Hell, Blake, I'm not married. Besides, you know how those girls are."

"Yeah, everybody knows. They sleep around and are pretty bold about it."

"Maybe I want a turn at sleeping around. What's all this shit anyway? You spent the past six months tryin' to get laid and finally did and you said it was great. Maybe I'm ready for a swim in those waters. Things with Ciera haven't been very good lately anyway."

"Fine, bro," Blake responded, "Just be aware that some changes bring about unforeseen circumstances."

"Speaking of unforeseen," I said, "You really were into Brother Conrad's sermon. That is an absolute first. What'd you find so impressive?"

"That he truly believes what he's sayin'."

"What!"

"It wasn't necessarily what he was sayin'. It was the strong sense that he totally believes everything he said. I could feel it. I'm not sure, but I bet not many people have that kind of faith. They might want to, but can't. It impresses me to see someone whose belief is so strong."

We were silent for the next couple of minutes until we pulled into my driveway.

"Blake," I said as I turned to him, "What's goin' on with us, bro?"

He sighed deeply. "Maybe adolescence sucks more than we

thought it would," he said, looking down at his steering wheel. "But we know it's more than that. I've started hopin' that I'll wake up one mornin' and all this crazy shit will disappear just as quickly as it appeared."

"But it won't, will it?"

"Nope."

Chapter Nine

BLAKE

Getting used to new surroundings was a challenge, but also kind of fun. Gardner High School was the oldest of the three school buildings in town. It was built in the early sixties, so it was on its way to a solid fifty. It had gone through some renovations, but was mostly the same. It was a one-story brick building, which was more than large enough to meet the needs of a community whose population had been in decline over the past couple of decades. Adjacent to the building was a nice gymnasium that had been built about ten years ago. An adequate parking lot sat on the west side of the building to serve both the school and the gymnasium. Students who drove had to buy a parking permit. Although there were no reserved parking spaces, there were designated areas for seniors, juniors, and sophomores. The teachers and administrators parked on the east side of the building in a smaller lot.

Krista and I were chillin' in the hall where the sophomore lockers were located. We were assigned bottom lockers—juniors had the top—to remind us of our status. Two students shared one locker. The seniors had single lockers, which were located down a hallway on the other side of the building. Krista wanted to share lockers with Cheryl, and I had no problem with that. I was a little concerned about the future of our relationship, so it was more comfortable that way. So Marsh and I teamed up, which suited everyone except Ciera.

Today was registration day, which was really a drop-in day before the real deal started tomorrow. Today, we checked in through the office and picked up class schedules, locker assignments, locks, and a few other things related to our student needs. Students could tour the building and find everything, but were encouraged not to loiter. The teachers were working in their classrooms, so you could stop in if you wanted to.

I wasn't real happy about my class schedule. I had some of the same courses as Krista and Marsh, but different class times. They had always been stronger students, mostly because they gave a shit, and I liked having them around. Marsh, Krista, and Rick had Geometry and Lit together. I was stuck with Jared, Tammy, and, luckily, Tyler. Jared Gavin was a pain-in-the-ass Marsh and I had somehow managed to develop a friendship with. He was a total phony, who specialized in sucking up to adults and somehow other students. Marsh said it was his insecurities and lack of confidence. I just thought he was an ass-kisser. He bordered on being a snitch, but he liked Marsh, so we were probably safe in that regard. Tammy Johnson was my ex-girlfriend. We were okay with each other, but it was still a little uncomfortable. She was a pretty hot brunette, who I'd still be interested in having sex with, but things were a little chilly there at this time. Tyler Franklin was one of the few black kids in our class. He was a cool guy and we shared the same taste in music. He was also my teammate on the basketball team and was a great player. He'd managed to grow almost three inches over the summer, making him the tallest player on the team at six-three. However, he weighed in under one-eighty, so he was a little light and needed some weight and strength.

Looking over our schedules, Krista and I took inventory of our teachers. Mrs. Ellery was our Geometry teacher and had a solid reputation as a good teacher, who wouldn't take any shit. Unfortunately, she was also a friend of my mom's. Mr. Wood was our Business Ed. teacher. He was a short guy and a little nerdy, but from what we heard, a cool guy. One name that was new to us was our Lit teacher. Her name was Ms. Huey, and she was a new teacher, so we knew nothing about her.

"Hey Blake, Krista!" Marsh said, coming down the hall. To my dismay, Jared was with him. "Have you guys seen the new Lit teacher?"

"No, but we were just talkin' about her," I said.

"Well, wait till you get a look at her!" Jared blurted out. "She is so hot."

I cut my eyes at Marsh, who gave me a quick nod of confirmation because Jared's opinion didn't mean shit to me.

"Oh, my God," Krista said, rolling her eyes, "Can't you guys use any other measure of a woman other than the way she looks?"

"Yes," Jared said, "I, for one, think all aspects of a person's makeup should be taken into account."

Marsh cut his eyes at me, shaking his head.

"Krista!" a familiar and unwelcome voice rang in from behind us.

"What's up, Cheryl?" Krista said.

"Well, girl, I've been checking out the yearbook staff, and it looks as if most of 'em are okay except, of course, the editor, Julie Pilgrim, who is a total bitch," Cheryl said. She paused a minute to look at Marsh, Jared, and me. "I see we have at least one version of the three mouseketeers."

"It's nice to see you, too, Cheryl," Marsh said. "You know, I can see now why you and Krista are such good friends."

"Is that right," Cheryl said with a smirky look on her face.

"Yeah, your friendship represents a perfect balance between opposites," Marsh said, using his solemn tone. "Krista is beautiful and you are, uh, well—you know."

Cheryl, who could always be counted on for a ladylike response, quickly flipped Marsh off and said, "Come on, Krista, let's go talk to Ms. Smith" —she was their cheerleading sponsor—"And leave the children here to play."

"Okay," Krista said and her eyes cut to Marsh for a second which, for no good reason, struck me as a little peculiar. She then gave me a peck on the cheek. "I'll be back in a few."

"I'll be around here somewhere," I said with a quick smile.

"Come on, Krista," Cheryl said, grabbing her arm.

"Alright, alright," Krista said, as they turned and walked down the hall.

"Okay, guys," I said, "Let's go get a look at this new Lit teacher." Marsh and I fell in behind Jared because he persisted in leading the way. He pointed out to us what teacher was in each room as we passed by them. I wondered how many times this morning he had made this trek in order to memorize all of this. Marsh just nodded as Jared went through all this trivial information. I just totally ignored him or at least tried to.

Arriving at room twelve, Jared turned, smiled, and pointed. After rolling my eyes, I poked my head inside the room and found myself frozen in place. She was beautiful! I mean the kind of beauty you rarely saw in person. Her eyes were bright blue, like mine; her cheeks nose and lips were like chiseled to perfection. She was about my height with long, bright blonde hair. Her legs—she was wearing a dress—were long, slender, and perfectly shaped. Her hips were beautifully curved and her tits were spectacular, sitting firm and high. This was a woman.

"Would you like to come in?" she asked, breaking the trance I was in.

"Well, uh, I uh, guess so," I stammered, knowing my face must be turning red. "My friends and I, uh, were just looking around tryin' to, uh, find our classrooms."

"Well, would your friends like to come in, too?" she asked. Even her voice was beautiful.

At that moment, Jared, our guide, bolted down the hall and disappeared. "I, uh, meant to say friend," I said, trying not to look as embarrassed as I was.

Marsh entered the room and gave her a little wave.

"My name is Ms. Huey and I teach English and Literature," she said with a warm smile. "Are you two gentlemen taking one of my classes this semester?"

"Yes, ma'am," I said, "My name is, uh Blake, Blake Coleman."

"And I'm Marsh Williams," Marsh said, trying to save me from myself. "We're takin' your American Literature class."

"That's great," she said. "Are you guys interested in any particular type of literature?"

"Well, uh, I'm kinda interested in, uh, poetry," I said, still unable to get it together.

"I'm impressed," she said. "It's rare to find a young man that will admit he has an interest in poetry. Are there any particular poets you like, or do you have just a generic interest?"

I wasn't sure how to respond, so Marsh came to my rescue again.

"We're both big fans of rap music, so I guess that's our main connection to poetry," he said.

"Now I'm really impressed," she said.

"Do you, uh, like rap music?" I asked, still trying.

"Actually, no," she said, "But I do recognize it as a form of modern poetry and many rap artists do actively write poetry. Many people are afraid of rap because some of the lyrics are offensive. And getting some segments of our society to look past that is almost impossible, so there's a prejudice against it."

That did it. I was falling in love. Not only was she the most beautiful woman I had ever seen, she was really sharp and super cool. I could see this was very likely to be my favorite class.

"That's really cool, Ms. Huey," Marsh said. "Most adults around here think we're on the road to hell. Oh, uh, excuse me."

"That's okay," she laughed a little. "I believe we can let that one slide. Besides, I have no doubt that you stated the truth." She paused for a second. "You know what guys, I have an idea. I'm the Literary Club sponsor, and we'll be meeting each day during the activity period. Why don't you two sign up and we'll see how some rap can translate into poetry. What do you think?"

We were both dumbfounded for a moment. Then, we looked at each other and smiled.

"Where do we sign up?" I asked, finally saying something without stammering.

"Step over to my desk, and we can take care of that in a quick minute," she replied. She led us over and we signed a form. She placed the form in the letter tray on her desk. "Well, it was certainly nice to meet you and I look forward to having you both in class and in the club. It ought to be a blast."

Meeting Ms. Huey was certainly an exciting and unexpected part of our day. Making our way down the hall, we ran into Tyler and Rick.

"What's up, guys?" I asked.

"We're just makin' the rounds tryin' to get acclimated to our new surroundings," Rick said. "Where've you guys been?"

"We've been to Ms. Huey's room signing up for the Literary Club," Marsh replied.

"Signing up for what?" Tyler asked, looking a little shocked.

"Literary Club," I replied to my teammate and fellow rap enthusiast. "The sponsor, Ms. Huey, said we'd look at the rap-poetry connection. And we get to look at her to boot. You ought to get in on the party."

"Can't do it," Tyler said. "I've already signed up for the Computer Club with Doug and Josh. We have some heavy web page stuff we want to put into action."

"I've already heard this Ms. Huey is hot," Rick said.

"She went past being hot a long time ago," I said. "I can't come up with a word or words that come close to describing how beautiful she is."

"Hell, Blake could barely even talk around her," Marsh said with a laugh.

"Damn, I've got to see that," Rick said. "Blake, are you bringin' your basketball stuff tomorrow? I don't know what we're supposed to do and I can't find Coach Randall."

"I haven't heard," I replied, "But I'll come prepared."

"Me, too," Tyler said. "We need to get off to a good start."

"What do we have here?" someone asked from behind us.

We all turned and were dismayed to see it was Matt Perdue and his band of merry men. It was always nerve-racking to be approached by seniors when you're a sophomore. But knowing Perdue, and how he felt about us—especially me—made this encounter all the more intimidating.

"I do believe we have some interlopers, who've moved into our domain," Perdue said as they encircled us. Perdue was accompanied by two other senior basketball players and, of course, Mutt. "You guys need some help gettin' familiar with your new surroundings?"

"I, for one, was okay with my surroundings until the last minute or so," Marsh said. "But now I feel like I'm enclosed by some kinda human blob."

"Williams, you need to learn very quickly that sophomores don't talk to seniors that way," Perdue stated, glaring at Marsh. He then turned to his friends and said, "What we have here, comrades, is a weird bunch of freaks. We have two wiggers, a nigger, and uh, hell I don't know what you are Thomas—probably a girl."

Tyler's face went stone cold and I could feel my rage building. Rick was frozen and Marsh—

"Matt, once again you've set new standards for yourself," Marsh said, staring at Perdue. "You've leaped past your previous high of blatant ignorance, continued right past blind stupidity, and landed on a level of idiocy that is beyond comprehension. But what's truly amazing is that you manage to function without the service of a brain."

His face darkening with rage, Perdue stepped forward and rammed the heel of his hand into Marsh's chest. The blow knocked him backwards into Rick and Tyler, who managed to catch him before he hit the floor. The impact was so hard; you could hear the wind go out of Marsh. Within a second, I jumped forward and, with all the strength I could muster, I threw both hands into Perdue's chest, sending him stumbling back into the wall. As he recovered, his glare met mine—

—It was so dark and cold. I could hear echoes of what sounded like some kind of heartbeat. My eyes tried to adjust but all I could see was darkness and it was so empty. Oh Jesus, the pain.—

"That's enough!" a loud voice shattered my vision.

As my eyes re-focused, I turned to see Coach Randall jogging down the hall toward us. A few other students had gathered around us.

"Now back off," Coach Randall said, as he walked up to us.

Looking back at Perdue, I was astounded to see him looking straight ahead, almost expressionless.

"Except for this group of guys right here" —referring to us— "Everyone else go on about your business," Coach Randall said, and the other students quickly scattered. "Alright, what's goin' on here?"

I spoke up first. "We had a little difference of opinion."

"Just how serious is the difference of opinion?" Coach asked, looking around at all of us. "Well, what about you Matt?" He turned his attention to Perdue.

"It's, uh, like he said," Perdue said, visibly shaken and a little pale. "We were havin' some fun, and it got out of hand, maybe."

"Okay, here's the deal," Coach said, "The fun is over and it better stay that way. And I want to see you two" —pointing at Perdue and me—"In my office at seven-thirty in the morning. Everybody got it?" We all said, "Yes, sir," in unison. "Good. Now find some place to be."

With that, Rick, Tyler, Marsh and I moved on our way. Krista and Cheryl were waiting just down the hall.

"Are you guys okay?" Krista asked, looking a little frantic.

"Yeah, I guess so. What about you, bro?" I asked, turning to Marsh.

"Yeah, I'm fine, I think," Marsh said, rubbing his chest, "I'm lucky he didn't knock me out."

"Hey, Blake, what'd you do, man?" Tyler asked. "Perdue stopped dead in his tracks like you shot 'im."

"Hell, I don't know. Maybe he had a dizzy spell or somethin'," I said, trying to sound convincing.

"Boy that was weird. He was just like frozen there," Rick said.

"Well, I'm glad he froze. Our life expectancy was droppin' in a hurry," Marsh said, once again intervening for me. "Let's get movin'."

We headed out to the parking lot. Rick and Tyler took off. Cheryl went back inside to work in the office, which was a perfect job for her. She was very efficient and a total horse's ass. Marsh, Krista, and I walked out to our vehicles.

"So, are you really okay, Marsh?" Krista asked.

"Yeah, thanks," Marsh said.

"What's up with you, bro? You're gettin' to be an 'in your face' kind of guy," I said, smiling a little.

"Yeah, I guess I better buff up or shut up. But Perdue asked for it by his mere existence. He's such an asshole," Marsh said.

"No argument about that," I said. "Well, wouldn't you know, the first day I get my pilot's license back, my dad puts me to work."

"Doin' what?" Krista asked.

"I've got to help him rearrange his office. Then, I get to mow and weed-eat the grounds. It's a bitch, but it pays thirty bucks."

"Call tonight, okay?" Krista asked.

"Of course," I said smiling.

"Hey, Marsh, you want me to drop you at your house since Blake's pointed in the opposite direction?" Krista asked.

"Fine by me, if it's okay with your boyfriend," Marsh said, smiling at me.

"I believe I can trust you," I said, rolling my eyes.

"What about trusting me?" Krista asked.

I gave her a quick kiss. "My trust can only reach so far."

She gave me a gentle shove and a smile. I returned the smile, but meant what I said.

Chapter Ten

KRISTA

Well, here I was in my car with Marsh, just as I had planned. Wondering, what the heck I was doing? My insides were churning to the point I was working hard not to tremble and appear nervous. At the same time I wanted to tear into Marsh. That shouldn't be hard to justify for a teenage girl. Except, the fact that he was my boyfriend's best friend should have counted for something. He was also a first class guy who had always been very respectful with me. That should probably count in there somewhere, too. Plus, he was dating a friend of mine who had never done anything wrong to me that I could remember. Boy, this counting was starting to be complicated. It seemed a lot simpler to just reach over and put my hand down his pants. That was, without a doubt, the totally wrong thing to do. And yet, that desire trumped all the counting going on in my mind. Maybe this was a test; maybe this was happening to challenge the way I viewed things; maybe I shouldn't have given a damn.

"You can turn the radio to whatever you like," I said, as I drove out of the parking lot.

"Thanks, but this is fine. You have a nice ride, Krista," he said.

"Thanks, I know it's just an economy car, but I like it. So, how're you and Ciera doin'?"

"Alright, I suppose. She's gone to West Memphis with her mother today. She did the early registration thing last week."

"Yeah, she told me the other day."

It was only a couple of minutes before I turned down 1st Street and cruised to his house and pulled into the driveway.

"Marsh, I know this is a little awkward, but I really need to use the restroom. Would you mind?"

"Of course not," he said. "C'mon in."

We went inside and he directed me to the restroom in his mom's bedroom. I'm sure hers was a lot cleaner and neater than his. That would certainly be the case at my house.

"I'll be in the den," he said sheepishly, which was kind of funny.

"Alright, I'll be out in a couple," I said.

After allowing enough time for a pee, I flushed and walked out in the hallway. I took a deep breath and was ready to go. I was so geared up, I was tingling.

"Hey, Marsh," I called out. "Where's your room?"

"Well, uh, it's kind of messy," he said, as he joined me in the hall. He has a sort of confused look about him and was obviously trying to maintain some composure. "I'm not very good at keepin' my room straight and don't want to bring embarrassment on me, my family, or my friends."

"Look, Marsh, my room wouldn't pass any credible inspection, either. And I doubt there are any guys your age who keep a neat room."

"Well, okay," he said after a moment of indecision, "But please don't let this lower your opinion of me."

I followed him down the hall and watched as he opened his bedroom door just enough to make a quick dash in there and clear things out of the way the best he could. I gave him a few seconds before I stepped into his room. I was immediately drawn to his DMX and Eminem posters on the wall.

"Wow; why am I not surprised to find a 'rap' haven," I said.

I stared at the posters for a few moments to give him time to do a little more "quick tidying up." Good grief, I could smell that male hormone scent in here which sent my urges spiraling out of control. He was shoveling stuff in his closet as I quietly walked over to him. He jumped a little when he turned and found me right in his face.

"Krista, I—," he managed to get out before I gently put the index finger of my left hand over his lips.

I slid my finger down to his chin and eased his mouth open.

I could tell he was trembling ever so slightly. I then brought my lips to his. I used my tongue to create a strong passionate kiss and establish some control. I pulled him closer and put my arms around him. Oh my God, I was on fire. I dropped my hands to his hips and pulled him even tighter against me. Wow, he was hard and I rubbed against it. When I finally broke the kiss, he appeared to be in a mesmerized state. I made sure to keep my eyes locked on his. I had control now and wasn't about to let it get away.

"Kris—," he tried again, but I used my mouth to cut him off. I did my best to take the kiss even deeper and could tell he was starting to melt. Easing my hands around from his hips, I found my way to his belt buckle. I had to work hard to keep from virtually attacking him—that was what I wanted to do. I unbuckled his belt, undid the button, and unzipped his pants. I then carefully slid my right hand inside his boxers and found him. Boy, he was bigger than Blake. Well, the head on Blake's was bigger but Blake wasn't this long.

I moaned softly, for effect, and began stroking him gently. I broke the kiss and he let out a long, deep moan. He was mine.

Suddenly, he pulled my t-shirt up and over my head and I responded by doing the same to him. We very methodically undressed each other. He was totally hot and the size of his junk was impressive. We eased into his bed and—

"Wait," he said, and rolled out of bed. He hurried over to his dresser, reached into the back of a bottom drawer, and came out with some condoms. He hurried back and started to get on top of me, but I rolled him over and got on top of him. I swear he had a frantic look about him. I took the condoms and he began aggressively groping my breasts which sent strong sensations rocketing through me.

I threw my head back and moaned—for real this time. I removed the condom from the package and methodically used it to cover his long, hard, pulsating penis. Rising up, I straddled him and moved him into position. He entered me a little bit at a time. There was very little pain as I eased all of him in me. What discomfort there was quickly turned into erotic feelings that started exploding inside of me.

He began lurching up and I fell into swaying motion with him. I could feel the heat coming from him. A flood of passion overwhelmed both of us, and we were swept away by currents that flexed with pure lust. I took him again, again, and again...

I had no idea how long I had been sitting here, parked in my driveway. How many times could I rewind this in my mind and make it not happen? It wouldn't go away. Why Marsh? Damn it, damn it, damn it. Did it have something to do with Blake? I just didn't know.

I'd known what I was doing from the moment I asked him if he wanted a ride home. For some reason, I couldn't stop—or didn't want to. I never thought I'd be capable of what I've done today. How could I do that? I didn't just take him once. I took him until he couldn't go anymore. This was about to make me sick. Hell, I was sick—with something.

Seeing him sitting there at the end of his bed after we'd finished and dressed; his elbows on his knees; fingers cupped together; and head down. Damn it, other than his mom, Blake was the most important person in his life. And I know he felt as if he had just stabbed him in the back—over and over. When I told him it didn't mean anything, he looked up at me and I could see the pain in his eyes. I left him still sitting there like that. As I closed his bedroom door, I stopped, and for just a moment, wished I was dead.

But I wasn't. I was sitting here wiping slow-running tears off my cheeks, trying to think of a way to make this damn thing inside me disappear. Hell, I talked as if it were some alien monster... one that took over my mind and filled me with passionate, lust-filled desires...one that drove me to the heights of ecstasy and then dropped me to the depths of despair...one that just came and went as it pleased. But the most disturbing thing was that none of that stuff today was done by an alien. It was done by me.

FALL

When securing the free and boundless;
With binding that's fraught and frayed;
There comes a finite attachment;
For wanderers who have strayed.

Then rumbles a subtle displacement;
Of all we have seen and known;
Foreshadows an ominous coming;
To devour of nature's own.

The great faiths will be shaken;
Their true essence open to take;
And the doctrines of humanity;
Crack and crumble from the quake.

Releasing the floods of distress;
Which cover all beacons of light;
Tramples across the realm of peace;
And prepares to inhale and incite.

BLAKE

Chapter Eleven

MARSH

I finally just walked away from Ciera in the hall before she really pissed me off. I hurried into Ms. Huey's room and back to our worktable where Blake was already seated. Ms. Huey arrived at the same time I did.

"Well, Blake, how are you and Marsh doing on your project?" she asked as I took my seat beside Blake.

"We're gettin' there, I think," Blake said.

Ms. Huey had given us a project to use our own rap lyrics and transform them into poetic verse. We were to try to tone down the offensive language and find ways to convert it into effective poetry.

"I think you guys are up to the task," she said. "Remember, our first publication is due out in about three weeks, and I definitely want you guys to be part of that. I expect it to add a special flavor to our paper."

"I hope so," he said, smiling at her.

She returned the smile and walked back to her desk as the other club members filled into the room. I wondered if Blake realized he was blushing. I thought it best to leave it alone.

"What's up, bro?" I asked.

"Not much. Lit class was good. Ms. Huey is such an awesome teacher."

"Hell, Blake, she's the only teacher you've bothered to listen to in I don't know how long. But she is pretty."

"Oh, Marsh, she so much more than just a pretty face."

"Well, that's true; she's got pretty tits, a pretty ass, and pretty legs."

"And you're pretty funny for an asshole."

I laughed a little and asked, "Hey, what'd you say to Jared in Business Ed? He is so pissed."

"The little kiss-ass won't stop askin' questions about stuff nobody cares about. I just suggested he stick his dick in a CPU and garner all the knowledge he can."

I laughed a little louder than I intended to which briefly caught everyone's attention.

"You gotta give him a break, bro," I said.

"I'm tryin'," he said. "How're things with you and Ciera?"

"Oh hell, I don't know," I replied as he started pulling our notes out of the files on our table. "She just keeps findin' things to bitch about. Sometimes, I wish we didn't have morning classes together. It's gettin' to be a pain."

"Yeah, y'know, at first I was kinda upset about not havin' any classes with Krista," he said, scattering some of our notes across the table. "But, I think it helped us a little, not bein' around each other all day long."

"Yeah, I bet that's better," I said, feeling some discomfort with him mentioning Krista. It had been two weeks since our 'rendezvous' at my house. She'd been making discreet overtures to me this week and I'd asked her to meet me at my house after school to try to get some kind of resolution.

"You know, bro, I'm startin' to feel better about Krista and me," he continued. "I mean I hope we'll work our way back into sex, but I think we'll get there. We just seem to be enjoyin' each other's company more and more, which is so cool. I'm startin' to trust us as a couple."

"It certainly sounds like a good, working relationship to me," I said, then paused for a few seconds. "Could I ask you somethin' kind of personal, bro?"

"Of course, always, you know that."

"You've always told me you didn't love Krista. Is that still the truth?"

"Well, I'm not sure I'm capable of lovin' any girl right now—at least by what I'd define as love. But I feel very close to her, and that feels good."

"Good for you, bro."

At that moment our eyes locked—

"Blake! Marsh! Are you guys okay?" some girl asked.

I looked around and saw Judy Wages standing beside our table, looking at us.

"What're you talkin' about, Judy?" Blake asked.

"You guys looked as if you were having some kind of a stare-down," she said.

"We're just tryin' to think through some rap lyrics," I said, as I looked over at Blake, who was looking down at the table. "You wanna join us for a little rap session?"

"No way; I don't understand that crazy stuff," she said, and then turned around and went on her way.

"What an air head," he said, looking up again.

"Damn it, Blake!" I said, looking around and keeping my voice just above a whisper. "You took one of those looks inside of me, didn't you? You did, didn't you?"

"Yeah, I guess so," he said with a deep sigh. "But it wasn't like I planned it. I never plan that shit."

"But, where in the hell was I while you were doin' this shit you weren't plannin' on doin'?" I asked, trying not to sound scared half to death, which I was.

"I don't have a clue," he replied.

"Well, w-what did you see?" I stammered a little.

"It's hard to describe; it was somethin' like a warm, red corridor with stuff comin' out of the walls."

"Well, what does that mean?"

"Hell, I don't know," he said with a kind of troubled look.

Dammit, I couldn't take this crap much longer. I was loafing through my classes and treating Ciera like shit. And this thing with Krista—Jesus! I just didn't seem to care about things that had always been important to me. Man, I was going to have to get a grip. I just had to figure out what I needed to grab a hold of.

Sitting at my kitchen table, I looked at the clock again. Well, it was three-thirty and she wasn't here. I decided I'd go fix me a snack and chill. I had to call Ray and line up some stuff. My bro and I needed some. I felt a surge of relief. Then why in the hell did I keep looking out the damn window to check the driveway? I walked back to the kitchen, grabbed a bag of chips, and threw them on the kitchen table. I then turned, walked back to the front room, and once again, checked the driveway. What the fuck was I doing? I was glad she wasn't showing up, but I still kept looking for her. I was such a coward.

This was the craziest shit I'd ever been through in my life. In about two weeks, I'd be sixteen. That was, of course, if I lived that long. The way things were going, I wasn't certain of anything. It was a beautiful day for late September, and I should be on the golf course. My game was a real rush right now. According to Todd, I was attacking the course with a mindset he'd never seen in someone my age. He claimed my growth into the game was extraordinary. Why was I not there?

I grabbed a soda out of the fridge and set it on the table beside the bag of chips. Then, I found myself walking back to check the driveway again. I was thinking back to the things Blake said today. He'd developed a new attitude about his relationship with Krista. He was beginning to trust himself concerning her and was, therefore, developing a trust in their relationship that I was sure had never existed. Boy, this was just great. My best friend got past his teenage lust and began to genuinely like Krista. During this period of change, his girlfriend and his best friend had engaged in a session of amazing sex. Now there's a reason to gain a new faith in the decency of humanity and the bonds of friendship.

Well, that's it—no car. Maybe she just decided it was over and Blake would never have to know. I was concerned about what happened this morning when he "looked inside me". I didn't know what he could see or, for that matter, how he could see.

And that made me uncomfortable, especially about this. Maybe only I'd have to live with what had happened. That was a heavy weight, but I'd earned it.

I turned to walk back to the kitchen when I heard it—the faint, but sure sound of a car pulling in the driveway. Without even looking, I knew it was her. Damn, I guess the time had come for a showdown. I watched as Krista, wearing a nice white blouse and jeans so tight they highlighted all the right places, walked into the garage to the back door. I opened the door before she had time to knock.

"Krista, I'd like you to sit at the table with me. We need to talk." She nodded.

"Would you like a soda or somethin'?" I asked.

"No, nothing for me," she said, taking a seat.

"Look, Krista, I can't do this stuff. You know how Blake and me are. This is totally wrong."

"What's so wrong, Marsh? All we did was have sex, which I might add was very satisfying. There are no commitments and it has nothing to do with Blake."

That rankled me a little. "How can you say that? You two have had a steady relationship for almost half a year. I know Blake pretty well and, to my knowledge, he's been totally loyal to you. That's pretty committed."

"I didn't say anything about Blake's commitment," she said. "I said there's no commitment between you and me. This has weighed on my mind, too, but I realize it has nothing to do with Blake. It only has to do with us."

"Krista, I talked to Blake today about you. He said he felt really good about you and mentioned trust, which is something that doesn't come easy with him. Of course, that's 'cause there are deceitful friends like me in the world that make a mockery of the word."

"I feel good about Blake, too," she said. "And I sometimes detest the dishonesty. But, my loyalty is to Blake as far as our relationship is concerned. I've just decided this isn't a violation of my commitment to Blake."

"Well, I think it is," I said. "I've reached a breaking point with this. It causes me more and more stress all the time. Hell, I'm half-assin' my classes and startin' to treat Ciera like shit. But none of those things come close to my situation with Blake. So, here's how I see it. I'd be lyin' if I didn't tell you that the sex we had was unbelievably awesome. And you're so beautiful; it's hard to put into words. But, this whole situation is tearing me up inside."

She was looking at me intently; maybe she was hearing me.

"So," I continued, "The only way I can continue doing this is if Blake and Ciera are out of the picture. I have to let Ciera go and you have to let Blake go. We can start from there and see what happens."

Things got quiet for a few moments and I nervously thumped the side of my soda can.

"Okay, Marsh," she said, "I get what you're saying. I've had some of the same thoughts and felt the same pain. For some reason, I just can't let Blake go. Maybe I'm growing into our relationship the same way he is. There's more to it, sometimes, but I don't know how to explain it. There's somethin' different about Blake and me. I can't let him go."

"Well, I guess that settles the issue," I said, not looking at her.

"Oh, c'mon Marsh," she said with a sudden fierceness that came out of nowhere. "What are you so afraid of? Blake's not gonna know."

"Well, I'm gonna know!" I said, raising my voice. "And so are you!"

"Well aren't you the righteous one," she said sarcastically. "You could've stopped it from the start that day, but you were too busy digging for your condoms."

Damn, that hurt. I looked down at my soda can, took a deep breath, let it out and said quietly, "I can't do it, Krista."

"Fine," she said and got up from the table.

"Uh, Krista," I muttered, looking back up at her, "There's no need for Blake to ever know about this, is there?"

"I don't plan to tell 'im," she said in a surly manner. "Do you?"

"No," I said softly and looked away from her.

"That's what I thought," she said abruptly and walked to the door.

"Krista."

"What?" she snapped as she turned back to me.

"Don't you care about him?" I said, my voice quivering a little.

As she looked at me, her hard expression suddenly changed. That fierce look eyes faded. Her aggressive posture changed. I was almost stunned by the transformation.

"Yes, Marsh, I do," she said in her normal sweet tone of voice. "I care about him very much."

She turned and walked out the door.

Chapter Twelve

BLAKE

Guys having a night out wasn't unusual, but this had a special flavor to it. Yesterday, Marsh had celebrated his sixteenth birthday and although he lobbied against it, as he claims, we had a small gathering at his house last night in his honor. The guests included Krista and me, Rick and his girlfriend, Jared, and Tyler. Marsh's grandparents were there and, of course, Ms. Becky. Ray skipped out, but had already given a generous gift in advance, which would add to our good time tonight.

The highlight of the evening was when Mr. TM presented Marsh with the keys to his new metallic gray Mustang. My family's gift was to pay for a top of the line sound system in the car. Marsh was excited, but not like I would've thought. He was going through some tough times right now. For the first time I could remember, his grades were in the mid-B range. That, of course, worked fine for me. But Marsh always did A's.

Compounding this was his sudden breakup with Ciera. They parted company less than a week ago after many months as a couple. Actually, I thought he initially handled it pretty good. But I'd been noticing a slow change in Marsh for a while. I still thought he was a little off center, but he hadn't said anything about it.

But Rick and I had a big surprise for our somewhat disillusioned friend. We had put together this guys' night out for Marsh. I even included Jared at Marsh's insistence. Marsh said it would be good for Jared; otherwise that champion ass-kisser would've never been included. But my hopes were high for a big night for my friend. With mid-terms and the start of basketball season quickly approaching, we all could use a big night.

Our first scheduled stop was Todd's. He lived in a nice little house just down from the country club—about halfway between the club and Mr. TM's house. He was grilling some burgers for all of us in honor of the birthday boy. From there, we were going to cruise Sikeston for a while and enjoy some choice weed courtesy of Ray—the aforementioned gift. After settling in on a good high, we'd make our way to the safety of the pool house. There we'd have a bunch of snacks and could kick back and enjoy a couple of good DVD movies. Ray had also thrown in a special movie titled "Here Cum the Brides". Also, Mr. TM had left us a couple of six packs of beer in the fridge, though if asked, he would claim to have no knowledge of it. That didn't include the gin Marsh had already swiped, which would at our disposal.

But the big surprise had been carefully orchestrated by Rick and me. We had decided to bring an end to Marsh's doldrums and his virginity. Through some discreet, strategic planning, we'd set up a late night rendezvous between Marsh and Lana McKay. She was more than willing to participate in the plan. She'd already set her sights on Marsh anyway. She arranged to stay with her cousin who lived in Sikeston, and was willing to chauffeur. We'd planned the pickup at ten-thirty. Marsh should be pretty loaded by then and ready to be swept into lustful paradise for a while. I was hoping he would emerge from this a totally different man, to say the least.

I was waiting for Marsh to come pick me up. I told him I'd be ready on time. He just laughed and said he'd arrive late just to make me feel more comfortable. I used the opportunity to make a quick call to the number Lana gave me.

"Hey, Lana, it's Blake."

"Oh, hi, Blake. Is everything okay?" she asked.

"Oh yeah; I just wanted to make double sure how this thing is gonna come off," I said.

"Sure; I've got the map you made me and am already in Sikeston. We pick 'im up on the corner you've marked at ten-thirty, right?"

"Yeah, but give 'im five minutes or so one way or another."

"No problem, I'm flexible," she said.

I bet that was true. But I was a little concerned because these girls shot from the hip, and I had serious doubts about their timing and sense of direction.

"Alright; I'll call if we fall behind schedule."

"Sounds great; later," she said and hung up.

I heard the horn in the driveway. Grabbing my bag, I headed out the door to load up in Marsh's car. It promised to be one helluva evening.

"Hey, Blake," Marsh said, as he pulled out of my drive, "Will ya do me a big favor tonight and try to be cool with Jared?"

"I'll put forth my best effort for you, bro," I said. "Just remember, though, everyone has a breaking point and ass-kissers push hard."

"I know, but I wanna have some fun tonight and not have to put out fires," he said.

I reached over and patted him on the shoulder. "You'll get my best effort—I promise," I said, smiling a little.

We stopped and picked up Rick first. I had to slide the passenger seat up so Rick, who was over six-feet tall, could squeeze in the back. He was a good friend and a really cool guy, who always helped keep things going at an even pace. I was glad he was with us just in case Jared got to be more than I could deal with. Jared's house was next. He lived on the other side of town from Rick, so we had to double back and get him. Driving across town in Gardner took a good four minutes. Jared had never really hung out with us outside of school, and I could tell he was really excited about it. He and Rick were still fifteen, but Rick was more mature. Rick had also smoked weed and drank with us before. Jared claimed he had some limited drinking experience, but had never smoked weed. So, we'd see how it went.

He was waiting in the front of his house, bag in hand, when we pulled up. He put his bag in the trunk with the others and climbed in the back seat beside Rick. We then headed out for Sikeston.

"Okay guys, here's the plan," Marsh said. "Our first stop is Todd's for a cookout. We'll hang out there for an hour or so."

"Now, what's Todd's full name, again?" Jared asked, leaning forward a little.

"Todd Little, but we call him Todd; he's cool with that," Marsh replied.

"Yeah, you guys'll like Todd," I said. "He's real cool about things, but try not to tear anything up. He has a nice place."

"Didn't you tell me he dates some hot women?" Rick asked.

"Yeah, Marsh and I have seen him with some really fine ladies," I said.

"Hell, there may be someone there tonight," Marsh added. "You never know."

"Hey, who do you guys think is the hottest chick in high school?" Rick asked no one in particular.

"That's easy," I said. "It's Ms. Huey, hands down."

We all got a laugh out of that.

"I think he was talkin' about students," Jared said.

"Okay, that's cool," I said. "But let's set some guidelines. Girlfriends aren't eligible, which eliminates Krista and Sally. We'll also exclude Ciera, because I'm not sure the period of mourning has ended."

"Very funny," Marsh said.

"Alright guys, the floor's open for nominations," I said. "We're almost to Todd's, so we won't have time to vote. Voting will take place later when we're all in a better frame of mind."

"Which means higher than hell," Rick said, smiling.

"Absolutely," I said.

"You think this is appropriate subject matter for a sausage party?" Marsh asked.

"What kind of party?" Jared asked, leaning forward again.

"A sausage party, dude," Rick answered. "Girls get together and have a hen party; guys have a sausage party."

"But why call it a sausage party?" Jared asked.

"You're right, Jared," I said, looking back at him. "In your honor, we'll call it a Tootsie Roll party."

Marsh gave me a stern look, while Rick laughed.

"What the hell does that mean?" Jared asked firmly.

"It means Blake likes Tootsie Rolls," Marsh said, drawing another laugh from Rick. "I have a nomination—Julie Pilgrim."

"The wicked bitch of the west," Rick said. "But she is hot."

Julie was a sandy blonde senior with a very pretty face and a decent body, featuring only fair tits but a nice ass. Krista and most the other girls said she was arrogant and, in general, a pain.

"And she's dating a college dude," I said. "So she must be putting out."

"Which is not a prerequisite," Marsh said. "Next nominee."

"I nominate Tammy," Jared said proudly.

"Oh, my God," I said, rolling his eyes about the nomination of my former girlfriend.

"She is pretty hot," Rick said, "And she's getting prettier."

"That's for sure; I'd bone 'er," Jared said, catching the rest of us a little off guard.

"You'd bone 'er with what?" I asked with a laugh.

"Well, whatever it was, it'd be more than you boned 'er with," Jared replied.

Marsh started laughing so hard he almost ran off the road. Rick was right in there with him. Hell, even I had to smile.

Well, well, well; a strange car was sitting in Todd's driveway when we pulled in. I'd say we were off to a good start. Marsh was loosening up, and even Jared was acting decent. But he was still an ass-kisser. We could smell the burgers grilling as we walked to the front door.

"Looks like we weren't the only ones invited," I said, as Marsh knocked on the door. "I bet she's hot."

Boy, did I hit it right. The front door was opened by a beautiful brunette with warm eyes, a brilliant smile, and a body worth fighting for.

"Well, come in boys. My name is Sandy. Todd is grilling on the back patio," she said and then looked at Marsh. "And you must be Marsh."

"Yeah, how'd you know?" Marsh asked, his eyes widening a little.

"Todd said you were a good-looking young man with bright blond hair," she said, "And you guys are?"

We each introduced ourselves and she led us to the back patio.

Todd was flipping burgers when we arrived. I'd had the opportunity to eat Todd's burgers before, and they were probably the best I had ever eaten. He cooked huge patties and seasoned them to perfection.

"Alright, the gang's all here," Todd said, as we walked over to the grill. "Okay, introductions are in order, and let me apologize in advance for not shaking hands. I'm a little greasy."

"Todd, this is Rick and this is Jared," Marsh said, pointing to each of them as he introduced them.

"Nice to meet you, Rick and Jared," Todd said.

"Nice to meet you, too, Mr. Little," Jared said in proper fashion.

"Thank you, Jared, but the mister is a formality which is not required and just call me Todd," Todd said, smiling at Jared.

I couldn't help but shake my head. Jared never ceased to amaze me.

"So, you guys grab a soda out of the ice chest over there," Todd said, pointing the way. "Chips and dip are out on the table, so help yourself. Burgers will be up in a few."

It was a nice evening for early October. We were wearing long sleeve shirts and jeans which felt just right as sunset approached. We sat at the table and started in on the chips. We couldn't help but stare when Sandy came out with her buns, uh, I mean the buns.

"You were right, Blake. That woman's the real deal," Rick said.

"Yeah, I guess I've seen him with three or four different women over the last year or so, and all of 'em were hot," I said.

"Todd is a great golf coach and a cool guy, who obviously has other talents," Marsh said.

"If that's what those talents produce, I'm willin' to learn," Rick said.

"Yeah, and he has a nice house in a nice place," Jared joined the conversation.

"The club we passed is less than half a mile from here," Marsh said. He then turned and pointed north. "Gramps' house is about a half a mile away."

"He doesn't have to travel far to work, does he?" Jared asked.

"No, the golf course runs almost up to his back yard," Marsh said, now pointing east. "It's just beyond that thicket of trees."

Sandy brought a plate stacked with huge burgers over to us, smiled and said, "Dig in guys."

A few minutes later Todd and Sandy joined us at the table. They asked each of us about our family and school. They were both really cool which gave me some hope for the adult world; despite some of the things we heard and saw from time to time. Our gathering provided me with an opportunity I'd been working up the courage to bring up.

"Todd, a few weeks ago you mentioned that Lake Wappapello had what you called a 'sordid history'," I said. "What did you mean by that?"

"Well, I was actually just makin' a little joke. One of my hobbies is to research folklore in this region of the country. I even have some contacts at SEMO that I trade info with. Three or four years ago, I heard there were some old stories about a region around the St. Francis River that is now Lake Wappapello, but never found out anything."

"Probably because there wasn't anything to find out," Sandy said.

Todd smiled and said, "I've found that there are grains of truth behind many old stories and legends."

"And we all know how big a grain is," Sandy said with a smirk.

Todd laughed a little and said, "Well, that's true; but strange things do happen. Of course, 'strange' can be a relative term."

"Yeah," Sandy chimed in again, "Depending on whose relative you're talking to."

We all laughed at that. But I didn't laugh very hard and neither did Marsh. We both knew something weird was going on and it wasn't some bullshit legend.

After the meal, Todd presented Marsh with a new pair of golf shoes. You know, the thing about Todd was he wasn't only cool; he was the kind of guy you looked up to. We thanked them for everything and loaded up, once again, in Marsh's new ride.

Marsh felt like it'd be better if we cruised the west side of Sikeston because there was more access to less populated areas on the outskirts of the city. I had a couple of blunts ready to fire up when the discussion I'd been anticipating got underway.

"Alright, Rick, I've got you and Jared rolled and ready to go," I said, handing the blunt to Rick.

"Look guys, I don't know about this," Jared said with some obvious discomfort. "I've never smoked weed and I'm not sure I want to."

"That's entirely up to you," Marsh said. "No one should do it unless they want to."

"Oh hell, Marsh, a few hits aren't going to hurt 'im." I said.

"That doesn't matter and you know it," Marsh said in a firm tone, letting me know he meant it.

"Alright, alright," I said, "Do what you like, Jared; I don't give a shit."

Everything got quiet for a few moments. Then I fired up a blunt and Rick followed suit. After I passed it over to Marsh, I heard a little cough from the back seat. I turned to look back there. Jared had just taken his first hit of a blunt. He passed it back to Rick who was smiling. I cut my eyes back to Jared and a really bad feeling suddenly swept over me. I didn't know what it was but I didn't like it.

"Jared, don't smoke that shit if you don't want to," Marsh said, using his rearview mirror to glance back.

"Hell, it's not a big deal," Jared said. "It's not like it's gonna kill me."

"Forget what I said, Jared. It was a stupid thing to say," I said with conviction. "Marsh is right; it's your choice and it's just as cool to choose not to."

But, Jared took the blunt from Rick for another toke. This time there was no cough.

"No, really guys, it's cool with me," he said, and then looked at me. "Thanks, Blake, but I made the choice."

I turned quickly and stared straight ahead, passing our blunt back to Marsh. Something wasn't right.

I didn't know how everyone else was doing, but I was coasting at a high altitude as Marsh pulled into his grandparents' driveway. Everyone appeared about the same, but you never knew sometimes. I was trying hard to forget about Jared and the blunt. Damn it, when I looked back at him with the weed, I felt something ugly. I tried to play it cool and everyone bought it, except maybe Marsh. He saw me better than others did and sometimes could pick up on my discomfort. Shit, I had to get this stuff out of my head and make this a fun night for Marsh. He needed one.

We quietly made our way to the pool house. Marsh used his cell phone to call his grandparents and tell them we'd arrived safely and were fine. He might have stretched the "fine" part. Somewhat disoriented might have been more accurate. The pool house was set up nice. It was more or less one big room with a hide-a-bed sofa, a couple of small recliners, a round game table, and a nice entertainment center featuring a cool sound system and small television. A kitchenette was partitioned off from the rest of the room by a small bar with three bar stools. The entertainment center was on the other side of the room across from the sofa and recliners. There was one full bath with a large shower. Two rollaway beds had been brought in to accommodate us. There were snacks on the kitchen counter with sodas and, of course, the beer in the fridge.

After we rotated through the toilet, we decided we'd break out the beer and get comfortable.

"Ms. Doty set this up nice, Marsh," Rick said.

"Yeah, this is so cool," Jared added, still flying from his first time high.

"Well, everyone just remember we have to be somewhat civil and hold the noise down to a roar," Marsh said.

"Guys, the weed was great, but I can't stand the taste of beer," Jared said, trying not to appear nervous.

"No problem, my young friend, I have a credible alternative," Marsh said, and then reached into his bag and pulled out a fifth of gin. "How about some gin and seven?"

"Now that's what I'm talkin' about," Jared said with a big smile. "I've done gin before and I like it. Thanks, Marsh." He gave Marsh a high five.

I chose not to say anything, but still felt uncomfortable with this whole scene involving Jared. I decided to shift gears.

"Hey, Marsh, let's do our new rap thing for 'em," I said.

"Yeah, I'm up for that," Rick said.

"Me, too, and I don't even like rap," Jared said from the kitchen, where he was mixing his drink.

Marsh smiled and said, "Let's do it."

So, with Marsh and I on one side of the table and Rick and Jared on the other, we put our best rap forward. With Marsh pounding out the beat on the table, I started:

"Man, oh man, I'm da' man;
Fly higher than a flight plan;
Tighter than a rubber band;
Attached to a hundred grand."

Marsh took over:

"Man, oh man, I'm da' man;
Large head, big face;
It's all a money race;
And leading in first place;
Sliding into home late;
Just a taste and you'll say;
'I can't find my face'."

Back to me:

"The whole pack will have you running back;
Game time fun, but I ain't done;
I'm just getting started, like hike;
Footballs fly by, 17.5's in the sky;
Landing on a super model, we run away;
We greet each other and shake hands;
Mine then travel below;
Her eyes roll, then say 'Oh no!';
But I say 'Hell yeah!'"

We teamed up for the finale:

"Man, oh man, I'm da' man;
She says I'm colder than a snowman;
Just break it down and I sell 1000 grams;
Smell me, if not, then smoke me;
I'll appear in your dreams chasing your cheese;
Demanding every dime and you're still behind;
That's when I take your life."

Rick and Jared gave us a big round of applause.

"You guys have really got it, whatever it is," Rick said.

Over the next half hour, Rick and I started on the beer, while Marsh, being the perfect host, joined Jared with the gin and seven. At about nine-thirty, it was time to spring the surprise.

"You guys want to crank up a movie while we can still understand the words?" Marsh asked. "We'll watch the fuck flick later 'cause the dialogue's irrelevant."

"Well, bro, we have a little treat in store for you," I said. "It's kind of a post-birthday present."

"Oh shit, what's up?" Marsh asked.

"In less than an hour, you will rendezvous with one Lana McKay, who plans to rob you of your feelings of remorse and your virginity," I said.

"What the hell are you talkin' about?" Marsh asked, staring in my direction.

"It sounded pretty plain to me," Rick said. "I'm about to get a boner just thinkin' about it."

"Look guys…" Marsh said, his voice trailing off as seemed to weigh some heavy thought. I wondered if the weed and booze had overwhelmed his capacity to comprehend how awesome this was. Then, after a moment, he shrugged. "Uhh, thanks."

Jared wasn't looking too good; the boy might have been too liberal with the gin, and it wouldn't taste as good the second time, which I thought he would soon discover. Rick and I had worked up a decent beer buzz. I was doing a little better than Rick, who looked as if he was staring right through the television. Marsh had been gone over an hour, so things with Lana must have been going well. I was glad, considering how lacking in enthusiasm he'd looked when he left.

Jared started to waver.

"Jared, you gettin' sick?" I asked.

"Yeah, I think so," he muttered.

"That means you are." I got up immediately and helped him navigate to the restroom.

Jared was my height and, fortunately for both of us, about ten to twelve pounds lighter. As he continued to struggle with his balance, it suddenly hit me that I was going to have to stay with him through this. I walked him over to the toilet just in time for the first heave. I managed to help him to his knees before the second heave. I held Jared and my nose until he finally heaved up all he had to heave. I then grabbed a cold wash cloth and ran it over his face a few times as he sat, propped up against the shower door. He looked up at me and said, "I'm sorry, Blake, I'm so sorry."

"Don't be sorry, dude. You just had too much to drink. You're not the first and you won't be the last," I said, as I continued wiping his face. "You'll go to sleep soon and be okay." I thought this wouldn't be a good time to mention the forthcoming pounding headache.

"You know, Blake, you're the coolest guy in school," he said, speaking very slowly.

"That's nice of you to say." Dammit, if he started crying, I was going to get sick.

"Really, Blake, I've always been jealous because you're so much of what I'd like to be," he said.

"You're okay, Jared. I just think you try too hard sometimes," I smiled a little. "Don't worry so much about what other people think, including me."

He looked up at me and met my eyes and—

—I was walking across an open field covered with lush green clover. It was peaceful, but eerily quiet, like no sound or movement. It was kinda serene, but was a little uncomfortable. Everything around me looked perfect, almost too perfect. Suddenly, a stream of water shot up from the ground on my right; as I moved away, a stream of water shot up from the ground on my left; then flames burst out in front of me, then behind me. All at once, flames were everywhere. Pitch black smoke billowed around me. I was looking around frantically. I wanted out...—

"You guys okay?"

What the fuck! I looked back and Rick, standing behind me, said, "I need to take a piss."

"Oh, yeah, okay," I said, regaining my senses. I moved away from the toilet. "Jared got a little sick."

"Yeah, I can smell it," Rick said. "Is he okay now; he looks totally wiped out."

In fact, he was staring straight ahead with a blank expression on his face.

"Yeah, he'll be alright," I said, and reached over to help him up. He jerked a little when I touched him. He looked up at me and then slowly let me help him up. "Let's put you to bed, big boy."

I managed to walk him to his rollaway and started helping him undress. He wasn't real steady, and a little of his gin and his dinner were splotched on his shirt and pants. I got a t-shirt and some gym shorts out of his bag. He was trying to help me, but was struggling. As I threw his pants to the side and started helping him into his shorts, I was suddenly frozen.

Sometime, in the midst of all this, Jared had come all over himself. Jesus, I wish I could switch places with you, Marsh.

Jared was sleeping soundly. Rick and I were watching the video magic of "Here Cum the Brides". It was a typical fuck flick, but the chicks were pretty hot. They had nice tits and other credible standard equipment. I wondered if they rehearsed before they filmed this shit. Seemed to me rehearsals could almost be counterproductive. Also, I wondered if they wore makeup on their "tools of the trade" for the close-ups. If so, who put that makeup on them? That job should pay pretty damned good. Rick was concerning me some with the way he was staring so intently at the flick and had nothing to say.

"Rick, you okay over there? You're not sayin' much," I said.

"I'm studying," Rick said.

I fell out of my chair, laughing so hard I nearly spilled my beer. I took a quick look over at Jared, not wanting to wake him up;

even though I wasn't sure a nuclear explosion could do that. As I sat up on the floor attempting to get myself together, I noticed my cell phone had fallen out of my pocket. Picking it up, I discovered it wasn't on. Damn it, I must have accidentally bumped the off button sometime tonight, probably when we were wrestlin' Marsh out the door. I turned it on, and noticed I had three messages and two other missed calls. The two missed calls were from Krista, which didn't alarm me, but the three messages were—holy shit—from Lana.

I immediately hit the first one, left at ten twenty-six: "Blake, you won't believe this." She sounded frantic. "We've had a wreck; it's not bad, but we're waiting on the police. The car is messed up some, so I guess we won't be able to make it. Sorry."

The second message at ten forty-one: "Blake, I hope you're gettin' these messages. I guess you already know we won't be comin'. Call me, so I'll know you got the message."

The third message at eleven: "Damn it, Blake, call me, so I'll know everything's cool."

"Rick," I said, breaking his trance on the current lesson, "I'm goin' to look for Marsh."

"Look for Marsh," he said with surprise. "What the hell's goin' on?"

"I don't know, but—"

The door opened and Marsh eased in. I ran over to him with Rick right behind me. "Marsh, where the hell have you been?" I asked sharply.

He just looked at me, then at Rick, and turned into the kitchen, heading for the fridge. We were right behind him. He grabbed a beer out of the fridge and, without saying a word, walked around and took a seat at the bar. Rick sat down beside him, while I stood across from him.

"Dammit, Marsh, where've you been? We know you weren't with Lana. What gives?" I asked, pressing the issue.

He took a swig of his beer, put it down, and began lightly

thumping the side of the can. "Don't do the eye thing, bro," he said, looking down.

"What's the eye thing?" Rick asked, looking at me.

"It's nothin', Rick," I said, never taking my eyes off of Marsh. He was scaring me. "No problem, bro, just tell us that you're alright and where you've been."

Without looking up, Marsh said, "Well, I don't think I've been alright since Dad died. As for where I've been—," He paused. "I've been roamin'; findin' my way back here."

I leaned closer to him. "Back here from where, bro?" I asked quietly.

"From who I am."

Chapter Thirteen

KRISTA

I certainly hoped that the yearbook was going to be a worthwhile venture. To this point, it had been an organizational nightmare. Mrs. Stakely, our sponsor, had been doing this for a long time. She claimed she had almost twenty years of experience in producing high school yearbooks, but so far, it appeared to me she had managed twenty years of one year's experience.

We were currently working on layouts for page designs for activity groups. We'd been given books to scan through with sample ideas. Cheryl and I were two of only three sophomores on the yearbook staff. The staff was dominated by seniors, which was probably the way it should be. To say that seniors relished their role at the top of the pecking order would have been an understatement. They ran around talking about making this the best yearbook in Gardner High School history. I felt things would be better when the seniors were history.

As intolerable as most of the seniors were, our editor, Julie Pilgrim, made the rest of them seem like angels. Julie considered herself a socialite in the purest sense. She was dating Chad Taylor, a college guy and she never missed a chance to let you know about it. She firmly believed that finishing high school was just an annoying bump in the road and actually a little beneath her. Most of the other seniors couldn't stand her.

Cheryl and I were working with a junior class member, Stacy, who was pretty cool. We had laid out some sample pages when we got a visit from Julie.

"Well kids, have you come up with something worth looking at?" she asked as she scanned the samples we had on the table.

"I guess not."

"Julie, why do we even do this?" Stacy asked. "Mrs. Stakely's just gonna go with what we did last year."

"My dear Stacy," Julie said in her usual condescending manner, "Mrs. Stakely is our sponsor; I'm the editor. Therefore, what was done in the past doesn't dictate what I may choose to do."

"So Julie, what do you envision?" Cheryl asked.

"Well, I'm working on that," Julie replied. "I'll be talking with Chad tonight and I'll have him check on some more elaborate samples at the college."

Cheryl, just warming up, said, "But Julie, we're operating on a tight budget according to Mrs. Stakely, so how can we afford to be elaborate?"

"I have some ideas about the budget," Julie said. "Chad is a budget major and will work with me on it. That's one of the advantages of having me as an editor."

"I see," Cheryl said, "So having you as an editor means we get Chad and his business expertise as an added bonus?"

"Without a doubt; he's such a dream," Julie said with a smile.

"Okay," I jumped in, attempting to head Cheryl off, "I guess we'll just wait and see what other information you come up with."

"Now Julie," Cheryl said, "Can Chad afford to work with us, go to school, be a dream and not be compensated?"

"Well, he'll actually just be working with me," Julie said.

"Well, that explains the compensation," Cheryl said, raising her eyebrows and waving me off as I tried to get her attention.

"Just what is that supposed to mean?" Julie asked, folding her arms.

"It means we get to look at more options and Chad gets to screw you."

"Listen, you little bitch—" Julie hissed, now furious.

At that moment, Mrs. Stakely arrived at our table and asked, "Well girls, how're things coming along?"

"We've just been talkin' about our options for the activity pages," I said, trying to cover the tension. "Julie was sharing some ideas with us."

"That's great," Mrs. Stakely said, patting Julie on the shoulder.

"Julie sure knows the ins and outs."

"I bet that's right," Cheryl said, and I immediately grabbed her arm and squeezed it.

Mrs. Stakely turned and moved on. Julie whirled and walked away. Stacy also thought this was a good time to take a break and left the table.

"Is there anything else you'd like to throw on the fire?" I asked.

"Yeah, Julie's ass," Cheryl said. "And Chad's, too, for not having any better sense than to get tied up with her."

"Speaking of tied up, how about you and your Sikeston beau?" I asked, taking the opportunity to change the subject. Cheryl had recently gone out with a senior at Sikeston High School she met through one of her co-workers at the video store.

"First, he's not my beau," Cheryl said. "Second, we're just barely past the introductory stages of dating. And third, he's nice, good-lookin', and not too sold on himself."

"Wow, how many more dates before you move past the introductory stages?" I asked, trying to keep from laughing.

"Now girlfriend, Scott and I are determined to do this the right way. So, I must defer to him because he is the oldest. I'll just sit on his lap and see what comes up."

It was nice to have some peace and quiet. I was lying on my bed waiting for my baby to come get me. Our first basketball game was Friday and I'd sure be glad when these mid-terms were out of the way. At least the Business Ed exam was relatively easy. My art project was good and an A was a lock there. Geometry was on tomorrow's schedule. Math had never really been a problem for me, but Geometry was different. I took Algebra last year, and it was easier for me than it was for most people. Geometry had a little more bite, or at least seemed to. Remarkably, Blake was catching on really well. He began the year a little intimidated, but he'd been gaining confidence ever since. This was just one of the changes I'd been picking up in Blake.

Another thing, Blake had never given a flip about his studies. Even before we got together, I noticed him doing everything possible to solicit help concerning his classes. Naturally, Marsh had come to his rescue many times. Rick, Tammy, and others had taken their turn answering his call for academic assistance over the past couple of years. And I virtually carried him through most of Algebra. For some reason, he had taken a different approach to his classes, as well as some other things.

Now, our Lit class had been made more interesting with the arrival of the new teacher, Ms. Huey. She was very pretty and didn't seem to mind projecting a sexy image. She dressed nice and strategically, at least from a girl's point of view. She wore bright-colored blouses, most of which were low cut, obviously to call attention to the cleavage of her upper body. She coordinated her blouses with her dark, curvaceous skirts or pants. I didn't think there should be any doubt of her intentions to energize the testosterone levels of every boy in her classroom.

As a matter of fact, I thought her conduct with Blake was a violation of professional ethics. I knew that sounded like a jealous girlfriend, but I didn't care. Everyone told me how she always gave Blake so much attention. Judy said her attention to Blake was so obvious in the Literary Club, it was almost embarrassing. She was probably just flirting, but that was very inappropriate and could be dangerous.

As if that wasn't enough, I was constantly trying to keep Cheryl from choking Julie every day during our yearbook period. And being a high school cheerleader was like belonging to the back-biters of America. Cheryl could jump right in there with them, but it just didn't seem to matter to me.

The biggest problem with cheerleading was the constant interference of some of the mothers. Betsy Tyler's mother was the worst. She was constantly in the middle of everything. I knew Mrs. Smith, our sponsor, had to be sick of her. Betsy, a junior, was cool. But she was dating Matt Perdue, which was not cool, in my opinion. Matt was an egotistical ass. He used to call me sometimes, but hadn't since that run-in with Blake at the beginning of school. He appeared to be pretty hung up on Betsy, but I wasn't real sure how hung up Betsy was with him.

My situation with Blake was, for lack of a better term, ongoing. I got a warm feeling from Blake that I got nowhere else. I loved for him to hold me and I loved to hold him. His kiss was the most wonderful I'd ever experienced. There was just this phobia in me about getting back into sex with him. For the life of me, I didn't know why. To be honest, it sort of bothered me more than I wanted to admit.

The changes in Blake made it more bothersome. Some of what I viewed as his basic nature had changed, like in our intimate moments. Before our sexual exorcism of each other's virginity, he was always gently pushing me towards sex, in his own way. Cheryl compared him to a dog in heat, which was a little strong, but he was pretty horny. But now, even though we were pretty intimate at times, he never attempted to push it.

But the biggest change I'd noticed was he seemed preoccupied so much of the time. I asked him what was on his mind and he said nothing, but I wasn't buying that. Lately, it had been even worse. I was still leery of looking into his eyes, except with quick glances. It went back to what happened that night between us, but I didn't have an explanation for it. I felt sure that qualified as a full-fledged case of paranoia.

I continued to have these unrelenting sexual urges, and they were getting more difficult to control. My time with Marsh had been my only relief. The heat and passion had been so intense, the pressure just oozed out, little by little, with the rhythm of the motion between us. The only emotion we'd shared was fueled by pure lust.

The sound of Blake's horn broke me free from these powerful thoughts. He used to always come to the door, but sometimes I just told him to honk, so we could avoid Mother. I hurried down the stairs and almost made it to the front door.

"Krista! Where are you going?" Mom asked, meeting me in the living room.

"Mom, Blake and I are going to grab something to eat and study for our Geometry mid-term," I replied, trying not to sound exasperated.

"This is a school night, and you need to asp permission to do that," she said, giving away the fact that she was sauced by the way "ask" came out as "asp".

That set off anger inside me. "I asked you yesterday and you said it'd be fine," I said sharply. "That must've been during one of your many cocktail hours and it just slipped your mind."

"Now, you listen here young lady—"

"No! You listen!" I snapped back. "You're a total drunk, Mom. It's reached a point that I'm scared for you to show up at any activity I'm involved in. I'm afraid you'll kill yourself driving to or from them without Dad, or you'll show up and not be able to talk."

I could see her fighting back tears. "Well, if you're ashamed of me, then I guess I won't bother to show up at anything you're involved in."

"Mom, you can't keep doin' this," I said, holding back tears myself. "You're sick and you need help. I want you to see it, Mom—please! If somethin' happens to you, what will Dad and me do?"

"I know I need to cut back," she said.

"Cut back! Mom, you've got to quit; period; end of story!" I said.

"Well, I'll talk to your father about it and we'll decide," she said.

"That's just great. You'll just bully Dad into seeing things your way and we'll just keep playing this game until someone dies."

"Your father and I are the adults here and are more caphable than a sixteen-year-old in dealing with these things," she said drunkenly, screwing up another word, and then turned and walked away.

I heard a light knock at the door. I grabbed my book bag and opened the door where Blake was waiting.

"Come on," I said, as I walked by him before he could say a word.

I quickly got into his truck, wanting to get the hell out of there.

Blake got into his truck and with a concerned look asked, "Krista, are you okay?"

"Let's just go, Blake," I said firmly.

"Okay," he said, cranking his truck. "Any place in particular you want to eat before we go study?"

"I don't care," I said, letting out a sigh. "Can we grab something and kinda disappear? I need some down time and I don't see getting it with Geometry."

"Sure, Babe, I know just the place," he said, as he pulled at me until I scooted over next to him. "I'm alright with Geometry, and whatever you wanna do is cool with me."

"Thanks," I said, and gave him a quick kiss on the cheek. He felt so good next to me.

We barely said more than a few words on our way out here. Blake made the turn on to the river road. He told me he had a special place out here. He hadn't even turned on any music. Quiet just seemed to fit better right now. We had eaten sandwiches at Subway—he'd eaten his and half of mine. He knew I was pissed and he just let me have that. It was getting hard to measure how important he was in my life right now. I felt really safe with him and I wasn't sure why. Maybe this was real love, or my first taste of it.

He turned off the river road onto a gravel road, which wound up to the levee. He found a place where it was safe to park, just off the side of the road. I'm not sure we would've been able to do this had it rained recently, but that wasn't the case.

It was dark now, but the sky was clear and the moon was full. When we got out of the truck, we felt the coolness of the air reminding us it was late October. A steady cool breeze out of the east justified the need for our light jackets. Holding hands, we maneuvered up the back side of the levee. When we reached the top, we had a moonlight view of the mighty Mississippi rolling south. It was a huge river at this location, with dangerous currents that could sweep someone away to oblivion in a few short seconds. Blake said that even when it raged from time to time, there was a majesty about it that was mesmerizing. And when it flooded, there were few acts of nature that could match its destructive force. We found a good clear spot in the grass and plopped down beside each other.

Blake leaned over and gave me a kiss on the cheek and said, "So, baby, you look like you're a little stressed and I don't think it's 'cause of the Geometry test tomorrow."

"I'd give anything right now if postulates and theorems were my only concerns," I said, looking straight out over the river. "You're right, baby; it's amazing out here."

"Yeah, I come out here alone sometimes to clear my mind," he said. "Do you wanna talk about what's goin' on?"

"Hell, I wouldn't know where to start, Blake," I said, still gazing at the river. "Everything is so screwed up. So much crap is going on at school. My classes are the easiest part of my existence. The yearbook class is a constant battle of egos and ideas, supervised by a woman who can't even run the new software program that's been implemented. Cheerleading is a hornet's nest, with our sponsor battling crazy mothers and all of us. I'm wading through mid-terms this week; our first basketball game is next week; and our first yearbook deadline is the week after that. There's got to be a better way."

"Wow! Do you feel any better after firin' those rounds?" he asked.

Well, actually that wasn't the biggest issue, but there was no way I could tell him about that. So I just smiled and said, "Actually, that did feel pretty good. So, how're things with you? You looked really good at the scrimmage the other night."

"Yeah, I guess," he said, as he looked out across the river. "I'm still gettin' accustomed to the pace of the game at this level, and it's a tougher game."

"Well, everyone I talked to said they thought you were the best player on the floor. And I'm talkin' about those basketball gurus in the stands."

"That's nice of you to say, but I'm still learnin'."

"How are things goin' with Perdue and crew?" she asked.

"He doesn't say much and he's a good player, so things are okay for now. They haven't even been givin' Tyler a hard time, and he's a competitive threat to Perdue and Alley. But Coach has been rotating them all, so everyone's been gettin' a lot of floor time, which helps. If everything falls right, we could have a pretty good team."

I was quiet for a few moments, and then finally asked, "Blake, do you think Ciera and Marsh'll get back together?"

"That's a good question," he replied, "There are some weird things goin' on with Marsh. I'm not sure about him and Ciera. He isn't talkin' about any other girls right now. Lana's tryin' to get his attention and may be makin' some headway. They're talkin' some."

"Well, that'd be great, wouldn't it?" I asked sharply, without thinking. "How can you let 'im get involved with a whore like that?"

"Hell, Krista, I'm not his dad," he said. "Things are crazy with him right now. He needs some kind of good experience to help 'im get out of this funk he's in."

Boy, how stupid could I be even raising the issue, much less reacting like I just did? This stuff was making me so irrational. What stuff? I had no idea what I was even talking about.

We sat for a few minutes watching and listening to the river's rolling waters. The moon reflecting off the dark, rolling waters really did have a settling effect.

I finally turned and looked at Blake and asked, "What about us, Blake. How are we doin'?"

"I guess we're doin' fine, Krista," he said, looking back at me. "You're still my girl, aren't you?"

I leaned over to him and our lips met. We fell into a deep, passionate kiss, which started me stirring inside—I mean really stirring. I couldn't let this get away from me and I realized it would if something didn't happen soon. I slowly broke the kiss.

"Let's go, Blake," I said suddenly. "I've got some things I have to get done at home." I gave him a quick kiss and then rose. I held out my hand, which he took and hopped up. We stepped carefully down the levee to his truck.

On our drive back to Gardner, I snuggled up really close and gave him soft kisses on his ear and cheek. I hoped it would help him forget that I'd never answered his question about being his girl.

Chapter Fourteen

MARSH

I supposed the time had come to address the matter I came out here to address. The high I was experiencing from some very potent weed should make this somewhat easier for me and, hopefully, Jared's high would make him more receptive. This was a very sensitive situation. But Blake insisted that I, due to my standing with Jared, deal with it now.

So, anyway, I'd done everything possible to make this comfortable for everyone. It had been a while since our "guy's night out" and Jared had been bugging Blake and me about getting some weed ever since. We had seen him talking to Bernie Talbut, a local drug dealer at the high school, a couple of times and Blake was getting all crazy about it. Hell, I had to do something because I was catching it from Blake about Jared and from Jared about weed. On top of all this, mid-term grades were out tomorrow and I knew Mom was not going to be happy. Now I found myself in this wooded ravine, which Gramps owned, located about a half mile behind his elevators. The elevators were in full swing during the harvest season and the air was full of grain dust. Parking my car under the trees helped keep some of the dust off, but it would still require a wash.

This place had a little history for Blake and me. This was where Ray first introduced us to the wonders of smoking weed about a year or so ago. The only thing that appeared significant for Jared and me right now was this really good high we had managed over the past hour or so.

"Jared, we need to have a little heart to heart," I said.

"If this is about money, I promise I'll get it for you by Friday, Marsh," he said, sounding a little nervous and absolutely high.

"It has nothing to do with money, dude. I'm not chargin' you for this."

"No, really, I know I have to pay. And I owe you and Blake for my share for the last time," he said, almost pleading.

"Look, Jared, you're not payin' for this. We'll all do it again sometime and you can kick in some cash on that. But there's somethin' else we need to discuss."

"Oh, okay," he said, settling a bit.

"We've noticed you've been talking to Bernie Talbut lately, and that can't mean but one thing."

He was quiet for a few seconds and then said, "Yeah, I know Marsh, but there's nothin' wrong with buyin' my own weed from him. Besides, you told me you guys dealt with him before."

"We dealt with him one time and won't do it again because it's dangerous." He offered no response. "Bernie's becomin' too well known for dealin', Jared. One of his older brothers and his first cousin are in prison right now. Hell, even his dad has been arrested for dealin'."

"So, plenty of people still buy from Bernie," Jared said.

"Yeah, and his days are numbered; you can bank on that," I said. "The police will be on 'im soon enough, if they aren't already. You can bet they're watchin' him, which means if you start buyin' from him, they may start watchin' you."

"There'd have to be a lot of people in front of me," Jared said defensively.

"That doesn't excuse you as far as the police are concerned," I fired back.

"Dammit, Marsh, I like this shit. It takes my mind off things and helps me with stress. You and Blake do it and it hasn't hurt you guys."

"We don't do it that much, Jared. And, besides, you don't need to depend on that stuff for stress relief all the time. It can lead to trouble at home and with the police."

"Just because I like it doesn't make me a pot-head," he said. "I'll know if it gets to be a problem."

"Yeah, well, I'm sure many people have said that. Look, dude, you can get high some, just don't let this stuff get away from you."

"I appreciate what you're sayin', Marsh. And I'll think hard about dealin' with Bernie. I'm not gonna get stupid about this."

I guess I'd made all the headway I could. I just hoped Jared would play it smart and stay cool. "Alright, it's time to head back. It's dinner time and I'm hungry."

"That's cool. Thanks, Marsh, for bein' a good friend," Jared said and then walked around and got into the car.

"No problem," I said, and climbed in behind the wheel.

We cruised back into town, listening to the Hot Boys. Just as I turned down the street to Jared's house, I heard the faint sound of my cell phone ringing through the music. Turning down the music, I looked at the caller ID and it caused me to pause for a moment. Then I took the call, "Hello."

"Hey, can we get together tonight?"

"Well, I don't know," I replied slowly. This was insane.

"It's up to you."

I waited a few seconds. "Okay, what time?"

"Say around eight?"

"Yeah, that'll work. Later."

I clicked off, wondering how in the hell I'd gotten myself into this. There was nothing right about it at all. Then why in the hell was I doing it?

I pulled over and let Jared out at his house.

"Thanks, again, Marsh," he said, getting out of the car. "Be careful."

"See ya', Jared," I said, and then took off thinking I better be careful and then some.

My God, these powerful waves of passion kept sweeping over me. It was an inside force that was burning out of control. I could barely control my body. I wanted to scream. My whole body was like a muscle in a constant cycle of tense and release; tense and release; tense and release. A series of tingling currents ran from my head to my toes, as I was caressed in ways which, at one time, would've scared the shit out of me. I was totally absorbed by erotic sensations that reached a level I almost couldn't stand. I was coming again! I couldn't believe it; I was coming again! Was this three or four times? Hell, between the two of us, we had come more times than I could count. A whirlwind of illicit desires had me spinning more and more and more. When did it stop? Why did it matter?

I shut my Geometry book and tossed it on the floor. I then reached over and turned off my bedside lamp. I laid back on my pillow with my hands cupped behind my head and stared at the ceiling. This had certainly been one hell of a day. To cap it off by trying to study Geometry was comical. But I didn't know how you'd begin to cap off a day like this. Maybe a toast—to me, Marsh Williams, one crazy son of a bitch.

The past few weeks of my life would make an interesting story. The question was who would believe it? Hell, I wasn't sure I'd believe it and I lived it. I was beginning to wonder if something was preordained here and someone forgot to tell me. It couldn't be God because He never forgets, does He? I think I might qualify for a few sessions with a shrink. Shit, no shrink would believe all this stuff.

I got it! I'd just go to my best friend in the world, Blake. He could look inside me or whatever that shit was he did; and maybe see everything. That would take care of all of it, with just a minimal amount of casualties. Let's check the casualty list. First, my virginity fell amidst great passion in all directions, setting into motion an unbelievable series of sexcapades; second, my academic prowess sailed south into the doldrums and, so as not to get lonely, was accompanied by my integrity; next, my girlfriend of a few months bit the dust for no reason that I could recall; and finally, after looking inside me and seeing all this, my best friend would hit me square in the mouth and promise to never speak to me again.

Then again, maybe while driving to school tomorrow, a 747 would fall on top of me, making all of this a moot point.

Chapter Fifteen

BLAKE

I honestly cannot remember the last time I arrived at school before seven-thirty. On top of that, Blake Coleman being at school for the purpose of working on a class-related activity was something my friends would have deemed impossible. But, here I was. One advantage to being here early was the number of prime parking spaces available. Hopefully, I'd be able to find some more advantages as I went along.

It was a chilly morning, but certainly not abnormal for the first half of November. It wouldn't be long until jacket weather would give way to a little heavier layer of clothing. Entering the building, I was caught off guard by the atmosphere of emptiness. The halls were relatively quiet when classes were in session during the day, but this was a different sort of quiet; one that wasn't very comfortable. That strange silence caused me to step up my pace down the hall and into Ms. Huey's classroom.

She smiled at me as I came through the door. I hoped I wasn't obviously gawking at her, but she was so damned pretty. She was wearing a red pullover sweater, which fit snugly and called attention to her firm high points. She had on black pants which, although they were not real tight, still managed to highlight the curvature of her hips. Shit, this was tough.

"Good morning, Blake," she said, as she looked through her file cabinet. "You're a little early."

"Yeah, and you have no idea how rare that is," I said, walking over to the table in the back I used during Literary Club. "It'd really hurt my image if it ever got out."

She laughed and said, "I'll never tell anyone. Grab your folder and I'll be right with you."

I had been writing some poetry independent of the rap stuff

Marsh and I wrote. He knew about it, but other than Ms. Huey, no one else knew. Even though it shouldn't matter, there was this perception that guys who wrote poetry were way outside the norm. The rednecks around here, who already detested my love of rap music, would have a field day with the poetry. They would certainly take pleasure in the name calling. Things like fag, fairy, gay, queer, and some other, less flattering names would be tossed in my direction. They were a bunch of stupid shitheads, but I already pushed the envelope a lot without adding more fuel to the fire. I knew Ms. Huey was trying to help me become more involved with my poetry, and she was taking extra time to help me do that. I had really developed a special feeling about my poetry, but I wasn't ready to start sharing it. I didn't know if it was good enough, and I just thought it would cause me grief.

I placed four poems on the table. Ms. Huey's help and encouragement had opened a door for me I never knew existed. She came over to the table and pulled up a chair beside me. I could smell the enticing fragrance of her perfume, which was a big distraction.

"Okay, Blake, here are some revisions I want you to look at," she said, reaching across me and picking up the four poems. She spent the next few minutes going through each of the poems and making suggestions. I worked real hard to keep my focus on the suggestions and not on her eyes, ears, hair, and everything else. "Remember," she continued, "Make adjustments you feel comfortable with and you have to like it. You are the poet." She leaned back in her chair, taking a deep breath and looking a little uncomfortable.

"Are you feelin' okay, Ms. Huey?" I asked.

"Yes, I'm just dealing with a lot of issues right now," she said, looking past me.

"Yeah, sometimes stuff can pile up and it really sucks, or at least it can in my case," I said, trying to say the right thing.

She smiled at me. "You have an uncommon insight, Blake,

which also shows up in your poetry. I believe your talents go far beyond the basketball court."

"Well, that's nice of you to say, and I hope you're right because I'm too small to have any real future in basketball."

"The way I understand it, you're the star of the team and you guys have won three of your first four. I plan to attend tomorrow night's game to see for myself."

"I don't think I'm a star. The team we play tomorrow is the best team we've seen so far and a big rival," I said, becoming more comfortable with the conversation. "I'm glad you're comin' 'cause we need all the help we can get."

She laughed. "I can cheer, but that's the extent of my contribution to basketball."

I decided to reach a little. "You know, Ms. Huey, it's hard for me to figure how someone like you ends up in Gardner. I mean, uh, I'm glad you did but, I don't know; I know it's none of my business."

"That's okay, Blake." She stared at me for a moment, almost like she was assessing me. "I'll tell you a little secret: I'm running."

"Running—from what?" I asked, probably too boldly.

"I was married for five years and it came to an ugly end last year. It just didn't work out and it took me too long to figure it out. He still hasn't figured it out, but that's another story. So, I'm living in Sikeston and moonlighting in Gardner. Life really is full of surprises."

"I'm sorry about all that. You really are a cool person and you're a great teacher. No other teacher has managed to get this much work outta me and made me like it at the same time."

She reached over with her right hand and gently ran her fingers across my forehead, around my cheeks, and over my lips. "Blake, you're a beautiful, gifted young man and don't let anyone ever tell you you're not."

I felt a warmth run all over me. Her touch sent surges of energy through me that stirred my emotions deep inside. I felt a sexual rush I hadn't felt in a long time. My testosterone levels had to be rising at a record pace.

She smiled with that warm smile again. I looked at the beauty of her cheeks, her chin, her lips, her eyes; oh my God, her eyes—

—I was swimming, gliding through clear, blue waters. Light seemed to blink on and off with rays refracting all around me. There was a feeling, comfort I had never experienced. I continued to swim, on and on, freely through the clear waters. Shadows lingered around the edges, but were cut off by the strength of the light. The current started surging and I was surging with it. The water seemed to flow in perfect motion with my body. It was holding me gently and then releasing me, only to gently tug at me again. I suddenly found myself swimming slowly toward the surface. Ripples of water began to lightly squeeze me as I continued to climb. The water got warmer and as I swam upward, now at a faster pace. Almost without warning, I rose faster and faster, while the water got warmer and warmer. The ripples squeezed firmer with more persistence. The warming waters caused an engulfing sensation; faster, warmer, faster, warmer. Suddenly, I broke the surface and there was an explosion of fire and water, and I, I,—

The table rattled as it scooted on the floor. I was in a daze, waiting for my vision to bring things into focus. It slowly returned and I scanned the classroom. Ms. Huey was standing at her desk with her back to me. She had hands over her face. Then she reached down for a Kleenex on her desk. She appeared to be wiping tears away. It was only then that I noticed that I was sweating a little.

"Ms. Huey, I—" I said, getting up from the table and—oh shit!...

Ms. Huey was gone for the rest of the day, and the substitute was like her exact opposite. I'd never seen this lady before and Marsh said she looked like the kind of person who should never go back to any place she'd ever been. She appeared to be fortyish; her hair propped up on her head in the shape of a beehive, and had to weigh almost as much as my truck. Without the guidance of our sponsor, the club members just grouped up and shot the shit. And a bunch of the girls in here could shoot a lot of shit.

I was still trying to come to terms with what happened with Ms. Huey this morning. I wanted to tell Marsh about it, but didn't feel that was the right thing to do—at least not right now. Right now I was trying to hold onto my sanity. This vision stuff, or whatever it was, was beyond anything I'd ever heard about. I was living some kind of science fiction movie or something. I wasn't sure what happened this morning, but whatever it was sent Ms. Huey home and left me feeling a combination of energized and hopeless. Those two things didn't even go together.

And it's not just about his morning. I was playing great basketball and felt almost no pressure. I was also writing some amazing poetry. Stuff was just coming out of me and that's not counting the ongoing wet dreams. I was doing so much better in my classes and things just sometimes came to me easier.

"Hey, bro," Marsh said. "I know you're into some heavy writing, but I really need to talk with you about somethin'."

I looked up at him a second—grounding my thoughts—and then turned my writing tablet over and put my pen down.

"Sure, what's up?" I asked.

"Well, I've received a couple of notes this week that are very interesting."

"Notes; someone's sending you notes?" I asked with a curious look.

"Yeah, I know it sounds a little 'junior high', but they actually came from a girl in the junior class."

"Oh, okay."

"Aren't you the least bit interested in who they're from?"

"Of course, bro, let's hear it."

"The notes are from Betsy Tyler and they're fairly explicit."

That got my complete attention. "Uh, Marsh," I said with a serious tone, "You do know that she's dating Matt Perdue, and he likes her a lot."

"Well, she obviously doesn't feel the same way about him."

"That may be true. If that's the case, then he'll figure the best thing to do is kill you, thereby eliminating the competition."

"Betsy is pretty hot, Blake; it might be worth gettin' my ass kicked."

"Bro," I said firmly this time, "I'm not talkin' about an ass kickin'; I'm talkin' about gettin' killed. Perdue is crazy about that girl and must think she's crazy about him. In case you don't know, women can make even a sane person do stupid things. And we both know Perdue is half nuts already."

"Well, whadda' you think I should I do?" he asked.

"If I were you, I would discreetly tell Betsy that you know she's dating Perdue and you can't get involved in that."

"What if she breaks it off with him?"

"In that case, give it a long cooling off period—like after Perdue graduates. There are other juniors that have shown an interest in you, bro. Go for one."

"Yeah, I should probably hook up with Lana before she gets to number five hundred," he said, rolling his eyes. "I wish Ms. Huey hadn't ditched today. Judy and these girls are more than I can handle, and this sub looks like death warmed over."

I said nothing and picked up my pen to start writing again.

"Dammit, Blake, it's five minutes to lunch. Give it a rest. You've been way too quiet all morning. Did someone die or somethin'?"

I paused for a few seconds and then closed my tablet. I very methodically placed the tablet in my club folder.

"I've got it," he said. "You're depressed because the beautiful Ms. Huey skipped out on us today. It was more than your heart could take."

"Marsh, I'm on overload right now about some things. I just need some time and space."

He looked at me, nodding his head, and said, "No problem, bro. You can have all the space you need."

The cool air slapped us in the face as we left the gym. Rick, Tyler, and I were leaving after practice.

"You guys think we're ready?" Rick asked, as we walked to the parking lot.

"There's no way to know as far as I can tell," I responded. "It's early and we don't know how we'll match up against them. Hell, we still don't know much about us." We played Charleston tomorrow night in our biggest game of the year thus far. Charleston was about twenty some odd miles from Gardner, so it was a natural rivalry. They were in the same classification we were, but played in the conference to the north. They had a good program and had had our number over the past three or four years.

"We're gonna find out soon enough," Tyler said. "I try not to think beyond that."

"I know last year they played rough," Rick said. "There was a lot of pushin' and shovin'."

"Yeah, I remember watchin' it," Tyler said, "Pretty heated."

We reached the parking lot and Rick headed for his car with a friendly goodbye.

Tyler and I loaded up in my truck and rolled out of the parking lot.

"Yo, Blake, how does the mood of the team seem to you?" Tyler asked.

"Okay, I guess," I said. "We're winnin' and that usually keeps things cool."

"Well, I'm gettin' some bad vibes from a couple of the seniors," Tyler said. "Perdue's the leader on the team and he's a scary dude. Just watch how sometimes he gets this look about him."

"Jesus, I try not to pay that much attention to him," I said, trying to disregard the eerie feeling I got when Tyler said that. "He's left us alone for the most part."

"Well, I can't help but to pay attention. He doesn't exactly like me or the color of my skin. I'm never comfortable turnin' my back to him."

"Yeah, I'm not a favorite of his either," I said, smiling a little.

"We have a history and it's all bad."

"Yeah, I know," Tyler said, "But, I don't think he really likes anybody except that girl. And I'd bet that's no more than a horny thing."

That was a very interesting comment. I hadn't really thought about it much. Perdue had only a few people who hung with him and you couldn't count Mutt, because he was a "gofer". "I never thought about it, Tyler, but you may have a good point."

We were currently stopped at one of two traffic lights in Gardner. Crossing in front of us in his old beige Impala was Bernie Talbut. Normally, that wouldn't mean anything, but it did today. Jared was riding in the car with him. Tyler noticed it the same time I did.

"Man, what's up with Jared?" Tyler asked.

"Looks like some stupid shit's up with him," I replied as the light turned green. I eased on through the intersection.

"Bernie's on his way to jail. He's gettin' bolder and bolder; and doesn't care who sees it," Tyler said.

"Yeah, well, Marsh and I've brought that to Jared's attention, but it doesn't seem to matter."

"That's a bad road to travel, dude. Bernie's into more than just weed. Does Jared know that?"

"Hell, who knows?" I asked in response. "Jared used to have more sense than that. He was always scared shitless about stuff like that."

"It's obvious he's changin'," Tyler said.

I pulled up to Tyler's house. "Thanks for the ride, as always," he said, getting out of the truck.

"Anytime," I said, as he closed the truck door.

I pulled out and started on my trek home. Man, I needed some good weed or a stiff drink. All of this shit was getting ready to catch up with me, so I better be prepared. That thing that happened in Ms. Huey's classroom this morning was beyond my comprehension. All I could remember was swimming, water, and fire. How could that be possible? Then, I was back in the room and my—this was so fucking crazy.

And what about Ms. Huey? I thought she was crying, and it worried me. She wouldn't look at me and told me I needed to go. I was so scared and embarrassed; I got out of there as quickly as I could. I was sitting in my truck in the parking lot when I saw her leaving school. Man, what had I done?

Then, there was this shit about Jared. He was doing some really stupid things. He had always been nerdy and an ass-kisser, but he wasn't reckless and crazy. If I thought it would help, I'd beat the shit out of his scrawny ass rather than see him doing this. I wasn't an expert, but I thought Jared was one of those people that needed to stay away from drugs—period. And I was the stupid bastard who goaded him into trying the stuff and then there was the vis-; I didn't want to even say the word. I wasn't sure how much more of this I could stand.

And where the hell was I with Krista? She said we were fine. What did that mean? I felt good around her, and I sensed she felt the same with me. I still felt the passion in our intimate moments, and I could tell she did, too. But then, as if programmed, we both backed off. I could tolerate it, but I couldn't understand it. I could address the tolerance with my periodic "masturbation marathons", but I was more frustrated by the lack of understanding. There was definitely something weird about our relationship.

Then there was Marsh. I had always felt I knew Marsh as well as I knew myself, but that was changing. There were important things he wasn't telling me. That thing at the pool house a month ago was still a mystery. But Marsh's demeanor was changing even before that. Whatever was going on, he was determined to keep it to himself. Of course, there were a few things I wasn't telling him either.

Tomorrow night, I would play in a really big high school basketball game for the first time. I knew I should be nervous. But, compared to all this other stuff, that basketball game didn't amount to shit.

Chapter Sixteen

KRISTA

It was the Friday before Thanksgiving week and a huge deadline in Yearbook period. I was happy to say that our "activity pages" group had met the deadline two days ago. So, today we were more or less hanging out, while the other groups tried to get finished. I noticed our illustrious editor, Julie, was headed our way. This was always a potentially dangerous situation with Cheryl and Julie in such a close proximity.

"Well, how's our leading activity group doing today?" Julie asked. "You folks earned a free day, huh?"

"Yes, Julie, we've finished our assignment and can't wait for the next one," Stacy said in an obvious sarcastic tone.

"That's great!" Julie said smiling, ignoring the sarcasm. She then leaned toward us and lowered her voice. "We were lucky to have Chad's help."

Here we go. Cheryl, who had been preoccupied, could not stay away from that one.

"Now, Julie," she said, "Maybe you can remind us exactly how it was that Chad helped us?"

"Seeing as you have a short memory, I would remind you of the sample books and magazines Chad got for us," Julie stated.

"Just how many of those did we look at?" Cheryl asked.

"That is not the point," Julie said in her authoritative tone. "We benefited from having access to those samples and gaining a better perspective on formatting."

"I see," Cheryl said and then turned to Stacy. "Stacy, what page format did we end up choosing?"

"Basically, the same as last year," Stacy replied. "Some of the names and faces changed, of course."

"I'll tell you one thing," Julie said, obviously flustered,

"Underclassmen are a species unto themselves. They are so short-sighted."

"What does all of this have to do with our eyesight?" Cheryl asked.

"That is such a stupid question, I won't dignify it with an answer," Julie replied.

"Now, wait a minute, Julie," Stacy jumped in. "I don't appreciate the comment about underclassmen. You were an underclassman once."

"She was a virgin once, too," Cheryl said. "But that ended when she was twelve and her ballet teacher convinced her they were really doin' a kind of pirouette."

Julie, red-faced, flipped Cheryl off with both hands.

"I'm not your ballet teacher," Cheryl said, as Julie walked away.

"Girlfriend, you never cease to amaze me," I said smiling. "You always manage to rain all over her world. So, what are you and Scott doing this weekend?"

"Oh, we'll probably rent a movie and crash at his house," she said.

"You said his folks are pretty cool, didn't you?" I asked.

"Yeah, they give us some privacy. His dad is kinda quiet but is always real nice to me. His mom always tries to make conversation and loves to talk about Scott's childhood. He, of course, hates that, and we quickly head for his bedroom to watch a movie and get comfortable."

"Didn't you say he has a little sister?"

"Yeah, but she doesn't say much around me. She's twelve and has always worshiped Scott, so she views me as an intruder."

"Getting back to the bedroom, just how comfortable do you guys get?" I asked with a smile.

She cuts her eyes at me. "Boy, the influence the 'snake' has on you continues to rear its horny head. Well, let's just say we're getting more comfortable all the time. The movies seem to matter less and less each week. So, what about you and the 'snake'?"

"We're doin' pretty good, overall," I replied. "He's so warm and loving. We lean on each other a lot and that feels good."

"How sickening; have you two been goin' to a joint confessional or somethin'?"

"No, that's just the way things are," I said. "Our relationship has gained substance, and I bet that's rare for people our age."

"The reason it's rare," Cheryl said, borrowing Julie's authoritative tone, "Is because people our age don't do relationships that way—at least the normal ones."

"Oh, I see," I fired back, "So all teenage relationships should be sex, drugs and rock and roll?"

"Not necessarily in that order," she replied smiling.

I rolled my eyes and shook my head. There was so much bullshit going on with me. I didn't like her talking about Blake like she did. I used to not let it bother me, but I was having trouble with that now. Along with all the other stuff going on, my Mom was getting worse. I heard her and Dad arguing last night about her drinking. Dad seemed to be holding his own this time. I hoped so.

It was good to be out of school. We had a home game tonight so I had some badly needed chill time. I was cruising solo around town using pretty strong tunnel vision. That was probably not the safest way to drive, but I needed to catch my breath. I just barely saw him out of the corner of my eye.

Mr. Dailey was waving both arms in the air trying to get my attention. He had stopped his jog on the side of the road. I pulled into an empty driveway, turned around and drove over to him. Even in his gray sweats, he was a hunk. I rolled down my window as I pulled up beside him.

"Hey, Krista," he said. "I hope I didn't alarm you."

"No, I was just cruising around," I said, suddenly drawn to the sight and smell of the glistening sweat on his face.

"Well, I was gonna call you a little later," he said. "We wanted to know if you could keep Cindy tomorrow evening. We have a dinner party in Sikeston. I was supposed to call you the other day and forgot."

Oh my God, it must be his testosterone! The churning inside me was off the charts. My legs were starting to quiver a little.

"Uh, sure, Mr. Dailey," I managed. "I can make it work. What time?"

"We need to leave at six," he said, "We should be back by ten. Is that okay?"

"Sure," I said, really needing to get out of there.

"Thanks, Krista," he said with a smile. "You're an angel."

Yeah, right.

Chapter Seventeen

BLAKE

Jesus, I didn't think Coach Randall would ever get tired of blowing that whistle. For the week of Thanksgiving, I was having a hard time finding much to be thankful for. It started this morning, when I had a flat on the way to school. With all the amazing advances the auto industry had made, dealing with the issue of flat tires had to be considered a failure. One of their space-saving changes involved a makeshift jack operation and a ridiculous excuse for a spare tire. It wasn't that the procedure wouldn't work; it just wore you out doing it. Of all the flimsy equipment, the lug wrench had to be the worst. You needed to have incredible physical strength to remove the lug nuts. All in all, it amounted to a total pain in the ass. Thankfully, using my cell phone, I was able to call the principal's office and give notice of the situation. Many kids in Gardner didn't have cell phones. Ms. Eileen, the secretary, took the message. She was a nice lady, who was once my Sunday school teacher. That didn't exactly work to my advantage. Due to some of our experiences, I wasn't sure she trusted me a lot. I hated it when that happened. Anyway, the message was delivered.

Things didn't get much better from there. Ms. Huey had been pretty distant with me since that mysterious early morning encounter we had. She did it in a professional manner, so it wasn't real obvious. Marsh had noticed it. He asked me about it, and I just told him I didn't know what was going on. Hell, I really didn't. But it had made my two plus hours in her classroom before lunch a little uncomfortable.

Ms. Huey continued to capture my attention. I just couldn't get over how pretty she was. It had begun to create some problems for me I wasn't expecting. I was very much drawn to Krista, even with some of the issues we had. But my attraction to Ms. Huey was taking on a life of its own. I was determined to find out what happened that day; I just had to figure out how to do that. There were still times, particularly during Lit class, when I caught her staring at me. She was quick to look away, but she knew I saw. There was something going on between us. I could sense it, but I didn't know what it was.

Many of these distractions led me to inadvertently do some irresponsible things. The situation that occurred after lunch today was a perfect example. I always walked Krista to class after lunch. The problem was making it back to my class without being tardy. Sometimes the halls were very congested, and my class was in a different wing. I'd made this point to Mr. Wood on the last two occasions I was tardy. I was disappointed to find him unsympathetic to the point of suggesting that maybe I shouldn't walk Krista to her class. What disappointed me even more was Marsh's attitude about the situation. He said using the reasoning I did with Mr. Wood was one of the stupidest things he'd ever heard. I could probably be upset with my best friend, but I just didn't give a shit—until now.

Today was my fourth tardy, which qualified me for a trip to see Mr. Evans, our principal. I did everything but beg Mr. Wood to give me extra work or something, but he was unreasonable and I was stuck. That meant I had to go see Mr. Evans before basketball practice. He then sent me with a note to Coach Randall explaining my situation. Coach Randall, being as sympathetic as he always was, told me to remain at the end of practice for some extra conditioning, which might help me get to class on time in the future. So, here I was.

"Mr. Coleman, I just cannot understand why you would create a problem like this when we're off to such a great start this season," Coach said.

"Sir," I said, stopping for a second to catch my breath and see if my legs would stop quivering, "It was not" —breath— "my intention" —breath—"to create a problem."

"Well, if it weren't for the generosity of Mr. Evans, you would've had to miss practice, unexcused, and couldn't have started the game Friday night," he said very matter-of-factly, like always.

"I know sir" —breath—"I'm grateful for that." God, I was dying here. "It won't happen again, Coach."

"I'm glad to hear that," he said smiling. "You're done."

With my back against the wall, I slowly slid down to the gym floor in a sitting position. My legs were gone. Managing to get to the dressing room would be the first major project. Then, getting in and out of the shower would be the next challenge. After a good shower, I should be able to make it to Krista's—I hoped. Right now, I was content to just sit.

Through the fog of my exhaustion, I recalled the "news of the day", which I heard before practice. My tardy situation ranked a distant second to the big story. It seemed that Betsy Tyler decided to end her relationship with Perdue. When I got out on the floor for practice, a little late of course, Rick and Tyler came over and filled me in. Apparently, Betsy told Perdue when he called her last night that it just wasn't working out and she had to break it off. He begged her to let him talk to her, which she did. According to the Gardner High gossip services, he was very upset and wanted to know why. She told him it just wasn't what she wanted to do anymore. That wasn't enough for him. He wanted to know if there was someone else.

Now, that was interesting. Two nights ago, I got a surprise phone call from Betsy. She'd asked if we could talk about some things confidentially. I'd said we could do that. After exchanging some pleasantries, she worked her way into the real reason she called. She wanted to know if, to my knowledge, Marsh was talking to any girls seriously. I told her I hadn't heard him mention anyone in particular. Ironically, just as Krista had done not long ago, she asked if Marsh and Ciera might be talking about getting together again. I told her the same thing I told Krista—to my knowledge, no.

I finally had to bring up the point that she was dating Perdue and, even if it was none of my business, I wanted to know her motivation. I justified that by reminding her Marsh was my best friend, and I didn't want to see him get involved in a mess with upper classmen. She said she understood and didn't think she and Perdue would be dating much longer, but to please keep that confidential for the time being. She thanked me for my discretion, and that was the end of the call.

So, she dropped the bomb on Perdue last night, not once, but twice. According to Rick, the gossip line said that Perdue went over to see her and had to be ordered to leave her house by Betsy's parents, so it didn't end very well.

Perdue was very quiet in practice, but did his work well. We were in a two-day Thanksgiving tournament in New Madrid this Friday and Saturday, and we needed Perdue to play well. He showed no ill effects in practice today from the disastrous fallout that took place last night. Maybe it was still sinking in, or he just decided it didn't mean anything. We had a good practice today in preparation for the tournament. We were seven and one and were excited about our chances. But we needed to be clicking on all cylinders, and that included Perdue.

Well, it was time to get up and make my way, however slowly, to the dressing room and showers. I was going over to Krista's when I left here. Her folks were gone and wouldn't be home until this evening, so we'd had some privacy. That sounded good to me. There was just one more day of school before Thanksgiving.

I finally made it to the dressing room and plodded over to my locker. I carefully managed to get out of practice stuff, step by step; then, slipped on my shower slides and grabbed my towel. My legs were still wobbly as I made my way to the showers. I had the showers to myself, since everyone else had gone home. I planted myself directly under a shower head and let the warm water pour all over me. It took at least five minutes before I decided to lather up and get clean. Going against the yearning of my body, I turned the shower off after rinsing and started back to my locker.

Suddenly, someone grabbed me by the neck and pushed me against the shower wall. I found myself pinned to the wall by the strong left forearm of Perdue, which was over my throat, pushing my head back. As painful as that was, I was more concerned about his right hand, which had a firm grip on my balls.

"Coleman, we need to have a talk," he said, actually sneering. "I have it from a reliable source you've been talkin' to Betsy. Is that true, Coleman?"

"Matt," I managed to grunt out, "Sh-she called me, man." The pressure on my neck was steady, as was the grip on my balls.

"Why would she call you, Coleman?" he asked, now almost growling. The pressure in both places increased a little.

"Sh-she just w-wanted to talk about me and K-Krista," I struggled to say. My eyes were watering up.

"That better be the truth, Coleman, 'cause if I find out different, this team'll need a new power forward and a new point guard. You got it?"

"Y-yeah, o-okay," I said, trying to keep from crying.

"That's good, Coleman, that's good," he said, releasing the pressure a little. "But, I may need to leave you a little reminder."

He then squeezed my balls together and twisted them with a hard jerk. A pain shot into me like nothing I had ever felt. As he released me, I fell to my knees with both hands cradling my balls. Tears were flowing down my face as I moaned and moaned, fighting the urge to throw up as tears streamed down my face. I couldn't remember hurting this bad, or the last time I'd cried this hard. After a couple of minutes, I picked myself up and staggered over to the locker. I got past the urge to throw up and slowly dried off and dressed. I went to the sinks and washed my face, trying to wash away the remnants of the tears. Looking in the mirror, I could see my eyes were still red and a little puffy.

"Blake! Let's go!" Coach Randall yelled, opening the dressing room door.

"Yes sir," I called back, trying to sound normal. I went back to my locker as quickly as I could. After locking it, I grabbed my bag and walked past Coach with my head down so he couldn't get a good look at my face. "See ya' tomorrow, Coach."

"Okay, Blake," he said, "be on time."

"Yes sir, I will," I said and kept moving. Jesus, just let me get to Krista's. So, with wobbly legs, aching balls, and a battered pride, I headed for my truck.

The pain had finally subsided. Krista's gentle kisses probably had something to do with that. Now I was fighting a frustrating mix of anger, fear, embarrassment, vulnerability, and an injured ego.

Sitting on the couch with Krista, I was contemplating whether or not to share with her what happened after practice. This was not the kind of thing that was easy for a guy to tell to anyone. I was supposed to be tough, not hurt and scared. But there was something strangely different about Krista. It was great comfort to have her snuggled in my arms. I felt a kind of security with her that I didn't feel around anyone else—I didn't know why.

She could fire me up and send my hormones into orbit, but it's almost like I regarded her with a weird kind of reverence. Whatever it was, it made for conflicting feelings unlike any I'd ever experienced or even heard of. How could something so warm and soothing go hand in hand with varying degrees of apprehension?

It was enough to make me speak.

"Krista, I had a little trouble after practice today," I said.

"Really; what kind of trouble?" she asked, her head lying on my shoulder.

"Matt Perdue kind of trouble."

She sat up immediately. "What happened, Blake? I heard about Betsy breakin' up with him."

"You know I told you Betsy called me the other night?"

"Yeah, you said she was asking you about Marsh."

"Right; well somehow Perdue got wind of the call and was curious as to why she was callin' me," I said, suddenly feeling a chill remembering the encounter.

"Oh God! I bet he was upset!" she said.

"Yeah, you could say that."

She turned my face toward her and, with her left hand gently massaging the back of my neck, asked in a very serious tone, "Did he hurt you, Blake?"

"Well, nothing really major," I said.

"What exactly does that mean, Blake?" she asked with a sudden look of anger on her face. "And tell me the truth."

After pausing for a few seconds, I said, "When I came out of the showers, he pinned me against the wall and wanted to know what Betsy called me about. I told him it was about you and me, and he seemed to buy that."

"What else, Blake? What did he do to you?" she asked, her eyes focused on me.

Jesus, she must be psychic or something. Plus, it was like something was tugging at me to tell her.

"Okay, he sort of crushed my balls."

"What!" she said, almost jumping off the couch. Her eyes then cut quickly to my crotch and then back to my eyes. "Are you serious?"

I sighed. "When he had me pinned against the wall, he had kind of a vice grip on my balls. He figured he'd leave me a little calling card and it was pretty effective."

"Just where the hell was Coach Randall?" she asked, with a fierce look about her.

"He was in his office across the dressing room; he doesn't know."

"Well, when were you plannin' on tellin' him?"

"I'm not. Look, Krista, I'm just a sophomore, but I'm the starting point guard on the varsity team. I have to be able to stand on my own. Plus, we have a good team and this kind of thing could mess it up."

"Team or no team, he can't get away with that. I'll just go to Coach Randall myself."

"No, Krista! This is between us. I wouldn't have told you if I thought different. But I needed to tell someone, and I knew I could trust you."

Her eyes softened and I felt a great warmth run over me. I didn't understand this at all, but this was the nurturing I was looking for and knew I would find here.

She looked at me for a few moments, and then ran her fingers gently through my hair. "Okay, Babe—for now. Are you okay?"

"Yeah, it's better now."

"I wanna make sure." She reached down and started undoing my pants.

"Krista! What are you doin'?"

"Making sure everything's okay," she replied as she slid my pants down just enough to give her room to look. She then pulled my boxers back so she could get a good look at everything. With her right hand, she ran her fingers gingerly over my balls, sending sensations darting through my whole body. Carefully returning my boxers to their normal position, she said, "I guess everything's okay, no swelling—uh oh; wait; I might've missed something."

Her reference was to the gradual rise in my boxers.

"Well, maybe there's a little swelling," she said, and reached down and wrapped her right hand around me on the outside of my boxers. She slowly began a gentle but firm massage.

"Krista, I—" I said, before moaning softly. She leaned to me and whispered for me to stay quiet as she continued her massage. I was so taken, I found myself helpless under her hold. I remained that way until it was done.

"Now," she said, "That's better."

Compared to the rest of my day, it was heaven and then some.

Chapter Eighteen

MARSH

Sitting on the edge of the bed, I slowly slid my socks on. I then sat for a couple of minutes with my hands anchored to the edge of the bed. My mind seemed to be spinning. Wonder if this was how you were supposed to feel after a few rounds of sex? Wonder if having one orgasm would ever be enough, after you'd become used to having three? Wonder if I'd ever be able to truly come to terms with what was going on? Wonder why the fuck I was wondering so much? I slipped on my shoes and made my way out of the bedroom.

"You okay?"

"Yeah," I replied, as I walked across the room. "I've got to hit the road to Gramps' house."

"Yeah, I've got plans tonight, too."

"Yeah, later," I said, as I grabbed my jacket and headed out.

It was cool outside; you could almost say it was cold. I thought I'd cruise a little bit, taking the long way to Gramps' house. Some good sounds should help me relax and get all this shit out of my head. So, I cranked up some Three 6 Mafia, and set out on my way.

Clearing my mind was damn near impossible. My mom told me that many people used to joke that Sigmund Freud thought most of our behaviors were related to sex. That's probably an exaggeration, but I was beginning to think that few things impacted our lives more than sex. At least that was the case for me at sixteen. I'd never been one to put much stock in some of the long-standing traditional beliefs I'd grown up around. The hypocrisy in this community, and I was sure in all others like it, was unbelievable. Blake and I marveled at some of the things we'd seen and stories we'd heard about the people who lived and worked around us. We heard gossip about people screwin' around all the time—some of it was pretty good. Of course, those stories could be lies or, then again, they could be true. But who gave a shit anyway?

What was fascinating was the way people thrived off talking about it as much or more than they would've enjoyed doing it. Great efforts were taken to keep all these things hidden or swept under the rug. By doing so, the natural purity of the traditions of rural living could be protected by the local pillars of society. Damn, I needed to remember I was too young to be thinking about all this stuff.

The point was I was gaining a better understanding of why all these activities went on, and the attitudes that existed around them. I'd become a very sexually active teenage, at least by the standards people would set around here. Everyone I knew would vehemently disapprove of what I was involved in. Hell, I didn't approve. But obviously, based on my ongoing behavior, approval didn't matter. Despite serious reservations, I had very strong, constant desires to revel in the sex. In spite of everything and everyone involved, the possible consequences of these sexual encounters served as no deterrent whatsoever.

There was some notable irony in that most people around me viewed me as a good kid. Those people had no idea that I drank alcoholic beverages, smoked weed, and was experiencing high-charged, illicit sex. The irony lay in the fact that, in my own way, I was becoming a viable part of the same hypocrisy that I was so quick to criticize.

It sure would be nice to have someone to bounce this stuff off of, but I wasn't comfortable with my options. Blake would be my obvious choice, but I didn't think he would take some of this very well, to say the least. Besides, he had enough shit going on around him as it was. I just didn't have enough confidence in anyone else.

I finally arrived at my grandparents', and looking at the vehicles

I was the last arrival. My mom, Aunt Tricia and Uncle Hal, Ray, and Michelle were already here. I might stay the night just so I could get some booze after mom left. I went into the house through the back door, as always, and made my way through the kitchen. It was sort of a tradition for us to gather the night before Thanksgiving for some non-traditional fare like steak and seafood. Tomorrow, we'd be joined by my grandmother's two sisters and their families for a big traditional meal. That would be an "eat and run" thing, now that I had my own wheels.

Michelle, Ray's little sister, ran to greet me when I entered the family room. She was only ten and represented an attempt by Aunt Tricia and Uncle Hal to do better than they had done with Ray. They were off to a great start because Michelle was a really good kid.

"Hey, Marsh," she said, as we hugged each other. "I've been waitin' for you."

"You have? What's up?" I asked, smiling at her.

"I helped cook the shrimp and they're really good, I want ya to try some."

"I can't wait. I bet they're the best we've ever had."

"Well, come on," she said and grabbed my hand, pulling me over to the serving table.

While I was sampling Michelle's shrimp, Grandma signaled for me to follow her to the foyer. Wonder what this was about? In the foyer, she gave me a big hug.

"How are you, Marsh?" she asked, sincere enough to make me curious.

"I'm fine, Grandma."

"Well, before we get started, your grandfather wants to see you in his office."

My mind went into overdrive trying to think of what this could be about. There's so much shit going on with me. Gramps was very sharp and seemed to know things, at times, you wouldn't think he'd know. I couldn't believe how nervous I was. Hell, this could be something good. Then why could I feel myself starting to sweat? As I knocked on the door to his office, I hoped no one would answer. But, I knew better.

"Come in," Gramps' voice rung out.

He was sitting behind his huge solid oak desk. Two large oak bookshelves lined parts of two walls. Family portraits made up most of the rest of the wall space. It was a very impressive office. To my surprise and alarm, I saw Ray sitting in one of the two chairs in front of his desk. Ray didn't look too happy and said nothing as I took my seat a few feet from him, also facing the desk. This couldn't be good.

"Marsh, I need to have a talk with you two before we eat to address some things and clear the air," Gramps said. "I'm probably supersedin' parental responsibility, but I hope to resolve this and spare them having to deal with it. I've never talked to either of you the way I'm gettin' ready to now. But never lose sight of the fact that I love you both with all my heart. Do you understand that?"

"Yes, sir," we said. I could feel the moistness in my armpits now.

"Ray, I'll start with you," Gramps said, rotating his chair toward Ray. "You're taking six hours of college credit at the vo-tech school and working for your father at the investment office. I've managed to find out that you're narrowly passin' those courses. Also, you're away from work almost as much as you're there." Gramps paused a second and cleared his throat. "I'm also aware of your drug use and your little side business."

Wow! This might really be bad. Ray was looking down and not uttering a sound.

"You see, Ray," Gramps continued, "I know many people in Sikeston, which you should already be aware of. I have some close acquaintances among various branches of law enforcement, and don't think they're unaware of some of the things you're doin'. They've been nice enough to come to me about it. You're not viewed as a big drug dealer, but you've come to their attention in and around other drug investigations."

Man. I had never seen Ray look so pale.

"Now, I've always been liberal with you about the booze, as long as you didn't over indulge or were drunk around family." He glanced over at me. "I've done the same with you, Marsh." He turned back to Ray. "I've looked the other way when bottles of liquor disappeared because it didn't happen too often. But I will not tolerate this drug business. You're living a fast life, Ray, and that's dangerous. I hope you'll choose not to become a drug addict, but that part's up to you. But this drug dealin's gonna stop. If this private talk won't do it, then we'll take the next step. Do you understand me, Ray?"

"Yes, sir," Ray said without looking up.

"Now, I have a question for you," Gramps said, his tone a little stronger. "Have you been supplyin' Marsh and Blake with marijuana?"

Oh shit! I looked over at Ray who was looking back at me. I knew I had to speak up.

"Gramps, Blake and I wanted that stuff and we bugged Ray about it. That's our responsibility."

Gramps turned to look at me. "I'm aware of that, Marsh, but I'm talkin' to Ray at the moment." I shut my mouth tight.

"Yes, sir," Ray said, looking up at Gramps for the first time. "I did that and I'm responsible. But buyin' marijuana can bring you into contact with some bad people and I didn't want Marsh dealin' with 'em."

"You're probably right, Ray," Gramps said, "But that's no excuse to provide illegal drugs to your cousin and his friend, especially when they're two years younger. That's unacceptable and will cease."

"Yes, sir," Ray said, dropping his head again.

Gramps now rotated his chair toward me. "Marsh, I've received word from people who work for me and farm my land that you and Blake have been smoking marijuana. Based on what you said a moment ago, I assume that's true."

"Yes, sir," I said, being careful to keep my head up and look at Gramps.

"That is also unacceptable. You two are sophomores in high school and we have enough teens doin' drugs. I'm also aware that your grades are not what they should be."

For some reason, I decided to speak up. "Gramps, we don't smoke very much and it has had no impact on my grades."

Gramps was quiet for a few seconds. He then said, "Look Marsh, I know life is a challenge for boys your age. I also know it's especially hard for you because you don't really have an adult male role model."

That flew all over me. Once again, I was unable to restrain myself from speaking, this time with some emotion. "I don't want an adult male role model! I deal with enough shit as it is; I don't need anyone else to have to deal with."

Gramps' eyes opened wide, and I noticed Ray was staring at me with amazement. Damn, I couldn't believe I said all that.

"Well, Marsh," Gramps said in a harsh tone, "Wanting and needing are two different things. And this dope smokin' had better cease, or you and I will take the next step. Now, do I need to contact Blake and his parents to address this further?"

Boy, Gramps was playing hardball. backing backed off immediately. "No sir," I said in a very soft tone. "I'll tell Blake, and please don't call his parents."

"That's a better approach, Son," Gramps said, also softening some. "We'll keep all this between the three of us—for now."

Damn, I almost ran my mouth into a complete disaster. I never used to do that stuff. Gramps lightly slapped his hands on his desk, smiled and said, "Now, let's go kick off a good Thanksgiving." He got up from behind the desk, came around and put one arm around each of us and led us out of his office.

Chapter Eighteen

As I walked to the dining room, I thought of all the things going on in my life. If Gramps knew about all of it, he'd have me committed.

Chapter Nineteen

KRISTA

It had been a long time since I read *The Night Before Christmas*. To make up for lost time, I had managed to read it six times over the last hour. Well, it was December which "tis the season". Actually, the real reason was to get Cindy to take her nap. She was growing fast. She had a truly sweet disposition and had a good time with whatever she was doing. And now, thanks to her, I could probably recite *The Night Before Christmas* by heart.

I went to the kitchen and grabbed a soda from the fridge. Then, it was back to the den to watch a little TV. Mr. Dailey would be back any minute. Just as I finished that thought, I heard his Explorer pull into the drive. I went to the window and, looking out, noticed he was very slow about getting out of the vehicle. God, he was such a hunk. He called when I got in from Mass and asked if I could keep Cindy this afternoon. He had to go to Sikeston to meet with a client. It was short notice, but cool with me.

Just as I heard his come through the back door and into the kitchen, their phone rang. He picked it up and I couldn't tell exactly what was being said but he was not happy. It soon became obvious he was talking to his wife and it wasn't a pleasant conversation. From what little I could put together from hearing just one side of the conversation, apparently she wasn't going to make it home until sometime tomorrow. I heard him saying something about her being on the road too damn much. He finally walked into the den after the call, looking a little flustered.

"Krista, would you have enough time to stay another hour?" he asked.

"Sure," I replied, "I came prepared to spend all afternoon."

"Thanks, I'd like to get in a good run while you're here with Cindy."

"No problem," I said.

"You're a jewel," he said smiling, and then hurried to his bedroom.

He was such a good guy, who barely looked his thirty-one years. It truly sounded like there was a conflict growing with his wife. How could she do that? This man had it all. He was a picture of physical perfection. He was obviously very intelligent and had such a cool manner about him. I didn't know what the deal was, but she would be crazy to put their relationship in jeopardy.

He bounced into the den wearing his winter running gear. That included a dark, slim-fit warm-up suit and a sweat band-ear muff combo to help combat the cold air. His physique was evident even in his attire. His youthful facial features, highlighted by dreamy blue eyes and coupled with his wavy brown hair, were captivating. It was enough to make me run after him, but I knew I couldn't catch him.

"I should be back in an hour and thanks again," he said, smiling, and headed out the front door.

I plopped down on the couch, trying to temper my growing desires for that man. These desires I had set off urges that were so powerful. Trying to contain them continued to be a problem. I felt like I was managing them better, but being around Mr. Dailey tended to make them difficult to suppress. I thought I'd give Cheryl a call to see what was up and try to chill out.

"Hey girl," I said, after she answered on the first ring.

"What's goin' on in your world?" she asked.

"I'm pullin' babysitting duty at the Dailey's."

"Well, how's the scenery?"

"He just went out for a jog," I said. "He asked me if I could stay for a while so he could run. Cindy napped down a few minutes ago."

"I see; so where's his lesser half?"

"She's out of town on business, evidently 'til tomorrow. I caught part of the phone conversation a minute ago, and he didn't sound too happy with her."

"Sounds like a disturbance is brewing in their marital bliss."

"Could be; it's hard to imagine any normal woman becoming very discontent with him."

"Listen girl," she said, taking on her snooty tone, "He may be the hottest man on this side of civilization, but he is a man. They're all a pain in the ass."

"Does that include Scott?" I asked, unable to resist.

"Of course it includes Scott. He's very sweet and has many positive characteristics, the most prominent obviously being his taste in women. But, you can bet I never forget he can be a lust-driven, heartless creature like all members of the male species."

"Cheryl, if you don't stop preachin' that junk, you may actually start believin' it."

"Start! I do believe it and it's not junk, girlfriend. I worry about you 'cause you have this very warped attachment to the 'snake', who's layin' around somewhere playin' with his dick, waiting his chance like the rest of them."

"Does the word cynical mean anything to you?" I asked.

"Not a damn thing. Does the word naïve mean anything to you?"

"I'm not naïve, girl, I just don't believe that guys are always totally consumed by lust. They have other interests."

"Well, they do have to eat. I supposed you can take an hour or so out of their day for that. Their other interests are just window dressing."

"Good grief; you know, Cheryl, we girls are capable of some lustful moments, too."

"You bet. I know I'm capable of some really kinky, perverted desires that would make many people sick. But I don't let it dominate my day like guys do."

"Well, I don't think Blake is absorbed by constant lust," I stated with some resolve, "Or Marsh, Rick, and most of the others, for that matter."

"They all have one-track minds and the tracks run around their dicks."

"You have such a quaint way of expressing yourself."

"Just one of my many wonderful qualities," she said, "Since Marsh's name came up, have you heard the rumblings that Betsy has her sights set on 'im?"

"Yeah, well, I wish she'd set her sights somewhere else. Matt's not givin' her up easily, and he's a loose cannon, to put it mildly."

"See, now that's another thing. Guys have to think they own you and view relationships as territorial."

"Girls can be just as bad," I countered, "and not all guys have that attitude to the level of Matt Perdue," I stated firmly. "Besides, he's a jerk."

"Now, you're comin' around to my way of thinking."

"Only about Matt Perdue." I stated firmly. "And if Betsy isn't careful, she'll get Marsh beaten up."

"I doubt it'd come to that."

"Well, I don't," I said. "I better get off the phone and play babysitter awhile."

"Maybe you should start playin' housewife."

"Very funny; love ya', girl."

"Back 'atcha."

In a few minutes, the front door opened and Mr. Dailey walked in. His hair was ruffled a little, and his skin glistened with a light sweat, which made him more attractive than ever.

"I'm not too late, am I?" he asked.

"Oh, no," I answered, "As I told you, I have no reason to hurry."

"Well, I'll get your money and —"

"No need to rush; I'll hang around until you shower or whatever, if you like."

"Well, thank you, Krista; that would be helpful," he said.

"You go ahead. Take your time. I've got no place to be."

I honestly had no idea why I just made that offer to stay. Cindy would nap another half hour or so. That was more than enough time for him to shower. I could no longer deny the urges I felt to get closer to him. He had shown no interest in me in regards to anything intimate. It's just that I was drawn to him. I'd felt this with Blake and Marsh, but not drawn like this. These urges were stronger in some way and would not be denied.

I decided this was a good time to check on Cindy. The fact that she was napping on her parent's bed had nothing to do with this or, at least, I was telling myself that as I made my way into the master bedroom.

Easing the bedroom door open, I quietly went in and walked over to the bed where I found Cindy sleeping soundly. The sound of the shower running filled the room. Looking up at the mirror on the dresser, I was momentarily frozen by the reflection of the partially open door to the master bath. That explained why the sound of the shower was so clear.

What it didn't explain was why I started walking over to that door. Why was I doing this? It would just take one second to turn and go out the bedroom door; then to the den for a few minutes; then out to my car and on my way home. This all ran through my head as I continued moving toward the bathroom door.

The door was about a quarter of the way open and my eyes were suddenly locked on the large bathroom mirror. In the mirror was the reflection of a slightly obscured view of the most beautiful body I had ever seen. Even with the detail precluded by the shower glass, his features were still easy to see. The muscle definition was so amazing. His shoulders were broad and their symmetry was perfect. He turned and I could now see the outline of his chest, with a dark patch of hair perfectly placed. I began to scan down his torso. His abs had a chiseled definition with a line of hair from his belly down to his—oh my. So that's what a man was supposed to look like.

The urges rose inside of me at an alarming rate. Damn, I wanted him. This wasn't only crazy, it was all wrong. It went against all accepted moral beliefs. Then why was I taking my shoes off? He had shown no desire for me, which offered me a quick out. Then why was I sliding out of my pants? This went against all social, religious, and legal rules for proper behavior. Then why was I slipping my shirt off? I was contemplating having a sexual encounter with a married man, which was more than a valid reason to turn away. Then why was I standing here totally naked?

I reached out and slowly pushed the door open. I eased inside, carefully making sure to close the door behind me. His back was to me as I approached the shower door. I quietly pulled it open and felt the little splashes of water against my legs and feet. His back was still to me as I stepped in the shower. He turned the water off and—

"What the hell, Krista!" he exclaimed, as he backed away about half a step. "What're you doing?"

I placed the fingers of my left hand over his mouth to silence him. "I'm a young woman looking for someone just like you."

He gently pulled my hand away, looking frantic, and in a whispered tone said, "Krista, this cannot happen; now I need you to please leave the shower and go get dressed, and I—"

Standing on the tips of my toes, I covered his mouth with mine and kissed him as deeply as I could.

He carefully grabbed my shoulders and pushed away from me, though he was virtually out of space. "Krista, please, we cannot do this."

I began running my lips over his nipples causing them to harden. I rubbed my breasts against his body.

"For Christ's sake, Krista—stop," he pleaded, but I felt his hardness against my stomach. His grip on my shoulders loosened. I ran my hands down his back and around his hips, which caused him to quiver. I started slowly sliding down.

"No, Krista," he said, panicking. He put his strong hands underneath my armpits to hold me up. But the wet shower floor gave him no traction, and he slid down with me, settling in a sitting position on the floor. To his obvious dismay, I was now straddling him, just atop a very impressive erection.

He looked at me, now almost eye to eye, and said, "Krista, I can't do this."

I gave him a quick, gentle kiss and said, "I can."

Chapter Twenty

MARSH

Really cold weather had finally arrived in Gardner. The high today might reach the freezing mark, which wasn't that unusual for the second week of December. The wind made it feel about ten degrees. I think weathermen came up with a good idea with the chill factor and heat index. It seemed to me how cold or hot it felt was more relevant than the actual temperature. You know, those guys who did the weather on TV had a great job. They didn't ever have to be right. I was pretty good at that already.

Sitting in the church parking lot with my Mustang running to stay warm, I was patiently waiting for Blake. This was the Christmas season, so the parking lot was full. Nothing filled the church like Christmas and Easter. The rest of the year was a crapshoot. Baptisms could occasionally bring in big crowds, depending on who was being baptized. Some attended to celebrate the occasion, while others were probably there on the outside chance that someone might drown.

Finally, Blake rolled into the parking lot. He was actually a little early. His improved attention to time was one of his interesting new qualities. He pulled in next to me, parked, and quickly jumped out of his truck and into my car.

"Man, it's cold this morning. I almost froze my balls off waitin' for my truck to warm up," he said, still shivering some.

"Well, at least you've still got some balls after lettin' Matt crush 'em for ya," I said, with obvious sarcasm.

"Are you still mad about that? I thought we hashed that out already," Blake said.

"We did and yes, I'm mad as hell. You waited over two weeks to tell me, and only told me then because I told you about the calls I was gettin' from Betsy."

"I wanted you to be aware of what you could be gettin' into. He's psychotic about Betsy right now," he said, looking over at me.

"That's fine, bro, but it's not what I'm talkin' about. He ambushed you and tortured you. I can't get over the fact you kept that from me." I was steaming up some, which was probably over the top because we'd already been through this once.

"Torture is a little strong," he said, "And I did tell you about it; and that's somethin' I wouldn't tell just anybody."

"I'm not just anybody, dammit!" I said, raising my voice.

"I know you're not," he snapped back, "And I told you! Maybe I shouldn't have 'cause you won't let it go. There's nothin' anyone can do about it now."

"Bullshit! I told you we'd go get his ass and I meant it."

"And I told you why we couldn't."

"Well, I don't believe the team thing matters in this case. And as far as provin' your manhood, you're more of a man than he'll ever be, so that doesn't fly either," I said, with a continued resolve.

"Look, can we just drop it?" he asked with some obvious frustration.

"Let me ask you somethin', bro; what if he jumped me and kicked the shit outta' me? You gonna just let that go? Well, are you?"

He stared out of his window for a few seconds and then said, "No."

I noticed something different in his expression, even in his demeanor. I was suddenly overcome by the strong emotions I sensed coming from him. It occurred to me that this might be hurting him. That immediately changed everything.

"Look, bro," I said in a very low tone, "You know how I am about you. When that son of a bitch hurt you, he hurt me. There's no way that shit's gonna happen anymore if I can help it. So, I'll respect your wishes, but I'm gonna be watchin' your back."

He smiled and said, "That's cool."

"You up for a little Christmas cheer courtesy of Brother Condrab?"

"I'd rather have some spiked eggnog, but I'll take what I can get," he replied. We got out of the car and hurried into the church.

The sanctuary was all dressed up for Christmas and was close to capacity. Blake and I worked our way to our familiar place on the back pew. James Kimball, a junior and loyal church-goer like us, was sitting in our regular spot. He was about forty pounds overweight, but filled out his clothes really well. He and all the other "back row kids" knew that we sat there, so I didn't know what was up with him today.

Blake made the first move by squeezing in tight to the right of him, while I placed myself snugly on his left. He looked at both of us like we were crazy, and then quickly got up and moved two pews up. He must not be very up close and personal.

I looked down the pew to our left and saw Jana and Lana in their normal spot. Jana saw me looking and nudged her sister who turned and smiled at me. I believe Lana's body was showing some sexy expansion. Her dress narrowly met the minimum standards of acceptability. She had always had nice hips and legs. It was her bust size that seemed to be expanding. I'd been receiving her LHS (let's have sex) signals for a while now, and the truth was I could do worse. There was just this thing about being in Lana's "who's who book" that left a bad taste in my mouth.

"Hey, Blake," I turned to him and whispered, "I think Jana's set on checkin' you out, no matter what the circumstances." She was really hot for him.

"Well, she needs to check in another direction," Blake whispered back. "Things may get that desperate, but they're not there yet."

I decided to shift my attention to any other section of the church. I spotted Mr. Harris on the far side. He worked at the bank. Blake and I saw him at the mall in Cape this past summer, and he was talking to a very pretty woman, who was not Mrs. Harris. They were nervously looking around as if they were guilty of something. We felt sure it was a perfectly innocent encounter, especially when we saw them in a car together later. It wasn't his car. Hey, that's just the way some of the world operated. I'm developing a clearer picture of that all the time.

"Marsh," Blake whispered.

"What?"

"When do you think we can end this weed embargo?"

"I guess anytime we feel it's worth the risk."

"What about Ray?"

"Oh, we can do that. Ray ain't changin'. We just have to be careful, bro. Gramps is not playin' around about this."

The service was now coming to order as the choir entered. Christmas hymns were the thing and we opened with *In The Bleak Midwinter*. No doubt it was a very popular hymn, but I bet our choir presented it in bleaker fashion than was ever intended by the writers. I tried to remember that church choirs were made up of people who liked to sing, not those who could sing. And I had to admit our choir represented a great diversity of sound.

We managed to survive the first half of the service, enduring the hymns, announcements, scripture reading, and, of course, the offering. I had to admire the strategic placement of the offering in the church service. It was placed to follow two or three hymns as an encouragement to give to those in need, and to precede the sermon, thereby insuring collections before many might be discouraged from giving.

"Brothers and sisters," the voice of Brother Conrad boomed out. "It is a blessing to gather and continue to worship in this special season."

That's a pretty generic, but effective start.

"You know, I was reading the other day about how many people were buying computers for Christmas and talking about how the internet continued to improve our world."

Is that in the Bible?

"Computers, cell phones, and other gadgets are the new way of life. The internet represented a new way of life and was changing everything. This article suggested that any major disruption in this ever expanding technology could bring the world to a standstill."

Uh oh.

"Did you hear that?" his voice rang out, "Bring the world to a standstill! Have we become so consumed with the magic of computers and the internet that we believe they can stop the world?"

So, we're going to do tech wars today.

"Well, I think the people of God have a different view."

From what floor?

"True Christians know that we're susceptible to the material creations we hope will improve our lives. This is not a new phenomenon, it's just the latest. Have you noticed they just keep getting bigger and, some like to think, better?"

I know of a few things in which bigger is certainly considered better.

He paused a moment. "It is certainly true that computers and other technological advances have expanded communication and given us more ready access to a wealth of information. There is no doubt it represents a prominent part of our new global society. However—"

You just knew that was coming.

"—Like every other great innovation of man, it is laden by a negative for every positive; for every plus, there's a minus; and Biblically speaking, for every Samson, a Delilah."

Whoa, now that's a zinger. We just alienated all feminists and every barber shop in the world.

"For all its good, its power to destroy is frightening. It is particularly frightening for the younger generation."

That would be me.

"Our young people now have more access to venues of blasphemous forms of music, greater sources of drugs, and blatantly offensive pornography."

When would we get to the frightening part?

"The communities we live in have always been far removed from the more decadent areas prevalent in our cities. This is no longer the case. And it's not just computers. Cable TV and video stores offer easy access to these venues of sin. We have radio stations which can reach us now that play lyrics with sex, guns, blood, violence, and profanity. Our kids are no longer safe from these things."

I'd just noticed Blake was paying very close attention and looked very unhappy.

"The most tragic part of this is that all of these venues do not only play these sanctums of sin, they promote them. Can you imagine? Right in front of our eyes, our children are not only exposed, but coerced and manipulated by these traps of damnation."

Sanctums of sin had a nice ring to it. Man, Blake looked really pissed.

"How can we be concerned about the world coming to a standstill over internet problems? Our young people are out there following a trail of marijuana smoke into the fires of hell. They are becoming entranced by this crazy music that promotes guns, drugs, and violence. They are being convinced that sexual activity is desirable and should be condoned."

I didn't know about condoned, but it sure was desirable.

"Our young people are being sacrificed even by their own peers who, influenced by this satanic force, draw other innocents into this ever growing web of self-destruction and spiritual annihilation."

I could live with satanic force, but I drew the line at spiritual annihilation.

"So, our own children have been corrupted and they're spreading this corruption. It will be a valiant test of faith to save our children and ourselves. And all of this at a time when we celebrate the birth of our Savior."

Exactly when would be a good time? I swear Blake was glaring at the pulpit.

"We will not waver in the face of this onslaught of evil!"

Condrab was rolling now.

"Our faith will more than sustain us. It will make the difference when things are darkest. It will give us the strength we need to stamp out the vile music and images that infect our young people. (louder) It will provide us with tools to overcome the forces which lead our youth to surrender their bodies to immoral temptation!"

Precisely what would be the terms of this surrender?

"Christ is born! We are saved!"

Amens filled the air. I'd move to second if this thing was over.

"Amen."

I so move.

The closing hymn, *Joy to the World* (the one a little older than the Three Dog Night version my mom likes), rubber stamped Brother Condrab's emotional message. Blake continued glaring throughout the hymn and closing prayer. When the service ended, he virtually bolted out of the sanctuary and through the exit. I tried to keep pace, but he had a big lead. I had to jog across the parking lot to catch up and he'd already started his truck. I went to the passenger side and hopped in.

"What the hell's up with you?" I asked, catching my breath.

"He was talkin' about us. It was all about us," Blake said stoically.

"Oh, come on, Blake. We've heard all that before. I don't think there's anything personal toward anyone. Just blow it off."

"I shouldn't have to tolerate open attacks on parts of my lifestyle in a place of worship by a bunch of pompous, self-righteous, back-biting, two-faced, judgmental, hypocritical bastards," he said, never missing a beat.

"Well, there is that."

WINTER

Not seeking or finding atonement;
Or knowledge of what lies in wake;
The haughty, gold treasures of virtue;
Can be found with ease to forsake.

As the pool of great thinkers scramble;
And fleet, flagging morals disperse;
What always once was is found to be not;
Pierced by a scourge of rebirth.

Encompassed by great shrouds of darkness;
The pitch will leave all seers blind;
Cover cries from the legions of prayerful;
Who are torched in the flames left behind.

Now blossoms a newfound existence;
Finding slivers of light in the night;
Straining for the will in order to deal
with the blessed and cursed gift of sight.

BLAKE

Chapter Twenty One

BLAKE

We won the Three Rivers Holiday Classic basketball tournament yesterday, beating Malden. The tournament was one of the biggest in southern Missouri. A big contingent of Gardner fans made the trip to Poplar Bluff for the game. Our team had become the focal point of the community. That happened when you won.

I was taking my time driving home from practice as the sun set. Christmas was good overall and the New Year was here. I was still dealing with some crazy shit and so was Marsh. There were things going on with Marsh. I could sense he was really troubled—and my ability to sense things was going off the chart—but he wasn't talking about it. We all changed, and this was a time in our life when changes could snowball. But his changes had affected so much of who he was.

Marsh had always been one to make sharp comments, but he was usually discreet. Now, he just blurted them out. He always worked hard enough in school to keep an A average. It now appeared B's were okay, no matter what his mom, Gramps, or anyone else thought about it. Everyone knew Marsh could cruise and make B's, and he'd decided to cruise. Despite my warnings, he continued to have phone conversations with Betsy, and it was only a matter of time before Perdue found out. Marsh had developed an aggressive attitude that was approaching reckless. I'd always been reckless, but he was catching me and gaining speed.

Krista's warmth was still beyond anything I'd ever experienced. She'd been holding me closer as of late. I wanted her so badly, but remained nervous about taking chances. Believe it or not, I wasn't willing to take any risks which might put our relationship in jeopardy. I'd never felt that way about a girl before.

There was another big change evolving in my life. In the past couple of weeks, I'd actually smoked weed with Jared on two occasions. I guess Marsh had convinced me that my concerns were unfounded. Of course, he didn't see what I saw that night at the pool house. But I was hopeful that Marsh was right about Jared. Jared had become a good friend and I felt a weird kind of connection with him. For some reason I couldn't explain, I was worried about him.

Marsh and I were slowly trying to build back our supply of weed and alcohol. Ray helped us out with some booze, but was still being careful about the weed. Gramps had a long reach and a death grip. Flying under his radar was a very wise and practical course of action.

I finally made it home and slowly pulled into the drive. The gang was all here and, no doubt, anxiously awaiting my arrival—I wished. Lugging my bag, I headed through the garage to the back door. Entering the kitchen, I was greeted by a typical Coleman household scene—Mom, Dad, and my sister Barbara sitting at the kitchen table. However, it concerned me a little that no one was smiling and all eyes were glued on me.

"What happened? Did someone die?" I asked, certainly hoping that was not the case.

"Have a seat, Son," Dad said solemnly. "We need to talk to you."

I dropped my bag behind the door and slowly pulled up a chair, sitting across from Barbara. I was flanked by Mom, who sat at the left end of the table, and Dad, who sat on the right.

"Son, I don't pretend to know what it takes to be a sixteen-year-old in today's world," Dad started. "And I know there are things I don't understand. But you and your sister are the most important things in our lives, and I feel we have certain responsibilities to you that we have not fulfilled."

"You and Mom have done fine," I said, feeling some discomfort inside.

"We both appreciate you saying that, Son," Dad said, as Mom reached over and patted my hand. "We've always been proud to be your parents. But, as Christian parents, we have certain standards that we're responsible for instilling in you and holding you to them."

I was getting a real bad feeling about this.

Dad shifted in his seat and, after glancing at Mom, said, "At the deacon's meeting this past Sunday afternoon, we discussed the fate of our young people. As you know, Brother Conrad has been addressing some of this in church. Now, you and I have discussed some behaviors you and Marsh had participated in that were unacceptable. I want to ask you now if you have ceased your involvement in those behaviors."

Well, here was one of those moments of truth, I guess. This would be a definitive moment in my relationship with my parents. Glancing at Mom; then Barbara; and then Dad; I said, "Yes, Dad, I'm no longer involved in those behaviors."

"That's real good news for us to hear, Son," Dad said, as Mom reached over and squeezed my hand. Barbara never changed expression. Dad now straightened up in his chair. "Now, Son, we need to address another issue."

There was a pause as dad placed three of my CDs on the table. "Son, I borrowed these three CDs from you and listened to parts of them."

I could feel my temper rising and said, "Dad, you mean you took my CDs from my room without even askin' me?"

"Well, sometimes parents have to infringe on their children's rights of privacy, if it's in their best interest," Dad said with confidence.

"So, nothin' I have is private enough to be beyond your reach?" I asked, trying to remain civil.

Dad sighed a little. "When it comes to your health and safety, parental rights supersede their child's right to privacy."

"And just how does listening to those CDs affect my health and safety?" I asked, this time with a defiant tone.

"Now, Blake," Mom interjected, "Don't get upset. You know how much we love and care about you."

"That's all well and good, Mom, but it doesn't answer my question."

"Son," Dad continued, "Your moral health and safety are just as important, if not more so, than your physical health and safety."

"And just how's my moral health and safety endangered by listening to those CDs?" I asked, trying to mirror my Dad's demeanor.

"My gosh," Dad said, "I just finished listening to that filth. It's all about taking drugs, shooting people, prostitution, and some other things I couldn't understand. There are some things on them I'd certainly hate for your mother to hear. Anyone who listens to that devilish garbage would be appalled at what they hear, to say the least."

"I see," I managed, still fighting my rising temper. "So, listening to that devilish garbage puts my moral health and safety in mortal danger."

"Of that, there can be no doubt," my Dad proclaimed. "Every one of those damnable things I listened to virtually glorify every evil activity which true Christians know to be spiritually destructive. It's time we stood up as followers of Christ and bring down this grave threat before it takes stronger hold of the souls of our children. And, as much as it pains me, I must face the fact that this infection has been residing in my own home."

I sat quiet for a few seconds, finally deciding enough was enough. "Please excuse me, Mom and Barbara," I started, "But, Dad, that's the biggest crock of shit I've ever heard."

"Blake!" Mom said, with a stunned look.

"Son, there's no excuse for that type of language," Dad said, his anger flaring, "And it serves as a perfect example of the influence I'm talking about."

"Really," I said, "I thought what I said was an appropriate response to the religious nuts who claim to speak for God about what's suitable."

"No one in their right mind would call that stuff suitable," Dad stated firmly.

"There seems to be some real discrepancies in what the church determines to be suitable," I said. "I know of no less than five adult members of our church who are involved in behaviors that make mine and Marsh's look like playground pranks. But I guess Brother Conrad and his 'deacons of damnation' aren't aware of that or, more than likely, choose to ignore it."

"My Lord, Son," Mom said, looking pale.

"Blake, I don't know how you think you can make such a malicious charge just to defend the immoral music you listen to."

I turned and caught his intense glare and matched it with my own

—A dark corridor opened before me. I began floating through an abyss surrounded by blank reflections. The reflections appeared to be covered by a tint of glitter which alternated between a sparkling glimmer and a shiny dullness. From this, I began to emerge into a faded bland landscape. The landscape slowly came into focus. I appeared to be in some kind of shallow valley. The most distinctive feature was how barren it was. There were spotty areas of grass and small trees, but it was predominantly rocks and stones. Looking in front of me, it was endless, with no horizon. I suddenly felt an inclination to look behind me. What I saw was breathtaking. A huge wall of stones towered over me. The stones were a sea of colors -gray, orange, brown, black, and silver. They were shimmering in different patterns. I could feel a rumble gaining momentum. Something was wrong. I suddenly noticed water seeping through the stones. My God! It's a dam! I turned and began to run. The rumbling was growing and growing. It's going to break. I was running faster and faster. There was an explosion—

"Blake! Bill!" a voice shrieked. "What's going on?"

I was jostled slightly around my shoulders. I turned and saw a hazy outline of my mother standing beside me. Things were slowly coming clear now. I saw Barbara beside Dad, who was also standing and staring straight at me. I rose slowly from the table. Then, in a flash, something hit the left side of my face with terrific force. The blow sent me stumbling backwards, falling to the floor and hitting my head.

"Bill! My God, Bill what're you doin'?" my Mom screamed.

"Daddy!" Barbara yelled, "You hit 'im! Are you crazy?"

I began regaining my senses and realized my father had struck me. I now began to feel the stinging on the left side of my face and a throbbing pain in the back of my head.

"Bill, you get out of here, now!" Mom screamed at him, while standing between me and my father.

The tears welled up in my eyes. He hit me; Jesus, he hit me. As my mom knelt beside me, I watched my sister lead my father, who now had his face buried in his hands, out of the kitchen.

"Oh Blake, I'm so sorry," Mom said, with tears flowing down her cheeks. She tried to cradle my head next to her, but I pulled away.

With tears slowly emerging, I jumped up, grabbed my CDs and bolted out the back door.

"Blake! Come back here, Son! Please!" Mom yelled, following behind me.

But I jumped into my truck, started it up and squealed my tires backing out of the driveway. I tried my best to choke off the tears. I would not cry. What was that shit I saw? Why did I see it? I couldn't believe he hit me.

There was no doubt I did many things I shouldn't. Driving my truck right now was one of those things. I was on my way to Sikeston after spending some time on the levee looking at the river. It was freezing outside, but I managed to keep warm, courtesy of my flask of gin. There couldn't be much left because I was pretty numb right now. Careful to move at a safe speed, I worked hard to stay alert. I needed to be somewhere, but I didn't know where to go.

I couldn't go home, at least not right now. My family had been calling my phone every five minutes. Dad left a message apologizing and asking for forgiveness. There was no doubt in my mind of his sincerity, but I wasn't ready to face him. If I could understand these damn trances, or whatever they were, maybe I'd know how to feel about this. But I didn't get it, and it scared the shit out of me. The only two places I felt safe were with my bro or my girl. But how could I justify dumping this shit on them? What kind of answers could give me anyway? It was a moot point because I couldn't find either one of them.

I'd tried Marsh three times with no response. I called Ms. Becky and she said he'd left and said he was going riding around town. She said he'd been talking to Betsy on and off all afternoon. So, I called Betsy's house and got no answer. I even drove by there and her car was there, but no lights were on in the house.

After climbing deeper into my gin cloud, I decided to call Krista. Again, I got no response. I called her mom, who said she thought Krista and Cheryl were going to Sikeston. There was also no response from Cheryl. Where the hell was everybody?

Passing the country club, I drove as deliberately as possible, considering I was experiencing a solid, gin-induced high. I passed Todd's and approached Marsh's grandparents' house. I came to a slow stop when I noticed Marsh's car parked in the driveway. Even in my dizzy state, I managed to punch in Marsh's number and still got no response. It now occurred to me that Marsh might be giving Betsy a tour of the pool house. Realizing that was a good possibility, I decided to drive on into Sikeston.

I had to make a pit stop, so I carefully pulled into a convenience store. Though not one hundred percent, I found that my sense of balance was manageable. I slowly made my way to the back of the store and into the restroom. I was always impressed by the selection of condoms offered in restrooms. It was like if you bought one of these specially designed condoms, the size of your dick didn't matter. Their masterful designs would guarantee explosive orgasms. In my only complete sexual experience, one wasn't required for a pretty damn good orgasm. I managed to hit the urinal and not splatter too much. With intense concentration, I was able to zip up, button up, and buckle up without getting tangled up. I then made my way out of the store and back to my truck.

Man, this was one hell of a buzz, and I needed one. At least the things running through my head couldn't run so damned fast. The hard hitting sounds of DMX helped me maintain focus, as I cruised down one of the main strips of Highway Sixty-One. Then, I saw it. I almost swerved off the road, but regained control and slowly pulled into the bowling alley parking lot on my right. What I saw was a billboard across the street advertising Gladewood Estates Condominiums.

Gladewood Estates was home to one Ms. Laurie Huey. She told Marsh and me about Gladewood in Literary Club one day. My mind was racing upstream against a gin-laden fog. Did I dare? Hell, she probably wasn't even there. I didn't even know which condo it was, but I could easily spot her silver Jetta. I saw the address on the billboard and knew exactly where it was. This rush had actually knocked down some of the gin buzz. Damn it, I was going to do it. I wheeled back out on the road and headed for the north end of Sikeston.

I arrived at Gladewood Estates within five minutes or so. Boy, they were nice. There were four rows of pairs of condos, and it looked like there was about a total of forty units. I eased into the parking area and began slowly navigating, looking for a silver Jetta. I needed to go no further than the second row. Parked in front of units fifteen and sixteen was Ms. Huey's Jetta. It was about eight o'clock and lights were on in both places. I parked next to the Jetta and pondered my next move. I had done some crazy things, but nothing like this. I really did need to land somewhere to ride out this buzz. To hell with it. I shut off my engine and took a deep breath. I checked my hair in the mirror and popped in a breath mint. Easing the truck door open, I was very quiet getting out and shutting the door. My age influenced my choice of condo number sixteen. Most of my nervousness was offset by the high I was on. There was a buzzer button and a speaker next to the door. Reminding myself to stay cool, I pressed the buzzer.

"Yes," a voice responded through the speaker.

"Ms. Huey," I said in a quiet tone.

"Who is this?" the voice asked, a little louder this time.

"Blake."

After a moment, I heard the lock turn and the latch released. The door opened and there she was, beautiful as ever, wearing a navy, light-weight sweat shirt and some really snug jeans. Her sparkling eyes, slender nose, and rich lips looked as if God had sculpted them to perfection. Her long blonde hair hung free and easy.

"Blake," she asked in a whisper, "What're you doing here?"

"I'm somewhat intoxicated and driving by myself. I figured that's a bad combination, so I needed a place to land, and I thought about you."

She stuck her head out the door, looked both ways, and said, "Blake, I—"

She then grabbed my arm and guided me inside. She walked me through a small foyer and into a fairly large den area, which contained a large sofa, recliner, two winged back chairs separated by a small table, a coffee table, and a big screen TV. A soft beige carpet covered the floor. Only one lamp and the TV were currently lighting the room.

She led me to one of the winged back chairs and sat me down. She sat in the other one, the small table separating us. "Blake, you shouldn't have come here. This is very inappropriate."

"I'm setting a record for 'shouldn'ts' today," I said. "I know I shouldn't be here, but I didn't know what else to do. I can't go home like this."

"What about your friends, Blake?"

"You know, that's a good question. The ones I trust all seem to be in hiding."

"What's that supposed to mean?"

"Your guess is as good as mine."

She was quiet for a minute, obviously weighing options.

"Okay, here's what I'm going to do," she said. " I'll call your parents and tell them you stopped here because you were sick. That way they can come and pick you and your truck up. I'll also —"

"Ms. Huey, I will not go home," I said, suddenly feeling a strong resolve. "I'll just leave and—"

"No, Blake, you're intoxicated and I can't allow you to drive. You can try to come to terms with your parents on this."

"My father and I have already negotiated terms today, and it ended with him layin' me out with a right cross."

"What!" she exclaimed.

"My father hit me," I said, looking down with my hands interlocked in front of me. "He's never done that before."

I looked up and could suddenly see she looked at me different. She reached over and touched a very tender place on my upper left cheek. I couldn't help but flinch.

"My gosh," she said, "Have you put some ice or something on that?"

"No," I replied, "I was outside for a while and it's pretty cold. That doesn't hurt like the back of my head where I hit the floor."

She reached over to the back of my head running her fingers through my hair until she found the spot and—

"Ouch!" I said, flinching away from her touch on an even tenderer spot.

"What a knot," she said, shaking her head. "I can't believe this."

"Join the club."

She was quiet for a few moments, contemplating again. Then she took me by the hand and led me to the sofa. "Take you jacket and shoes off and lie back on the sofa," she instructed. "We're going to get some ice on you."

Wow, I was up for some TLC. I followed her instructions,

making myself comfortable and inclining my head and shoulders against a large cushion pillow on the end of the sofa. She returned with a small ice pack covered with a small towel. Lifting my head, she gently placed it under me and slowly eased my head back on it. Then she pulled the coffee table up next to the sofa. She took a seat on it, and with a small, ice-filled, cloth-covered baggie, began gingerly dabbing the sore area on my face for a few minutes. For those few minutes, I believed that maybe I'd died and gone to heaven.

With her left hand, she started caressing my forehead and flicking locks of my hair. The power of her touch made my whole body tingle. The tingling continued to grow stronger. I had an erection that was rock hard and knew it showed, but made no attempt to hide it. Looking at her, she seemed entranced, almost like she was somewhere else. I slowly reached up and gently ran my fingers across her cheek.

Then, as if in rhythm with her caress, she leaned over and brought her mouth to mine. Her tongue filled my mouth, which set into motion the evolving of the deepest, most sensual kiss of my life. The kiss continued to gain depth, never stopping and sending waves of tingling sensations through me. My body was squirming a little, trying to maintain control against the power of the sensations. She finally released and I felt my breath release. I could tell I was quivering.

She looked at me with those beautiful eyes and asked, "Are you okay, Blake? You're shaking."

"I'll be okay," I said, trying to breathe normally.

She then got up and walked out of the den for a minute. She returned with a huge quilt. I watched as she carefully spread the quilt out on the carpet floor. She picked up the TV remote, switched to a music station and raised the volume. Then she scooted the coffee table out of the way and offered me her hand. I took it and eased up slowly from the sofa. We stepped over to the center of the quilt.

She stood facing me and peeled off her sweat shirt, which revealed she was braless under her t-shirt. Next, she slowly removed the t-shirt, exposing the most amazing breasts I had ever seen. After waiting a moment, obviously to give me time to soak up this phenomenal sight, she unbuttoned her jeans and slid them down to her ankles. She then stepped out of them, using her right foot to toss them to the side. Using her thumbs, she very deliberately removed her panties, exposing a small patch of light brownish hair. The sight of her was almost surreal.

She now stepped up to me and, starting at the top button, began methodically unbuttoning my shirt. I was frozen in place. Reaching the top of my jeans, she unbuckled my belt, unbuttoned my jeans, and slowly opened my zipper. Without taking her eyes off my face, she removed my shirt. She ran her fingers across my hairless chest and down to my jeans. Falling to her knees, she used both hands to pull down my jeans, allowing me to step out of them. Carefully pulling my boxers out around my erection, she removed them.

Taking my hands, she pulled me down to my knees, bringing me face to face with her. Our mouths met again with me trying to lead, but she took over once again. I could feel her breasts rubbing against me, igniting crazy sensations inside me. She reached down and gently maneuvered my erection up and down her smooth patch of hair. I couldn't stand this for long.

She must have sensed that, because she slid down to a sitting position and slowly laid flat on her back, taking me with her the whole way. With me propped up on my hands atop her, she opened up and, with her left hand, guided me in. I entered her smoothly, beginning a steady driving rhythm. Displaying amazing flexibility, she pulled her knees back, enticing me to drive deeper. I drove as deeply as I could at a frantic pace. Through all of this, I fought off my own desperate need to release. I could feel her wanting more, but I couldn't hold it any longer.

I let out a long, low groan, experiencing a release like never before. My toes were curled so tight, they almost cramped. My breathing was hard and deep; my heart was beating fiercely. If there was ever a good time to die, this would be it—in total ecstasy.

After pulling out, I eased down, laying my head just below her breasts and whimpered, "I'm sorry, but I couldn't hold it any longer."

"You were wonderful," she said, and gently began running her fingers through my hair, being careful to avoid the tender area in back. For the next few minutes, it seemed as if I were floating in space, totally free of the world.

Then, with a renewed sense of purpose, I lifted up just enough to start tenderly kissing her nipples and caressing them with my lips. I could tell by her light moans that she was very sensitive to this. In response to her, I worked more aggressively and began to feel the heat from her as her body started to twitch.

Suddenly, she began gradually rolling me over, putting me on my back and looking up at her straddling my newfound erection. With an ease that was both sensual and fluid, I went inside her. She began taking me with a vigorous motion. Her breathing was fast and furious. She laid her head back, stretching with everything she had. I arched up as much as I could to enhance the rhythm. Suddenly, I felt her melt from inside. With four or five short screams, she seemed to succumb. My release followed immediately. It was all of me—everything.

She leaned down, gave me a quick kiss, and smiled. I smiled back with fulfillment. With a great exhibition of agility, she came off of me and sprang to her feet. She offered her hand, which I took and eased myself up. She leaned to me ear and whispered, "You were truly wonderful."

I looked at her, smiled, and said, "You must be an angel from heaven."

Then, once again serving as my guide, she led me back to a bathroom and provided me with everything I needed to shower.

The warm shower was great. After such a crazy day, I felt a reassuring comfort. After my shower, I put on my clothes, which she had placed outside the bathroom door for me. I then went back in the den, sat on the sofa, and waited for her to emerge from her shower in the other bath. I had never felt such a wonderful exhaustion.

A few minutes later, she came in dressed in a full sweat suit and sat down beside me.

"Are you okay to drive now, Blake?" she asked.

"Yeah, I'm okay now," I replied.

"Okay, I've got tell you something, and I don't want you to interrupt me. Will you do that?" She seemed shaken.

"Yes, ma'am."

"What I did tonight was wrong and it was all my fault. You are a beautiful and gifted young man, and I had no right to do what I did."

I started to speak but she raised her hand to silence me.

"I enjoyed what happened and have to face the fact that I'm developing very strong feelings for you. These feelings are deemed inappropriate because I'm twelve years older than you are, so I must come to terms with that. If you decide to talk about this, I'll have to face whatever consequences are warranted. You have the right to do that, and it won't change how I feel about you. That being said, I realize the responsible thing for me to do is resign and leave. I'm already giving that serious consideration. I just don't know how to handle it at this time. I've fought strong feelings about you for months now. I don't know what's going on with me, but I will not bring harm to you."

"Can I say something now, Ms. Huey?" I asked.

She sighed and nodded.

"When I came here tonight, I felt lower than anything on this earth. I've got so much shit goin' on with me, I can barely see straight. I was drunk and meant what I said about havin' no place to go. I wasn't forced to do anything here tonight. I wanted this to happen, too. So, as far as I'm concerned, you saved my life tonight. And I'd rather die than do anything that would bring harm to you."

A tear ran down her cheek. "Thank you for saying that, Blake. I'll decide soon what's best for me to do."

I looked at her for a moment. "Okay, Ms. Huey; but please take into account that I believe you're one of the best things that has ever happened to me, as a teacher more than anything. It seems like I'm losing my grip on a lot of things lately, but I pray to God that I don't lose you." With that, I put on my jacket and walked out the door.

Making my way back to Gardner, I was almost sober. I finally turned on my phone and saw I had amassed countless calls from home, Marsh, and Krista. I could only deal with one right now, so I chose Marsh. Boy, this would not be easy. I punched in his number.

"Okay, where the hell are you?" Marsh answered.

"I'm a couple of miles out of town, bro, wondering if I can crash at your place. It's been a bad day," I replied. Of course, that wasn't totally true.

"Yeah, I want you to come straight here, now!"

Damn, he's mad. "Look, bro, I've—"

"I know what happened; your mom called my mom. I've been callin' and drivin' all over this county lookin' for you. So, you come on over right now. I'll meet you in the front yard because we're gonna fight, and I don't wanna tear up the house."

Oh shit. "Look, bro, I just don't have the energy to fight."

"Well, good, that way I can beat the shit outta you. What the hell were you thinkin'? I thought you were dead or somethin'."

"For a while, I did, too. And I did call." Jesus, I was so tired.

There was silence for a few seconds.

"I know you called, bro," Marsh said in a quiet, sensitive tone. "Please just come on in, so I can see you in the flesh and know you're okay."

"On my way, bro. Will you have your mom call my mom and tell her I'm fine and stayin' over with you? I'll go home tomorrow."

"Will do; anything else?"

"Yeah, give Krista a call and tell her everything's cool and I'll call her tomorrow."

"Got it."

"Be there in a minute."

About five minutes later, I pulled into Marsh's drive and parked behind his car. I walked to the front door where he was waiting on me. I went in and followed him back to his bedroom, shutting the door behind me. He turned and looked at me. Tears started flowing down my cheek. I fell into his arms and he held me.

"I'm with ya, bro," he said. "No matter what, I'm with ya."

Chapter Twenty Two

KRISTA

One of the many good qualities my good friend Cheryl possessed was her subtleness. Ha! We were loaded up in my car on our way to pick up Betsy. From there, we would drive up to Cape Girardeau to spend the afternoon watching college cheerleading squads perform. The performance took place on the campus of Southeast Missouri (SEMO) and might be fun. Mrs. Smith, our sponsor, gave us tickets for the event, so the three of us decided to make the trip.

After one honk, Betsy came bouncing out of her house to my car. She climbed in the back seat behind Cheryl.

"Hey girls," she said with a bright smile, "Are we ready to roll?"

"It's not noon yet," Cheryl said, "So I ain't rollin' for nobody."

"It's close enough to noon for you to stop being grumpy," I said, as I pulled out on the road and started us on our way.

"I like being grumpy on Saturday morning," Cheryl said. "No self-respecting teenage girl should be up before noon on Saturday."

"What about the guys?" Betsy asked.

"First of all, few teenage guys are worthy of any self-respect," Cheryl replied. "Second, the ones who're awake on Saturday morning are jackin' off, and the ones who're asleep are dreaming about jackin' off."

"Don't you think you're stretching it a little bit?" Betsy asked.

"No, but I'm sure they're stretching it all the time," Cheryl replied.

It was time to come to Betsy's rescue. "You see, Betsy, Cheryl thinks all guys do is eat, sleep and sex. She has this warped view of guys in general, except for Scott, of course, who gets a free pass."

"Now, girlfriend, that's a very narrow view of what I think about guys," Cheryl said in a mockingly serious tone. "Guys our age are at this transitional period in their life. They lack the capacity to control the radical hormonal changes goin' on in their bodies."

"Cheryl," I said, exasperated, "What is this vain attempt at an unbiased scientific explanation about the biased prejudices you harbor against guys?"

"Now that was very unfair," she claimed. "Here I try to provide Betsy with a perfectly sound reason why guys are such single-minded, lust-filled creatures. I think I'm bein' very fair to the guys by acknowledging the fact that the desires that drive their lives are natural."

"And, I can't tell you how much I appreciate your efforts," Betsy said, "Even if I don't happen to totally agree with your ideas."

"I wasn't seeking support from either of you for ideas that I know are universally true," Cheryl retorted. "And as far as Krista's earlier reference to Scott getting a pass, that is absolutely untrue. Just like all guys, Scott thinks usin' his head correlates directly with unzipping his pants. Being older, his lustful energies are more refined, but they're there."

"Just out of curiosity, does Scott know about these deeply embedded ideas you have about guys, including him?" I asked.

"We don't discuss it, if that's what you mean," Cheryl responded, a little defiant. "Some things a girl keeps to herself when it comes to a relationship."

"Yeah, and besides, you certainly wouldn't want to say anything that might break down that correlation to unzipping his pants," I said.

Cheryl now turned to Betsy and said, "Now see, Betsy, that's the kind of thing that comes from spending too much time with a creature like Blake Coleman."

"Alright girl," I said firmly, "first of all, Blake's not a creature. Second, you expect me to buy into that 'girl keeps to herself'" crap, which is BS. And third, any reasonable person would be able to see that you're battling your own prejudices."

"See what I mean, Betsy," Cheryl said, shaking her head. "Because of Blake, Krista exhibits completely irrational thinking."

"I think Blake's cute and basically a nice guy," Betsy chimed in, "And his best friend is really hot, as far as I'm concerned."

"Uh oh," Cheryl said. "Do I sense a new romance in the air?"

I didn't want to seem nosy or meddlesome, but I felt I needed to address this. "Betsy, are you sure Matt's accepted the fact that your relationship with him is over?"

"Matt's okay, despite what many people think," Betsy said. "We had a good time, even though our relationship was pretty tame. He actually conducted himself in a very proper manner. It was just that I could tell he wanted more, and I just didn't wanna go there."

"Well, everyone knows about the scene he made over at your house, and that didn't sound too good," I said.

"Yeah, and he still calls sometimes wantin' to know if we can work somethin' out, but I never lead 'im on, and I do remind him it's over. He hasn't been callin' as much lately, so I think it's sinkin' in."

"Just another example of how teenage boys can mess anything up," Cheryl said.

"Betsy, are you sure Marsh is safe from Matt?" I asked pointedly.

"I think so," she replied. "He pops off a lot, but it's mostly for show. He'll latch on to someone else pretty soon."

"Yeah, well, I think he's crazy and dangerous," I stated. "I don't know him as well as you do, but he's big enough to break Marsh in half."

"Good God," Cheryl said, "Then we'd have two of 'im."

"Not funny, girlfriend," I shot back.

"I'm not laughing," she said, with a phony surprised look on her face.

"Look, girls," Betsy said, "Matt barks loud, but doesn't really have much bite. And I certainly wouldn't do anything intentionally to put Marsh in danger. Marsh and I've been talkin' every day, and I think we're ready to go out. He said he wanted to and I do, too. He's such a dream."

"Only if it's a wet one," Cheryl said smiling.

"Well, I hope you're right," I said.

Things got quiet for a minute. We were just a few miles out of Cape. We had plenty of time to stop and eat before going out to the college.

"Hey, Krista?" Betsy asked, breaking the silence.

"What girl?"

"I know you and Blake have dated a long time. So, you're bound to know some things about Marsh. Is there anything maybe I should know?"

"Marsh is a great guy," I said in a very serious tone. "He's one of the most real people I've ever met. You can't do much better."

"God help us," Cheryl said, rolling her eyes.

God help me, I thought, if Cheryl was going to be like this the entire day. The trip was supposed to be fun, and I really needed some fun after yesterday.

Last night was a game night and the team had been on the road. That meant I'd had only two hours after school before our bus left for the game. When I got home, my mom told me Mr. Dailey had called, which caught me a little off guard. Since our fateful shower scene last month, he hadn't spoken more than a few words to me. I'd been over there to baby sit a few times, but our interaction had been quick and chilly. I had no real clue as to what that meant. Mrs. Dailey had been the one calling as of late, so this call aroused my curiosity.

I went to my room and returned the call. He wanted to know if I could babysit, but I told him we had a game. He then asked about this afternoon. Once again, I had a conflict. After a few moments of silence, he said that was all he needed and would check with me another time. It left me with a really weird feeling.

Then, things didn't go well at the game. Blake hurt his ankle and sat out the second half. He said it felt better after the game, but there was still some swelling. So, when we got back to Gardner, I was all set to play nurse, and maybe take his mind off his sore ankle. But, when Blake and I got to my house, things went bad.

Mom was on another drinking binge and had already been into it with Dad. Blake was hobbling, and I had to get his ankle elevated and iced. I got him settled in on the sofa with his ankle up on a couple of pillows. Mom was planted at the kitchen table, like she always was after a few drinks and a fight with Dad. But, lately, Mom was being unusually hateful when she was drinking, and last night had been no exception.

She told me not to use all the ice because we needed some. I immediately took issue with her. She said she wasn't running an emergency ward in her living room. I countered with a comment about her inability to run an automatic dishwasher, much less an emergency ward. She said I was being belligerent, and I asked her how she could tell. I'd turned to get the ice pack when she crossed the line. She said I never talked to her in a disrespectful manner until I started dating "that boy". Then she said she'd heard rumors that he was a pot-head and couldn't do much else but bounce a basketball. Firing back, I told her that she didn't know what she was talking about. He was not a pot-head and, as a matter of fact, was a genuinely good person. I became furious. Furthermore, I said, he'd had to endure a lot of grief and pain recently and wouldn't take any shit from her or anyone else when I was around. She tried to speak, but was so drunk and upset she couldn't put any words together. I then took the ice pack and returned to the living room. We didn't see her for the remainder of the evening.

So, though I didn't pretend to know what this day might hold, I was certainly hopeful it would be better than yesterday. Mom didn't have anything to say this morning about what happened last night. As a matter of fact, she'd been very cordial. She probably couldn't even remember what happened. That's how far gone she was sometimes.

I'd talked to Blake a few minutes ago, just before I picked up Cheryl. He said his ankle was sore, but the swelling was down and he could get around on it. We didn't talk about the thing with his dad much, and I'd never said a word to anyone else about it. But I'd never look at Mr. Coleman the same.

My mom, now Blake's dad. And my best friend turning into a complete man-hater. Life was kinda turning to shit.

Chapter Twenty Three

MARSH

A short break in the sexual action, for some crazy reason, led me to think about my unwillingness to pursue different options. I used to just shake my head when Blake took senseless chances when there were less risky options available. Well, my recent exploits put me right up there with my bro. I'd become a pretty big risk taker. I guess the level of risk depended on the motivation.

Fear was a great motivator. I'd never been one to fly in the face of danger and would shift directions in a hurry. My emotions could also motivate me. When they were the driving force, my logic and reason took a back seat. I would have to include greed on my list of motivators. Like most people, if I wanted something bad enough, I'd do almost anything to get it. Plus, I didn't mind lowering my standards to make it work.

But I knew what was motivating me now more than anything was my own vulnerability. I hated to admit it but it was the truth. I was making choices at the moment that, aside from being reckless, bordered on insanity. What was really weird was it sometimes actually helped me keep my shit together. Boy, I could sugar coat anything. There was a void in me being filled—a void I didn't even know existed. I mean, I kind of knew. For the life of me, I had no idea how to get a grip on this stuff. And I had plenty of attractive options.

First, there was the rough and ready Lana. Her looks were okay and she had a nice body. She offered certain enticing advantages. There was never any doubt about the ultimate goal of any date or even moment of privacy. The normal frills of dating were more or less disposed of. Sex was not a prospect, it was an absolute. I would have to wonder about finding enough time to satisfy her sexual desires. Of course, there would be no issues about loyalty because there wouldn't be any. Other temptations wouldn't be considered conflicts of interest.

Another, more appealing alternative was Betsy. She was a pretty girl and, as far as I knew, a virgin. That's what I'd heard anyway and that made her even more desirable. She met all the standards of our community culture—good family, good student, and good values. We'd been talking some and she had a great personality. Plus, she was chasing me which was good for my self-esteem. However, I wasn't sure Blake's warnings weren't warranted—Perdue could be dangerous.

There was another alternative that I believed was still open for me. That would be my old flame, Ciera. She went for a ride with me in my car the day after Christmas, even though we didn't tell anyone. She wasn't the prettiest of the girls, but was first class in my eyes. I knew I still cared about her. Many of the intangibles belonged to her.

Any normal person in my situation would undoubtedly choose one of those three options as opposed to where I was now. But, regardless of anything, there was something here I wasn't sure I could get anywhere else.

"Can you go again?"

"Y'know," I said, "I don't know exactly where the point 'I can't go again' is."

"Well, I guess anyone can be 'spent'."

"I guess that's true. Do you think we can ever make any of this stuff okay?"

"I don't think it matters."

"That's probably the way to look at it," I had to admit. "But it's hard to shake all these feelings of guilt sometimes."

"Yeah, I know."

"I just feel like I'm tempting fate; y'know what I mean?"

"Yeah, well you're not tempting any more than I am."

Well, I knew that was true. I had a little time before I was supposed to pick up Blake and take him to the gym and treat his ankle—probably just enough time to see if I could manage one more...

Riding around Gardner to kill time had to be one of the most monotonous tasks a person could ever undertake and a cold Sunday afternoon was really taxing. I had Master P supplying some great sounds which made it somewhat bearable. Taking a loop out by the elevators added two or three minutes, but that was it. Blake asked me to come into the gym with him while he went through treatment for his ankle, but I respectfully declined. I told him that even though sitting and watching while he rotated his ankle between hot and cold treatments sounded exhilarating, I just wasn't up for that much excitement. The whole thing should take less than an hour, so I told him I'd cruise around, then circle back and pick him up.

The down time gave me a chance to relax my mind. I had to admit I was getting excited about going out with Betsy. We were going to have a casual get together this evening, after she got back from Cape. I guess you could call it a date, even though we just planned to ride around and spend some time together. I could have gone cruising with Blake and Jared, but this was way too appealing. Blake said he and Krista would probably join up later, but he was going to cruise with Jared awhile. He and Jared got along really well now. As a matter of fact, Jared almost worshiped Blake, though he was discreet about it. What was really funny was that Jared was with Blake's old girlfriend, Tammy, at the game last night. How strange life could be.

I couldn't help but admire my best friend concerning this thing with his dad. Blake's father had always been a little bit fanatical on the religious end, but he'd always been a nice guy. He was a highly respected man in the community and, though he was a little over the top at times, was regarded as a calming force. Some of our deacons viewed themselves as authoritative, exalted spiritual leaders. Mr. Coleman had never done that. Mom said he was a good person to have for a deacon, because he had a cool head. Well, so much for that. But, it was strange, especially knowing what I knew about it.

Blake told me about doing that thing he did with his eyes when this stuff happened with his dad. He said it worked like a trance and tried to describe the things he saw. I didn't understand it, but I knew there was something to it. He had done that with me before and the first time was quiet memorable. I'd told him about the time lapse, but not the rest. He was defensive about his father because of this. Outside his family, only Mom, Krista, and I knew about it.

Also, Blake was the unquestioned star on our basketball team. The only bad game he'd had was at the holiday tournament the night after the deal with his dad. He never said anything about being the star, but I knew it was hard on him. Through all of this, his academic performance for the first semester bested mine and that was a first. Plus, he was writing some unbelievable poetry in Literary Club. Ms. Huey, who was kind of cool towards us for a while, was now very actively helping us both with improving our work. She had a special influence on Blake. I thought it was just because she was hot, but he really respected her, and I believed she was the driving force behind his grades improving so much. Boy, he'd had a hell of a year so far.

January was a cold and dreary month in this part of the country. I truly hated this month. Oh, I liked a good snow every once and awhile, but not as much as I used to. But the cloudy, dreary days stirred up memories of great loss, including the greatest loss of my life. My father had died in a car wreck during this month six years ago. It was a cloudy, cold day—a setting that I would always equate with tragedy. I didn't think I'd ever be able to see it any other way.

Well, I'd just about driven my limit of laps in and around Gardner. It was time to cruise back over to the school. Blake should be finishing up soon. We should have plenty of time to fire up a joint and mellow out for a while. Between the two of us, we had managed to discreetly latch on to some weed through Jared. Jared was cool with it, but Blake and I didn't like dealing even indirectly with Bernie. Plus we didn't like Jared getting caught in the middle. I suspected he might be dealing some, anyway. His parents came close to making Mr. Coleman look liberal. If they found out Jared was using weed, it was very likely he would be chained to a tree in his back yard and given only bread and water. But Jared just didn't seem to care. He'd become bolder than I would have ever imagined possible.

Making my way into the parking lot, I pulled into a spot not far from the gym's side door, so Blake wouldn't have far to walk. It was too cold to stand outside, so I was content to kick back in my car, close my eyes, and soak up the sounds of 50 Cent.

Suddenly, my car door swung open. I felt the rush of cold air and—

"Get out, punk," clamored the unmistakable voice of Matt Perdue. He was standing inside my open door.

I turned the music down, and slowly laid back in my seat again. Without looking at him I said, "Matt, I'm very comfortable right where I am. Now, would you kindly move away from my door; I'm losin' valuable heat here."

"Well, Williams, I'm sorry about you losin' heat, but I'd say you stand to lose a lot more than that," he said in a very disturbing tone.

I looked in front of my car where Perdue had parked his truck. Not surprisingly, Mutt was sitting in the cab. "Look Matt, I don't know what your problem is, but I really can't think about anything we need to talk about."

He leaned slowly down close to my face and said, "You can get out of your car, Williams, or I can help you get out."

I smelled beer on his breath and I seriously doubted he'd had just one. I began quickly weighing my options. I could ease out of my car and make a break for the gym door. But that son of a bitch would probably trash my car. I decided to play it one step at a time and turn off the engine. He took a step back, giving me just enough room to get out of the car. I eased my door shut and found myself face to face with a lunatic and nothing between us but a couple of feet of air.

"You've been talkin' to my girl, Williams, and that's way out of line," he said, glaring at me.

"First of all, Matt, you need to be more specific," I said, scanning the area hoping to see someone drive up.

"I know you've been talkin' to Betsy, so don't try lyin' about it."

"I see," I said, working hard not to show I was scared shitless. "So you've been monitoring my phone calls. Just how have you managed that?"

"I ain't monitored a Goddamned thing, you little shit," he said, raising his voice. "People talk around here."

Come on, somebody—Blake, Coach Randall, anybody; this wasn't looking good. I had to try to distract him, somehow. "Well, I'm glad to hear that, Matt. But I don't see how who I talk with on the phone concerns you. I don't ask you about any of the obscene calls you probably make."

"Always a smart ass, aren't you, Williams?" he said, not as loudly. "Well, if I hear about you callin' my girl again, I'll shut that mouth for ya."

"Matt, my understanding is that Betsy is no longer dating you. Have I been misinformed?"

"We'll work things out if people just stay out of our business," he said, looking away from me for a few seconds. One would have to wonder what could be going through this idiot's head while he was blankly staring into space.

"It's not my intention to be in your business, Matt, but I would think that Betsy's free to decide things for herself."

"And I'm free to do whatever's necessary to protect my interest," he said, staring at me again. "So, Williams, I suppose I can count on these calls between you and Betsy comin' to a halt."

Jesus, I hated his shit. He was running all over me and I wanted to tell him to go to hell, but I had a strong commitment to self-preservation. "I'll put it this way, Matt; I'm not going to interfere in anyone else's relationship."

"Well, I sure hope that means you aren't plannin' to have anything to do with Betsy, 'cause you've never had an ass whippin' like I'll give ya."

"Y'know Matt, that might be true, because I didn't know they had a scale for ass whippin's. Once again, I'll stay out of your business and you can do the same for me."

He stared at me for a few seconds. "Williams, the day's comin' when that mouth of yours is gonna get you beat to death. The only reason I don't stomp your scrawny ass now is you're a punk sophomore, and I have other things more important to me than you. But, if I find out anything in the future that puts you near Betsy, those things won't matter." He paused for a second. "You know, I bet your father ditched himself on purpose after realizin' he had a pussy for a son."

What rose inside of me was unlike anything I had ever felt. With a burst of fury, I threw a roundhouse right that hit Perdue square in his face. He staggered back a couple of steps, obviously caught totally by surprise. I came right back with a quick left, catching him again in the face.

"God dammit, you son of a bitch!" he yelled.

I stepped up to swing again, but he blocked it, rushing me. Before I knew it, he had me around the neck with his left arm. With his right arm around my waist, he lifted me off the ground. Grunting hard and with amazing speed, he whirled and slammed me to the pavement.

I screamed when my left shoulder was rammed into the hard surface. Intense pain shot through my shoulder. I tried to roll over, but I'd lost the use of my left arm.

"Oh shit! Shit! Shit!" I yelled with tears streaming down my face. I crawled back toward my car using my right hand only. Through my tears, I saw the gym door crack open a little. Oh God, please, somebody come.

"We're just getting' started," Perdue growled as he pounced on me again. He grabbed me by my hair and shirt, pulling me off the ground.

I screamed through the tears. "You broke my shoulder! Shit! Shit! Shit!—"

He got me up, turned me around and caught me with a solid right, sending me sprawling onto the hood of my car. I knew I screamed, but it sounded so distant. The side of my face was numb and my vision was coming and going. My left arm was quivering.

"That's enough!" I heard someone yell.

"Alright, Mutt, let me go," I heard Perdue say.

Using my right hand, I tried hard to pick myself up off of my car. I couldn't keep my balance and slid down the side of my car, using my right hand to ease my fall.

"That's what happens when you tangle with a real man, little boy," Matt said.

Through all the pain, I managed to raise my right hand and flip him off. He then lurched forward and rammed his boot into my groin. I tried to scream, but nothing came out. Pain shot through my midsection like someone had stabbed me with a knife. I turned on my right side trying to cover what was left of my balls.

"Hey, what's goin' on here!" a voice cried out. It sounded miles away.

Then, I felt it coming. I managed to raise my head up just before I began to heave up what was in my stomach. The pain was making me light headed as I heaved again and again. Somewhere in the midst of the agony, what was left of me yearned for a safe haven to hide in forever.

In a moment, I could hear whom I guessed was Coach Randall yelling at Perdue. I couldn't understand any of it. Then, he was there. I turned to see my bro kneel down next to me. I groaned as he gently lifted my head and scooted his legs underneath me. He then laid my head gently on his lap. Through all the pain, I could actually feel a comfort from him.

"Let me see about 'im, Blake," Coach Randall said, as I looked up at him.

He knelt down beside us, reached over and gently grabbed my left shoulder—

"Oh God, don't," I grunted loudly. "My shoulder's messed up."

"Marsh," Coach said quietly, "Tell me where else you're hurtin', Son."

"My balls," I grunted out again, "He crushed my balls. God, they hurt so bad I can't move."

"Okay, Son," Coach said, "You stay still." "Blake, I'm gonna call his mom and see what she wants to do and I'll go in and get some ice for 'im."

Blake took off his jacket to cover my upper body and leaned down close to my ear.

"I'm here, bro," he whispered, "You're gonna be okay. And that son of a bitch'll never touch you again."

Chapter Twenty Four

BLAKE

Emergency rooms were always depressing and the one here in the Southeast Missouri Medical Center was no different. This was a little hospital, a branch of the big one in Cape. I hated being in the waiting room surrounded by all these people who were either sick or waiting on people who were. I found a place in the corner as far away from everyone as I could manage. More people were arriving to see about Marsh. His mom was in there with him and the doctors. They better be helping him. Mr. TM and Ms. Doty were here visiting with my parents who had arrived a few minutes ago. I finally got Krista on her phone and she was on her way, riding with her folks. Ray and his parents were just now coming in. Todd Little was right behind them. Scanning the room, he spotted me and waved. I waved back. It was really cool that he was here. They all sort of huddled up together across the room from me. Every now and then some of them would turn to look over at me. I could literally feel their eyes on me and I didn't like it. Somebody just tell me Marsh was good to go and I'd be fine.

I tried to shift my thoughts to better things. It appeared my ankle would be okay, which was a relief. More important than that, Ms. Huey had decided to stay. She was so awesome. She was beautiful, smart, articulate, and compassionate. I hated that her Lit class ended even though I made an A. But I still had her for Literary Club every day. She claimed my poetry was really taking off. If that was true, it was all because of her. Hell, even Marsh agreed with her that I should try to get some of it published. Not a word about "that night" had passed between us, but her warm smile let me know everything was okay. God, she made me feel so much better about myself.

Another really cool thing concerned my dad. We talked out the incident that happened between us. I told him I forgave him and that I knew how much he loved me. Dad's mood was so much better. He and Mom were even going out more lately. This morning I overheard him telling Mr. Gleason, another deacon in our church, that the church needed to gain some new perspective about what was happening in the world today. Man, Dad was stepping out a little.

Uh oh, here was an interesting visitor. Mr. Davidson, Gardner's police chief, had arrived. He immediately went over to the group. Jesus, I knew he would want to talk to me. I laid my head back and looked at the ceiling. My mind was navigating its way back to the present and I could feel the rage fueling back up inside me. As I suspected, in a couple of minutes, my dad walked over to me.

"Son, you need to come over here. Mr. Davidson needs to talk to you."

Without saying anything, I got up and followed my dad over to the others. Mr. Davidson was older than my dad, about four inches taller than me, and really needed to lose some weight. He was wearing a sport coat that was one full size too small. My dad put his hand on my shoulder and stood with me.

"Hello, Blake," the chief said, smiling a little. "You're okay, aren't you?"

"Yes sir." I was so tired of answering that question. Hell no, I wasn't okay. How did that sound? Some idiot just almost killed my best friend.

"Blake, I talked to Coach Randall about the fight," he continued, "So I know what he saw."

"Yes sir," I said. "He was there before I was."

"Did Marsh say anything to you about what happened?"

"No sir, he wasn't able to talk much."

"Blake," he said, looking at me intently, "Do you know anything that could have caused this to happen?"

Yes, I did—the existence of a piece of shit like Matt Perdue. He tried to murder Marsh. The fact he breathed the same air we did should be against the law.

Instead, I replied, "No sir, I don't know of anything." I was sure someone else would tell him about Betsy.

"To your knowledge, have the two of them had any previous problems?"

"No sir." I conveniently forgot about the incident at the beginning of school.

He looked at my dad, gave Mr. TM a quick glance, and said, "I think that'll be all for now. I may need to talk to you later if there's an investigation."

"There won't need to be an investigation," I said loud enough to draw the whole group's attention.

"Well, why wouldn't there be a need, Blake?" the chief asked.

"Because I'm gonna' kill 'im," I said, glaring right at Mr. Davidson.

"Now Blake, honey," my mom said, as she walked over and put her arm around me, "We know you're upset, but let's be careful what we say."

"I was," I said.

"Son," the chief said, "You let us take care of this situation. You just steer clear of this; we'll deal with it."

"Y'know, Mr. Davidson," I started, louder than I intended, "Of all the people in this room, I was the only one there. I had to hold his head up so he could spit out the blood. He could barely move his left arm. His balls hurt him so bad he was curled up to try to stop the pain. I put my jacket over 'im to try to stop him from shakin'. Try dealin' with that."

Before anyone could say anything else, Ms. Becky came into the waiting room. All eyes turned to her.

She took a deep breath and let it out slowly, "Okay, here's what it is. Marsh has some slightly torn ligaments in his shoulder that should not require surgery. It doesn't appear his jaw is broken.

"His"—she paused a moment—"His testicles are severely bruised. They're going to let me take him home after they get him bandaged up and get a sling for his arm. He'll see an orthopedic on Tuesday morning about his shoulder and they'll take another look at his jaw."

Everyone was quiet, and I turned to walk away.

"Blake," Ms. Becky said, so I stopped and turned back to her. "Through everything back there, Marsh didn't say a word. Then just before they started to work on him, he grabbed my arm. He said for me to tell you to leave it alone and let it go."

"I don't know that I can do that, Ms. Becky," I said, and then walked past her and went outside into the cold night. I stood with my hands in my jacket pockets looking up at a starry night. It seemed so peaceful. I heard someone approaching from behind me.

"Blake, can I talk to you a minute?" Mr. TM asked.

"Yes sir," I said, turning to face him.

"I want you to try to follow Marsh's wishes. What he needs now, Blake, is his best friend in the world to be there with him. He's always admired your strength and resolve. He will be stronger and heal faster if you're there with him. Vengeance can be self-destructive, Son. Leave that to others. Will you think on that for a bit?"

"Yes sir," I said.

He then came forward and hugged me. I could sense and feel a great strength in him. I had so much respect for him. He turned and went back inside. I turned back and looked to the stars again for a couple of minutes. I turned to go back inside and was startled a little as I ran right into Ray.

"Oh shit," I said. "You scared me."

"Thanks for bein' there for cuz, Blake," he said, with the most sincerity I had ever seen on his face. I could actually tell he was fighting tears.

I nodded.

"You do like he said, Blake," he said.

"Like who said?" I asked.

"Like cuz said," he replied. "Leave it alone and let it go. And don't worry; that son of a bitch'll get his, I promise you that."

Chapter Twenty Five

KRISTA

"Wow, Krista, that's really good," Mrs. Jackson, my art teacher said, looking at my canvas. "You've gone beyond contrasting dark shades; you've created a striking image."

"Thank you, Mrs. Jackson," I said. "I'm still working on it."

We were working on painting with contrasting dark colors. Mrs. Jackson had given us the freedom to do with as we wanted. Most the students had just chosen different designs combining shades of dark blue, black and gray. These designs were more or less like bizarre landscapes. But I'd had an idea and just ran with it.

"Well, it's an extraordinary piece of work," Mrs. Jackson continued, "What are you doing with the background?"

"I'm not real sure just yet," I said.

Boy that was an understatement. I was building what started as a dark gray cloud-like entity in the background that had an undefined air about it. It was like a shape that seemed intent on re-making itself, if that made any sense. It had started as no more than a wisp of smoke. But as I tried to fade it down, I just kept bringing it back bigger. I didn't know why, nor could I explain any of it—I just went with it.

"I can't wait to see the finished product," Mrs. Jackson said as she walked away.

That would make two of us. The forefront of the work had started as one great dark shadow that had gradually evolved into three dark figures in human shapes. I knew the figures were me, Blake and Marsh, though no one else would be able to deduce that. I thought Marsh was the last figure to form for at least a couple of reasons. One, the sex I had with him was more than memorable. Secondly, I was greatly affected by Perdue's attack on him. He was getting better, but he still suffered from it.

I couldn't put my finger on any particular thing that was driving the thoughts and behaviors that were such a big part of my life right now. Maybe I wasn't supposed to know. Sometimes, it was like I would just zone out without really zoning out. Of course, that made no sense at all. But I wasn't sure anyone could make sense of all this. I guess I would have to start being more up front in my confessions.

"How's it coming, Krista?" Katy asked, walking up beside me. Katy was a friend in art class. She wasn't part of the crowd I hung with, but I really liked her. With her discreet help, I had made a very secret change in my life that my regular circle of friends knew nothing about—I started on the "pill". This was another secret part of my life I was dealing with, but I felt it a risk worth taking. Katy was a little on the heavy side and battled complexion problems, but was a genuinely good person whom I respected and trusted. Unlike even some of my closest friends, she wouldn't give me a hard time and would not run her mouth.

"Oh, I'm not sure Katy. I'm still tryin' to finish."

"Gosh Krista, it looks pretty much done and pretty amazing, if I do say so myself."

"Thanks Katy; I saw yours and it's great."

"Thanks, but it's just bands of dark shaded colors bending in the wind."

"Don't play it down, Katy. It's really good."

"No, what you have here is really good. What's goin' on in the background?"

"I wish I knew," I sighed. "It's just something that kinda showed up. I'm not sure what to do with it."

"Y'know Krista, this may sound crazy, but it's almost like your three shadowed figures emerge from it and—wait a second—it kinda looks like water."

You know it was taking on the look of a smooth, dark blue surface that could be water. That gave me pause for a second when— "Hey girlfriend," Cheryl said from behind me, startling me some.

"Cheryl, what're you doin' here?" I asked.

"I had all of Spanish class I could stand," she said. "So I told Ms. Perez I needed to take some stuff to you concerning the yearbook."

"She bought that?" I asked, smiling.

"Are you kidding?" Cheryl said. "I could tell her that her house was on fire and I needed to go to the office and call the fire department. She would just say 'Okay honey, you go right ahead'."

Katy and I had to catch ourselves to keep from laughing out loud.

"Girlfriend, you are awful," I said.

"Yeah, well," she said, "Here's one of our old yearbook folders. I had to show it to Mrs. Jackson so she'd let me in."

"Jeez, speaking of yearbook," Katy said, "Julie Pilgrim came by here yesterday during activity period claiming the art samples we sent her were hideous. She is a pain."

"Don't worry about her, Katy," I said.

"Yeah," Cheryl chimed in, "She's just in the world to remind us of what we never want to be—her."

"I'll try to remember that," Katy said with a smile and walked away.

"Wow, girlfriend," Cheryl said, looking past me at my work, "Is that yours?"

"Yeah, it's our latest assignment," I said

"That's pretty awesome stuff," she said, "Especially those dark shapes."

"Well, they're no one in particular."

"Yeah they are. That's you on the left, Blake in the middle, and got to be Marsh on the right."

"Cheryl," I said, with what had to be a shocked look about me.

"Well girlfriend, you've always said you can't have one without the other. What's that in the background?"

"I'm not really sure," I muttered, still trying to process what she'd said about Blake and Marsh.

"Well, whatever it is, it's a lot bigger than the three of you."

"Ah, Cheryl," Mrs. Jackson said, walking over to us. "Have you made your delivery?"

"Oh yes, Mrs. Jackson; thank you," Cheryl said and hurried out of the room.

I was staring intently at my work when Mrs. Jackson told us to tidy up. It was just about bell time. That broke my focus and reminded me of the task that would soon be at hand. I had a very important, discreet rendezvous after school. It was a combination of fearful and exhilarating. I'd found I could mix those two pretty well.

I noticed he was working hard to maintain his composure. He'd actually had no control a couple of minutes ago. It was amazing how such a macho guy could be brought to such a degree of submission by a young lady like me. This was without a doubt, the boldest step I had even taken, but the risk seemed to enhance my urges to levels which excited me like nothing else. The fires that burned inside me seemed to glow brighter at every turn I made into different avenues of immoral conduct.

He squirmed a little as I refused to let him go just yet. The ability to hold this power was addictive. The more it was put into play, the greater the yearning. I continued to make him plead for more, while preparing to use his own compulsive weakness against him. All of this was being managed by a sixteen-year-old girl now playing in a big game where the stakes were high. In spite of being older, bigger and stronger, he was so easy to manipulate. He couldn't even manage a little resistance. That had to be a blow to the male ego.

"Well, do you understand our agreement?" I asked as I continued.

"Y-yeah, anything y-you say," he responded, unable to control his trembling.

"Good, I guess this is enough for now," I said smiling.

"Oh God, no; p-p-please," he said, shaking.

"Everything goes the way I say?" I asked, looking squarely at him.

"Yes, yes, yes; I-I swear, e-everything," he said, panicking.

"Okay, but just a little more..."

Chapter Twenty Six

MARSH

One thing was for sure—my mom could grill a burger. Her seasoning was great and she cooked them just right. Todd's were better, but not much. We were piled around the kitchen table, five of us, eating enough food to satisfy the appetite of ten. Jared, Tyler, Rick, and Blake were circled up with me. You'd think Tyler, who seemed to be growing an inch per month, would out eat everyone. But Jared and Blake were setting the pace. My appetite was a little better, but I couldn't eat like these guys.

A cookout on a Thursday night in February would normally mean some type of celebration was underway; but not in this case. Mom just decided to cook for all of us. She said we were too busy on weekends to be in one place at one time, so this was the best way. Keeping this bunch in burgers and fries would be a challenge for a group of cooks, but Mom hadn't missed a step.

I knew the motivation behind this was the consensus of concern about my psychological well-being. Physically, things were much better. As my attack on this meal could attest, my jaw was in fine working order. Actually, the outward signs of my damaged jaw were gone in about five days or so, but the soreness stayed with me for two weeks. My shoulder was a work in progress. I was in the midst of the painful process of rehabilitation. It really hurt. I needed to be working on my golf game by March, but that was up in the air. My golf swing required full range of motion in my left shoulder, and the doctors said that could take a while. I didn't like to think about the prospect of missing the high school golf season this spring.

My balls, as one could imagine, had been a very sensitive issue. It took two full weeks for them to really look and feel normal again. I harbored this underlying concern about my continuing ability to do some things guys really wanted to be able to do. Most of those concerns were alleviated yesterday afternoon with a special visit after school. The gentle caressing of my balls set into motion all of the things it should. When the caressing extended to the boner I had, all the regular sensations went into gear. The strength of those sensations erased all the doubts and reservations I had. The oral sex that followed led to a climax that left no doubt that everything was in working order. So, physically, I had conquered or was conquering all the obstacles to recovery.

The other part was more difficult to deal with. It took two solid weeks for my fight with Perdue to come off the lead as the number one news item in town. Regardless of the motivation, I did hit him first. The controversy centered on the difference in our ages and what constituted a threat. The school finally settled their part of the issue by giving me three days of in-school suspension for fighting on school property and suspending Matt for three days for the same. The legal issues were a little more complicated. It was eventually settled by basically giving Matt what amounted to a restraining order to stay away from me. I didn't want it pushed any further, despite the wishes of some of my family and friends.

Maybe the biggest controversy was kept pretty quiet. Coach Randall suspended Matt from the team for two games in addition to the one he missed due to the school suspension. The problem was Blake. He told Coach Randall he wouldn't play on the team if Matt was allowed to return. When I was made aware of this, it led to the most emotional confrontation Blake and I had ever had.

I understood how Blake felt, because I would've felt exactly the same way had the roles been reversed. But, as I argued, Blake quitting the team would negatively affect a lot of people and that wasn't fair. Blake's contention was he couldn't be around the s.o.b. I reminded him there were other people on the team, and they depended on him. The standoff reached the point that I finally told Blake that I wanted this to go away so I could stop hurting, and that him not playing would just make it worse. It was a tearful confrontation for both of us, but he was still playing.

There was no doubt my greatest hurdle was the fear and anxiety that haunted me. As hard as it was for me to admit, I was still scared. I was having night sweats. I wouldn't sit alone in my car when parked. Then, I would look around frantically before I got out. At school, I tried not to look where I might see Matt's truck, because I was having flashbacks that caused me to shake. I had kept all of these problems to myself, even though Mom and maybe even Blake had to be suspicious about some of them.

Some things I knew were visible to those close to me. I'd always liked being a wise ass around my friends, just for fun. I had no motivation to do that now. I'd been abnormally quiet and reserved, which I blamed on my physical injuries, but that was a hard sell. Mom and Gramps had talked about getting me some counseling, but I wasn't interested in that.

My friends had been great. I never realized the importance of friendship to the degree I did now, though it could get a little out of hand. It started when Blake insisted on escorting me to school. But, he gave in on the basketball, so I relented on the morning escorts. While in school, everywhere I went I had a sort of entourage—of Blake, Jared, Tyler, and Rick; no less than two of them would be walking me through the halls and to lunch every day. The girls were in on it, too. Even Judy, one of our Literary Club members, had been waiting on me hand and foot during club meetings. Hell, I never knew she cared.

And, of course, there were people whose concerns went a little deeper, both at and away from school. I had been receiving calls from Betsy, Lana and even Ciera on a fairly frequent basis. But with all of them, there seemed to be something in the way, which was hard to explain. Basically, I was psychologically prohibited from Betsy, physically intimidated by Lana, and somewhat guilt-strapped about Ciera. And all of this failed to take into account another, more dynamic relationship, which was the most stable and totally nuts.

"You guys save some room," Mom said. "The hot fudge cake will be out in a few minutes."

"Room's not an issue, Ms. Becky," Tyler said, putting the finishing touches on what amounted to three burgers and half a pound of fries.

"Ms. Becky, your burgers are really good," Jared said with his mouth half full.

"How could you tell, Jared?" Rick asked. "You didn't eat them, you inhaled them."

"Yeah, dude, how can you eat like that and not gain thirty pounds?" Tyler asked.

"I have a real wholesome lifestyle," Jared replied, and we all cracked up. This is another example of the new Jared. He used to be so self-conscious. Now, he just weighed in.

"Speakin' of lifestyle, Jared," I said, joining the conversation, "How're things goin' with you and Tammy?" Jared had started dating Blake's ex and no one was happier for him than Blake.

"Well, it'll help when one of us is old enough to drive and gets some wheels," he answered. "I prefer to go over to her house to watch TV. My folks won't give us much privacy. We can't go to my bedroom, so we have to fight traffic in the living room. Mom tries to keep my little brother and sister away, but they can out-maneuver her. We can actually manage some make-out time at Tammy's."

"Well, are you makin' any headway?" Rick asked.

Jared looked around to make sure Mom wasn't in hearing range. "We're makin' progress. I'm gettin' more allowances all the time. She loves to squeeze my dick, so I think we're close."

"She's probably just makin' sure you have one," Rick said, which drew some laughter.

"Probably so," Jared said. "Send Sally over to see me, so she can get a feel of a real dick." That drew more laughter.

I noticed Blake was smiling, but not saying much. I knew he was watching me to see how I was interacting with everyone. I needed to try harder, but I had to be careful because he could tell if I was faking it.

"So since we're all takin' World Cultures, whadda you guys think about Mrs. O'Connell?" I asked.

"I thought she was pretty cool until we had that test yesterday," Rick said.

"Yeah, I don't like it when they schedule a big test on the day after a game," Blake finally spoke up.

"That is not cool," Tyler said. "Plus, why can't the lady give us some multiple choice? I like havin' a hint or two every now and then."

"You, my gosh, Tyler," Rick said, "You never make less than a B on anything. It's the rest of us that need help."

"I told you, Rick," Jared said, "Just send Sally over." You gotta love it.

"Okay, guys," Mom said, walking in with a huge pan of chocolate fudge cake, "See if you can wipe this out."

Mom made a fudge cake that was out of this world, if I did say so myself. It was the perfect combination of cake, ice cream, and whipped cream, which tasted heavenly and had no nutritional value whatsoever. We dug in.

"Okay guys, what's the deal on the game tomorrow night?" Jared asked between bites.

"Portageville's the third place team in our conference, and they played us close down there," Blake said.

"Yeah, and the conference tournament is down there next week. They've got a couple of good inside guys that play tough," Tyler said.

"I think we'll take 'em," Rick said, "We're back at full strength and—"

He realized what he'd said and stopped. He was referring to Perdue's return to the lineup. I could tell he suddenly felt uncomfortable.

"Well, you guys are the first place team," I said, coming to the rescue of my friend, "So, tough or not, I like our chances."

"So, Marsh, how's the shoulder rehab comin'?" Jared asked, astutely following my lead.

"It's comin', and that's about all I can say. It hurts like hell, and I'm really just getting started."

"Blake, you're his personal trainer; whadda you think?" Jared asked.

"Well, we've been through a few sessions and the patient can be very difficult to the point of being verbally abusive," Blake said.

"Some of that may be the approach of the trainer," I said. "It appears Blake has a hidden passion for inducing pain."

"I just follow the directions given by the doctor, in spite of the verbal barrage that falls down on top of me," Blake said.

As unbelievable as it seemed, the five of us had almost devoured a fudge cake made for twice as many people. Everyone hung out for a while, but it was a school night, so they didn't stay too long. When the guys went to thank Mom, I motioned for Blake.

"Hey, bro, can you stay a little longer?"

"Yeah, let me see if Rick can drop Tyler?"

Blake checked it out with Rick and everything was cool. So, after they cut out, Blake and I went back to my bedroom. Blake plopped down in what I called my "slouch chair". It was an old recliner, but it was one of the best chairs to lay around in ever made. I hopped on my bed and kicked back.

"That was a fun time tonight, I thought," I said.

"Good food; cool friends; great time," Blake said.

"Boy, Jared's really comin' into his own, don't ya' think?"

"Without a doubt, but you gotta remember, Marsh, he doesn't turn sixteen until April. Hell, I'm nine months older than he is which means you're six months older. Maybe he's just catchin' up."

"I don't know, Blake. It's like the whole makeup of his character has come one hundred and eighty degrees. You know what I'm talkin' about?"

He paused for a few seconds. "Yeah, well, things happen. So, what's up?"

I paused for a moment, looking down and contemplating how to say something no guy my age would ever want to say. Even though it was Blake, it was still hard to say.

"I need to tell someone about what's goin' on with me."

"Okay."

"I'm scared, Blake."

He immediately shifted to the edge of the chair, facing me. "What're you talkin' about? Did that bastard say somethin' to you?" he asked, with anger showing on his face.

"No, no, no; it's not that. He hasn't said a word to me or come near me for that matter," I said.

"What's scarin' you, bro?"

"Everything," I replied. "I don't like bein' by myself, even in my own house. I'm wakin' up some nights in a sweat. Three times in the past week, Mom has come in here in the middle of the night because she said I was yellin' in my sleep."

"Hell, Marsh, you've gone through some tough shit. Anybody would be messed up about it."

"It's more than that, Blake. The other day, I was sittin' in class and happened to glance up when Perdue and some of his buddies walked by in the hall. My hands started shakin' and I started sweatin'." Blake was looking at me with great intensity. I could feel my eyes watering a little. "And yesterday, in the cafeteria, I was sittin' beside you when I looked across the room and saw him. On impulse, I scooted closer to you."

"So."

"So, hell, Blake, that's like a wimpy kid leanin' on his best friend for protection."

"Bullshit, Marsh, you're just comin' out of some heavy stuff. You're beatin' the physical part, step by step. You'll get past this the same way. And time takes care of a lot."

There was silence between us for a few seconds when I said,

"Mom knows I'm havin' trouble. She wants me to think about seeing a shrink. Jesus, I went through that shit when Dad died."

"Well, see one if you want to. I just think you need some time."

"But how much time?" I asked, talking to myself more than to Blake. "You know how important golf is to me. It's going to be close whether or not I'll physically be able to compete this spring. But, there's no way I can play golf with all this shit goin' on in my head."

"I think you're sellin' yourself short, Marsh. We're gonna have your shoulder in good shape in plenty of time. And Todd'll move mountains to help you."

"I have all the confidence in the world in you helpin' with my shoulder and Todd does more than move mountains, believe me."

"And the mental part'll get better; you have lots of friends."

"I know that, too. No one's luckier than I am in that regard. I'm just tired and ashamed of bein' so scared."

He got up and came over to sit beside me on the bed. "Y'know, bro, we're a pretty tough pair. Together, we're unstoppable."

That made me smile. God, where would I be without him? I turned and saw him smiling back at me. I could see the love and caring in his eyes, oh my God, his eyes...

Chapter Twenty Seven

BLAKE

It had been one hell of a night, so Marsh and I were capping it off by sharing a blunt. We'd won our conference tournament tonight over Portageville by ten points, and my bro and I were cruising on the outskirts of Gardner. We'd dropped off Krista and Betsy a few minutes ago, barely making their midnight curfew.

Marsh had made a tremendous psychological recovery. I knew it had something to do with our vision experience last week. But there was something different about this vision. I never saw the others coming. This time, I felt the strong desire to look into Marsh's eyes. Man, this was some crazy shit. Somewhere; somehow; some way—this all had to mean something. Maybe it was a seizure of some sort. But I'd never heard of anyone sharing their seizures with someone else.

Marsh said he couldn't remember anything. I told him it happened and he believed me. It just didn't seem to bother him much. He came out of it laughing his ass off. I sure didn't remember anything funny about it. I just remember a dark cavern with the walls spewing red stuff. A strong wind was blowing and eventually a roaring fire broke out. I shared it all with Marsh and he just nodded.

Nonetheless, Marsh had his swagger back, so to speak. With all the pressure on Perdue since the fight, I thought he was safe, and he was making good progress with his shoulder rehab. His biggest move had been with Betsy. Considering everything that had happened, you'd think he'd dodge her. But, to a degree, I understood. Marsh had put himself back together and wasn't going to let Perdue dictate his life. I'd feel the same way.

So, romance seemed to find its way back into Marsh's life and I was glad. Hell, I thought he'd settled on a path of celibacy, seeing the way he kept turning down Lana's advances. It was time my bro had some serious sex in his life or just any sex at all. Maybe this thing with Betsy would be a sexual awakening for both of them.

I'd had a pretty good game tonight. Tyler had a great game, while Perdue was awful and he knew it. He pouted all the way back on the bus. I noticed him reaming out Mutt in the parking lot about something. Why Mutt put up with that, I'd never know. Mutt was bigger and stronger, but still followed every order Perdue gave him. I almost felt sorry for him because he was kind of socially backward, but it was his choice to hang around that stupid bastard. As long as Marsh and I were out of Perdue's reach, I really didn't care.

My phone rang, which was a shock to both of us since it was after midnight. Marsh turned down Eminem so I could answer.

"Yeah."

"Blake," whispered a voice I recognized immediately.

"Tammy?" I asked, just to make sure. Marsh quickly shot a glance my way.

"Yeah, listen, I know this is weird, but it's kind of an emergency," she whispered. Her voice was trembling.

"Sure, it's okay, Tammy."

"Well, you know, Jared and I rode to the game with Beth and Leesa," she started.

"Yeah, I know."

"Well, when we got back to town, we went to the Dairy Freeze to get some food and stuff. It was pretty crowded, so Jared walked inside to put in our order. When he came back out, Bernie pulled in and parked directly across from us. He waved Jared over to his car. I couldn't tell what was being said, but Jared didn't look too happy." She whimpered a little.

"Are you okay, Tammy?" I asked.

"Yes, thank you," she replied. "Well, so Jared started walkin' away when Bernie jumped out of his car. I could hear him yell at Jared to come back. So, Jared went back and some words were exchanged—I don't know—but they both were mad. Jared turned to walk away again and Bernie grabbed his arm. Jared pulled his arm away and, and..." She was starting to cry.

"Tammy, tell me," I said.

"Bernie hit him in the face. Then he pushed him down and started kicking him. I jumped out of Beth's car, screaming. Everyone was lookin', so Bernie went back to his car and left. Jared got up and walked over to us, holding his side. His nose was bleeding and his side was really hurtin' him. We got some ice for his nose. Then, we went to Beth's house 'cause her folks were already in bed. I told him we needed to go to his house and tell his parents what had happened. He got really upset and said they couldn't know anything about it. I told him we had to do somethin'. So, he called his house and told his mom he was stayin' at Marsh's house tonight. She said that was okay. He tried to call Marsh, but couldn't get an answer."

I turned to Marsh and asked, "Where's your phone?"

"It's in my jacket pocket in the back seat," he said.

I reached in the back seat and grabbed his jacket. I got his phone out and there was a notice of two missed calls.

"Marsh's phone was in his jacket pocket and we didn't hear it," I said to Tammy.

"Okay, well, he's really hurt, Blake."

"Let me talk to 'im."

"He's not here," she said, starting to cry again.

"What! Where is he?" I asked loud enough to, once again, draw Marsh's attention.

"He left. He said he was gonna walk over to Marsh's house. Oh, Blake, it hurts him to walk, but I couldn't stop 'im."

"Okay, Tammy, it's alright. We're gonna find 'im right now. I'm glad you called."

"Thanks, Blake; tell him to call me in the morning, will ya?"

"No problem, see ya later," I said and hung up. I then turned to Marsh.

"Jared left Beth Parker's house on foot headed to your house."

"What the hell!" Marsh said.

"Bernie kicked the shit out of him at the Dairy Freeze earlier. Tammy said he was hurtin' pretty bad."

Marsh hit the gas and we headed for 1st Street a lot faster than we should have. On the way, I filled Marsh in on the rest of what Tammy told me. When we turned down 1st Street, we saw him walking slowly, holding his side. Marsh pulled up beside him and I hopped out of the car.

He looked up in surprise. "Blake, I, ah—"

"We know, Jared. Get in the car," I said, and climbed in the back seat. Jared grimaced as he sat down slowly in the passenger seat and shut the door.

"Jared, it's okay now," Marsh said, reaching over and gently squeezing his left shoulder.

"Marsh, I—," Jared was clearly fighting back tears. "I told Mom I was stayin' the night with you. I didn't know—"

"That's cool; it's okay for you to stay. Dude, it's cold out there. You've got to be freezin'," Marsh said.

"Hell, I hadn't even noticed it was cold," Jared said, settling some.

"Don't worry about it now," Marsh said as he pulled into his drive. "Blake, you gonna stay over?"

"Yeah, I told Dad if I wasn't home by twelve, I was stayin' with you."

"Okay," Marsh said, and then looked at Jared. "Let's get you inside."

Once we got to the house, Marsh and I set about the task of getting his room prepared for a three-person sleep over and tending to our wounded friend. Jared's nose, though a little swollen on the left side, didn't look too bad thanks to the ice treatment applied by Tammy. The problem was where Bernie had kicked him—once in the ribs and once around tip of his left pelvic region. We worked hard at being quiet in getting everything ready. After prepping Marsh's slouch chair for me to sleep in, I retrieved the ice packs Marsh had made in the kitchen. While Marsh gathered some snacks and sodas, I propped Jared up on one side of the bed and, using baggies and towels for wraps, applied ice to his injured areas. Finally we all got settled in.

"Okay, Jared, what was all that shit with Bernie about?" I asked.

"He wanted me to go with him to make a drop. I told 'im I was with Tammy and couldn't go. He got pissed. The truth is I'd bailed on him the last couple of times he'd asked me to do that. I always came up with an excuse...I just don't wanna do that anymore."

"That's a wise decision and I'm glad to hear you made it," Marsh said.

"Well, Bernie didn't take it so good. He called me some names, which didn't bother me, but then he brought you guys into it."

"Us! What about us?" I asked.

"He said he knew how to get word to the right people about you guys and me, which would get us in big trouble. So, I told 'im I'd just call him a God-damned liar and tell whoever that it was all bullshit. Plus, I told 'im anyone with any sense would believe us before they ever believed him."

"Pretty damned good, Jared," Marsh said.

"Yeah, well, he punched me. I never saw it coming. Bernie isn't big and bad, but I should've been more alert. He clipped my nose, pushed me down, and used me for a soccer ball."

"That's okay, I'll introduce 'im to boxing by punchin' his ass out," I said, suddenly very angry. I hadn't forgotten the call I got from Jared the night after Marsh was beaten up. He told me even though he wasn't big and tough, if I was going after Perdue, he wanted to go with me. And, tonight he showed he's a pretty tough guy. He'd become a good friend and needed to know we looked out for our friends.

"Chill out, Blake," Marsh said, "We've gotta be careful here. We'll get his ass, but it has to be handled right. There're some things we'd rather he didn't say and, even though he's not big and bad, he can still be dangerous."

"Well, he's not gonna get away with this," I shot back.

"I didn't say that, Blake," Marsh said sternly. "I said we'll get his ass. My guess is he'll try to make amends with Jared at some point 'cause it's in his best interest."

"Fuck him," Jared said.

"You have to be smart here, Jared. I don't want you fuckin' with that guy either. But we have to make a statement, and we choose the time and place," Marsh said.

"Ouch," Jared said as he shifted positions to get some chips. "Damn, this thing hurts. What kind of statement?"

"You fuck with one of us and you get fucked up by all of us," I said.

Chapter Twenty Eight

KRISTA

Of all the babysitting I had done for the Dailey's, this arrangement had never been used. Mr. Dailey called me this morning to see if I could keep Cindy this afternoon. Once again, his call had a strange feel about it. But the feel had cautious warmth to it. These surges that I worked so hard to keep at bay had a powerful, almost intoxicating force, which erased any attempt at resistance I might make.

The cheerleading bus left for the Regional Tournament game at five o'clock. That was fine, he said, because he only needed me to sit for two or three hours starting at one. I felt an unusual twinge of reluctance, but I could think of no reason for it. It was just his behavior over the past month had been mystifying. He'd called about a month ago and wanted me to work on a weekend in which I had conflicts. He wasn't rude, but seemed put off. I hadn't heard another word from him until this morning.

One noteworthy difference was allowing me entrance to his home when no one was there. According to Mr. Dailey, Cindy would be arriving shortly after one. He should be finished with his meeting before four, so I could go. Nothing really seemed out of sorts, it was just a departure from the norm.

I got in my car and started over to the Dailey's. I decided to give Blake a call and let him know what I was doing.

"What's up, baby?" he answered.

"Just wanted ya' to know I'm babysitting at the Dailey's for a while this afternoon, so I guess I won't see you before we get to the tournament."

"Okay; I just dropped Jared at Marsh's and am on my way home to get ready to leave," he said. "Jared's riding with Marsh to the game."

"Jared seems to have gotten over his deal with Bernie," I said.

"Yeah, he's okay now."

"Bernie's just a weaselly dope dealer. You and Marsh tried to tell 'im and he wouldn't listen."

"Don't be so hard on 'im. He screwed up, but he took a stand against Bernie. And Bernie had best leave him alone."

"Now Blake, we're just getting past this stuff with Matt Perdue. We don't need to start fires with Bernie," I warned.

"There's not gonna be any problems right now, unless Bernie tries to hurt 'im again. Besides, Perdue's on the sidelines right now; goin' after Marsh would get him in too much trouble."

"That may be true, but you and I both know Perdue's a lunatic—that part's still the same."

"I know, but I still think things are okay." He paused. "So, I'll see ya after the game?"

"Of course, baby," I replied. "We'll be celebrating a big win."

"I'm all for that."

"Well, I'm here at the Dailey's, so I'll see you tonight, Babe."

"Okay, see ya then," he said and was gone.

Following Mr. Dailey's instructions, after parking my car in the drive, I went into the garage and found the key on the shelf where he said it would be. I let myself in through the back door. The house was nice and warm, but empty. I went into the den and sat on the sofa. With remote in hand, I turned on the TV and began scanning channels.

It was very difficult to try and deal with these conflicting feelings competing for control. I should probably be going crazy or falling into some kind of catatonic state, based on what was going on with me. There were so many things bouncing around in my life. Some of them were normal and some weren't.

Classes were going really well in school. My art works, according to my instructor, were displaying a unique, exquisite nature she considered amazing. She asked me if she could take a couple of my landscape works to a college professor she knew in the art department at St. Louis U. It was fine with me. I didn't know enough about it to have an opinion. I did know that I lost myself in my work sometimes.

I personally thought Blake's poetry was really special. I didn't understand it all, but it was an amazing read. The voluptuous Ms. Huey, whose intentions I considered to be dishonorable, had become a powerful force in his writing. She's hot for him, though—a girl could just tell.

The yearbook was coming together nicely. Julie, the scourge of the staff to many, was actually a pretty good editor. She was just always arrogant and prissy, which continued to alienate all those around her.

Cheerleading had been a blast. Following a winning team was always fun and Blake had been all-everything. I knew I was biased, but he was really good. Betsy had joined Cheryl and me as a trio of friends on the squad that hung together. She's been able to hold her own with Cheryl, which took some doing. Her mother was the biggest busybody I'd ever seen, but she was super nice to Cheryl and me.

So much for all the normal things. Mom, despite her constant claims of moving toward sobriety, had continued to have her share of binges. I was a little worried about Dad. He had battled this stuff with Mom for a long time. He worked hard at his job and I knew all this wore on him. My dad was as resilient as anyone I knew, but everyone had a limit.

Everyone, that is, but me. No matter how bizarre my thoughts and desires seemed to be, I just managed to take them in stride. There were times when I thought I had lost complete touch with the foundations of my faith. I had been very coy in my confessions and had kept them to a minimum. That was a sin in itself. I believed I had to offer a full confession at some time to have any hope of redemption. At least I still believed that.

My journey of thought was brought to an abrupt end by the sound of the back door opening. Well, I guess it was time to hit the deck and have fun with my little angel, Cindy. She just got cuter every—

Mr. Dailey came in, dressed in his running gear, and had obviously been running.

"Hello, Krista," he said, and then took a swig from his water bottle.

"Hi," I said, standing and looking behind him. "Where's Cindy?"

"Well, Krista, I'm afraid I'm guilty of a little deception. Cindy's with her mother and won't be back until eight or nine tonight," he said, watching me carefully.

"I see. Then why the deception?"

"Because I needed to talk to you. If you don't want to stay, go ahead and go. I'll understand."

Ah ha; what we had here just might be a little soul cleansing. Naturally, the proper thing to do was to politely take my leave. Unfortunately, that all too familiar churning had already started, so I thought I'd see what he had to say.

"No, I've got time to talk."

"Okay; just so you'll know, I ran from my office and came down a back path so no one knows I'm here," he explained.

"That's cool," I said.

"Krista, what happened between us has been a big weight on me that I've been tryin' to shake and can't. Originally, I thought it would be best if you didn't work here anymore, but I didn't know how to explain that to my wife or Cindy." He took another drink of water and sat down on the chair just over to the right of the sofa.

"Go ahead, Mr. Dailey," I said, trying to help him get this out. It sounded like it was going to be good.

"You see, the big problem is that our experience in the shower was the best sexual experience I've had in years. There's nothing right about it, and I won't try to rationalize it. Last month, my sole purpose in asking you to babysit was to see you alone. When it didn't work out, I thought maybe fate had played a hand in my favor. But as time went by, it became obvious it hasn't. I almost called you this morning five different times to cancel this and again right before I left my office."

"Why would you not want to have this talk?" I asked.

"Because I knew I would start having the feelings I'm having now, which are totally unacceptable."

"Why're those feelings unacceptable, Mr. Dailey?"

"Because Krista, you're sixteen. In the eyes of society, you're a child."

"Then society needs to have their eyes checked," I said with confidence. "Do you see me as a child?"

"Well, yes; I mean, no; you're only—"

"Mr. Dailey, do you see me as a child or not?"

"I guess I don't see you as a child, but it doesn't matter how I see you, because—"

"Oh, but I think it matters very much how you see me. The question of how I'm perceived will be answered by those who perceive me. I view myself as a young woman, but that's my view. And I think you view me the same way. Am I right?"

He sighed deeply. "Yes, Krista, I suppose I see you as a young woman, but, in the eyes of the law you're a minor, which means what happened between us was wrong from a statutory, social, and moral standpoint."

"I've heard that all my life, Mr. Dailey. I don't believe we've done anything wrong," —actually, I wasn't at all sure about that, but my urges were now in full control—"But, as you point out, many people would consider it so. And I supposed if something goes crazy in my life down the road, I could always blame it on what happened between us. That would be very convenient and totally ludicrous."

"But Krista, I've taken advantage of you and—"

"That's even more ludicrous, but I know that's what people would say. What do you propose we do about this situation, Mr. Dailey?"

"Well, I want you to know that I consider what happened to be my fault and hope it hasn't caused you undue harm, physically or psychologically. If you feel you want to talk to someone about this, then—"

"You know what I want, Mr. Dailey?" I interrupted, reveling in the anticipation of what I was about to say.

He looked at me and said nothing.

"I want you and me to go to bed together right now." I was in charge, and I loved it. "And I know that's really what you want, too. So, let's go."

I turned and walked back to the master bedroom. I sat down on one side of the bed and undressed. He came into the room as I finished and came out of his clothes quickly. We fell into bed together.

We kissed each other deeply as he held me close to him. His hold was firm, but easy. I could sense the energy running through him and it was amazing. His hands rubbed up and down my back. His kisses were so sensual; they caused me to tingle all over.

He was struggling to control himself. His grip on me tightened and loosened, over and over. It was like there was an animal inside him that he was releasing slowly. But it might be getting away from him as he tried to pace himself. He began to work my breasts with his mouth, which started more tingling sensations. The passion built as I ran my fingers through his hair.

Driven by my growing urges, I pushed his head down little by little, as he continued working me. He suddenly reached a place where—oh my god! It felt like flames were exploding inside of me. I began twitching as the flames grew stronger. These were powerful feelings and I was trying to control myself. Soaking all of this up, I gradually became steadier.

I gently pulled him up, opening my legs as he rose. The explosions grew stronger as he entered me. He began powerful thrusts, which created a new level of passion. I could tell by his determination he was accustomed to being in charge. The urgings inside of me continued to build. His breathing was rapid as he began to perspire all over—working hard to bring me.

He moaned loudly as he came inside of me. His release was huge and went on and on. After a slow, smooth withdrawal, he fell beside me on his back. I turned over and kissed him with a tenderness meant to comfort.

"Oh, Krista," he whispered, still recovering. "What can I do?"

"Be resilient, Mr. Dailey," I replied softly. "Just be resilient."

An hour later, after a flurry of passionate sex, I managed my release. Then I quietly dressed and left Mr. Dailey totally exhausted.

BLAKE

Crack! Crack! The sound of the pistol firing rang out. There was no reason for alarm. Hell, there was no one out here to be alarmed. Rick, Jared, and I were sitting on the bank of a slough just off the river. This was a popular fishing hole in the spring when it was full of water. But the fishermen wouldn't be here for another two or three weeks. Rick brought his dad's .38 pistol and enough rounds of ammunition to fill up our Friday afternoon. From a technical standpoint, we were probably breaking a law or two. Well, you might as well make that three, since we were making the rounds with our second blunt.

It was a cool afternoon, but the sun was shining, which made it tolerable. We did have to create some fun activities around the first of March in Gardner. Our basketball season ended last Friday night when we lost in the regionals to a really good team. I didn't have a very good game and, honestly, was over matched. Tyler was the only player we had who played worth a shit, and we got pounded by twenty points. But we'd had a great season and felt good about our future.

Crack! Crack! Crack!

"Damn, Jared, you can't hit shit," Rick said. "That bottle isn't even movin', it's just floatin' in the same spot."

"I wasn't aimin' at the bottle," Jared said.

"Well, then what the hell were you aimin' at?" Rick asked.

"I was shootin' at the water, and I hit it all three times."

I couldn't help but laugh.

"You're so full of shit, Jared," Rick replied. "Give me the pistol so I can show you how to shoot."

Jared handed over the pistol. Rick took aim at the bottle floating about fifteen yards away. He shattered it with his second shot.

"I certainly hope you were payin' attention to how it's done, Jared," Rick said smiling.

"It's not really a fair competition because you have a distinct advantage," Jared said.

"Besides just bein' a better shot, what other advantage could I have?"

"I'm not used to holding somethin' that small in my hand and you are," Jared said.

Once again, I had to laugh.

"Oh, is that right?" Rick asked. "Do you wanna compare dick size?"

"No," Jared answered, "Let's trade blow jobs, but you'll have to go first 'cause I don't know how."

"For God's sake, shut up; both of you," I said, holding my gut from laughing. "We don't have anything out here for you to measure your dicks with but a Zippo lighter, which would probably work."

"Well, excuse me, Mr. 'big dick' Coleman," Rick said. "I guess we can't all be a thoroughbred stud like you."

"Mother Nature is just kinder to some than she is to others," I said smiling. I took another drag off the blunt and passed it on to Jared.

"I read the average length of a male's penis is six inches," Jared said with a contemplative look on his face. "Assuming that means length at erection, just how was the data for that conclusion collected?"

"They probably used a random survey," Rick said.

"Jesus, Rick, what guys would admit to having a dick less than six inches?" I asked.

"Okay, they took volunteers from all over the world who were willin' to get it out and get it up," he responded.

"Well, just how many guys with little dicks do you think would volunteer?" Jared asked.

"I don't know," Rick responded and then looked at Jared.

"Would you volunteer?"

"Only if you did, so at least I'd know I wouldn't be the smallest," Jared replied.

"Enough, guys," I said, "Let's find somethin' else to talk about. I don't want to waste this high discussin' dick sizes."

Things got quiet for a couple of minutes as the blunt continued to make the rounds.

"How's Marsh's rehab comin'? Jared asked. "He always says it's okay, but is it really?"

"Well, the range of motion in his shoulder is almost there," I said. "He works really hard because the golf team's crankin' up next week."

"Yeah, I know the golf season is the biggest thing of the year for him," Rick said.

"Well, based on his last examination, his range of motion is over seventy percent, which is okay and basically on schedule."

"What do the doctors say about him regainin' full range?" Rick asked.

"They feel like he should be one hundred percent no later than the middle of the month or so, if he keeps at it. But Marsh doesn't wanna wait that long to get ready 'cause he's afraid he'll be behind. So, he wants to speed up the process and that can be counterproductive."

"So, what does all this add up to?" Jared asked.

"It means, realistically, Marsh has a good shot at more than half a golf season which, of course, is unacceptable to him."

"Yeah, and Perdue will be making local headlines as a pitcher on our baseball team like nothin' every happened. He's a good pitcher," Rick said.

"But, you know, his basketball play suffered at the end and he felt it," I said.

"I say we take Rick's pistol and shoot him in the shoulder, so his baseball season goes down the tubes," Jared said.

"Sounds like a good idea," I said, "But he's not worth it."

"You know," Rick said, after a toke, "This is damn good weed."

"Yeah, Bernie's tryin' real hard to make up with Jared with some free weed as a gesture of friendship, and he's bein' totally rejected," I said.

"Fuck him," Jared said.

"See what I mean," I said. After pausing a moment, I continued. "Actually, a plot's bein' hatched for good ole' Bernie. Marsh has taken sole responsibility for the plan. He said he had a way to pay Bernie back big time and, at the same time, ensure he keeps his mouth shut. I still want to punch him out. Marsh has promised me one punch. He said his role would be the most challenging and memorable. He can really be creative and devious. In the meantime, we're glad to accept Bernie's peace offerings."

"Fuck him, again," Jared said.

"Jared has many good qualities, but his regard for Bernie undercuts them all," I said with a smile.

We took a few more shots with the .38, finished off the blunt, and loaded up in Rick's car. Jared discreetly asked me if he could talk to me later, which I said was fine. It stayed daylight until six or so now, which was about an hour away.

"What time are you guys goin' to the bowling center?" Rick asked.

"It'll probably be eight or so before Krista and I get there," I replied, "'Cause she went to Sikeston to get some things for her mom. She said it might be close to eight before she got back. I don't know what takes so long; it's a girl thing, I guess."

"You and Tammy are comin' over with Marsh and Betsy, aren't you Jared?" Rick asked.

"Yeah, but I think we're coming late, too," Jared said.

"Probably so," I said. "Marsh's workin' on his golf game this afternoon with Todd. By the time he gets in and gets ready, you guys'll end up leavin' close to when we do."

"In that case, I'll just tell Sally we'll go grab something to eat first and go over there around eight."

"Well, Rick, go ahead and take me to my truck. We've burned enough of your gas and used up all your ammo," I said. "I'll take Jared home on my way."

"No problem, and you know the gas and ammo were my treat," Rick said. "Besides, you guys supplied the weed, which was the best thing of all."

"Now remember," I said, "The weed was a gift to Jared from Bernie."

"Fuck him," Jared said. We all laughed.

Rick pulled up to my truck in the school parking lot and let us out. Jared and I got in my truck, and I cranked it up to let it warm a second.

"What's up, Jared?"

He looked at me very seriously and said, "I need to talk to you sort of serious like."

"That's cool."

"I want to ask you about some things that are very personal and private, if that's okay?" he asked, looking at me intently.

"You know it's okay."

"Some of it's about Tammy and me; is that alright?"

"Absolutely; you know I'm glad you and Tammy are together." Boy he was really nervous.

"Yeah, well," —he stopped for a few seconds—"Okay, you know Tammy and I've been doin' some stuff."

I nodded.

"Well, we've been feelin' around each other, but it's all been on the outside, if you know what I mean."

Once again, I nodded. He was keeping a close eye on my reactions.

"I'm not sure, but we may be close to takin' the next step. And, I, ah—" He paused again.

"It's okay, Jared," I said, trying to sound reassuring.

"I wanna make sure I know what I'm doin' and, there's somethin' else, too."

"Alright, let's take 'em one at a time."

"I know where everything is; I just..."

"Look, Jared, everybody goes through this the first time. Hell, it's her first time, too, despite my best efforts. Just go slow and be gentle. Never stop lovin' on her. She'll help you into all the right places and you do the same for her."

"Yeah, you're right," he said, "I just need to hear it from you 'cause, well, you're you."

"Whatever that means." We both laughed a little. "And the other thing?"

He took a deep breath. "Boy, this is a tough one. See, Blake, I'm not much of a stud; hell, I'm not even close. As a matter of fact, I think I'm small."

"According to who?" I asked.

"Hell, Blake, at the pool house last fall, you and Marsh treated the whole place like a locker room, walking around with nothing on. Let's just say that was pretty humbling for me."

"Listen Jared, you've got all the dick you need. Didn't you say Tammy's been checkin' you out?"

"Yeah."

"And things just keep warmin' up?"

"Yeah."

"Then she obviously wants what you've got and wants it pretty bad. Sounds to me like you've got all you need and then some," I said smiling.

He smiled back. "Thanks, Blake."

"No problem."

Krista hopped into my truck, slid over next to me and gave me a quick kiss. She snuggled up to me, placing my right arm around her and cradling her head against my shoulder. She lifted her right knee almost up into my lap and put her right arm across my stomach with her right hand tucked behind my left side. I was literally wrapped up.

"Okay, we can go now," she said softly.

"I guess I'm supposed to be able to drive like this," I said.

"You can manage," she replied, snuggling tighter.

"Well, I think I can steer with one hand, but you'll have to start the truck."

She did, and I strained to reach over and put the truck in reverse. I slowly backed out of her drive. Then, once again, I strained to shift the truck back into drive. We could now start on our way to Sikeston. She began gently teething the side of my neck creating almost unbearable sensations.

"Uh, Krista, I don't think I can make it to the bowling center if you keep doin' that. Keeping still enough to drive will soon be impossible, and I'm so hard it hurts."

She reached down with her right hand and softly squeezed me. "Well, baby, I think a nice massage will relieve some of the pressure."

"I've no doubt about that, but I'd be a little uncomfortable at the bowling center with my boxers plastered to me."

"Yeah, I suppose that's true," she said and put her right hand back around my side, providing me with more than a twinge of disappointment.

"You seem tired, baby," I said.

"I've had a hectic afternoon. I've been running around Sikeston doing this and that. Mom just wasn't up to making the trip, if you know what I mean."

I never really knew how to talk to Krista about her mother. I knew the situation was getting worse. Her mom didn't get out much anymore. We used to see her whenever Krista was involved in anything. But she never seemed very happy. Krista's dad was a great guy. Marsh and I would see him at work a lot and he was always good to us. I really didn't think her mom liked me very much. Krista said it had nothing to do with me—it was that she hated herself so bad, she couldn't like anyone else. That might be true; I knew her mom had sort of a sad feel to her whenever

I was around her. "Is your mom okay, Krista?"

"No, she's not. Her drinking's about the same, but her attitude is worse. I wish she'd get help before it's too late. I've talked to Dad about it. He just said he'd keep tryin'."

"Does your dad know why she got into drinking so heavy or did it just happen over time?" I asked.

"That's a good question, which I have asked on more than one occasion. He just shakes his head and says nothing. Let's talk about something else."

"Sure, Babe, I'm sorry."

She hugged me tighter. "So how's Jared doin' with the Bernie situation? I saw him talking to Bernie after school."

"Oh, Bernie keeps trying to make up, but Jared isn't going for it. He just listens and walks away."

"You don't think Jared will fall in with him again?"

"Nope," I answered firmly. "Jared's fallen in with us and he won't go back 'cause he has no desire to."

"Jared has really changed over this school year, hasn't he?"

"Yeah, but he got a late start because he was younger. He used to whine a lot, but I think that was just because he wanted to belong and felt intimidated. I was an asshole to 'im and that was wrong."

"Well, everybody wants to fit in. The battle to do that is harder for some than it is for others. Some people never really fit."

"That's true, but Jared seems to be fitting in now. Plus, he and Tammy are gettin' pretty tight and that's helpin' some."

"Yeah, Tammy's pretty cool."

"She's always been a really nice girl."

"Careful."

"Oh, come on, Krista, you know what I mean."

"I know; I just don't like the idea of sharing your affections."

Neither of us said anything for a couple of minutes.

"How's Marsh doin'?" she asked.

"He's okay; just worried about being ready for golf season, and it's kind of up in the air."

"He's practicing, isn't he?"

"Yeah, but he can't take a full swing and probably won't be able to for a month, which makes him very unhappy."

"I know that's tough for him."

"I'm hopin' spendin' more time with Betsy will be a healthy distraction and get his mind off some of his troubles."

"I bet Marsh can find his way. You've always said he was resourceful and more capable than everyone else thinks."

"That's true, but this golf thing is a big deal."

"You know, Blake, I'm still concerned that this thing with Perdue may not be over. He's not dating anyone according to my very reliable source, Cheryl."

"Well, I just think he has too much to lose by causin' problems. On top of that, Marsh is never around him and, now that basketball is over, neither am I."

I had managed to drive us to Sikeston in a very difficult driving position. We'd be at the bowling center in a couple of minutes.

"Cheryl said she and Scott might drop by for a while."

"Oh, that's just great."

"It won't be too bad," she said. "When Scott's around, she tends to be less talkative."

"Well, I'd like to see that."

A minute or so later, I carefully pulled into the bowling center, never taking my eyes from the rear view mirror. Watching, as Perdue's truck cruised on by, I wondered how long he'd been following us.

Chapter Thirty

MARSH

We finally had a decent day to hit a golf ball. It had taken until mid-March to get sixty degrees and sunshine. We'd used the driving range three days last week and it was too damned cold. But our golf coach, Coach Maben, insisted that we take the range time allowed by the Sikeston Country Club and Todd. She, of course, was absent from the sessions, thereby depriving us of her expertise in golf. She could probably do that in about one minute. Her job as golf coach was, more or less, comparable to a hall monitor.

Todd took of his own time to come out and give us tips about our game. He was more than qualified and a good teacher. He also provided us with driving range time and special access to the course. Sikeston also had a nine hole public course which we sometimes used, but the eighteen hole course here was our preference. I had a sneaky feeling that the fact that Gramps was the club's most prominent member played a role in our extensive use of the facilities.

Today, we got to play our first round on the course, though we only had enough daylight to play nine holes. There were six team members—including Blake and me. Everyone was pretty cool, and there wasn't any crap directed at us sophomores.

As excited as I was about playing this spring, I was worried about my being ready. My rehab was going well, but I was frustrated and impatient. While we were swinging last week, I was limited to half swings, chipping and putting. My bro worked hard on encouraging me, but not being able to fully participate was driving me crazy. It was reaching a point that I was pissed about everything. Golf was one of my loves and I didn't have very many loves. It was getting to be tiresome trying to put up a good front about all this. I hated it.

I'd had to apologize to Mom twice this week over stupid remarks I'd made to her. I really didn't want to be around much of anybody and seemed determined to make them feel the same way about me. Hell, I'd been popping off at Blake about everything and he just let it go. But he damned well didn't deserve it. Todd tried to show me something about my putting stance earlier and I told him I didn't give a shit. He and Blake made all these allowances for me and that just pissed me off more.

The course was officially closed today, so we had it to ourselves. Todd broke us up into threesomes. The older guys would tee off on hole ten and play the back nine, while we sophomores, would tee off on one and play the front. I would mostly just chip and putt around the greens.

Blake rode in the cart with me. Taking his first official swing of the season off the first tee, he pushed my drive into the trees off the right side of the fairway. He was long, but playing off the fairway tended to negate length in most cases.

"You hurried your swing and that's why you pushed it," I said dryly.

"Yeah, I'm probably a little anxious," he said. "Jimmy hit a good drive though."

"He's a lot like you—he'll screw up his approach and mess up a good shot."

"Well, I'm workin' on that, startin' today," he said.

"Then again, hitting approach shots from the trees is somethin' some people need to practice, 'cause they play from there a lot," I said, looking straight ahead.

"Look bro," Blake said, dropping his club into the bag, "I want you to help me, but the sarcastic shit is somethin' I can do without."

"I was just makin' a valid observation; you can't be so sensitive and be good at this."

"Yeah, okay, whatever you say," he said, showing his frustration. He needed a six iron for my next shot and had to negotiate a very small opening through the trees. This would not be easy. Despite his best effort, his shot clipped a tree branch and dribbled just a few yards out into the fairway.

"Shit," he said, as he walked back to the cart to look at changing clubs.

"Why don't you just use the same club?" I asked.

"I wanna make sure of my lie and distance," I replied.

"With your game, the difference in this case won't really matter," I stated firmly.

"What's that supposed to mean?" he asked, with a little anger rising.

"It means you need to use the six again."

God, I was being an ass. I wanted Blake to tell me I was being an ass. Stop being nice about it and flip me off or something. But he just let it go. He hit his next shot pretty well but pulled it, landing about ten yards to the left of the green. He walked back to the cart as Jimmy hit his second shot, which missed the green to the right.

"Well, you guys got the green surrounded," I said, a comment he totally ignored.

"Well, so how're things going with you and Betsy?" he asked.

"Well, they're goin', I suppose," he replied. "She meets all the criteria—pretty face, good tits, and a nice ass. She's a fine representative of the female species."

"Thanks for that really generic, descriptive response."

"Generic, bullshit questions deserve generic, bullshit answers."

He brought our cart to a halt. "Damn it, Marsh, it's obvious that you're determined to be a horse's ass. Do you plan to do this the entire round?"

Well, I got the response I'd been looking for and I felt even worse. After a few seconds of silence, I said, "Let's just play and not talk."

"Fine with me." He hit the pedal and on down the cart path we went.

Over the next three holes, he managed to bogey two holes and double bogey another. We stuck to our agreement about not talking; we were both very cordial with Jimmy. The par five fifth hole shaped up to be his best hole so far. He was looking at an eighteen-foot birdie putt. Jimmy was lying five about twenty-five feet from the cup. Todd drove up in his cart and was watching. I decided to pick up my ball and go over to see him.

"Well, how's it goin'?" he asked as I sat down beside him.

"Oh, it's goin' just great," I said. "I'm really good at bein' an asshole."

"You're gettin' there, Marsh," he said. "I bet you'll be ready in a couple of weeks."

"Boy that makes me feel better already." After a few moments of awkward silence, I added, "Sorry, Todd. I just feel like shit and I guess I want everyone else to."

"Recovery takes its toll on anyone," he said. "It's a tough road, but you're almost through."

"Yeah, I wish it'd move along; I don't know how much longer Blake can take bein' around me."

"Let me tell you somethin', Marsh," he said intently. "What Blake is doin' with you is as clear an act of pure love as I've ever seen. No one in the world could have a better friend."

I felt my eyes start to water. How could I be such a fucking idiot? My bro, who had all kinds of crazy shit going on in his life, was going the distance for me. Todd was right. It suddenly hit me that Blake was a lot more important than golf was or ever would be. Jimmy pulled up beside me in his cart.

"Hey Marsh," Jimmy said. "I'm gonna run to the clubhouse for a soda and snacks. Blake gave me a couple of bucks to get him somethin'. You want anything?"

"Yeah," I said, hopping out of Todd's cart. "I'll ride with ya'. Thanks, Todd."

"You bet," he said.

I got in the cart with Jimmy and we headed for the clubhouse.

I saw Blake waving goodbye to Todd as Jimmy and I arrived from our snack run. I walked over to our cart and gave Blake his soda, candy bar, and his two bucks.

"Man, that Todd's the coolest guy," he said, as I got into the cart and he started driving to the sixth tee.

"No, he's the second coolest," I said, looking straight ahead. "I'm sittin' next to the coolest."

We had a blast the rest of the round. Blake managed to par three of the last four holes with me coaching him along the way. We competed around each green, with him playing alongside me. We welcomed Jimmy into the camaraderie, and we all enjoyed some fun golf.

After we returned the cart, we stopped by the pro shop on our way out to say good-bye to Todd. Once inside, we ran into, of all people, Ray.

"What's up, guys? How was life on the links?" Ray asked.

"Not bad," I replied. "I'm still a little handicapped, literally, but Blake had a good round."

"I'm not surprised; another major coup by the dynamic duo." Ray said with a smile.

"Thanks, Ray, what're you up to?" Blake asked.

"I've been knocking the tennis ball around some; nothing special; how's your shoulder, cuz?"

"It gets a little better each day, but it needs to hurry up," I replied.

"Ah, patience is a virtue, not that I have many virtues myself," Ray said.

My cell phone, which had been quiet all afternoon, rang. It was Jared.

"Hey, what's up Jared?" I answered.

"Where are you?" he asked, sounding a little frantic.

"I'm at the country club with Blake; we—"

He cut me off and proceeded to tell me why he called. The more he talked, the more I felt sick and angry. I kept glancing at

Blake, who could tell something was bad wrong by my demeanor. I had Ray's and Todd's attention, too.

"Okay, Jared, we'll check on it." The call ended.

"Well?" Blake said, looking intently at me.

"Matt Perdue jumped on Rick after baseball practice."

"Let's go," Blake said immediately, then turned and headed out the door.

I was right behind him.

Blake had the look of someone possessed as he drove. You could tell it was a combination of deep concern and anger. I could identify strongly with those feelings. We were closing in on Gardner when I asked, "What's on your mind, bro?"

"What's on my mind is how we can let this stuff keep happening," he replied. "Perdue's a fucking lunatic and we need to do away with him."

"Come on, bro, when it gets right down to it, do you really think you could kill somebody?"

"He's not somebody. He's a God-damned rabid animal, and I have no problem puttin' rabid animals out of their misery. He's gotta be brain dead already."

"We're gonna be home in a minute and we both have gotta get a grip."

"I know; I can do it. But we gotta do somethin'."

"Let's just keep it cool; we'll call and check on Rick."

"Fine, but this is all fucked up. You and I both know what this is about—he's tryin' to hurt us. We're gonna have to come up with a plan of action."

"Well, I think our plan of action is to defend ourselves. He's crazy and I think, eventually, he'll come after us." I paused for a moment. "Blake, do you think Betsy and I should cool it for a while?"

"Hell, Marsh, that doesn't matter anymore. The lines have been drawn. To tell you the truth, I think he wants me more than he wants you."

That wasn't exactly news to me. I'd already come to that conclusion. Perdue liked Betsy, but not as much as he hated Blake. He hated everything about Blake. Perdue wanted to be the man; hell, he had to be the man. Blake had everything Perdue wanted. He had Krista, for one. And this was supposed to be Perdue's year in basketball, but everybody talked about Blake and Tyler.

No, he wanted to hurt me to get at Blake. Betsy was just an excuse. He jumped on Rick for the same reason. And I had a feeling that raving lunatic was planning to do more than hurt Blake. And that wasn't going to happen. What that bastard didn't know was that even though Blake might or might not possess the ability to kill him, I did.

"Well, bro," I said, "I think he carries a mutual hatred for both of us and it's not gonna just go away."

"Nope, it's not."

"Well, do you think we should share this with our folks?"

"Yeah, we could," he said, "But exactly where would they go with it? The police have already been brought in about you. And the thing with Rick will probably just be considered a school-yard fight. They might think we were just tryin' to cause trouble. Plus, I don't think Chief Davidson likes me very much."

"That's probably because you ride around Gardner drinking booze and smoking pot, which is in violation of the law," I said smiling. "Didn't you know that ?"

We checked on Rick and he was gonna be okay. The coach and players broke it up pretty quick. He said Perdue kept calling him names and talking about us being "faggots", so he finally told him that he was the one who couldn't keep a girlfriend and that did it. He said Perdue blacked his eye and bloodied his nose, but that was it. I could tell Rick was shaken pretty bad and Blake and I both told him we had his back. He said he knew that and that Perdue could go fuck himself. But I knew he was scared and so was I.

Blake and I decided to grab Jared and go to my house and talk it over. When we rolled into the house, completely unannounced, my mom took it right in stride. As always, we were starving and she came to the rescue. She heated up a roast she had in the fridge and made us some two-inch thick roast beef sandwiches. She threw in some fries and anything else she could scrape together. I explained to her that we had to discuss some private matters, so we would be dining in the confines of my bedroom. She just rolled her eyes—she was so cool sometimes. We grabbed our food and headed for the bedroom.

"Okay, Jared, whadda you think about all this?" I asked.

"I think Perdue jumped on Rick 'cause he's friends with you guys," Jared replied, very matter-of-factly, as he often does.

"We're absolutely sure of it," I continued. "It now appears obvious that bein' friends with Blake and me makes you an automatic enemy of Perdue."

"Yeah, I know," Jared said, and then calmly took a big bit of his sandwich.

Blake and I looked at each other, a little surprised by the ease with which he took what I had said.

"Ah, Jared, this could be a pretty serious situation with you becomin' a target simply because you hang out with us," Blake said.

He nodded as he swallowed a tremendous mouthful of food, and then followed that with a big swig of soda and a healthy belch.

"Excuse me," he said, wiping his mouth with his hand. "The situation is pretty clear to me. I know there's a possibility that he could try to do somethin' to me. I also know he could break me into little pieces. And if he comes after me, I'll run like hell. But I'm not runnin' away from my friends and he won't scare me away from 'em. Plus, if you wanna go kill the sick bastard, count me in."

We couldn't contain our laughter. "Damn, Jared, you sound like you've been thinkin' this through," I said.

"Yeah, me and Tammy have talked about it some. I basically told her the same thing I told you—except about the killin' part."

"Jared, what in the world has come over you?" Blake asked, trying to keep from laughing again. "You're becomin' one bad boy."

"Oh, I'm not bad," he said. "I just figure there's no need in gettin' all crazy about it. He's not that important. You guys are important."

"Jared, you're a diamond in the rough," I said, as I wadded up my napkin and threw it at him, who managed a smile even with his mouth full.

"But, we've got to take precautions," Blake said, and then looking at Jared, "Marsh and I think it'd be better if you rode to and from school with us whenever possible. Will that be a problem with your folks?"

"No, they won't care," he replied. "They like you guys."

"Well, we've got to bind together even tighter than normal," I said. "Should we tell the girls?"

"Hell, Krista already knows," Blake said.

"Tammy'll be cool with everything," Jared said.

"Okay, we'll do our best to keep up with each other," I said. "Hell, maybe this shit'll blow over. Maybe Perdue'll find somethin' else to occupy his feeble mind."

"I tell you what I think," Jared said.

"What would that be, bad boy?" Blake asked.

"I think this is the best roast beef sandwich I've ever had."

SPRING

The blindness of love's all consuming;
Setting leery imposters to flight;
Taking no count of the wounding;
Which leaves them resolved to their plight.

When the merciless set out to draw feelings;
That the bands of the faithful indulge;
Then watch with a foresight unyielding;
The fears of their fate to divulge.

Pain stakes the heart, though forbidden;
With a barrage of travails to defeat;
Beauty hides what needs to be hidden;
And dishevel what yearns to complete.

The reaches of trust and devotion;
That struggle to take part of what's whole;
Fall victim to mindless emotion;
Leaving just threads of your soul.

BLAKE

Chapter Thirty One

KRISTA

There was no better example of controlled chaos than the lunch hour at Gardner High School, at least from a girl's point of view. Students rushed into the cafeteria to try to get a good spot in one of the two lunch lines. Whatever teachers were unlucky enough to draw lunch duty did their best to monitor the lines for those that might try to break in front of someone else. Our principal, Mr. Evans, or one of the male coaches patrolled the tables, keeping a wary eye out for student stupidity.

There were many complaints that could justifiably be lodged against the lunch program here. One was the insistence of the administration on calling it a lunch hour when, in fact, it was only thirty-five minutes long. The limited time meant that students could count on about ten minutes or so to eat, except for those who made it to the front of the line. Of course, some students chose to bring their lunch. Cheryl and I fell in that category most of the time. This allowed for twenty minutes or so to eat. What I found interesting about this was that it promoted eating at a very fast pace. I was raised that it was healthiest to eat your food slowly and not stuff your mouth full. Then, I started high school and eating lunch was almost like entering one of those pie eating contests under the clock.

Naturally, another issue was the food itself. School food service programs were now required to meet certain nutritional guidelines, but what qualified as "nutritional" was apparently open to some interpretation. Debating this was really a waste of time. The only thing I would say about the guidelines was that starchy foods must be very important. Sodium and sugar levels were monitored closely. They were also astronomical.

One other point about food service involved downsizing. For

example, when we had roast turkey, it was amazing that turkey could be sliced so thin you could see through it. To make up for this, there was usually a double helping of mashed potatoes. Now that was nutritional balance. Following my normal routine, I made my way to the tables we always sat at. "We" meant Blake, Cheryl, Marsh, Betsy, Rick, Sally, Jared, Tammy and me. Jared and Tammy had just recently joined us. As was normally the case, the girls had avoided today's meal, bringing lunch from home or opting for vending. The guys were in line for a scrumptious meal consisting of two corn dogs, pinto beans, coleslaw, and some kind of yellow cake with icing. What was both fascinating and frightening was the way the guys would inhale that food. And Jared, who was the smallest of the guys, was the biggest eater.

"So, Betsy," I said, "I guess this weather will cancel out golf today for our guys."

"Looks like it," Betsy said. "It's been raining all morning, and it isn't supposed to stop."

"Yeah, that means they'll probably have one of those pow-wows this afternoon, so I know where Jared'll be," Tammy said, joining the conversation.

"You can bet on that," Cheryl chimed in. "He's one of the four mouseketeers, which means many things, none of which are good."

"Why do you say that, Cheryl?" Tammy asked, showing concern.

"Because she has a habit of opening her mouth and tripping over it," I said.

"You have such a way with words, girlfriend," Cheryl said, sneering a little.

"No, but really," Tammy said, "This thing that Jared talks about with Matt Perdue scares me. He says he started that stuff with Rick 'cause he hates Blake and Marsh and that he might come after him."

"Rick has a strange attitude about that," Sally said. "He claims

Matt keeps tryin' to do little things to intimidate him since their fight. Rick tries to play it off, but I can tell it bothers him. His baseball isn't goin' too well and I think that's why. But, for God's sake, don't tell him I said that."

"That's what I mean," Tammy said. "And look how bad he hurt Marsh. He'd kill Jared." She was on the edge of becoming emotional.

"I share you concern, Tammy," I said, "but the guys are sticking pretty close. They're aware and'll be careful."

"Well, it all sounds like lunacy to me," Cheryl said. "I'm not disputing that Perdue's a worthless piece of shit, but I just don't view him as homicidal."

"I don't like to think of him that way, either," Betsy said. "I don't say anything to Marsh about it, and he won't bring it up around me. But I do know he's very concerned. He's the same way about golf."

"Well, I don't know anything about the homicidal part," I said, "but I firmly believe Perdue's crazy, which makes him capable of almost anything."

Blake, Marsh, Rick and Jared finally arrived at the table. Blake had managed to hijack two additional corn dogs. He gave one of them to Jared.

"Well, what's goin' on girls, and Cheryl?" Marsh asked, smiling as the guys took their seats.

"Things were goin' great until you guys arrived and polluted the table," Cheryl said.

"Now that's a really cruel thing to say," Marsh responded. "I would never consider you a pollutant. Maybe sewage, but never a pollutant."

"Would it be possible for you two to give it a rest while we finish our lunch?" I asked. "I'm sure everyone would appreciate it."

Blake and Jared, who were attacking their food as opposed to eating it, had paid no attention to the conversation at all. Jared was getting taller but, despite a phenomenal appetite, not much bigger. His face was more slender now and, with his wavy, sandy brown hair, he was getting better looking. The truth was Jared wasn't as physically mature as the other three guys, but he was starting to blossom.

"So, Marsh, has this rain washed out golf practice?" Betsy asked.

"Probably so," he replied, "Which gives my shoulder another day to heal. I can take a pretty good swing now. Next week is the first week of April and I'm hopin' I can get cleared for full use."

I didn't know if Marsh said that for our benefit or for his. "You guys have a match next week, don't you, Blake?" I asked, trying to pry him away from his food for a minute.

"Yeah, things start to get serious next week," he replied.

"Okay, everyone is here, so I've got the latest bit of juicy gossip," Cheryl chimed in.

"Oh, I can't wait," Marsh said, earning a nudge from Betsy and a glare from Cheryl.

"Well, as most of you know, Ms. Huey is out again today. And a reliable source"—Marsh coughed suddenly—"Said that she overheard one of the teachers say she was having personal problems involving her ex-husband."

"Wow, what kind of problems?" Sally asked.

"Well, of course no one knows for sure, but it seems he's trying to play her, while taking care of another female interest."

"Oh, he's in search of the best of both worlds," Jared finally joined in.

"Yeah," Cheryl shot back at him, "You guys are always good for stuff like that, no compassion and total irresponsibility."

"Now, Cheryl, you're not stereotyping us, are you?" Marsh asked.

"Wait a minute," I said, throwing my hands up in the air, "Let's not get into a 'battle of the sexes'. I just don't think I can handle it."

"Alright; well, anyway, that's the gossip," Cheryl said. "Oh, and she may not be comin' back to teach next year."

"I think Ms. Huey is a cool teacher. I hope she stays," Jared said.

"Yeah, she's pretty good," Tammy said.

"She's a good teacher," Marsh said. "Unlike most teachers, she won't condemn things before givin' 'em a chance."

"That's just because she lets you and Blake play with that rap shit all the time, and you guys are all google-eyed over her," Cheryl said.

"You know, Cheryl, I guess Blake and I should be offended by that comment, but we know you're battlin' personal stupidity, which prevents you from being rational. Besides, you're so good at being stupid."

"Look, Krista's right," Betsy said. "You two are more than enough to drive sane people crazy. Now, cut it out."

"You're right, Betsy," Marsh said, "I'll be good."

"Now, you want me—," Cheryl started.

"Cheryl!" I almost screamed. "Give it a rest."

The bell sounded, bringing an abrupt end to this wonderful lunch and all the pleasant conversation. I didn't get what was going on with Blake. He normally would've jumped in with Marsh against Cheryl. He just sat quietly and watched.

"Are you feeling okay, Babe?" I asked, as we walked out of the cafeteria together.

"Yeah, it's just kind of a dreary day," he said. "That just makes everything drag."

"I know what you mean," I said. I knew Blake had a lot on his mind. He came over last night and was so tense; it just rubbed on him for two hours. This thing with Perdue continued to bother him. He was always on the lookout at school, or just riding around. But that wasn't all of it. I was worried about him.

The thing with Marsh and his shoulder was also a constant source of stress for him. I knew he worried about Rick and feared for Jared. On top of all this, he'd start playing golf matches next week and, with Marsh on the mend, the team really needed him.

Then there was me. He was always careful to see how I was and how things were going with Mom. And I felt the same way he did about Perdue. Perdue intended to come after Blake and would hurt him worse than the others.

Well, I was ready to breeze through these afternoon classes. I had big plans for this afternoon after school; and was already churning inside just thinking about it.

His powerful hands trembled as he tried to be gentle and careful. This was, without a doubt, beyond anything he was prepared to deal with. Despite his age, there was an attractive innocence about him. I knew this ordeal had opened a new world for him— one he'd never seen before. When people depended so much on the image they projected, I believed they lost touch with what was real and what wasn't. If they discovered or uncovered truths they had hidden from themselves, serious conflicts arose.

These conflicts caused confusion. This confusion could lead to a lack of control over parts of their lives they'd previously taken for granted. Depending on the person and situation, this lack of control led to all kinds of behavior driven by the strength of their feelings. It was that behavior that had to be watched closely or things could really get out of hand.

"They're s-so beautiful," he said. There was a kind of special gentleness in his manner when he was like this.

"That's nice of you to say," I said, with a quaint smile.

I was sitting on his lap facing him. He was reclined and totally fascinated with the sight and feel of my breasts. He was carefully navigating them with his fingertips. This would actually feel better if he were a little bit firmer.

"What's the situation now?" I asked.

"There are b-bad signs; it's s-scary," he replied. His focus had shifted to my nipples which stirred me some.

"Do you think somethin's getting ready to happen?" I asked. I could feel his huge erection beneath me, which gave me a rush.

"It's h-hard to say; I j-just know things are g-gettin' c-crazy," he said.

Sensing the need, I began a slow swaying motion from my sitting position up and down his erection. He shuddered a couple of times and let out a low moan. This was the time to press the issue.

"Can you deal with this craziness?" I asked.

"Y-yeah, I think s-so," he said, now starting to breathe faster and his hands tensed a little around my breasts, which fired off more feelings inside me.

"We have to be sure," I said, suddenly stopping my motion.

His face showed immediate alarm when I stopped. "N-no, p-please don't stop, please," he begged.

"I have to be sure you can follow through. I can't do this unless you're sure," I said, scolding him a little.

"Yeah, I c-can do it; I-I mean I'm s-sure," he said in desperation.

I slid back just enough so I could undo his pants. His erection already reached past the boundaries of his underwear. I began working him slowly but steadily. He continued to be mesmerized by my breasts, even though his body began to quiver. His breathing became more rapid.

"Promise me," I said, speeding up my pace.

"Yeah, yeah, yeah; I promise, I—yessss!"

Well, it had certainly been an interesting afternoon. It was a little invigorating for a bit, but faded with a wad. I had to smile a little with that thought. My phone rang as I entered my house and, seeing the number, hurried to my bedroom to take the call. No one needed to hear it, especially my mom, who'd started one of her happy hours.

"Hello."

"Well, how are things?"

"Not too good; I'm afraid it's gonna get bad sooner than later."

"As I've told you, it's inevitable. The guy is obviously unbalanced, unstable, and capable of all kinds of destruction."

"I know you're right; it's just hard to believe he would go this crazy over a girl that was never really that close to him."

"Oh, the girl is irrelevant; she was just a trigger mechanism."

"Good grief, somethin's gotta give here."

"It will. You just keep doin' what you're doin' and keep me informed."

"I will."

"Okay, be careful."

The call ended. Huh, just keep doin' what I'm doin'—that's amazing. This whole business is so far outside the box, I couldn't even see the box. Maybe the warming spring weather would bring us some peace and sanity. Maybe feelings would change and everyone could ride this out. Maybe it would all turn out to be a bad dream.

Maybe not.

Chapter Thirty Two

BLAKE

The day had been just fine until Cheryl said that shit today at lunch about Ms. Huey. I hoped her problems had nothing to do with me. I still carried very warm feelings about the night we had together. But the contributions she had made to me and my writing had placed her close to my heart. Damn, I didn't want her to leave.

That's the primary reason, I supposed, I found myself driving through Sikeston on my way to her condo. Mom and Dad had taken one of their movie nights, which meant they'd be gone until about ten. I told them I had to pick up some stuff for school at Walmart in Sikeston and would be back after a while, giving myself most of the evening to check on Ms. Huey. That's if she would see me.

The clouds and the rain had brought darkness a little early, providing me some cover as I pulled into her parking lot. Once again, I found her car parked in the same place. As I pulled in to park beside her, I could feel the nervous tension within me. I didn't call in advance for fear that she might tell me not to come. The hard rain helped with my nervousness because I had to jog to her door. Working hard on my composure, I pushed the buzzer.

"Yes," she answered.

"It's Blake, Ms. Huey."

I heard the latches turn quickly. She opened the door and grabbed my arm firmly and pulled me inside.

"Good grief, Blake, what're you doing here? Did something happen?"

"Yeah, to you," I replied. "You've been out for two days, and I heard a rumor that you're havin' some problems with your ex."

"Where did you hear that?" she asked. She was wearing a loose fitting sweatshirt and those skin tight jeans. She was not made up, which exposed her natural beauty.

"Someone overheard a faculty member sayin' that. They also said you might not be coming back. That's why I'm here."

"Gossip, gossip, gossip; faculty lounges are as bad as small town beauty shops," she said, showing her disgust. She suddenly stopped and looked at me. "Oh, Blake, you're soaking wet. Get those shoes off and come with me." She led the way to one of the back bedrooms.

"There are towels in the bathroom and, here—" She tossed me a t-shirt and some gym shorts from a dresser drawer. "Change into those and bring me your wet clothes. I'll dry them for you." She then turned and left the room, closing the door behind her.

The shorts fit fine and the shirt was a little big, but worked. I came out, having dressed, and gave her my wet clothes. She told me to have a seat in the den while she threw my clothes in the dryer. I chose the sofa, grabbed the remote, and turned on MTV, hoping for some good sounds.

She returned in a couple of minutes and smiled when she saw the TV. "Let's turn that down for a minute. Can I get you something to drink?"

"No ma'am, I'm okay, thanks," I said, turning down the TV.

She took a seat beside me. "Okay; now Blake, you know this is a bad idea. You shouldn't be here."

"I guess, but I wanted to make sure you were okay. And I don't want you to leave."

"I appreciate your concern, but it's misplaced, Blake. You can't just come over here like this. It could be disastrous for both of us."

"It was important to me that you were okay. Risk or not, I needed to know."

She sighed deeply and turned to me, looking right into my eyes—

—There was a flashing of light and I was disoriented for a time. I started floating through a bright channel. Slowly coming into view below me was beautiful blue surf. The surf was rolling softly, barely white capping in places. On both sides of me, lush green flora slowly emerged into existence… A light breeze blew across the flora as I continued to float.

Above me was a bright white sky that was lined with streams of flickering illumination. There was a strange warmth, which seemed to surround me and began a gentle soothing. A wind suddenly whirled into my face, taking some of my breath away. Bits of flora appeared to break off in fine strands that blew into my face and ears. There was a tingling as they danced across my skin. Floating; floating; floating; with a fluctuating motion that had no line of direction.

There gradually came a feeling of descent. It was a feeling foreign to me and it brought a slight chill. As I looked around, the flora was turning into an even darker green. It was becoming more and more displaced by a growing breeze. I continued a slow descent. The chill evaporated into a warming feeling. As the warmth pulsed faster, my descent became more pronounced. Now I saw the blue surf looming large as I approached the surface. The waves seemed to be creeping.

Down, down, down I went; until I felt the surf tickle my feet, causing me to tense up. The surf gradually engulfed my legs, then my chest, then my head, and I was suddenly submerged into the soothing warm surf. The warmth did not relieve the tenseness and—

"Oh God!" I faintly heard her voice.

My eyes came into focus looking at what appeared to be a white—ceiling, it was a ceiling. I looked around me and found I was reclined on the sofa. What had happened? I sat up and saw Ms. Huey standing, facing away from me. As I leaned forward, I was surprised to find I had a hard on, which was clearly visible as a rise in my shorts.

"Ms. Huey, what is it? Are you okay?" I asked tentatively.

She turned around and faced me, obviously shaken and said, "Can you tell me what it is, Blake? This is the second time I've lost myself with you. I have no idea what happened. It's like I just seem to stop existing. Then I wake up and I-I-I—"

"You what?" I asked, almost pleading.

"I have you in my mouth, Blake," she said, looking away.

"Oh, I didn't know." I felt a pang of embarrassment.

"I had you in my mouth that morning at school, too. It was almost more than I could take. Nothing like that has ever happened to me. What are you doing?"

"I don't know what it is or what I do, Ms. Huey," I said, trying not to tremble. "But it's scaring me to death and I don't—" I could feel tears welling up in my eyes. My emotions were running so high. I needed to let go.

She came back over to me. She pulled me into her arms and I started crying. Her hold was so warm. Tears continued to flow as I let go of all my feelings.

"Oh, Blake," she whispered. She gently patted my back and rocked me a little. Over the next few minutes, thanks to her tender attention, I regained my composure. She slowly released me. I tried to lower my head, but she lifted my chin with her left hand.

"It doesn't matter, Blake," she said. "I don't know why, but it just doesn't matter." She began caressing my hair with her right hand, providing me with a comfort I couldn't remember having before.

"I didn't know," I said.

"I believe you," she said, continuing to comfort me. "Blake, I'm so strongly attracted to you, and I just don't think I can deal with it."

After a few seconds of silence, I said, "I need you, Ms. Huey. I need you in my life right now. I know how people would view this if they knew, but I don't care." Then I said something I can't believe I had the nerve to say. "I wanna go to bed with you."

She pulled back for a moment and gave me kind of a bewildered look. I could feel something in the gaze between us, but had no idea what it was. She then eased up and nudged me up with her. Taking my hand, she led me to her bedroom. Once in her room, she slowly removed her sweatshirt and bra. Standing by the bed, she slipped out of her jeans and panties and slid under the covers. Breaking from a momentary trance caused by viewing her beautiful body, I quickly shed my clothes and joined her.

We moved together and she started consuming me with the depth of her kisses. Jesus, she was taking over again. But then, with a sudden surge, I turned her on her back and began orally caressing her breast. This brought on deep moans and twitching movements, just like it did before. Taking my time, I slid on down and continued working her. She started quivering and breathing fast. All of a sudden, she tensed up and let go a quiet scream. My God, I did it.

She grabbed me and pulled me up into her. She grabbed my hair and held on as I moved in and out of her. I drove hard and fast. The feeling was so intense. Despite my best effort, she took charge and handled my explosive release with ease.

With everything I could muster, I tried to gain control again, but she was too strong. I began to fall under her power. She was forceful, but kept a nurturing passion as she took me, and took me, and took me...

An hour or so later, I was so drained it took intense concentration just to put my clothes on. The rain had stopped and it was time for me to head out. I had to beat mom and dad home.

Once I dressed, she walked me to the door. She kissed me on the forehead and promised me she'd return to work, which made me smile.

I was so totally exhausted; I walked in slow motion to my truck. It was going to take a great effort to get home. Once there, I knew I'd go straight to my bedroom and pass out, falling into a peaceful sleep. Ms. Huey was safe.

Chapter Thirty Three

MARSH

This was not the way we would normally choose to use our Saturday morning, but Gramps called and snapped Blake and me to attention. He needed some plants picked up at the nursery in Sikeston and delivered to his house. We were then needed to help in planting them in the flower beds. I knew this was a Grandma thing. She'd got her flower beds worked up and ready to go and it was supposed to start raining around noon. We had to pick up more than one hundred plants. This meant we had to go out to the elevators and get a company pickup.

Blake and I decided to recruit Jared to help, which he was more than happy to do. It was nice that one of us showed a little enthusiasm. Much of that depended on Grandma's temperament. She always had a plan, but it was subject to change about every fifteen minutes. We'd keep Jared closest to her because she barked orders at Blake and me like a drill sergeant. But, she didn't know Jared that well. He'd be eager to please and she'd like that.

My shoulder was better. The team played a match this past Thursday and won. My bro was pretty damned good. He shot a seventy-nine, which was the fourth best score in the three team event. It was hard to sit and watch. But I was confident now that I'd be back this week, and I knew we'd have a good team.

I picked up Blake and Jared and we drove out to the elevators. There, we loaded up in a long bed pickup and headed for Sikeston.

"So, since I've never done this, what exactly do I do?" Jared asked.

"It's pretty simple," I said. "We load up the plants at the nursery; take 'em to Gramps' house; unload them and plant them in the flower bed."

"But I haven't ever planted anything that I can remember," Jared said.

"You just stick with Grandma; she'll show you what to do," I said, and noticed Blake turned and looked at me. He knew Jared was in for a really thorough lesson in planting from Grandma, but someone had to do it.

"Marsh, have you talked to Ray?" Blake asked.

"Yeah, he's got some gin for us, but he's still holdin' back on the weed."

"Well, shit," Blake said with disgust.

"It's just too much right now, bro," I said. "He knows Gramps has eyes and ears all over the place."

"Well, then how do we keep the booze hidden from 'im?" Blake asked.

"We don't," I replied. "He just doesn't care about the booze, unless it gets out of hand. He's just old school and weed doesn't work for him."

"It's not workin' for us either," he said. "What about Bernie, Jared?"

"Fuck Bernie," Jared said. "I talk to that bastard a little bit just because Marsh said I need right now."

"I thought he was being nice to you," Blake said.

"He is; he offered me some weed twice this week, and a ride when you guys went to your golf match."

"Be patient, Jared," I said. "I have plans for good ole' Bern. The time's not right, yet."

"That's fine," Jared said, "It just sucks bein' around him."

"You're right, Jared," Blake said. "He's a piece of shit and I'm going to bust 'im in the mouth. I'm just havin' a weed craving."

"Well, there are some other possibilities, which I became aware of when I was hangin' with Bernie," Jared said. "But, I didn't think we wanted the exposure."

"We don't," I said. "Things'll ease up before long. I just wanna keep Bernie on a leash until it's time."

The truck was a very rough ride. I wondered if the damned thing even had any shocks. I didn't push it very hard because I was afraid it would start coming apart.

"What'd you and Krista end up doin' last night?" I asked Blake.

"Well, we went to eat at Western Sizzlin' and had planned to return to her house. But her mom wasn't in a very hospitable mood, so we went over to my house, which is under tighter supervision. That's how it goes sometimes."

"Do you and Krista wanna go with Betsy and me to a movie tonight?" I asked.

"Sounds good to me," Blake said. "Krista's goin' to Cape today to do whatever, so I'm not sure when she'll be back."

"You wanna just do a nine-thirty show then?"

"Yeah, it'd probably be best. Krista's as bad about time as I used to be."

"You and Tammy are goin' to the bowling center, aren't you Jared?" I asked.

"Yeah, her folks are takin' us. We're leavin' around seven. There's just nothin' like a family outing. My family's goin' to a revival in Blytheville, so we'll miss a good opportunity to sneak over to my house."

"We all go through it. It's one of the things that sucks about bein' our age and livin' in the Bible belt," Blake said.

"Yeah, but at least we have extra protection for our souls," I said. "With all those flagrant sinners in other places, we should be able to slip through the pearly gates while everyone else is preoccupied."

"That's an interesting observation and somewhat insightful, Marsh," Jared said.

"And totally riddled with holes caused by bullets of bullshit," Blake said.

"Blake, I do believe you need a religious retreat or somethin'. You may be straying from the path of salvation," I said.

"Straying, hell; you've got to find the damn thing before you can stray from it. Besides, I don't wanna really start lookin' for it right now."

"Hey guys," Jared said, "I just thought of somethin'. Snakes aren't out yet, are they? I've heard they like those big flower beds."

"Sufferin' from a little snake phobia, are we?" Blake asked.

"I hate the damn things," he said. "I'm almost as bad as Bernie is about spiders."

"Bernie doesn't like spiders?" I asked.

"Mortal fear is more like it," Jared replied. "I was ridin' with him one day and pointed one out on his floorboard. We almost wrecked when he wheeled off the road. He jumped out of the car shoutin' for me to kill the damn thing. Hell, it was just a tiny spider."

"Does it matter to you if the snake is big or little?" Blake asked.

"Hell no; a snake is a snake. But spiders—now, come on," Jared said.

"Well, Jared, I don't think we'll run into any snakes today," I said. "It's not quite time for 'em, but never say never."

"But if I do see one, I'll bring it over to ya," Blake said.

"Come on, Blake," Jared said. "I'm not kiddin', dude. I'd probably go ballistic and piss myself or somethin'."

"He's just kidding, Jared," I said, "Hell, we're not crazy about 'em either."

"I like the little ones," Blake said.

"I think that's a case of mistaken identity," I said.

"Now, that's hitting below the belt, bro."

"The truth hurts sometimes."

It was amazing what a person could do with their mouth. The tongue was a pretty fascinating tool, also. Sometimes, I could see why the church had the attitude it did about sexual behavior. Besides eating and sleeping, why would anyone want to do anything else? This shit was a curse. Before I did it, I thought about the reasons not to. After I did it, I felt like shit because of the guilt and shame. But while I was doing it, I reveled in an ecstasy that rivaled all other forms of gratification. I guess my Achilles' heel was my dick.

Earlier today I was ankle deep in potash and now I had sensations of sexual fire running through me like balls of fire. My body had reached an almost unbearable level of rigidity, as had my erection, while I tried to hold my release as long as possible. It wouldn't be much longer. I was trying to control my breathing as the rest of me prepared to explode. I arched up, up, up and—

Jesus, how was this shit so wired into us that it could make us submit to almost anything. My breathing and pulse rate were slowly returning to normal. I sat up in the bed and looked at the clock—

"Shit!" I said. "It's almost seven."

"Yeah, we kind of lost track of time."

"Kinda, hell, we lost it," I said, trying to put my clothes on in record time. "Damn, we've got to be careful about this."

"Well, I'm not sure bein' careful will help much with the time."

Finally getting my tennis shoes tied, I grabbed my phone off the dresser and turned it on. There were three calls from Blake and a message. I played the message.

"Damn it!" I said.

"What is it?"

"Blake left a message to call 'im back now, which means somethin's wrong."

I punched in his number.

Chapter Thirty Four

BLAKE

"Blake!" my mom's voice rang out, bringing me out of a good nap.

"Okay, Mom, I'm awake," I called back, still waking up.

Boy, this morning's flower bed work for Ms. Doty had taken more out of me than I thought. Jared handled it all well and Marsh was really doing better—so well, in fact, that when we finished he was headed for the club to get some practice in if he could beat the rain. I'd helped Mom move a few boxes when I got back. Maybe that was why I'd crashed so hard. It was as good a reason as any.

I crawled off the bed and stretched out. Looking out my window, I noticed it hadn't rained yet but it looked rainy. Realizing there was no rush, I went to the kitchen, grabbed a sandwich and a soda, and returned to my room to chill. Just before I slipped my headphones on to get into some Jay-Z, my phone rang. I scooped it up to answer, pausing just for a moment because I didn't recognize the number.

"Hello," I answered quietly, my curiosity peaked.

"Blake."

"Who is this?" I asked.

"It's Jared," he said, and I did recognize his voice, but he didn't sound good.

"What's up, Jared. Are you okay?"

"Blake, I'm sorry."

I could tell he was crying and asked loudly, "What's wrong, Jared? Where are you?"

"I'm at the old Haskins barn," he said, really struggling, "Can you come get me?"

Something was bad wrong and he was hurt.

"What the hell are you doin' out there?" I asked.

"I'm really sorry, Blake," he said, now crying more.

"I'm on my way, Jared. You hold on."

I wasn't sure what was up, but Jared was in trouble. As I got ready to go, I punched in Marsh's number and got his voicemail. Shit. I went to my closet and got my old baseball bat—something told me I might need it. I was in my truck and on the road in a hurry. The old Haskins Barn was out east of town off Seventy-Five and wasn't far. This really smelled like Bernie. If he'd hurt Jared again, I'd beat that drug dealing bastard until he wished he was dead. I punched in Marsh's number again and, again, got voicemail. This time I left a clear crisp message—"Call me now!" I felt someone should know where I was going, so I called Krista. I got her voicemail. Where the hell was everybody? A couple of minutes later, my phone rang.

"Hey, bro," I answered.

"What's up?" Marsh asked.

"Jared called me and was cryin'—I mean bad. He said he was at Haskins barn—this has Bernie written all over it."

"Give me a few minutes, max, and I'll be there," he said.

"No time, bro, I'm almost there, now."

"Dammit, you wait on me, Blake!" he yelled.

"He's hurtin' bad, Marsh, and I'm closin' in on the barn now."

"Blake!"

I turned off the highway onto an old dirt road which led to the barn. I could see it now and—

"Yeah, there it is—Bernie's fuckin' car. I'm gonna beat the shit out of 'im, Marsh."

"You wait, Blake, it's dangerous!" he was still yelling.

"I gotta' go, bro; hurry on out."

I ended the call.

The sun had set as I pulled up behind Bernie's car. I grabbed my bat and walked around to the closest entrance to the barn. I eased open the creaky, broken door. It was dark, but I could see a lighted area past a row of stalls on my left. This place was old and there were places that were rotting out. Still, many a private party had been held out here by kids from Gardner and other places.

I held my bat steady in my right hand as I walked past the stalls toward the lighted area. As I turned to the left beyond the stalls I saw Jared sitting on an old crate. What looked like a battery-powered lantern sitting on the shelf above him was providing the light. As I moved toward him I noticed he didn't have any clothes on. I moved closer, more than a little wary, and—

"That's close enough, Coleman."

Out of the shadows from just behind Jared stepped Matt Perdue. I noticed he had some kind of wooden club in his hand. Then something moved behind which caused me to jump. I turned to see Mutt closing in. When I turned back around, Bernie stepped out of the shadows across from Perdue. This was not looking good.

"Toss the bat to Mutt, Coleman," Perdue said, "Or I'll pop your little friend in the face with this club, and he's already having a bad day."

I knew there was no need in contesting the bat, so I tossed it back in the direction of Mutt.

"That's better, Coleman. Y'know, we've been tryin' to set this up. Your friend happened to just make it easy for us. Seemed he wanted to get some weed from Bernie."

Holy shit, this was my fault. Jared was trying to land some weed for us, and this was what he got for it. I moved a little closer to Jared and could see him trembling.

"Why are his fuckin' clothes off, Perdue?" I asked.

"Well, you see, Coleman, little Gavin here seems to have taken advantage of Bernie's kindness. Bernie took the little twerp under his wing when no one else, including you, had much time for 'im. Then, he just turned his back on Bernie. The problem is he was involved in some business transactions with Bernie and had become somewhat of an asset. Bernie tried to renew their friendship and Gavin just blew him off. Therefore, he became a liability."

I was looking for an escape route for Jared and me, but I couldn't find one at the moment.

"So," Perdue continued, "Just in case Gavin ever decided to share information he shouldn't, Bernie needed a deterrent. So, we managed to convince young Gavin to undress and pose for a few revealing photos, even though, I must say, there's not much to reveal. His dick must have stopped growin' when he was in third grade. Now, if he's willin' to behave himself and even occasionally help out, there'd be no need for anyone to ever see the photos."

Jared hadn't said a word. He was just sitting there with his head down and his right hand covering himself.

"All I wanted him to do is give you a call," Perdue said, "But even the photo threat wouldn't convince him to do that, so I had to resort to other measures."

"What did you do?" I demanded, my eyes moving back to Jared.

"Not much, really," Perdue said. "I just took the middle finger of his left hand and snapped it at the knuckle. That still didn't convince 'im, so I had to do the same thing to his index finger. He became more cooperative. I was kind enough to snap them back in place for 'im."

I moved a little closer to Jared and noticed his trembling left hand sitting on his left knee. Those two fingers were swollen. I suddenly felt a rage building inside of me like some kind of eruption.

"You sick perverted bastard!" I yelled at Perdue. "You think you're tough, but you're just a big fuckin' coward! You want some of me; well, here I am, you worthless piece of shit!"

He smiled real big, dropped his club, and moved toward me. He took a cut at me, swinging with his right, but I ducked under it. Spinning down to one knee, I whirled with a right jab which hit him square in the balls. He screamed with pain, falling to the floor, holding himself.

A fury grew inside me I didn't know was possible. I was up immediately and landed a full kick to his face that sent blood splattering. I screamed a scream even I didn't recognize. Out of the corner of my eye, I saw Bernie break and run. I whirled again and landed another full kick to the left side of his head which sent him tumbling over groaning in agony. Then I saw his club, hopped over him, and picked it up.

"Now, you bastard, it's over!" I growled as I raised the club and—

"Blake, don't!" Jared screamed. His voice stopped me just before I split Perdue's head open. "Remember, he's not worth it. Let's just go—now."

The sight of my injured friend and the sound of his voice froze me and, after a few seconds, brought me back to my senses. I tossed the wooden club aside and walked over to Jared, who looked really pale. I knelt down and helped him get into his underwear and jeans. I slipped his tennis shoes on him and tied them. He was still trembling.

"Can you walk okay?" I asked.

"Yeah," he muttered and picked up his shirt.

Suddenly, his eyes widened as he looked past me. I turned just in time to see Perdue hurdling into me. The impact knocked me into Jared, who went sprawling into the side of a stall, screaming as he hit.

I went down hard to the floor with Perdue on top of me, screaming like a mad man. He had me pinned to the floor on my back, his weight crushing down on my chest, his hands around my throat, choking me. I flailed at him with both fists, but couldn't reach him. Squirming and kicking with all I had, I still couldn't budge him. God, I couldn't breathe! I was dying and I knew it. My face felt like it might explode and my vision was fading. My arms dropped to my side and everything started going black—fading—

All of a sudden, Perdue flew off the top of me. I could hear him scream as I rolled over and got on all fours trying to breathe again. I coughed to the point of almost puking. Someone touched my shoulder which startled me. I looked up and saw Jared.

"Are you okay, Blake?" he asked.

"I think so," came out real hoarse and burned some. I slowly turned to get up and saw Perdue lying on the floor about fifteen feet away. I eased up from the floor. What the fuck happened to Perdue? Jared was at my side when we became engulfed by a huge shadow. I turned and could barely make out who it was. My God, it was Mutt.

"You t-take your friend and g-go now," he said. Those were the first words I believe I had ever heard Mutt speak. He took out Perdue. I couldn't believe it. Mutt saved my life. He saved my fucking life. But why?

"Let's go," Jared said, gently tugging at my arm.

"Thank you, Mutt," I managed to get out in a gruff voice.

"D-Don't thank me," he said, "Now g-go before he g-gets back up."

With Jared tugging at my arm, I turned and we fled the barn. We jumped into my truck. Bernie's car was gone. I started the truck and we spun out on to the dirt road leading to the highway.

As we approached the highway, there was a car turning in. It was Marsh's Mustang. I flashed my lights and we both came to a screeching halt.

"We're goin' to my house!" I yelled out my window. Man, that hurt to yell.

"You guys okay?" he yelled back.

"We'll live, come on!" I yelled, rolling my window up and then pulled out on Seventy-Five. I waited until Marsh was behind me before hitting the gas hard.

"What are we gonna say happened?" Jared asked.

"What do you want us to say?"

"I don't know; Bernie still has those—"

"I know, so as of now, it's your call."

"What if the truck door slammed on my fingers?"

"That's what it will be if you want, at least for now."

"I'm sorry, Blake; I called him to get some weed. I fucked up."

"No, you didn't, I did. You were tryin' to get some weed 'cause I was whinin' about it. It was my fault." I paused for a moment and glanced at my friend. "I'll tell you somethin', Jared; I think I would've caved in after the first finger. You're one tough dude."

He closed his eyes and laid his head against the back of the cab. As I drove on, my thoughts were dominated by one searing question—why did Mutt save my ass?

Chapter Thirty Five

KRISTA

I had finally tired of this tug of war between desire and dread. It's one of those rare instances where I was on a journey I was anxious to make, yet had great apprehension about it.

I had decided to go to confession at the church in Cape Girardeau. It was a very large church and I hadn't attended mass there in years. It was important for me to be sure of anonymity because of the things I was prepared to confess. These unrelenting feelings I had now were gaining more control. I could tell by the impulses which rose inside me, and it was frightening. They were going crazy when I was over at Blake's last night. I even felt them with Jared, though I liked to think that was more about feeling sorry for him about his fingers.

I had skirted the issue in my previous confessions in hope that I could somehow contain these lustful desires. Once contained, I'd feel more comfortable about coming forth with them. This was a weakness in my faith of which I was well aware. I'd been wrestling with this long enough.

It was Sunday afternoon and I told Mom and Dad I wanted to go to the mall in Cape to shop for a couple of things. And, in fact, that was exactly what I had done. After all, I had enough on my plate for confession today without adding anything. My first stop was the mall for a quick salad and a visit to a couple of shoe stores. I could always use another pair of shoes.

After I'd browsed long enough and bought one pair of shoes, I left the mall for the church. Pulling into the church parking lot, I couldn't help but feel nervous. I figured you should always be a little nervous before confession.

The only person who knew I was doing this was Cheryl. I felt the need to share it with someone, and I could completely trust

Cheryl. She had no idea of the things I was about to confess, or she would have come with me. Cheryl had always taken issue with me about the practice of confession. She contended she would only confess to God and claimed even that was a waste of time, because He already knew. Plus, she had issues with some of the things that were considered sinful. Religious discussions with Cheryl were enough to qualify as a true test of spiritual resolve.

As I made my way into the church, it was my resolve that would be put to the test. I was wearing a nice white blouse and a fashionable skirt. I had my hair tied back and was wearing a scarf. This might be considered over doing it, but I needed to feel safe. I paused for a moment before entering the confessional. Many thoughts were racing through my head. People such as Mom, Dad, Blake, Marsh, Cheryl, Mr. Dailey, and others all crossed my mind. Everything I treasured in the world now ran through me. I had great respect for the practice of confession in the church. And, regardless of all the recent events impacting my life, I believed in the power of God. I entered the confessional.

"Bless me Father, for I have sinned. It's been three weeks since my last confession. More importantly, I have sins which I've yet to confess that have occurred over the past few months."

"I see, Miss—"

"Krista, Father, my name is Krista."

"Certainly, Krista, and what is the nature of these sins you have chosen to withhold from your confessions?"

"They're sexual in nature."

"I see; how old are you, Krista?"

"I'm sixteen, Father. I lost my virginity just after my sixteenth birthday to my current boyfriend."

"Has your sexual activity been confined to your boyfriend?"

"No Father, I have also had sex with his best friend."

"Excuse me; did you say his best friend?"

"Yes, Father."

"Are these two young men still best friends?"

"Yes, Father, the sex with his best friend has been kept a secret. I felt discretion was best."

"Best for you or him?"

"Best for all three of us. I didn't feel my lustful desires should disrupt the close relationships between the three of us. After all, one knowing about the other could create damaged feelings, which could then spread between the three of us in varying degrees. Therefore, the hurt between two of us would become a hurt between the three of us. The hurts would be different for each of us, making them difficult to resolve, especially since they would certainly overlap. This just seemed way too much for three sixteen-year-olds to deal with."

"Krista, I'm a lot older than sixteen, and I know I couldn't deal with that without God's help. And it might take Him a minute to break that one down. Have there been others?"

"Yes, Father, I have had sex with an older, married man."

"How much older?"

"He's thirty-one years old, Father."

"And how did you come to meet this man?"

"I baby sit his three-year-old daughter."

"I see."

"Father, I know what I've been doing is wrong. But I'm driven by powerful desires that seem to grow in strength all the time. When they reach a certain level, nothing else, including my faith, matters."

"Is there anything, as far as you can tell, that precipitates these powerful desires?"

"At first, they seemed only to occur when I was close to someone that I had a natural attraction to, but now, it seems like the sun coming up can set them into motion."

"Have you had sex with anyone else?"

"No, Father; not yet."

"Has protection been used?"

"Yes, Father; in all but the first encounter."

"I see."

"Also, Father, I can tell I'm falling victim to the power induced by these illicit desires. I'm aware of this, but my awareness has not been enough."

"Krista, you said a few moments ago you knew all of this is wrong. The situation with the married man is a very serious transgression and is unlawful. You have been entrusted with the care of their child in support of their family. Yet, you have become involved in a behavior which could destroy that same family. This activity should be halted at once. As for the others, the church doesn't condone such activity, but realizes we're all sinners. Therefore, we all face challenges to our faith and obstacles which we strive to overcome. God doesn't expect us to be perfect. His desire is that we work to strengthen our faith and never stop trying to overcome those obstacles."

"I understand what you're saying, Father, but I just don't see how, as a child of God, such things can be part of my life. I feel I'm in danger of losing my faith."

"Oh, Krista, you won't lose your faith. It's obvious God has a prominent place in your life."

"How so. Father?"

"Despite all these challenges that you're facing, you're here taking account for your actions before Him. You came to the place your heart led you to, which reflects the strength of that faith you're talking about. You have reasons for concern in your life, as I do in mine, but the loss of your faith is not one of those concerns."

Chapter Thirty Six

MARSH

It was a rare occasion when Gardner warranted a front page mention in the Sikeston newspaper. It was just as rare to find our little community mentioned in the Cape Girardeau paper at all. The St. Louis Post Dispatch was a pipe dream. However, we had managed to get prominent space in all three of those papers and air time on three TV stations over the past three days.

On top of this record publicity, we had been host to a sort of law enforcement convention. In addition to our all-too-capable local police force, we were playing host to officers from the Mississippi County Sheriff's Department and the Missouri State Police. We found out this morning the F.B.I. had joined in on the efforts. What could bring all of this about—the disappearance of Matt Perdue.

This past Sunday afternoon, Perdue's truck was found parked along the Mississippi River levee about two miles north of Wolf Island. That was less than twenty-four hours after Blake's fight with him in the barn. According to the ever growing rumor mill, they had gathered forensic evidence from the cab of the truck, but no official news about that had been released. Because of the heavy rain early on that Sunday morning, any credible evidence around the truck and on the levee had washed away. They found a couple of partial footprints around the truck, but that was about it. It had been unofficially stated that the prints matched Perdue's shoe size.

I had sort of a special interest in the case. So did at least four other people I knew of. In an assembly at school two days ago, Chief Davidson, doing his best Harrison Ford impersonation, and a state police officer asked for any student that had any information they thought might be useful, to please come forward. To Blake, Jared, and I, that was a precarious offer. I would assume it was even more precarious for Bernie. Due to these unforeseen circumstances, our situation with Bernie was on hold. However, he would be badly mistaken if he thought we were letting this thing go. But for now, Perdue's disappearance had to take priority.

The police had already taken Mutt in for questioning. The story we were getting was that Mutt told them Perdue dropped him off close to his house about ten o'clock Saturday night. Evidently, Mutt's family had confirmed the time. He told the police they had been riding around until then. Mutt lived on the east side of town about five miles from the Haskins barn. The fact that no official had attempted to contact Blake or Jared seemed to indicate that Mutt had made no mention of the barn incident— at least to this point.

So, where was Perdue? One theory circulating was he was drunk and ended up strolling into the Mississippi River. Supposedly, there were some beer cans in the back of his truck. Some speculation was that Mutt said they'd been drinking some.

One thing we were sure of was that Perdue was alive when Jared and Blake left that barn. We were back at Blake's house that night by a little after eight. I remembered that distinctly because we had to piece together a story not only about Jared's hand, but where he'd been over the previous hour or two. Tammy and her parents had been looking for him. Our story about him ending up stranded at the park, calling Blake, and then accidentally slamming his fingers in my truck door was flimsy at best. It only worked because of all the concern about his fingers.

Blake's dad got Dr. Martin, who lived just down the street, to come check his fingers. After stabilizing them, he instructed us to keep ice on them for twenty-four hours. He would meet him at his office the next day and x-ray them. Jared held up well through the whole thing. He called his parents later that night and, after some extensive lobbying and some help from Blake's mom, got permission to stay the night with Blake. The girls came over and we hung out at Blake's house until twelve.

Blake's throat was sore for a couple of days, but he played it off. No one but Krista noticed the two light bruises on his neck, and she accepted a lame excuse about it happening while he was helping his mom move boxes. So, the barn incident was covered—we hoped.

There had been an eerie atmosphere around school all week. Like Perdue or not, it was a strange feeling when a part of a small school was inexplicably taken away. The seniors were the most affected, but the entire school was shaken. I really wished the bastard would show up, but for different reasons than most other students. Mainly, I didn't like not knowing where he was.

For some reason, Blake said he sensed that he wasn't coming back. And I knew you couldn't discount anything Blake sensed these days. We weren't sure about the river story and, even though they were dredging, they hadn't found a body. It was difficult to feel bad about it, but to a degree, I actually did. It hadn't been that long since he'd damn near killed me, but death still seemed like such a foreign thing.

Blake finally arrived at my house. Our golf match was canceled today and school dismissed early due to the events going on around our school and community. Blake and I would normally be on the course right now, but we needed to have a private meeting, which included Jared. The police, who had been talking to a few students, had requested an interview with Blake and me late this afternoon. It was common knowledge that we weren't Perdue's favorite people and that we basically detested him. Under those circumstances, I guess we warranted an interview. Our parents would be with us, along with Gramps. Blake said he was glad Gramps would be there. I was, too.

I heard Blake come in through the back door. Mom would be at school for another forty-five minutes or so, which gave us some privacy. Blake, soda in hand, came into my bedroom.

Jared was kicked back in the old recliner, his fingers still secured with splints, a big bag of chips in his lap, and his soda sitting on the window sill next to his chair. I was sitting up on the left side of my bed, leaning against the headboard, my shoes off, tossing a golf ball from one hand to the other. He sat his soda on the bedside table, slipped his shoes off, and hopped up on the bed beside me.

"Okay, guys," I started, "We have to make sure what we're gonna do concerning this Perdue situation and we all need to be on the same page."

"Well, let's look at what we know about this shit," Blake said. "First, evidently Mutt hasn't said anything about the barn fiasco, or they would've called us in before this. Second, Bernie's sorry ass has been left out completely as far as we know. You know, he and Perdue never had anything to do with each other before— that's one hard thing to figure."

"Not to me," I said. "It just goes to show you how bad Perdue wanted to get at you. The son of a bitch is or was outta' his mind. But I think Bernie's sittin' this one out for a couple of reasons."

"Like what?" Blake asked.

"Well, for one, he's probably scared to death about what we're gonna do. He can't be sure how strong his hand is, even with the pictures. And, for another, he could be involved in Perdue's disappearance."

"Yeah, Bernie cut out pretty quick. It's possible they could've gathered later to discuss his cowardice," Blake said. "Whadda' you think, Jared?"

"Fuck Bernie," Jared said, "I wish they'd kill each other." He managed to get that out even though he had to have at least eight chips in his mouth.

"Well, somethin' could've happened," I said. "I still can't believe Bernie did that picture shit. He's gone crazy, too."

"Yeah, Bernie's crazy," Blake said, "But I don't think he's involved in the Perdue thing, unless it was an accident."

"Anyway, here's what it comes down to," I said. "We can come forward with the story, calling Bernie's hand. He can talk about us being pot smokers and give Jared some unwanted exposure. But, we probably still win in the long run."

"The problem I have with that is it probably has nothin' to do with Perdue's disappearance," Blake said. "If someone did do Perdue in, I just don't see it bein' Bernie. He's too big a coward. Plus, I don't see riskin' this stuff with Jared—not right now."

"Hey guys," Jared interrupted, "If it causes a problem for either one of you, then don't worry about the damned pictures. You do what you need to do. Just tell me what I'm supposed to say and that'll be my story—period."

"We know, Jared," Marsh said, "And I promise you Bernie has no idea what all this shit's gonna cost him. When we get through with 'im, he'll never come near you again."

We were silent for a moment.

"Perdue's gotta be dead, Marsh," Blake said. "He would've shown up by now. I can't see anyone kidnappin' him. And, if he was hidin' out, thinkin' we might go to the cops, he'd know by now that we aren't goin' to."

"So, you think our best option's to pretend the barn incident never happened?" Marsh asked. "That'd mean you and Jared never saw Perdue that day at all."

"I think it's the best way, but this is just as much Jared's call, if not more."

We both looked at Jared. He was quiet for a few moments, and I noticed his eyes glistening a little.

"Y'know," Jared said, "I hate what happened so bad, that I almost get sick sometimes. As morbid as it sounds, I find myself hopin' he's dead and burnin' in hell. The memory makes me feel so ashamed. I feel like total shit when I think about them makin' fun of me during those pictures. It was the hate I had for 'em that kept me from cryin', 'cause I wanted to."

I could see the emotion rising in him.

"It's okay, Jared, I feel the same way," Blake said. "It makes me angry because of the way it makes you feel. But you shouldn't feel any shame."

"He's right, Jared," I said. "Don't give 'em the satisfaction. You're a great guy and they're trash."

"I appreciate you guys sayin' that," Jared said, his eyes starting to water, "And I've let some of it go. But the hardest thing is rememberin' that I gave up one of my best friends and he almost got killed."

"You gave up nothin'," Blake said sternly. "He tortured you. The crazy bastard would've broken all your fingers. I would've called you. How do ya think I feel knowin' he did that to you 'cause of me?"

"The things you endured and the call had nothin' to do with givin' up Blake," I said. "It just showed how much you love your friends."

"So, you be pissed as much as you want," Blake said, "But fuck the shame 'cause that's bullshit."

"In that case, as far as I'm concerned, the barn thing never happened," Jared said.

"Then, that's our story," I said.

"Okay," Blake said, "C'mon, Jared, I'll run you home; then I'll go get ready for the third degree."

"Okay," Jared said. "Oh, ah, Marsh, I sorta ate this whole bag of chips."

"That's cool," I said, "Mom always kept enough food for four people because of Blake. Now, since you joined the family, she buys for ten."

I'd been to city hall many times before, but it was always to pay the water bill or run some related errand. Blake and I had never been behind the secured doors of the police department. Even though I realized this was Gardner and the Gardner Police Department probably belonged on one of those "believe it or not" programs, I was still nervous.

It's funny, but a week ago, my greatest concern was getting back on the golf course. Life could change really fast.

The one constant I had in my life, my illicit affair, involved deep secrecy, and I had little doubt of its destructive capabilities. Before this school year, I couldn't think of one thing of any consequence I kept from Blake. In the year of my father's death, I cried a few times. One of the great blessings I had at the time was I never had to cry alone. I did a couple of times by choice, but the rest were with Mom or Blake. Most were with him. Sometimes, he cried with me, and he was there every single time I needed him. No guy liked to cry around another guy, but with Blake, it didn't matter. Hell, it shouldn't matter anyway.

There had just never been secrets between us. When he was stealing Mrs. Tremble's spelling tests in the fifth grade and never got caught, I was the only one he told. When we were thirteen, one of Barbara's friends, Marilyn, taught him the real art of masturbation. He had her teach me one night when she managed both of us at one time. I was sure Barbara didn't know about that, and I seriously doubted Marilyn would ever tell anyone.

We had done so many things that we shared with no one. Yet, this year something had changed. We still shared things, but not all things. I could tell there were things he was just not telling me. But I knew whatever he was withholding from me was of no greater magnitude than what I was keeping from him. There had been times I had wanted to tell him. It was so heavy, and we had always been there for each other when things got heavy.

But, I was justifiably afraid. His friendship was more important to me than anything else I had. To lose him would hurt so bad, I wasn't sure I could take it. I was unable to find the courage to do so. I was practicing deception with the last person on earth I would ever knowingly wish to deceive.

And now recent events were compounding the issue of secrecy again. I actually had very little problem with this situation specifically. It was just having to deal with another deception, and this one could have important consequences. But we didn't know that for sure. It just seemed like I kept piling on things to keep to myself and it wasn't healthy. Also, in this case, there were too many other people who knew at least some of what happened. That was a recipe for disaster.

For right now, this interview held the key. If Blake and I could keep the barn incident out of it, I thought it would fade away. We decided we should give short answers and say as little as possible.

We were led into a conference room two doors down the hall. The room had a long table that could comfortably seat twelve people. We were seated on the long side of the table away from the door. From left to right, it was Mr. Coleman, Blake, and Ms. Kathy, Mom, me, and Gramps. Across from us were Chief Davidson, Sergeant Cavitt, and an investigator for the state police. Sergeant Cavitt looked very official in his state issue sport coat, shirt, and tie. It quickly became obvious he was conducting the interview. He introduced himself and asked if there was any objection to him recording the interview. Our parents said that was fine as long as it was understood we could refuse to answer any question, if we so desired. Cavitt agreed to the condition and said the interview wouldn't take long. He also said some of his questions would be based on information from interviews with other people. Blake and I gave our names and verified we were students at Gardner High School. We also verified that we knew Matt Perdue.

"Okay, guys," Cavitt said, "Please try to speak clearly, if you would. Do you mind if I call you by your first name?"

We both indicated that would be fine.

"Okay, Marsh, I'd like to start with you. How would you describe your relationship with Matt Perdue?"

"Nonexistent," I replied.

"By that you mean you didn't associate with Matt Perdue," he said, almost glaring at me, probably put off by my curtness.

"No, I didn't. Let me save you a little time, Mr. Cavitt," I said, staring right back at him. "I hate Matt Perdue. He's a bully who I happen to think is crazy. He hurt me and is a threat to me and my friends."

Cavitt was quiet for a minute and then continued, "During the first week of school this past August, were you involved in an altercation with Perdue?"

"I don't know that you'd call it much of an altercation. I said something he didn't like and he hit me in the chest, knocking me down."

"What'd you say to him?" he asked.

"I don't remember exactly. He was calling us names, so I threw it right back at 'im."

"And are you aware that Blake then attacked Matt Perdue?"

"He did no such thing," I snapped at him. "He stepped in and pushed him away from me—that's it. That wasn't an attack, he was defending me. For God's sake, the guy towers over both of us."

He paused for a second to write something down. "Okay, now, earlier this year you had another altercation with Matt Perdue; is that right?"

"Yes."

"Is it true that you punched him in the face twice, precipitating a fight?"

"Hey, wait a minute!" Blake said, loudly.

"Do not interrupt us," Cavitt said, harshly. "You'll get your chance in a minute."

Blake sat back in his chair, glaring at Cavitt.

You better be careful messin' with my bro, Cavitt.

"Yes," I stated. "I punched him twice. He said somethin' about my father and if he says it again, I'll punch 'im again."

"I understand you were hurt pretty bad," Cavitt said.

"Capsule version," I replied, "He busted my shoulder, my jaw, and my balls."

"Mr. Cavitt," Gramps jumped in, "Just what does this have to do with the disappearance of the Perdue boy?" First Blake, now Gramps; Mr. Cavitt, you're pushing it.

"I was just verifying some background information, Mr. Williams," Cavitt replied. "Now Marsh, when did you last see Matt Perdue?"

"A week or so ago at school, best I can remember," I answered.

"And where were you this past Saturday evening?" he asked, "If you don't mind me asking."

"I don't mind. My girlfriend, Betsy, and I spent the evening at Blake's house with some of our friends. I took her home about twelve. We were in her driveway for a few minutes maybe doin' some things I'd rather not discuss around my mother. I then went home and went to bed."

"Marsh got home around twelve-thirty or so," my mom interjected. "I wait up on him when he's out. Sergeant, my son obviously knows nothing about this. I explained this to Pete, uh, Chief Davidson, on the phone the other day. For whatever reason, you've managed to dig up some things that are not easy for Marsh to talk about—I guess that's your job. It's my job to protect my son. Now, are there any other pertinent questions for him?"

Now, you did it, Cavitt. That's Blake, Gramps, and Mom— you're toast.

"No, Mrs. Williams, that'll be enough for now," Cavitt said.

He then turned in his chair to Blake. "Okay, Blake, what about your relationship with Matt Perdue?"

"We had a very distant association revolvin' around basketball and mutual hatred," Blake said.

"What served as the basis for this mutual hatred?"

"For my part, he was always tryin' to pick on me. If he didn't pick on me, he picked on my friends. You'll have to ask him about his part of the hatred."

"Did you ever call his girlfriend?"

"No, but she called me."

"Why did she call you?"

"That's personal and it had nothing to do with Matt Perdue."

"Okay, now you seemed to get along fine with Matt Perdue during basketball season until the incident between him and Marsh," Cavitt said.

"It wasn't an incident; he tried to kill Marsh," Blake said with a little fire in his voice.

"Well, I'd call that a little strong to say a school yard fight was attempted murder," Cavitt said.

"Well, you weren't there."

"No, and I'm conducting this interview in a professional manner and expect the appropriate courtesy in return," Cavitt said, getting flustered.

"Sergeant Cavitt," Mr. Coleman spoke up. "You raised an issue that represents a very traumatic time in my son's life. I don't want my son to ever be disrespectful to an adult. However, I'll not have my son being harassed about something that affected him very deeply. What happened to Marsh is a very sensitive issue with Blake and needs to be handled carefully. I don't see its relevance to why we're here, but my son's feelings have to be respected, too."

Way to go, Mr. C.

"Okay," Cavitt said, obviously upset, but trying to be careful, "Let's just get straight to the pertinent issue. Is it true that you openly stated you planned to kill Matt Perdue?"

"Now, hold on a minute," Ms. Kathy said.

"No, Mom," Blake said, "I'll deal with that. I did say that and, at the time, I meant it. Look, if Matt Perdue tries to hurt Marsh, then I'll do everything in my power to stop 'im. But that's not exclusive to Perdue, it goes for anyone. I've never killed anyone and hope I never do. I don't like to fight and don't want to, but Marsh is my best friend. So, if someone goes after 'im, they better be prepared to take me on as well."

Cavitt was quiet for a moment staring at the table. "Where were you last Saturday night—if you don't mind me asking?"

"I was at my house with a group of friends. My parents were there. My friends, with the exception of one who stayed the night, left around twelve. That was my Saturday night."

"Do you know if Matt Perdue drank alcoholic beverages or used drugs?"

"I don't have any idea if he does, or has done, any of those things," Blake stated.

"Well, I have information which suggests that you do both."

"I do not! Who said that?" Blake asked quickly.

"Well, it's common knowledge among my officers that young Mr. Coleman here is a marijuana user and a drinker," Chief Davidson chimed in.

"Is that right, Chief?" Blake's dad shot back. "Do you have any proof of such a charge?"

"We hear things," Chief Davidson replied.

"So do I, Pete," Gramps suddenly said. "I hear lots of things." Gramps was staring hard at Chief Davidson. The chief leaned back in his chair without saying anything else.

"Well, I guess we've covered enough for now," Cavitt said, looking disgusted. "I know these are trying times for everyone. I appreciate you folks coming in."

Blake's parents and my mom were cordial with everyone as we left. Gramps was having a private conversation with Chief Davidson in one corner of the room. I didn't know what was being said, but Gramps was doing all the talking.

Blake and I walked outside together.

"You were pretty good in there, bro," I said. "I wanted to come over there and kiss you right on the mouth."

"Let me grab a couple of breath mints first," he said.

Chapter Thirty Seven

BLAKE

It only took Krista and me about an hour and a half to put the finishing touches on our papers. We had both chosen Middle Eastern countries to write about. She had chosen Iraq, and I had picked Iran. They were both anti-American and didn't care much for each other. Thanks to the internet, our research, which was pretty general, wasn't very difficult. The organization was the biggest challenge and mine was better, thanks, in no small part, to Ms. Huey.

Our Literary Club had finished our publications for the year, so we were just working independently. This past week, Ms. Huey gave me some helpful ideas for the organization of my paper. There was only one minor incident, and it was Marsh's fault. After Ms. Huey left our table—she had been working with me a few minutes—I asked Marsh to get some papers out of the file cabinet for me. He knew I didn't want to walk across the room because I was a little sexually aroused, and he gave me a hard time—pardon the pun—about it. He eventually bailed me out, but gave me shit about it the rest of the day.

So, Krista and I had a little touching up to do, and it came together pretty quick. We worked in her room, but had to leave the door cracked because her mom said that was proper. We sprawled out on her bed with our papers scattered in organized fashion. Due to the number of papers and working setup, we were forced to change positions numerous times. There were other motivations around the position changes, but they were strictly sensual in nature.

Krista took my socks off and began strategically massaging my feet, which she knew drove me crazy. My feet were sensitive and when they were handled with an easy touch, others parts of my body tended to be stimulated. To be blunt, I usually got a boner that got so hard it hurt. To make sure things worked as she wanted them to, she would periodically reach over to my crotch and gently squeeze me. I told her that was torture, which just made her smile that almost devilish smile she displayed sometimes.

There was no doubt I might be the luckiest sixteen-year-old in the world. I had been sexually involved with two of the most beautiful women that walked the earth. My feelings about the two were very different. I was crazy about Krista, more than I really thought I ever would be. It was like we had become part of each other. We fussed over each other in ways different from most teenagers. Our relationship was typical in some ways, which meant basically lust driven. But the devotion we had to one another was not as typical.

Then there was Ms. Huey. She was like a goddess. I didn't consider us equals in any way. I didn't want to be her equal. She could enslave me if she desired—I couldn't stop her. But, instead, she treated me like a king and made me feel special.

I guess Marsh was right earlier today when he said I looked after a lot of people. I felt a sense of responsibility for many of the people close to me. Marsh and Krista occupied a special place in my life, but there were others. Jared had become a big part of my life now. I was very defensive about him and would protect him at all costs. I had similar feelings for Rick and even Tyler, though not strong. But I would go to war for them. Those feelings came from deep inside.

"Well baby, I think that's a wrap," Krista said, still driving me nuts messing with my toes. "You got anything else you need to do?"

"Yeah, I need to do something about this boner you've caused me to have," I said. "You're pushing me into sexual convulsions."

"Now Blake, you can't let a foot rub send you into lustful delusions," she said with that smile again.

"Yes, I can, and I'm coming apart inside out," I said. "But, under these circumstances, I'll just have to suffer."

"If we had more privacy, I'd be able to work on your suffering through this mysterious connection that runs from your toes to, ah, other parts of your anatomy."

"Well, we don't have any, so let up on me, pleeease," I pleaded.

"Okay, babe," she said and moved over next to me. She then brought her mouth to mine and we kissed passionately. With her right hand she reached down, grabbed me again, and began gently squeezing.

"Come on, Krista," I said. "I don't want to do it in my pants."

"Then don't, baby," she said, gently stroking me through my jeans.

"Krista, stop, please." But she had me and she knew it. She kissed me again and—

"Krista!" her mother called, breaking us up immediately and saving me a private laundry session later.

"What, Mom?" she called back.

"Aren't you guys about through? I need you to help me in the kitchen."

"Good grief," Krista said to me, and then called out, "Okay, Mom, on my way!"

"I'll call you tonight," I said, slipping my socks and shoes on. "You go ahead; I'll show myself out. Your mom sounds put out."

"She's probably wiped out," Krista said. She kissed me and I grabbed my papers and headed out the front door. I was just about to step off the front porch when—

"Hey!"

I turned and saw Mrs. Baker coming around the corner of the porch toward me.

"I want to know if you're taking advantage of my daughter," she asked sternly, as she walked up to me.

"No ma'am, I wouldn't do that, Mrs. Baker," I said, trying to hide the fact that I was scared to death.

"Yeah, well, I know how young men are, and I know my daughter just thinks you're wonderful," she said with a smirk. "But you don't fool me a bit."

I backed down a couple of steps. "I like Krista, Mrs. Baker; I wouldn't do anything to hurt her," I said, lowering my gaze.

"Look at me, young man, when I'm talking to you," she said and our eyes met—

—*A fog was all around me. It was thick and murky. I was walking aimlessly, unable to see more than a couple of feet in front of me. I could hear a strange whispering breeze, but could not feel it. The ground felt crunchy under my feet as I continued to walk.*

The fog began to fade a little, even though my vision was still limited. I walked on and on, the ground still crunching under my feet. Slowly, I began to see what looked like trees on my left and right. Small bushes began to come into view. I guess I was in some kind of forest, but there was something peculiar about it.

The fog began to disappear, leaving dim shadows above me exposing more of the forest around me. What was it about this place? Suddenly, a sliver of light cut through the shadowy sky providing a little light. Wait; now I knew what it was. The trees and the bushes around me were all dead! Another sliver of light shot through. I looked down and saw what was causing the crunching sound—the grass I was walking on was dead. Another sliver of light pierced through; then another and another.

I now saw the trees and bushes touched by the light began to sprout rich green leaves that multiplied rapidly. More and more slivers of light shot through, dispersing the shadows. The grass began to green under my feet. The whispering sound gave way to the sound of a steady breeze rustling through the new leaves. More and more light appeared all around and—

"Oh, my God!" she screamed. "Oh my God!"

Things began to come into focus around me as I blinked my eyes. Krista's porch came into view.

"Ohhhh John," Mrs. Baker cried. She was on her knees on the front porch trying to hide the flowing tears with her hands.

Suddenly, the front door opened and Mr. Baker burst out, coming to her.

"Sweetheart, what's wrong?" he said, as he dropped to one knee and took her in his arms.

"Oh, John, I'm so sorry," Mrs. Baker whimpered. "It's all my fault; please forgive me, John. I'm so sorry."

"It's okay," Mr. Baker said. "It's all okay." He began rocking her gently.

"What happened?" Krista asked loudly as she came out the door. "What is it, Mom?"

"Oh, John, please forgive me," Mrs. Baker continued to plead through her tears.

"There's no need for that, sweetheart, I love you," Mr. Baker said, his eyes watering. "Come on now." He got her to her feet and held her closely, as they walked back in the house. "It's alright, now," he said, as they disappeared into the house.

"What happened, Blake?" Krista asked, almost glaring at me.

"I don't know; she just fell to her knees crying—I just don't know," I said, trying to be composed.

She looked at me with a strange, hard look. Then, without saying a word, she turned to go back into the house.

"Krista, I—" I got out before the front door slammed. Goddammit, I didn't know what happened. My eyes started to fill with tears as I walked out to my truck.

Marsh had just about driven down every highway and road in Mississippi County. He'd played every rap song I loved. He now had the radio tuned into classical music, trying to break this funk I was in. He'd just come off the driving range when I called him, and told me to meet him at the club. When I got there, we got into his car and had been cruising ever since.

I was so damned scared. I told him what had happened. He was working hard to get a grip on the story of another of my trances—this one with Mrs. Baker. It was pretty damned frightening to him, too. But there had to be an explanation for this shit. I just slumped down in the seat and stared at the dash.

"Blake, I think we need to call Krista," he said.

That brought me back to life. "No way, bro, she wants to kill me. You should've seen that look she gave me."

"I don't care; you didn't do anything, at least anything that can be rationally explained," he said.

"Oh, that's real good, Marsh," I said, "Let's just start filling out the commitment papers now."

"You gotta chill out about this, bro. I don't know what it is, but we'll ride it out." He reached over and opened the glove compartment. "Grab that bag of weed and let's roll up."

I grabbed the bag and said, "Well, maybe we can look at this thing from a different perspective."

"Damn, bro, let's get high enough we don't have to look at all."

Chapter Thirty Eight

KRISTA

I was more anxious than I had been in a long time. Mom and Dad had been back with the doctor for a while. Wow, it was already after nine. I was relieved that Mom had consented to come to the SEMO Regional Rehab Center here in Cape. But I wanted to understand some things. Cheryl wanted to come up here, but Dad said no one needed to come right now.

The thing that happened with Blake this afternoon had me both confused and afraid. He was standing there like he was in a daze while Mom was crying. I just didn't get it. He hadn't tried to call, and I'm glad because I just couldn't talk to him right now.

My phone rang. I checked to make sure it wasn't Blake. It wasn't.

"Hello, I thought you might be calling," I answered.

"Well, I've been waiting to see what's gonna happen concerning the long, lost Perdue."

"Do you think he's dead?" I asked.

"I have no idea."

"He's crazy and dangerous, but I hate to think of anyone that young dying," I said.

"Well, there are numerous possibilities. By the way, how'd your contact do?"

"He did okay," I said, though that wasn't one hundred percent true.

Blake and the guys had no idea that I knew all about what had happened at the barn. I was mad as hell when I was told about it and made it clear that sick crap like that should never be allowed to happen. However, things overall turned out okay.

"You don't think he's in the middle of this disappearance thing, do you?"

"No, I don't think so," I said. "But, he's really scared."

"I'm sure he is."

"Well, we'll see. I just want this thing to be over, with or without Matt Perdue."

"I prefer without."

I hung up, pushing down the ripples of fear.

"Krista," Dad called from the door to the doctor's office. "We need you to come back here now."

Shaking off everything but what I needed to focus on now, I got up and walked to my father, who put his arm around me and led me down a corridor. We took the door on our left about half way down. Mom was sitting on a little couch on the right side of the room. No one was sitting at the doctor's desk. Mom motioned for me to sit beside her. She was smiling a very generous smile. When I sat down beside her, she took my hand in her left hand pulling me close to her. Dad sat in a chair across from us.

"Krista, I want you to know that I'm okay," Mom said. "I'm going to be staying here for a while to get back on my feet. But, first, I want to tell you a story. Is that okay?"

I nodded. My eyes were watering already.

She looked at me lovingly. "You were the most beautiful baby and you're even more beautiful now. After you were born, your father and I determined we would wait until you were three or four before we had another child. We were very careful. When you were a little over a year old, I found out I was pregnant again." She squeezed my hand and looked across the room at my dad's comforting smile.

"But, you see, Krista," she continued, "I was pregnant with another man's child."

I tried very hard to hide the emotions that sprang to life inside me.

"I'd been seeing this man off and on for some time. I won't go into all the particulars now. Suffice to say I was at my wit's end. I had been unfaithful to the most wonderful man in the world and was with child. The man I was involved with said he would

handle it any way I wanted to. I knew I had to make a decision."
I could feel a tear run down my cheek.

"With no regard for the people I loved, my church, or my faith, I decided to abort the baby. I decided I would rather face damnation than to accept what I had done. Naturally, this had to be a deep dark secret, so I found a small, obscure abortion clinic to take care of the matter. That turned out to be a big mistake. There were complications after the abortion. I was passing blood and had to go into the hospital for emergency surgery. The end result of this was I would no longer be able to have children."

Tears rolled down my face as Mom squeezed my hand firmer.

"Of course, your father had to be told now. I told him I would tell the rest of the family and I would understand if he wanted to leave me. His love never wavered and he told me we would tell no one, unless I wanted to. He said we would continue to build our life together, and we would make it. As you already know, your father is an extraordinary man, who serves as an example for everyone to follow in living a life next to God."

I pulled myself even closer to my mother.

"So, that's what we did. Your dad got the job in Gardner so we could make a fresh start in a new place. Things were fine for a while thanks to your father and you. But, I couldn't stop the pain I felt, so I found a way to medicate myself and you know what that turned into. Suddenly, for whatever reason, I found a part of me today that has been dead for years, and I'm ready to come to terms with the issues that have haunted me. I came to realize that even though I turned my back on God, that He would not turn his back on me. He gave me your father and you—the greatest gifts anyone could ever receive. I wanted you to know that, my sweet baby. I'll get well now and be the kind of mother you deserve."

We cried together for a couple of minutes, and I felt a warmth from her I can't ever remember feeling.

"You're right, Mom, it'll all be fine."

"It sure will," she said with a smile. "Oh, and Krista, you apologize to Blake for me. I know this had to upset him. He really is a good boy, and I've got some making up with him to do, also."

We hugged and kissed each other. Then she went with the staff to be checked in. My dad and I went to our car and began our drive home—a home I knew would look a lot different now.

I felt strong feelings for all things dear to me. My mom would find her way now. As bad as it was, it could've been worse. I had hope now for some of the issues I'd been facing. That hope was a gift from my mom and dad.

I would call my friends when I got home to tell them that my mom was okay. And then I would call Blake and tell him how much I loved him.

Chapter Thirty Nine

MARSH

I found myself doing a lot of personal inventory as of late. There were few better times for me to do this than the first half of today's church service. The ability to zone out the music was something Blake and me had become really good at. In and around the church choir's attempts at hymn destruction were the various announcements and other trivial matters brought before the brethren.

The end of April usually served as the beginning of the late spring-summer lull. Christmas and Easter were both by the boards, the weather was starting to warm up, and people stared finding reasons to miss. I'd always remained stalwart in attendance, even outdistancing my mom. I wished I could say it was because of my deep Baptist faith, but that would be sinful. Blake was under a clear requirement to attend due to his father's standing as a deacon. I would not desert my bro, so here I was.

It had been three weeks since Perdue's disappearance and over two weeks since our interview with the police. There had been no break in the case, as far as we knew. We heard they'd been hounding Mutt, but there was still no body. Then again, the Mississippi had swallowed many a body. It was a scary thought to think he might be lurking somewhere, but I seriously doubted it. As the school year moved into its last month, there was still a dark cloud over us, and it didn't look like it would be going anywhere soon.

We celebrated Jared's sixteenth birthday at a pool house sleep over last weekend. We confiscated some beer and gin, and I surprised even Blake with some good weed from an anonymous source I refused to divulge. I'd had trouble touching base with Ray lately. Blake, Rick, Jared, and I had a pretty good time. Rick had worked his way past the fight with Perdue and seemed like his old self. Blake and I had made a concerted effort to bring Rick closer to us since that fight. With Jared's permission, we had shared with Rick what had happened at the barn. His initial response had been much like Blake's—he wanted to go find ole' Bern and stomp him in the ground. But we convinced him to wait with us.

Jared's fingers were getting better every day. They were out of the splints and he was gaining more use of them. Blake and I helped him with his flexing exercises. Until just recently, Jared wouldn't let anyone else touch them, not even Tammy. I could tell he was still bothered by what happened, and who could blame him? The Jared I used to know would have had a nervous breakdown. He had to see Bernie around some and, even though Bernie kept his distance, it still served as an ugly reminder. Getting revenge wouldn't cure the painful memories, but Bernie would soon face a reckoning.

Things with Betsy and me were heating up. I was allowed more "rights of exploration" as time went by. She had a nice body highlighted by sturdy, firm breasts. I had only seen one girl who was better equipped overall. My allowance of touch into areas previously off limits had brought flares of passionate lust that were new for her. Another area of progress was her hand finding me—something she had never done—which brought us closer to new horizons. These erotic thoughts were probably out of place in church. Wonder if Lana, who was sitting just down the pew, would think so?

Blake was rolling right along. His golf game was really good, which had raised our golf team to a higher level of performance. His grades had continued to approach excellence, beyond anyone's expectations. Ms. Huey had made a significant contribution there. There was something about her and Blake, but I couldn't figure it out and he offered no clues. He and Krista were now the steadiest couple in school. My bro was doing great, but the visions still haunted him just like they would me or anyone else. I'd been thinking about the visions and was tinkering with a wild theory. I wasn't ready to go to Blake with it just yet.

Of course, my struggles could rival his and anyone else's, for that matter. My shoulder was great, and my golf game was off and running. My grade performance had normalized over this second semester, which provided some relief with Mom. There was every reason for me to feel good about all these things and more. But I just couldn't feel good about myself, and I really didn't think I should. I needed to be strong enough to make some decisions, be honest, and go on with my life.

Well, it was time for another message from the dealer of devotion; the leader of laity; the patron of piety; the sultan of spirituality; the one and, thank God, only Reverend Elias Condrab. My bro, sitting beside me as usual, was tuning in and I still didn't understand why. His only explanation was his continued fascination that the good reverend so firmly believed in what he was preaching. Personally, I found that somewhat alarming.

He began. "My brothers and sisters in Christ, it is once again a blessing for me to be sharing with you another day the Lord hath made. We bear witness to another example of the boundless generosity of our Savior..."

I, myself, could use a few more examples.

"...As always, our Father displays the rewards we can garner through the power of giving..."

This had all the earmarks of "dialing for dollars".

"...Even in the toughest of times, we have so much. How can we ever question the numerous gifts we are allotted through His love and caring? But we do. We don't measure gifts through love and caring; we measure them by our greed and selfish need..."

Wonder if they had to be in that order?

"...We are continually taken in by our vast capabilities to consume everything, which can fuel our worldly desires for material things that we come to believe make us better, and we like to label as means of progress..."

Which could be transposed to "progress of means" and not lose any punch.

"...But when do we stop to think about the progress of spiritual growth in our lives and the importance of the church in our lives..."

It was enough of a challenge to stop and think, period.

"...We find ourselves taking our church and all it provides for granted. When looking for a place to cut back our expenses, the church falls easy prey to our reduction in expenditures. We tell ourselves we'll make up the difference next week. This is the same as waiting for tomorrow, when we know tomorrow never comes..."

It was already tomorrow in New Zealand.

"...Until one day we look up and there is no church to make provisions for. All of this because we couldn't even put one dollar out of ten aside in support of the one entity in our lives that asks so little and, yet, can give so much..."

Sounded like a slot machine to me.

"...But we, as true followers of Christ, will not let this stand!" Brother Condrab's voice rang out, waking up at least three members of the choir. "Our church family has faced greater challenges than this! The influence of the worldly desires will never win out! When our backs are to the wall, we always find our way, we find the way, we find His way!"

Ah, but can we find the money?

"...This is yet another example of the tremendous challenges we face to maintain the true principles of our Christian faith. We continue to be bombarded with the influences of evil, which are determined to cloud our minds, harden our hearts, and sever our soul..."

That didn't leave a whole lot, did it?

"...Through all of this, our faith remains stalwart. It is, as it always has been, the backbone of our existence. It continues to sustain us through all of our trials and tribulations. We must resist complacency in our obligations to the church that provides a bastion of sustenance on which we can always count..."

"Bastion of sustenance" sounded like a worthy attribute to have in my sex life, if only my sex life was worthy.

"...So let us look past those wanton desires that lead us to stray from our obligations to our God, our faith, our church..."

Carnal desires weren't wanton, were they?

"...And we can walk hand in hand with the Father, the Son, and the Holy Ghost to the end of eternity."

Or the end of the block, whichever came first.

"Amen."

Whew, I survived another one. I didn't know what Brother Condrab was doing for my spiritual well-being, but he was certainly strengthening my "staying power".

After the service concluded, Blake and I walked out to our vehicles. It was a warm, cloudy, and breezy day.

"Well, I'm going over to Gramps'; then, to the club to hit some range balls, if it doesn't rain. Maybe I can round us up some more weed."

"That would be good," he said, showing little interest.

"You doin' okay, bro?" I asked. "You look more than a little preoccupied."

"Yeah, I guess," he said. "Hell, I don't know, Marsh. All this shit going on. I'm just tired of it."

"It's a lot of shit to deal with. And I know it's extra hard on you. You look out for a lot of people—mainly me—and it means more than I can say." I felt tears starting to fill my eyes as I looked at him. "I don't really believe in many things in this world, but I believe in you. You're as much a part of my life as my mom is. I know I'm a burden to you sometimes, but I can't help it."

We stood for a moment in front of our vehicles.

"You're not a burden, Marsh," he said. "You're my bro."

Chapter Forty

BLAKE

The mystery of the disappearance of Matt Perdue still persisted. But, with no body and evidently few clues, it had become a dead end. It had apparently become dead enough for Bernie Talbut. Yesterday, he contacted Jared and said they needed to meet. Jared told him to fuck off. Bernie then brought up the pictures. Jared played it like Marsh told him to and begrudgingly agreed to meet him. Their normal pick up spot was an alley just down from Jared's house. It was shielded by what was left of an old warehouse and a line of tall hedges. Naturally, Bernie warned Jared that if he saw any sign of us, he wouldn't stop. If that happened, he told Jared he might be surprised to see some interesting photos start to pop up. Jared agreed to the stipulation. Marsh and I didn't.

This whole situation with Bernie had never left my thoughts. I was waiting for my shot at him and couldn't wait. Marsh kept telling me he was building a plan. The plan had grown in scope and in line with events which had occurred over the past few weeks. And Marsh said it all came together after the Perdue thing. The big question was when to put it in play. We'd been counting on Bernie helping us with that, and he finally did. Marsh could come up with some devious stuff and Bernie was in for a bad day. I still wanted to just beat the shit out of him.

The prom provided the perfect backdrop. It gave us a free afternoon and the time to make this happen. Rick was right in the middle of this thing with us. Marsh gave him an important role. Rick's father had a really nice digital camera. It was a handy tool that would serve our needs. We had another friend who would also make a major contribution.

But, first things first. It was just after noon, so Bernie should be here any time. I was hidden in an open slit in the hedge row on one side of the alley, while Marsh was positioned behind a broken opening in the old warehouse's wall across from him. Jared was pacing back and forth about fifteen feet into the alley. Jared said Bernie would always pull in, allowing him to get into the car without being seen. He would then slide down in the seat until Bernie got out of the neighborhood. This little procedure would fit our needs perfectly. Bernie would see Jared and pull in. We could then begin phase one of Bernie's demise.

Jared continued his methodical pace. His attitude reflected a quiet determination. There was a furrow in his brow, which represented an intense focus. Jared suddenly halted. He started backing up toward the warehouse, just in front of where Marsh was hidden. Now, I could see Bernie's car slowly pulling in. His window was down, which was another good break for us. The passenger side window eased down and Jared approached the car. Jared leaned down into the open window.

Now was the time and I slowly emerged from my hiding place. Jared had Bernie's attention drawn to him. In a flash, I was at the driver's side window and popped Bernie in the side of his face. It was flush and you could hear the smack. I opened the door and pinned Bernie down in the seat. Jared had moved away from the passenger side door and Marsh opened it and slid into the seat.

"Get off of me, you shitass," Bernie yelled.

"Fuck you, Bernie," I said, my left hand pressing Bernie's head into the seat. My right fist was drawn back ready to strike again.

Marsh, literally sitting next to the top of Bernie's head, said, "Now Blake, let's give Bernie a chance to be cooperative before we mess his face up."

"What's it gonna be, you piece of shit?" I said.

"Okay, okay," Bernie said, obviously convinced I would be happy to beat the hell out him.

"Turn on your stomach," I ordered.

Bernie slowly turned so he was flat on his stomach. Marsh then grabbed his left ear, which was facing up, as I released his head.

"Ow! That's my fuckin' ear, man," Bernie squawked.

"I'm aware of that, Bernie," Marsh said. "I know you don't want to make me tear it off, so be still and shut up."

"Jared," I said, as I continued to straddle Bernie right by the steering wheel while Jared slid into the back seat with a duffel bag we had tucked away by the warehouse. "Give me the duct tape outta' there."

Jared handed me the roll of duct tape. I jerked Bernie's hands behind him drawing another yelp from him. Marsh twisted his ear hard, bringing an agonizing moan.

"I told you to shut up, Bernie," Marsh said.

I wrapped Bernie's wrists together firmly with the duct tape. Marsh then helped me sit Bernie up in the seat between the two of us. I then settled in behind the wheel and Jared sat quietly in the back.

"Now Bernie," Marsh said, "We're goin' for a little ride. You need to sit tight and be quiet 'cause we don't like you, and might react violently if we thought you were bein' disrespectful."

"Look," Bernie said, "I—uh!" I fired an elbow into his ribs.

"He said to be quiet, Bernie," I said. I slowly backed the car out of the alley. We started on our trek out of town. I turned the radio to one of the few stations that played rap and cranked it up. We were careful to take some side streets until we hit the outskirts of town and headed north. I'm sure Bernie never noticed that Rick, driving his car, had fallen in right behind us.

After about ten minutes, we made a right off the highway and down a favorite farm road of ours. The road wound around to the old farm house where we'd fired up more than a few joints. I eased the car around the house, where it would be shielded from view. Rick came in behind us. Marsh got out of the car and waved Rick over to an area beyond us to park his car. Jared then got out of the car, bag in hand.

"Bernie, now I want you to slide over toward me and I'll help you out of the car," Marsh said. "I'm afraid Blake might hit you again if you slid the other way."

Bernie did as he was told. He was trying hard to be cool, but you could tell he was scared shitless. Marsh slowly got him on his feet.

"Now, you walk with me very slowly toward those steps over there," Marsh said, pointing at the steps leading onto the front porch. Rick walked behind us carrying his bag. Jared was beside Marsh, while I walked on the other side of Bernie. As was prearranged, we did all of this in silence. This, no doubt, added to Bernie's fear and discomfort.

We made our way into the old farm house. Of course, there was no electricity, but plenty of light was provided by the windows, along with the cracks in the walls and ceiling. Marsh and I walked Bernie over to a sturdy wooden chair. It was the only piece of sturdy furniture in the whole place. I motioned for Jared to bring the bag over to me. I opened the bag, reached in, and pulled out a very impressive hunting knife, along with the roll of duct tape.

"I guess that's supposed to scare me," Bernie finally spoke.

"No, it's not," I said, "Now shut up and turn around."

Bernie slowly turned away from me, probably sensing the fact that I'd be more than happy to cut him into little pieces. I used the hunting knife to cut the duct tape that bound Bernie's wrists.

"Now, sit in the chair, Bernie," Marsh said, looking at him face to face.

"What if I don't want to?" Bernie asked, showing some defiance for the first time.

"We don't give a shit what you want, Bernie!" I said loudly. "Now, sit down or I'll sit your ass down!"

Bernie glared back at me for a moment, but slowly sat down in the chair.

I moved behind him. "Raise your hands over your head."

Bernie complied. The chair had a high back, which reached the back of Bernie's neck. With Marsh holding the knife and standing in front of Bernie, I wrapped duct tape around his upper body and the back of the chair numerous times, so he was attached to the chair. I pulled his wrists behind him and secured them with duct tape again, then taped his ankles to the front legs of the chair.

"Rick, will you have enough light to snap from the right side?" Marsh asked.

"Let me see," Rick said. He pulled out the digital camera. His dad was a photography nut and had all kinds of neat gadgets. Rick connected the flash attachment, which had a flash meter. "It reads low but it'll work okay."

Bernie wasn't looking too good, but tried to put up a good front. "You guys takin' pictures don't scare me. You're just a bunch of freaks, anyway."

"It's time to see just how freaky we can be," Marsh said.

He handed the knife back to me, then reached down and unbuttoned and unzipped Bernie's pants.

"Oh, I see, I'm going to get a blow job from you guys," Bernie said.

"It's more likely that I'll cut your dick off and stick it in your mouth," I responded.

"We're going to take a few photos," Marsh said.

"Well, you take all the pictures you want," Bernie said. "I've got some pictures of my own, though my subject didn't have much to show."

"Y'know, Bernie," Marsh said, "That's bold talk for a chicken-shit pussy like you."

"Fuck you, Williams; fuck all of you," he said, but was obviously very nervous.

"I sure hope our dates feel that way tonight after the prom," Marsh said. "Now, let's get down to business. First, we require that you apologize to Jared and beg his forgiveness; then, you return the pictures of Jared; finally, you'll have a choice as to how you want to pose for the pictures."

What the hell was this choice thing about? Marsh hadn't said anything to me about that. I looked to Jared and Rick who also looked a little confused.

"As I said, fuck all of you; I ain't doin' any of that shit," Bernie stated.

Marsh motioned for Jared to bring the bag to him. He removed a small set of tongs and a brown paper sack from it. He was standing about three feet in front of Bernie and had his undivided attention. Then he removed an old pickle jar from the sack which contained a nice healthy wolf spider that was about two inches in diameter.

"Oh fuck!" Bernie said when he saw the spider. He then went into frenzy, and I had to hold the chair to keep it from tipping over. "Get it away from me!"

"Now Bernie, I'll be glad to put the spider away, if you adhere to our requests," Marsh stated calmly.

"Alright, alright," he said, with beads of sweat popping out on his forehead.

"First, the apology and ask for forgiveness," Marsh said. "And look at Jared when you say it."

He turned his head toward Jared and said, "I'm sorry dude; I really am. Would you forgive me?"

"Please," Marsh said.

"Please," he said.

"Fuck you, Bernie," Jared said.

"Oh well, Bernie, at least you tried," Marsh said. "Now about the pictures."

"Okay, okay, you can have 'em," he said, eyeing the jar in my hand. "I don't have 'em in my car or on me, but I swear I'll get 'em to you whenever you say." Man, he was shaking.

"Well, that's nice, Bernie," Marsh continued, "Unfortunately, I just can't find any reason to trust you, so we need some insurance; therefore, the choice. I want a picture of you posing for the camera while kissing the end of my dick."

Oh my God! I almost couldn't believe what I just heard. But I had to smile a little thinking about just how vicious Marsh could be. I glanced at Rick and Jared, who were totally stunned.

"You're fuckin' crazy, Williams; I ain't kissin' no one's dick," Bernie said.

"You have no idea how crazy I am, but I had to offer you a choice," Marsh said. "Assuming you're takin' the other choice, Rick, get your camera ready. I'm going to remove the spider and put it inside Mr. Talbut's underwear."

"No fucking way!" Bernie screamed, and went into a frenzy again. Boy, this was something to see. "No! No! Nooo!!"

Marsh began unscrewing the top of the jar.

"Wait, wait!" he said, starting to look really pale. "Look, I swear I'll give you the pictures. To prove it, there's three hundred dollars under the front seat of my car. I've got to have that money, but you can keep it 'til I deliver the pictures to you—I swear. There's some weed under there, too, that you can just have."

"You know, Bernie," Marsh said, "That's an enticing offer. But, as I said, I just can't trust you. So, we'll take pictures of you with a spider sucking on your balls or of you kissin' my dick."

"Come on, Marsh," he pleaded. My God, he was shaking. "Don't do this, man, don't do this."

"Goddammit, Bernie, you don't get it, do you?" Marsh yelled. "How do you think Jared felt when you made him strip and pose for those pictures? You sons of bitches laughed at 'im! Then you watched while that crazy bastard snapped his fingers! And you have the fuckin' nerve to ask me for some kind of mercy? No way! We can't trust you about the pictures, but we can play the same game. Now—last chance—what's it gonna be?"

Bernie had tears in his eyes and slowly dropped his head. "Put the spider away."

"Okay," Marsh said, "Rick, get positioned and get ready."

Marsh gave the jar to Jared, then undid his pants and put his hand inside to work himself up. Amazingly, within a few seconds, he plopped out a pretty good semi-hard. This was one of the most awesome events I believe I'd ever witnessed.

"Rick," Marsh said, "Get just his face and my dick in the picture."

I suddenly jerked Bernie's head back by his hair, holding the point of the knife right to the edge of his left eye. "Bernie, you even think about trying to hurt my friend, and I'll stick this knife in places you don't want to think about."

I eased Bernie's head back down, but kept a grip on his hair. Without hesitation, Marsh straddled up to Bernie's face.

"You've got to lean to me a little, Bernie," he said, "And don't close your eyes."

The camera began flashing, recording a truly magical "Kodak moment."

This had been one of those days that refused to end. I didn't know how I could ever explain to anyone what a great day this had been. This afternoon's "Bernie pictorial" with Marsh was an event I would never forget. The prom was better than I would've ever imagined.

All the girls looked hot. Krista was so beautiful. She looked like God's valiant attempt at beautiful perfection. It had been a hard time because of her mom's stuff. She said I'd been her hero but, to me, she was the hero. She'd been handling the whole situation better than I could have.

The DJ was good; he played a little good rap, which gave Marsh and me a chance to embarrass our girlfriends on the dance floor, by showcasing our rap moves. We topped it all off with the cookout here at Mr TM's. Yes, this had been one hell of a day.

Chapter Forty One

KRISTA

Some days were just so special; they were easy to separate from others. I've had two of those over the last three days. The other day, I visited my mom, and she looked really good. She said she was feeling better and was clearing her heart of all the pain that had weighed on her. She asked about everything going on with me. She laughed when I told her about Blake and Marsh doing their rap dance at the prom. It was so good to hear her laugh so hard. It was so refreshing to talk to her. She wanted to know all about my upcoming finals and my plans for the summer.

Today had been the other special day. Watching my baby on the golf course was a thrill. He helped Gardner High School make it to state in two sports. Though he seemed a little distracted, he still kept his composure and played like a champion. Some thought he was disappointed in his play, but I didn't think that was it. This was a crazy thought, but Blake just felt different to me, and that feeling seemed to be getting stronger. And I wasn't the only one who felt that way.

I got a most curious phone call two days ago from Marsh. First, he asked how Mom was doing. But then he asked, in a very nice way, if she had other problems besides her drinking. Knowing Marsh as well as I did, I knew he had some special purpose. So, I told him my mom had some demons in her life she had to overcome. He explained that Blake was worried that he had unintentionally caused some problems. I assured him that wasn't the case. I also knew there was more to it than that.

Things were going better for me personally. The rise of the sexual urges had subsided somewhat. I had to be careful, though. Some of the desires were tempered by my interaction with Blake, and Mom's situation had been a helpful distraction, but I had to be vigilant, because of the power the urges possessed.

Anyway, our golf team had placed fourth today in the state. The tournament was held in the West County region of St. Louis. Betsy, Rick, Sally, Jared, Tammy, and I had managed our way up there and we had a blast. After the tournament, we divided up between Blake's mother's Olds and Rick's car to make the trek home. But first, we stopped for a big meal. Mr. TM had given Marsh more than enough money to feed the eight of us at the Angus Steakhouse.

We were finally being seated for our meal. Tables for eight could take a while and it was a Saturday. I was hungry; Blake was famished; Jared was on the verge of needing life support. One thing I had to admit about the guys—they were all good looking. I hoped that wasn't my urgings churning up. Blake was beautiful with his dark hair, which he was starting to grow long for some reason, his sparkling bright blue eyes, and those amazing lips. Marsh, with his bright blond hair, which was also getting longer, deep brown eyes and smooth, unblemished face, was getting more of the "Hollywood look" than ever. Rick had a mane of curly black hair almost as dark as Blake's, a dark complexion, and even darker brown eyes. Jared, whose sandy brown hair was also growing long, had a "baby face" and was actually—God, he would hate this—pretty.

They all had one feature in common that I was just really picking up on. None of the four had a real beard even starting to appear. Rick had a few stray whiskers, but not much. Marsh and Jared were baby-faced. Strangely, Blake, who was showing the beginnings of a beard earlier this year, had stopped at the beginnings.

"You guys were great today," Rick said.

"Yeah, my God, Marsh, you're the number three golfer in the state," Jared added.

"Thanks, but you have to realize that it's hard to truly gauge that just playin' one round," Marsh said.

"That may be true," I said, "but everyone out there had the

same opportunity and only two topped you and they just barely did that. Plus, they were seniors. You were great and so were you, Blake."

"That's nice of you to say," Blake said, "but if I had played worth a shit, our team would have had a top three finish—hell, we might've won the thing."

"Hell, Blake, the team finished fourth in the state, and your score was better than a lot of those guys out there," Rick said.

"That's true, Blake," Betsy joined the conversation, "And Gardner has never done so well in golf."

"The truth is that Blake's the reason we're even in the state tournament," Marsh said. "One, his golf game is phenomenal. Two, if it weren't for him, I would've never been able to hit a golf ball this spring. And most importantly, his presence makes the whole team play better. That's because, as he proved during basketball season, he's a great leader."

"Great job, Marsh," Blake said, "You said that just the way I wrote it down for you."

Everyone at the table laughed. It felt as good as the laughs I had with Mom. How do we always manage to overlook the importance of good friends? The waiter brought the appetizers. The cheesy ranchero dip and salsa gave us some relief from our hunger and temporarily removed Jared from all the conversation.

"Did you guys hear that the police called Mutt in again yesterday?" Sally asked.

"Well, that's ridiculous," I said. "The guy may be a little socially backward, but that doesn't make him some kind of killer."

Marsh cut his eyes at me, which made me feel a little awkward.

"Yeah, I don't know if Mutt did anything," Rick said, "But if he did, you can bet Perdue had it comin'."

"I don't think you should ever kill anyone," Betsy said.

"What if they leave you no choice?" I asked.

"That's a hard question," she responded, "But murder seems to me an alternative that should be avoided at all costs."

"That depends on the costs," Marsh said.

The table got quiet for a few seconds.

"Just think, we have finals this week," I said, breaking the weird silence.

"Yeah, and I'm okay with everything, except maybe Algebra II," Betsy said.

"Well, I've got to ace the Biology final to pull an A in there," Jared said. "My dissection work knocked my grade down a notch."

"That's because you insisted on trying to perform vasectomies on frogs," Tammy said with a disgusted look.

"Don't blame it all on him, Tammy," I said. "Blake and Marsh, the Frankenstein brothers, were behind most of that."

"It was just a suggestion," Marsh said. "Jared's smart; I thought if anyone could do it, he could."

"And I didn't say a word," Blake said.

"No, you just kept sneaking him specimens," I said. "He should've experimented on you two."

"Ouch, that hurts just thinkin' about it," Blake said.

Our steaks finally arrived and the conversation subsided. About the only thing said for the next twenty minutes or so were Jared's persistent requests for more bread. When we finished our main course, only Blake and Jared were interested in dessert, which was a surprise to no one.

"I know this is a touchy subject, but I think maybe it's somethin' most of us have an interest in," Tammy said. "I haven't even told Jared."

"Hey," Jared muffled out, and then swallowed his mouthful of cheesecake, "You said we wouldn't keep anything from each other."

"I was talkin' about food, sweetie," Tammy said with a smile. The whole table cracked up. "No, seriously, one of my mom's friends works in the state police office in Cape. She told Mom some interesting things about Matt Perdue."

"What kinds of things?" Blake asked abruptly.

"Well, we need to keep this quiet; even though I'm sure it'll be public knowledge soon. The Perdue's lived in McCrory, Arkansas, before coming to Gardner when Matt was in the seventh grade. Evidently, he had serious behavioral problems as a child. He had violent outbursts and could be hard to control. His parents put everything they had into getting help for him. He was institutionalized for a while and with extensive therapy and medication, he got better. Following the recommendation of his doctors in Memphis, the family relocated to give him and them a fresh start. Matt still saw a psychiatrist, who kept him on medications to help control his anger. His parents said everything had been okay until the beginning of school this year. For some reason, the tantrums started coming back. His medications were adjusted and would work for a while, but then problems would start again. His family has spent everything they have to try to get him whatever he needed."

"Can you believe that?" Sally asked.

"You'll do anything for the people you love," Jared said.

"I'll be damned," Marsh said, almost under his breath and giving Jared an odd look.

"Anyway," Tammy continued, "His mother told the police it was like his body just kept rejecting everything the doctors gave him."

I noticed Marsh had centered his attention on Blake. My baby was staring down at the table. He was troubled and looked like he was afraid. For some reason, I was, too.

Chapter Forty Two

MARSH

If someone had told me a year ago that I would play in the state golf tournament, I would've thought they either had a vivid imagination or had taken too many drugs. We placed fourth today in the state, which was an unprecedented accomplishment in our school's history. I played well enough to place third overall with a seventy-four. It was a banner day, though it didn't start out that way.

When hitting on the practice range before the round, I was trying to get the kinks out of my swing. I had been pulling the ball a little. Todd was there, trying to get me to keep my left shoulder in. It had just rubbed me the wrong way, and I snapped at him. It caught Blake's attention, and he stopped his practice. Trying to maintain my composure, I backed off. Todd walked away.

Blake came over to see what was wrong. I told him it was nothing, but he knew I was lying. It's just that I seemed to have these flashes of anger. I knew it had to do with the conflicting feelings I was dealing with. There had to be a way to bring some resolution to all this shit. I was afraid there was going to be an emotional tidal wave.

Nonetheless, Todd's advice proved invaluable, just like it always did. My day picked up considerably from that point. I played as fine a round as I'd ever played. My focus was strong, and I played with an aggression that had recently become a trademark of my game.

Blake's demeanor caught my attention when I saw him during the round. He played okay, but something was wrong. He played best when he was kind of loose and free. That was unusual in golf, which usually required a quiet, focus-oriented approach.

But my bro's game didn't work that way. Maybe it was because he was playing with some guys he didn't click with, but I didn't think so. No, some things had to be addressed. He had always been there for me and I was damn well gonna be there for him.

I'd been pondering this thing with Blake and this "trance" of his. Based on my own experiences and what he'd shared with me, I'd developed a theory. The problem was I had no explanation. But the time had come for Blake and me to take this thing on. Now, how to approach it was another issue. Blake was understandably very uncomfortable with the whole thing, so I had to be careful. I knew there were things he hadn't told me about. Fear was a great motivator. Blake didn't scare easy, but he was frightened by this.

We'd dropped the girls off and were almost to our pool house safe haven. It had been a long day and a long ride home but we were going to tackle this thing. I knew Blake was on edge. When we traded his mom's car for his truck, he'd asked me to drive. He just didn't look good. It was almost midnight when we arrived at Gramps' and made our way back to the pool house.

"I'm totally wasted," he said as we went inside, "And I haven't smoked any weed or drank a damned thing."

"I know; me, too," I said. "Grab a shower while I put sheets on the bed."

He took a long shower and I knew he needed one. I took a pretty long one myself and when I got out, he was sitting up on the bed with his eyes closed. I noticed he'd already grabbed a beer and appeared to have dozed off.

"Hey, bro," I said, shaking his shoulder to roust him awake.

"Yeah," he said, looking up at me, "I'm zonked."

"I know, but it's time to get to the bottom of this shit," I said, as I took a seat on the bed beside him. "Now, look at me."

"I am."

"Look at me, Blake. Really look at me"...

Boy, this would be a challenge to explain, but it felt like it was right. It was hard to accept something like this when you didn't know how or why. We always needed to know hows and whys. But I didn't think they applied in this case. Whatever this was, there was nothing rational about it, therefore explanations just might not ever be available.

I'd been awake for over half an hour, while Blake continued to snooze. He would wake up soon enough. Hell, it was only a little after eight. So, I was content to just lie here, uncovered, on the bed beside him, staring at the ceiling and trying to comprehend what was incomprehensible. When I awoke, I was snuggled up right next to Blake and we were both naked. We had bunked together on this hide-a-bed more times than I could count, but had never been in that position and had never slept nude. A quick review of everything seemed to suggest that snuggling might not have been the extent of things. But I had no memory of it and, unless I missed my guess, he wouldn't either.

Blake's accounts of these "vision journeys" he went on had baffled me and still did, but I had a theory. And, based on what had happened here last night, it was past time to take a serious look at all of this. I just hoped he could deal with it. I had an advantage on him, and this was still a load for me.

He moaned as he slowly shifted in his sleep, turning on his right side toward me. His eyes blinked open.

"Marsh," he managed, his voice grudgingly waking up, like the rest of him.

"Yeah, bro."

He yawned widely and then opened his eyes a little wider. "Uh, Marsh, I know I'm probably groggy, but do you realize you're lying on the bed beside me with nothin' on—like naked."

"Yeah, well, that's okay," I said, "You don't have anything on, either."

"What!" he said, pulling the sheet up for a look. "Damn, what in the hell possessed us to sleep in the nude, uh, like with each other?"

He was calm so far. "Well, bro, it appears we may have done more than sleep, based on the evidence on the sheets, and elsewhere."

"Shit," he said, and quickly pulled himself up in a sitting position. The sheets had dry splotches scattered everywhere, and we both needed a little washing off in places as well. I waited anxiously as he took visual inventory.

He suddenly looked straight ahead with a deep furrow in his brow and asked, "What did we do, Marsh?"

"Well bro, I don't remember a thing from the time you took the 'eye express' inside me. So, your guess is as good as mine."

He was silent. I could tell he was running all this through his mind. Even in the face of this, his resolve astounded me. Then he asked, "Uh, we didn't ah—"

Wow, that was quick. "Hell, bro, I don't know what happened."

"Well, this is just fucking great! Every damned thing that has happened over the past year, and now this. You know what? This whole thing is a bunch of shit. I started last summer wantin' to have sex, and have managed to set records for wet dreams and dive into sexual perversion. I don't need to watch those perverted fuck flicks—I'm creatin' my own."

"Well, bro, you don't have exclusive rights to that shit. But before we go there, can I talk to you about my theory on these trances?"

"Why not," he said and threw the sheet off, leaving both of us lying naked on the bed uncovered. "Maybe the rest of the golf team'll come over, since we're dressed for it. I just don't give a shit."

"Fine; neither do I. Now I know you've experienced these trances with me, Krista, your dad, Jared, and Krista's mother. Is there anyone else?"

"Let's not forget Perdue," he said, "I probably caused his death."

"Bullshit. Anyone else?"

He was quiet for a few seconds and then said, "Ms. Huey."

"No shit," I said, genuinely surprised. "How far did that go?"

"Further than we did last night, I hope."

"What did you see inside of me last night, bro?"

"Fire everywhere and some kind of thing where I dove in the ocean and kept flying to the surface and then into the air and back down again. That kept repeating as far as I can remember."

"That's a new one—the ocean."

"Not really; Ms. Huey's involved the ocean."

I paused for a second. "Okay, here's what I think is happening. You go inside people and break down barriers."

"What?"

"You break down barriers."

"What kind of barriers?"

"The kind that are born inside us, and the kind we build inside of us."

"What are you talkin' about, bro?"

"Look Blake, we're human and we have a conscience. When we're faced with dilemmas or obstacles, our conscience helps determine how we deal with 'em. Based on the natural barriers we're born with and the ones that are built into us, we make decisions as to what we're willin' to do and how far we'll go. You with me?"

"So far," he said. "Should we be holdin' hands?"

"Shit, Blake, I'm being serious here."

"Okay, okay—just tryin' to make light of all this perversion I'm into."

"Whatever. Anyway, some barriers are stronger than others and almost all are based on fears and insecurities. Some of them are related to personal beliefs. What keeps almost all people from taking senseless high risks? They have barriers that live inside them that block that behavior. We get furious and want to hurt or destroy someone or somethin', but a barrier inside of us stops us." I paused to see if he was really listening.

"Go on," he said, making it obvious that I had his attention.

"Okay, I don't know how or why, but through this trance, as you call it, you go inside someone's conscience and drive them through barriers. This means they become willing and able to do things they would never have done, at least not at this point in their lives." I could see he was listening by the look on his face. "Think about the various things you've told me you see, bro. Something is always breaking; explosions of fire and smoke; breaking the surface of oceans; dams giving way. I believe you're witnessing the fall of one or more barriers that reside within people."

"Then, for whatever reason, people start changin'," he said.

"Right; look at people like Jared. Jesus, he's a completely different person. Hell, look at the changes in your own father, bro. Krista's mom went to rehab—somethin' she'd been fightin' a long time. And you have no idea of all the things that have happened with me."

He turned and looked at me. "What about Perdue?"

"I've been thinkin' about that. You told me you looked inside of him and it scared you really bad. I think two things happened. One, you were just gettin' your feet wet in whatever the hell this is. Second, your trance with him was prematurely interrupted by Coach Randall."

"Did I fuck him up?" he asked.

"He was already fucked up, bro. I do think you might have disrupted things inside 'im, but that's not your fault. However, it may have inadvertently played a role in his intense hatred for you, and he probably never realized that. The tragedy is I think you could have actually helped him if the situation had been different."

"What do you mean?"

"Breaking down barriers can be a good thing or a bad thing, bro. It depends on the person and the situation. You might have been able to help him overcome some things—like your dad

314

or Krista's mom. Now, there's another part of this we need to address."

"Okay."

"At times there appears to be some type of correlation with the trance and sexual responses, but I'm not sure."

"I think there is," he stated. "You know about Krista. Well, Jared came all over himself. Now, with you—"

"I came the first time in Krista's driveway," I interrupted, "I just didn't wanna tell you."

He went silent for a minute and then said, "Things got sexual with Ms. Huey, too."

"I'm not surprised. I really don't know what these sexual responses have to do with it or what determines when they happen, but they play some kind of role. I'm still not sure about any of this, but it's my best shot."

Blake thought for a minute looking straight ahead, and then turned to me and said, "I think you're on to somethin'. Thanks, bro."

"It may all be bullshit," I said.

"Yeah, it might be, but I don't think so."

"It's close to nine, bro, and I have more to share, but I need some breakfast. So, let's shower and head down the road to Todd's. He's cookin' breakfast for us."

"Okay, but does Todd—"

"Yeah, I told him some of what's been goin' on and my theory. Hell, I needed to tell someone I could trust before I tried it out on you."

"But, he doesn't know about last night," he said.

"No, and I'm not sure what all that entailed."

"Great choice of words, Marsh."

Chapter Forty Three

BLAKE

I honestly believed Todd might be the best cook I have ever known. When Marsh and I arrived at his place, he had a smorgasbord prepared for us. We had fresh fruit and bagels, biscuits made from scratch, and a scrambled egg casserole that was awesome. In spite of everything, I had a healthy appetite and dug in. Breakfast conversation centered on our tournament play yesterday. If I left for hell in the next few minutes, at least I'd had a great meal. We helped Todd clean up until he shooed us out of the kitchen.

A few minutes later, Todd joined us in the den. He sat across the room from Marsh and me. We were on the sofa.

"Well Todd, Blake and I had an interesting experience last night related to his trances I told you about," Marsh said.

"Okay; how interesting were these experiences?" Todd asked.

To my utter astonishment, Marsh shared everything about how we found ourselves this morning. I was trying hard to hide my embarrassment.

"I told him what my theory was about his visions, and he seemed to think it was plausible," Marsh said.

"I know all this sounds crazy, Todd," I said.

"Not at all, Blake," Todd said. "I believe in the paranormal—always have. Remember, folklore is one of my hobbies and I've run across many interesting people and stories that reach outside the world we live in. And I think what Marsh has told me is plausible; there's just a lot still unknown. But, it may always be unknown."

"I need to share something else with you, bro," Marsh said, with an uncharacteristic quiver in his voice. "And I need to know you'll still love me."

"I love ya', bro," I said. "Nothin'll ever change that."

Marsh took a deep breath. He looked really troubled.

"Look, Marsh, if this is about last night, that didn't mean shit," I said. "Neither of us even knows what happened, so we can't know how to feel about it. Hell, we don't do gay stuff."

"I do," he stated quickly.

I knew my feelings of disbelief had to show on my face as I looked in his direction. "What did you say, bro?"

"I've been with a guy, Blake—still am," Marsh said, looking devastated.

"Wait a minute, wait a minute," I said, and got up and walked to the front window. I was working hard to stay cool. "If that's true, Marsh, then who is this guy?" I turned and looked at my bro.

He looked up and cut his eyes at Todd and then back. I began to feel an explosion of emotions.

"You, Todd! You!" I screamed. "What the hell have you done to him, you bastard!" I instinctively started toward him.

"No, Blake!" Marsh yelled and jumped in front of me. "It was my choice—no one forced me."

"That doesn't mean shit!" I yelled over Marsh's shoulder at Todd. "You're his mentor, his confidant! He trusts you and counts on you. Then you do this shit! No way, Todd! You're a damned pervert, you son of a bitch!"

"He may have opened a door, but I chose to go in," Marsh said, not giving an inch. "He has apologized many times and suggested we stop, but I didn't want to stop—I mean, sometimes I do, but then I change my mind. It's my choice and involves my desires."

"Dammit, Marsh," I said, now looking at him. "He's an adult; he took advantage of you and your feelings. You're not gay!"

"I don't know if I'm gay or not, but I'm obviously not straight, either," Marsh said. "Right now, I'm not sure where I fit. These feelings I share with Todd had to be inside me somewhere. Somethin' just happened that cut 'em loose."

I felt the tears well up in my eyes. Oh my God, had I caused this, too?

Suddenly, Marsh grabbed me with a forceful hug and spoke quietly, "You didn't do anything wrong, Blake. You've never hurt me in my life and I love you with all my heart. It's not about you; it's not about Todd; it's about me."

I stepped back, with tears rolling down my cheeks. What was wrong with this world? Hell, what was wrong with me?

"Todd has never wavered in the way he's treated me and helped me. I have mixed feelings about this, but I know he genuinely cares about me," Marsh said.

I walked back over to the sofa and sat down, hanging my head. I managed to utter out, "When did this—"

"Start?" Marsh responded. "That night after my birthday when we all stayed at the pool house. Todd saw me by the road and picked me up. There was nothin' planned, it just happened. We were also together the night that shit happened with your father."

"I was with Ms. Huey that night," I said, without looking up.

"What a coincidence, huh," Marsh said. "The two of us involved in illicit affairs at the same time. God, if He's out there somewhere, really does have a sense of humor."

I nodded my head, still looking down, not able to begin digesting this recent revelation. After a few moments of silence, I looked up at Marsh who was standing, looking back at me. I could feel the yearning in his eyes. He needed my acceptance and I didn't know how to give it to him.

He slowly turned to face Todd. "I think we need to clear up a couple of other things while it's just the three of us."

Todd shifted to the edge of his chair. "What do you mean, Marsh?" he asked, sounding a little uneasy.

"I wanted to wait until Blake was here with me before I brought it up. And I wouldn't bring it up now, if I didn't feel like I had a pretty good hunch about what's happened, or at least some of it."

I looked at Marsh and then at Todd. No one I knew had better instincts than Marsh. Whatever this was, it was important.

Looking at Todd, Marsh continued, "Last week, I happened to notice your phone bill on the bedside table while you were in the shower. It wasn't my intent to pry, but I saw a familiar number. So, I scanned the bill and noticed you'd called that number more than once."

Todd was looking down, his hands interlocked in front of him. He did not appear comfortable.

"What reason would you have for makin' calls to Krista, Todd?" Marsh asked.

"You what!" I shouted and stood up, my anger rising again.

"Hold it, Blake," Marsh said, holding his right hand up in front of me. "We need to hear what this is about, so chill out a minute."

I went silent, but continued glaring at Todd.

"Let's hear it, Todd," Marsh demanded. "Blake has a right to know."

Todd let out a long sigh and then looked up at both of us. "Krista and I were working together to keep tabs on Perdue. She felt, as I did, that he was a danger to both of you."

I was infuriated. "Just how did you do this 'keeping tabs'?" I asked, using a disrespectful tone.

"I did some personal surveillance and she—," Todd responded, and paused a second before finishing, "—she recruited some help."

"Recruited some help!" I said loudly. "And just who did she recruit?"

Things got quiet; then Marsh spoke up, "It was Mutt, wasn't it?"

Todd sat silent.

"What the fuck!" I exclaimed. "How in the hell did she recruit Mutt?" Things got quiet again. My temper continued to rise. "We'll just see about this shit." I reached in my pocket and got my cell phone.

"Blake," Marsh said.

"No way, Marsh," I snapped back, "I'm callin' her right now."

She answered on the second ring, "Hey, Babe."

"Where are you?" I asked abruptly.

"I'm on my way to Mass. What's wrong with you?" she asked in a sharp tone.

"Well, Marsh and I have been having a revealing conversation with Todd that just keeps getting better all the time. You know Todd Little, don't you?"

"Yes," she answered quietly.

"He claims the two of you decided to protect Marsh and me from Perdue and you recruited some help. Popular opinion seems to be that you recruited Mutt. Whadda' you think?"

"Yes, I did," she answered, matter-of-factly.

I could feel my face turning red. "And just how did you get Mutt to agree to help you, Krista?" I asked, virtually yelling into the phone. There was silence for a moment. "Did you fuck him, Krista? Did you?"

"No," she fired back, "But I would have if it meant protecting you!"

"I'm not worth that, Krista!" I screamed.

"You're worth a lot more than that to me!" she screamed back.

I clicked my phone off and threw it on the sofa, turning my back to Marsh and Todd, so they wouldn't see the tears starting to flow again. In a few moments, I felt Marsh's hand gently squeeze my shoulder. I was trying to stop trembling.

"Love, or at least the perception of it, makes people do strange things," Marsh said. He turned back to Todd. "You've been tellin' me you love me, Todd; is that really the truth?"

"Yes," Todd replied.

"Last night, a good friend of mine said people'll do anything for someone they love," Marsh said. "With that in mind, Todd, do you think they'll ever find Matt Perdue?"

I slowly turned so I, too, was facing Todd.

He stared at both of us. "Not a chance."

The rolling waters of the Mississippi could take you to a different plane of existence. Sitting on top of the levee, I wished I could find that plane and stay for as long as it took. For what? For the cycle of life to roll back around and give me another shot at my sixteenth year; or just let me go back and delete a few days. You know, I always thought reflecting on things gave me a chance to see them more clearly. But, as I looked back, there seemed to be a curtain of shadows around some things.

In less than twenty-four hours, my world had turned upside down—again. It just wouldn't stop turning. Why was I always on the ass end of the hourglass? Let the damned sand fall on someone else for a change. Matt Perdue was dead. Todd killed him. He never said he did, but he did. He did it because he loved Marsh, or at least because he thought he did. But did I seal Perdue's fate that first day of school? Krista gave up things she wouldn't tell me in order to save me. My best friend was in a same-sex relationship, which had him totally confused. He was afraid to talk to me about it for fear of losing my love. Speaking of love, I found myself loving two different women for very different reasons. On top of all this, I might have some kind of power that caused people to alter their behavior in various ways, maybe based on their own fears and insecurities. At least that's what Marsh thinks, and he's right a lot.

I'd walked out of Todd's alone. The last thing Marsh said to me was, and I quote, "Let he who is without sin." Like I said, he's right a lot. So here I was attempting to fall in line with the peace that comes from one of nature's majestic wonders. I barely heard footsteps coming up behind me. I turned and saw my best friend.

"Could you tolerate some company?" he asked.

"Hell, you're not company, bro," I said, patting the ground beside me.

He sat down beside me and pulled out a baggie with four huge blunts in it. "I thought you might want to float over the river for a while."

"That could keep us up there until tomorrow morning," I said, trying to smile a little.

"That's true; we could get some more and ride them all the way through finals," he said, as he fired one up.

I looked at him, tilting my head some, and said, "Your hair's gettin' long, bro."

He toked up, handed me the blunt. "I know; the only reason I haven't cut it is I don't want to. Hell, have you noticed Jared's?"

I shook my head in the midst of a toke.

"Hell, it's longer than yours and mine. His mom and dad said somethin' to him about it. He told them Jesus had long hair and so did Blake."

We both had a good laugh at that.

"I just don't want to cut mine, either," I said. "How'd you know I was here?"

"Krista said you'd be here," he replied. "God, she loves you. You are one lucky dude."

"I don't feel lucky; and this vision shit, Marsh—hell, I don't know."

"Let me tell you somethin', bro. I don't know what all this is about. But if some power has given you this, they gave it to the only sixteen-year-old in the world who has the strength and courage to handle it."

I reached over and squeezed his arm.

"Hey!" we heard someone yell from behind us, and turned just in time to see Jared top the levee on the dead run. Rick was right behind him. Jared came to a skidding halt and went to his knees right beside me.

"What's wrong, Blake?" he asked, trying to catch his breath. He was still wearing the clothes he had worn to church.

"Yeah, what's goin' on, guys?" Rick asked, sitting down beside Marsh.

"Well, currently, we're attempting to smoke down this blunt," Marsh said.

"Krista called me and said Blake was havin' a tough time," Jared said. "She said you were here, so I called Rick."

"Yeah, he was frantic," Rick said. "So, I went to get 'im as fast as I could. Hell, he left his lunch on the table."

"What!" Marsh and I exclaimed in unison.

"I can eat anytime," Jared said. "Now, what's wrong?"

"Lots of things are wrong," I said, and then took another toke. I turned and looked at Jared and said, "But none of 'em have anything to do with you, bro."

He smiled. I had never called him "bro" before. I offered him the blunt, which he took and sat down beside me.

"Do you still wanna work with us this summer, Rick?" Marsh asked.

"Can't do it," he replied, "The legion team plays all summer. We got a new coach and he's all gung-ho. He's really changin' things."

"Yeah, it seems that lots of things are changin'," I said. "Nothin' stays the same."

"And that includes us," Marsh said.

The four of us sat on the levee overlooking the mighty Mississippi and watched as the great river rolled on.

Epilogue

I really liked my bro's ride. I mean, my truck was cool—but not this cool. We were almost to Cape and I was glad because I really needed to piss. That soda I had earlier ran through me in a hurry. Marsh and I were hitting the mall for some Ts and shorts. We were teamed up for the Memorial Day Four Ball Tournament at the club day after tomorrow so Marsh said he wanted to make this run in the morning. That would give us time to practice this afternoon. Personally, I could've slept through the morning and most the afternoon.

Finals this past week turned out to be a breeze and I made good grades for the second semester in a row. Most of my friends did really well, too, but that wasn't unusual. Getting through this "Todd thing" with Marsh was not a breeze and was ongoing. Part of the week we were barely speaking to each other. I was still mad as hell about the whole thing; I was also scared to death. We reached a temporary truce yesterday and I stayed over with him last night.

We took our exit and closed in on the mall.

"Blake, I need to tell you somethin'," Marsh said.

Oh shit; I wasn't sure I could take much more.

"Just don't hit me with too much, bro," I said, "Cause I really need to piss."

"We're meeting with someone at the mall."

"Who?" I asked, a little sharply.

"A guy Todd knows that..."

"No fuckin' way," I interrupted, looking away from him. "I'm not meetin' with a pervert."

"He's not a pervert, Blake," Marsh said calmly.

"You don't know that," I said. "Todd's a perv, so his friends probably are."

"Blake, we're not goin' down that road again," he said firmly.

"This has nothin' to do with Todd."

"Then what does it have to do with?" I asked, showing a little attitude.

"It has to do with you."

"I don't have shit to do with any of Todd's friends."

"Blake, will you just listen a minute?" he asked as he drove into the mall parking lot. I didn't say anything. "Thank you; this guy's a college history professor who travels around and gives lectures about Native American cultures. Todd's had a couple of classes under 'im."

"Wonder what else Todd's done under 'im?" I asked.

"Dammit, Blake!" he said loudly as he pulled into a parking place.

"Okay, okay," I said, "But why do we need to talk to this guy?"

"Todd said this guy is half Cherokee and knows about a lot of stuff that you don't find in history books, like legends and things like that. And he knows stories about places around where we live, including the lake."

"Marsh, this guy's a history teacher. He'll think we're nuts if we tell 'im about my stuff."

"We're not gonna tell 'im. We're gonna say we're doin' some research about the lake and heard he had some interesting stories about it."

"Hell, Marsh, what do Indians and the history of the lake have to do with anything?" I asked.

"What have we got to lose?" he asked. "Basically, we don't know shit anyway, do we?"

"No," I sighed, "We don't; but I know I gotta piss."

"Okay, you go piss," he said as we got out of the car, "And then we'll see what this guy has to say."

"Fine," I said, breaking into a brisk walk, "Maybe he can tell us about peyote so we can get somethin' useful outta' this."

We made our way into the mall and I used the first restroom I saw. I had never seen so few people in the mall, but I'd never been here this early before. I was not feeling good about his. History was not my favorite subject and I saw no purpose in this at all. There was probably something supernatural going on with me, not historical. Hell, I didn't even believe in the supernatural and hearing old Indian stories sounded more than a little boring.

We found this guy sitting in the far corner of the food court. He looked pretty much like a white guy to me and was dressed like us except he was wearing jeans as opposed to our shorts. His name was Zachary Wing, which didn't sound Native American to me. Marsh handled the introductions—turned out Mr. Wing's mother was a full-blooded Cherokee and his father was white. I was respectful and tried to look interested. Marsh brought a pen and a small notepad to play up his part.

"So what would you guys like to know about the lake?" he asked. "Todd said you were interested in Lake Wappapello."

"Well, Todd said you had some stories about the region that were kinda out there," Marsh said. "We'd like to hear about those."

"Oh, okay," he said with a chuckle. "There's nothing like some good Native American folklore to spice up history."

Hell, I didn't know you could spice up history.

"That'll work for us," Marsh said, really playing it up—he was so good at this with adults.

"Okay," Mr. Wing said, "Now, you do know that Lake Wappapello was formed when they dammed up part of the St. Francis River in the 1930s during the Great Depression."

Marsh nodded; I didn't know that at all and I seriously doubted Marsh did.

"Okay, I guess I'll tell you about the legend of Yusgovey Tsi," Mr. Wing said.

What in the hell was that? I cut my eyes at Marsh.

"That's Cherokee for 'Pale Eyes'," Mr. Wing continued, "He was a white boy who was captured by a Cherokee raiding party in Kentucky in the late 1700s. He was seven years old and his parents were killed. What makes this interesting is that he normally would've been killed, too."

Interesting to whom?

"Anyway, according to the story, he not only survived living with the Cherokee, he supposedly did quite well—that was unheard of. Even more amazing was that he was liked and admired by his peers in the tribe."

That's no more amazing than the fact that I'm sitting here acting interested in this bullshit.

"When he was around you guys' age, he had grown into a strong young man. One night, he and a group of boys and a few girls disappeared into the night. The tribe searched, but couldn't find them. Not long after that, a hunting party from the tribe was found slaughtered. A search for the culprits turned up nothing. As you could imagine, there was great concern among the tribe."

Boy, it was getting to be a challenge to act interested in this shit. Marsh would write something in that little notebook now and then—that was pretty funny.

"Some time later, a Cherokee raiding party from the tribe attacked a group of settlers who had settled on the tribe's land. The story goes that the raiding party was slaughtered, but not by the settlers. The tribe's chief offered the settlers the right to keep the land they'd settled on in return for information about what they saw. The settlers claimed it was a group of Indians that swept in on the raiding party. The Indian group appeared to be led by what they called a 'white Indian'. That told the tribe all they needed to know."

That's all I need to know, too. I wish he'd wrap this up.

"So the tribe sent war parties out to find them, but they either came up empty or ended up dead. Finally, a few months later, a young renegade rode into the tribe's village. He claimed he'd left the group. He told the chief that the group was indeed led by Yugov, uh, Pale Eyes, and they had now crossed the 'great river'. The chief, following the directions of the young renegade, took a large war party and went after them. They would've probably crossed the Mississippi River somewhere close to where you two boys live."

Good for them; can we stop now?

"With the help of Shawnee scouts, they located the group near the St. Francis River about where Lake Wappapello is today. That night they attacked with a force that outnumbered the young renegades five to one. When the dust settled, the entire group of young renegades—including Pale Eyes—had been killed. Unbelievably, all but four of the Cherokee war party had also been killed, including the chief."

"That does sound extraordinary," Marsh said, "But not really strange or weird."

Come on, Marsh, don't encourage the man.

"Well, there's a little more to the story," Mr. Wing said. "The young renegade that had left the group warned the tribe about a few things. He said Pale Eyes claimed that his spirit was immortal and could never be destroyed—that if he were killed in battle, he would find a way back. The renegade said Pale Eyes had great mystic powers that could manifest themselves emotionally, psychologically, and even sexually."

Whoa; sexual mystic powers did catch my attention. I suddenly felt a tinge of discomfort as my senses seemed to reach some kind of alert status. This was the kind of weird shit that popped up in me at times. I shifted my gaze directly on him.

He must have also sensed something because he shifted his gaze back at me and continued, "But most importantly, he could look into your eyes and travel to your soul, breaking down all your fears and inhibitions. He could cause great change in people. They would often become bolder, fearless, and sometimes reckless."

Oh my God! I knew my face was probably flush as I slowly soaked up what he just said. I looked at my bro who was looking back at me with a look of pure fear in his eyes. I was sure the same look of fear rested on me.

"So," Mr. Wing said, though his voice now sounded like a distant echo, "For those who believe in such things, be warned. According to the legend, somewhere beneath the waters of Lake Wappapello, lurks the infamous spirit of Yusgovey Tsi, looking for a way back."

Author Biography

William G. Anderson was born and raised in the South-Central United States. He spent much of his life living in and around rural areas which gave him great insight into the life and culture of the region. His middle class upbringing in a Christian home has served as a great influence in his life and is reflected in his writing. He has a degree in American Studies and is retired from private business. He is a proud parent and new grandparent.

If you want to get on the path to be a published author by
Influence Publishing please go to
www.InfluencePublishing.com

Inspiring books that influence change

More information on our other titles and how to submit your
own proposal can be found at
www.InfluencePublishing.com

CPSIA information can be obtained at www.ICGtesting.com
Printed in the USA
LVOW04s0856061114

412019LV00008B/19/P